C000094336

The Lethal Touch © 2024 by Candice Wright

Cover design by Dez @Pretty in Ink Creations.
Editing by Tanya Oemig
Proofreading by Briann Graziano

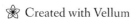 Created with Vellum

The Lethal Touch

CODENAME: RANA

Apex Tactical
Book 4

Candice Wright

For Bree,
Your attention to detail amazes me every time.
I'm over here forgetting everything from my characters names to
their hair color. Meanwhile, you remember which characters
ordered Dr Pepper three books ago
We are not the same.
There isn't a chance in hell I could pull this off without you.
So thank you for everything you do, my anally attentive friend and
fellow book nerd.

Chapter One

Lara

It's been a week.

A week since my life veered drastically off course. Not that there'd ever been anything stable about my life. Just as the embers of hope had started to glow, things were changing again.

Coming here terrified me from the get-go. It might seem silly to those born free, but when life in captivity is all you've ever known, that small cage can feel comforting when facing a huge unknown.

I came here for the kids. Because in a world of chaos, I have been their one constant. I didn't care what happened to me as long as the kids were safe. That's what I thought until Avery brought us to Apex and threw us into a makeshift family full of men who strive to protect people instead of seeking to destroy them.

Two of them, Crew and Wilder, had paid more attention to

1

me than I was comfortable with. Not because I sensed anything bad in them, but because they made me feel things I'd never felt before. Things I had no idea how to deal with.

But as Bella innocently reveals my father's identity, I feel their anger cut through the calmness of the room and swallow, wishing I'd been less nervous. I wish I'd enjoyed their lingering looks and soft touches instead of panicking. I might at least have had a nice memory to take with me when they kicked me out.

The contempt in Wilder and Crew's expressions makes my stomach cramp as they back away from me.

Tears prick my eyes as Avery calls my name. I turn to look at her.

"Is it true?" she asks, looking at me.

There's no reason to deny it anymore. It's true, he contributed to my DNA, but he was never my dad. Still, that's not what they want to hear.

I nod. "But he isn't just my father." I glance at Salem and bite my lip, wondering if I should keep my mouth shut. But I figure she should know. "He's yours too."

The room goes so silent you could hear a pin drop.

"You're my sister?" Salem whispers. And I nod again, unsure of what else to say.

She starts crying, but before she can say or do anything else, Wilder and Crew step between us.

"Then I guess the question is, are you here to help us or hurt us?" Wilder growls.

I let go of Bella's hand and cross my arms over my chest, shielding myself from his anger.

"I would never do anything to hurt these kids."

"Yeah, and why should we believe you?" Crew huffs, making whatever had sparked between us fade into nothing.

"Because I am one of these kids."

"Lara, how old are you?" Zig asks quietly as I angrily swipe at the single tear that slipped free.

I close my eyes briefly and blow out a breath before I open them again and focus on Zig. He let me into his home and could just as easily kick me out of it.

"Seventeen," I whisper.

Out of the corner of my eye, I see Wilder and Crew back up even farther, but I don't pay them any more attention.

"I'll go as long as you protect the kids."

"No. If you leave, I'm leaving too," Alfie snaps, moving to stand in front of me.

I fight back a sob as I smooth my hand through his hair. I pull Alfie behind me when Zig steps toward me, making everyone else freeze.

I frown, unsure how to proceed. "He's just being protective. He doesn't mean anything by it," I say, hoping they won't punish him for speaking out of turn.

"You don't—" Zig starts, but he's cut off by Alfie.

"I'm not staying without Lara."

"Me either," Bella says.

"And me." Delaney moves closer as Noah approaches me and wordlessly takes my hand.

This time, I don't have a chance in hell of holding my tears back.

"I'm not going to make Lara go anywhere," Zig tells the kids softly as his eyes move from them to me. "It was never my intention to make you feel that way. But you have to understand that a lot has happened to us because of your father."

"A lot has happened to me because of him too," I murmur, though clearly not quietly enough because Wilder steps forward.

"Like what? What are you talking about?"

I pull my shoulders back and lift my chin, remembering the way he looked at me just moments ago, like I was something that needed to be scrapped off the bottom of his shoe.

"Nothing that matters now."

"If it concerns—"

I hold up my free hand and cut him off. "It doesn't concern your family."

I look back at Zig, my focus solely on him, not ready to see the condemnation in anyone's eyes just yet. I might only be giving myself a slight reprieve, but it's enough for me to fortify the walls around myself once more.

I take a deep, calming breath and feel each of the children relax around me. "Can I go back to my cabin? Is that still allowed?"

"Of course, but—"

"Maybe the kids should stay somewhere else," Crew cuts in, making my temper flare.

"Like with you and Wilder?"

"If needed, yes."

"Because you don't trust me with them, or because I'm a child myself?"

When he doesn't answer, I feel something harden inside me.

"Lara—" Avery starts, but I ignore her, my glare on Crew instead.

"So it's okay for them to stay alone with two strange men

rather than me, the *child*"—I spit the word at Crew— "that raised them?"

He opens his mouth and shuts it again as I stare at him. Shaking my head, I turn back to Zig.

"If they can't stay with me, they stay with you."

"They can stay with us too. Bella is al—"

I whip my head around to look at Avery when she speaks. But whatever she sees on my face has her shutting up.

"You said we'd be safe here."

She flinches at the tone of my voice, and I see Zig take another step closer out of the corner of my eye.

The kids push closer to me, acting like a shield when it's my job to shield them.

"My mistake for thinking that included me," I say to her before turning to Zig. "I don't even care anymore. Kick me out, lock me up, do whatever you want, but you *will* keep the others safe, or my father will be the least of your worries," I snarl at Zig before I get down on my knees to talk to the kids, ignoring everyone else in the room.

"I'm sorry. I didn't mean to make everyone mad at you," Bella cries, throwing herself into my arms.

I hold her to me and breathe her in, sending a wave of calmness to her and the other kids. I keep it small, not wanting any of the others to feel it. They've already proven that I can't trust them, so I won't be revealing anything else, not when it will only be used against me.

"You didn't do anything wrong," I tell her, pulling back and wiping her cheeks.

"But everyone is mad at you now."

"That's not your fault or mine. We can't change how people

feel, Bella." I hold back a wince because, in my case, that's not exactly true. "All you can do is be who you are, and here, you'll be free to do just that."

I take Delaney in my arms and give her a hug when Bella steps back. When Delaney moves, Noah wraps his arms around my neck and buries his face in my hair. I let my calming power soothe him while I look at Alfie.

"I am so proud of you. You're always looking out for me and the others. And you're the kindest, bravest, and most courageous ten-year-old I've ever met, and I've met a few in my lifetime," I tease as his face takes on a shocked look.

Usually, when a lot is going on, Alfie slips on a pair of noise-canceling headphones to drown everyone out. Being here, in a more positive environment, he obviously felt like he could do without them for a little while. But as his hand slips into his pocket, I know he's dying to put them back on.

As a boy who remembers every word said to or around him, he's had the unfortunate luck of listening to some of the vilest things anyone could hear. What just happened is nothing compared to what he's been through. But when Alfie loves, he loves hard. And Alfie loves me. He won't like that I'm hurting or that the people he so desperately wants to like and trust are the ones to do it.

"One day, you'll grow up into an amazing man. But right now, you don't need to worry about me or them." I motion to the other adults in the room with my thumb. "You just need to worry about you. They won't hurt me, and they won't hurt you guys either."

He moves closer. Alfie isn't a hugger. Hell, he isn't a talker—well, he never used to be. I hold still as he dips a little and presses his forehead to mine. We stand like that for a few minutes, with

Noah wedged between us, and talk silently to one another. The message needs no words, only feelings, but I whisper to him anyway.

"I love you. I'm proud of you. Everything will be okay."

He doesn't say anything. He just stands there and absorbs my words, storing them away for later.

I pull back and kiss his head before getting to my feet. I set Noah down beside Alfie, who instantly takes Noah's hand and smiles softly at him. I feel pride shine in my eyes as I watch them.

Looking around the room, I skim over Wilder and Crew, jolting back when their expression isn't anger or disgust like before. It's something else entirely, something I can't put a name to because I've never witnessed it before.

I clear my throat and move my eyes to Zig, who's been joined by his brother Oz and Greg.

"If you need me..." I let my voice trail off because, even if they need me, they won't ask for my help. I see that now.

I keep my expression blank, refusing to let them see the pain they're causing me. It's stupid. I'm stupid. I've been hurt before by worse people, so why does it feel much more painful this time?

"I'll walk you to your cabin," Greg states.

"You're in no state to—" Oz starts, but Greg glares at him.

"I will walk her to her cabin and then head to mine to rest. I've lost my appetite all of a sudden. The smell of bullshit has that effect on me."

Before anyone can say anything, Greg walks over to me and bends his arm, offering me his elbow.

"Milady."

My lips twitch with the urge to grin, but I fight it back. My smiles are just that. *Mine.* I refuse to give these people more of me when they've already judged me so harshly.

I slip my arm through Greg's and feel him tremble slightly. I realize this is taking a far greater toll on him than he lets on, so I take a little more of his weight and lead him toward the doors.

I can hear the murmur of voices as soon as our backs are turned, but I ignore them. I need to get out of here. When I get outside, I'll be able to breathe through the pain. Once I'm alone, I'll allow my foolish tears to fall, but only for a moment. I've learned my lesson. I always do.

"Just hold on a little longer, sweetheart. We're almost there," Greg whispers as we get to the doors.

I jolt at his words, guessing I'm not hiding as well as I thought.

"You're doing fine. It's only because I can feel you shaking. Trust me when I say I know what it's like—not wanting to seem weak in front of others. Grab the door."

I hesitate for a second before opening the door and holding it while Greg steps through first and tugs me after him.

He takes a deep breath once we're outside, and I do the same.

"You'll come home with me."

"I... Umm... Look, I'm not sure what you—"

He chuckles. "Am I that terrifying? You could take me down with your pinkie finger right now."

I relax at his words because they're true. It's just that logic and panic rarely co-exist.

"I have a two-bedroom cabin. Bedroom two is a guest room-slash-office. It is yours for as long as you want, be it one night or one hundred."

"Why?" I whisper. "I already have a cabin."

"A cabin you share with children. Children make a mess, and

they make noise. Without them, that place will feel very lonely, and I know a thing or two about loneliness."

"How can you be lonely? You have so many people who love you."

"So do you."

"I do not—"

"That boy would take a bullet for you."

I growl at his words. "Nobody will be taking a bullet for me, especially not one of my kids."

"Calm down, Mama Bear; your babies are safe."

I blow out a breath and nod but still feel tense.

"He stood in front of you. The boy who hides from the world stood in front of you to protect you."

I swallow back my tears.

"Alfie, is it?"

At my nod, he continues, "I'm sure he has many reasons to be scared of people. And because of it, he is shy and reserved, but with you, he is just a boy, and he loves you wholeheartedly. Same with the others. They take your words as the gospel truth, no question at all, and they do so because they trust you. And after what they've been through, I know that trust was not given lightly but earned."

He uses his free hand to pat mine.

"They are your family, and they love you. So for you to go home and them not be there..." He shakes his head.

I bite my lip because he's right. I've been raising children for so long—not just these ones but the ones who came before them—that I don't know how to be me without them.

"That still doesn't explain why you want me to stay with you," I tell him warily. "I know you don't trust me—"

"Oh, I trust you, Lara. I know how this is going to play out."

"I'm sorry. I'm lost. How what plays out?"

He looks at me and grins, though it has an edge of pain to it. "Those men in there are the best men I know. I would die for them, and they would die for me. We are bound not by blood but by choice, and our bond is far stronger because of it. That doesn't mean that I don't see them as the fucking idiots they are sometimes."

Without meaning to, a burst of laughter escapes me, surprising us both. Greg grins before tugging me along to his house.

"Stick with me, kid. I have a few stories I think you might like to hear. It all started with Zig and Oz and the day they saw a photo of Salem..."

Chapter Two

Wilder

Avery whirls on us as soon as the door closes.

"Seriously?"

I cross my arms over my chest and look at Hawk standing beside her.

"Don't tell me you don't have the same concerns."

"I trust her." Avery juts out her chin, daring me to argue.

"You didn't exactly speak up for her," Astrid says from where she's standing. "This isn't me trying to place the blame on you, but you're the only one here who knows her. So when you didn't step in..." She trails off, not needing to say anymore. Avery's lack of defense made our actions seem more justified.

"I was shocked. It wasn't because I don't trust her. It was finding out who her father was and her real age. I was more focused on that than anything else." Avery sighs, running a hand through her hair.

"If she's telling the truth, then he's my father too. Are you all going to start treating me differently because of it?" Salem aims her question at us as Zig walks over to her, placing his hand on the small of her back in silent support.

"Of course not, but we know you. And you were not raised by him like she was."

"I think *raised* might be pushing it. The age thing shocked me because she doesn't look or act seventeen, and she's been working for the department as long as I've been there. Hell, she was there before I was," Avery tells us, making me tense.

"She was working there when she was a child? What the fuck?"

Avery shrugs. "She's always looked after the kids. I assumed she was older because of it. I didn't realize she was one herself."

I feel my gut clench at that. When I first laid eyes on Lara, I knew I wanted her. One look at Crew, and I knew he was feeling the same way. Finally, we would get what the others had. But I guess the joke's on us. Seventeen years old. Fuck, I'm nothing but a pervert.

"Will she be staying with one of us?" Slade asks. The man had been remarkably quiet until now, which is unlike him.

"She's seventeen, not seven, and probably more mature than all you guys here put together," Salem huffs.

"She's still a kid," Crew grunts out.

"Not really. Jesus, when I think back to what I got up to at her age." Oz shakes his head. "We had Luna following us around everywhere, but we were still shitheads. I can tell you this: we didn't have anywhere near the patience with her that Lara does with those kids."

"I think you're overreacting because of the shock of finding out that Salem's Penn Travis is so much more than we thought he was," Ev states, his eyes moving to Avery. "I need to know whatever you have on her."

"Well, since I didn't know how old she really was, clearly I don't know much."

"What's her gift?" Jagger asks, making everyone quiet down.

I look over at the kids, who are all now watching TV. Alfie glances over at us warily before facing forward again, so I lower my voice.

"That's a good question. We should know what we're dealing with."

"*Who,*" Astrid fumes. "*Who* you're dealing with. Thirty minutes ago, you looked at her like she had the answer to world peace. Now you're acting like she's the enemy. It's like you guys are destined to repeat each other's mistakes," she mumbles the last part.

"It's not the same," Crew huffs. "She's seventeen. We won't be going anywhere near her."

"She won't be seventeen forever. And honestly, if she isn't worth waiting for, then she isn't the one for you." She turns and walks out. Slade, shrugging his shoulders, follows her.

"I'm not telling you her gift. That's up to Lara to share," Avery states.

"If we didn't have a houseful of kids, I'd wait. But we do, and we need to make sure we can protect them." Oz sighs.

"If you think the kids need protecting from Lara, then you haven't been paying attention at all." She storms out.

Creed curses. "I'll go talk to her. Explain things."

"Good luck. Lara had no reason to leave the Division, but she still came here for them." Salem gestures to the children. "She did that so she could keep them safe, and you just shit all over that by insinuating that they need to be protected from her." Salem takes a deep breath before continuing. "Revealing a gift, one you might have been hiding for safety or because you've had to use it against your will, is traumatic enough without having someone do it for you. I have a feeling that girl hasn't had many things in her life. Don't take something else from her."

"Salem," Oz sighs as he steps closer, but she knows him as well as I do. He won't back down on this.

"Do what you want, Oz. You always do. I'm going to check on our son. I hope to fuck someone shows him more kindness than we showed Lara."

She leaves, shoving past Oz.

"Thanks for having my back, brother," Oz grumbles at Zig.

"No point in her being pissed at both of us." Zig shrugs with no remorse. "Besides, I'm not sure I'm on the same side as you guys are."

"What do you mean?" Oz asks.

"Exactly what I said. She hasn't done anything other than take good care of those kids. She's quiet, polite, respectful, and jumps in to help with anything without being asked. What she hasn't done is make any demands, prod for answers, or dig for information. Despite these two here"—he points at me and Crew— "hovering around her, she's kept her head down."

"Well, that won't be an issue anymore."

"Like Astrid said, she won't be seventeen forever. But that's up to you. What I don't want to do is isolate a young woman and treat her like she's the enemy. If we do, I'm not sure we can say we are any better than they are."

"Knowing what her gift is would go a long way to calming this down." Jagger sighs. I'm not sure I agree, and apparently, neither does Zig.

"Yeah? And what if her gift is something dangerous? Is that going to make you feel better? No, it won't. So what then? We lock her up, pretend it's for her safety, and make her stay there until she proves herself to us in some arbitrary way? Yeah, because that worked out so well the last couple of times." He lifts an eyebrow.

I stare at Zig in surprise. It's not often that there's a divide between us. Most of the time, we're united in our feelings. But he does have a point.

"Can you honestly say that having her around our boy without knowing what her gift is doesn't faze you?" Oz asks incredulously.

"Yeah, I can, because those kids in there love her. There isn't a single ounce of fear in them directed at Lara. In fact, after the stunt we just pulled, I think if they're scared of anyone, it's us. What I also find fascinating is that for the last week, not one of you questioned her ability to look after those kids or be around Aries. None of you asked what her gift was, but the second you find out who her father is, she's dangerous. Since when did we make the child pay for the sins of the father?"

"I can't believe you're not more concerned." I shake my head.

"One of us has to be level-headed."

"So, what the fuck do you expect us to do?" Oz snaps.

"Did any of you just think to ask her?" Zig sighs.

Nobody says anything because, of course, we didn't.

"I'm sure she'll be really open to sharing now," Oz grumbles.

"What the fuck is your problem?" Zig snarls at him.

"You. We have kids here to protect."

"Yeah, and Lara is one of them," Zig replies.

Ev leans against the counter. "Let's just pull back and think for a minute. How did she act when Bella spilled the beans about her father? Frustrated? Guilty? Pissed that all her wicked plans were foiled? I saw her face, and I can tell you I didn't see any of that. I saw embarrassment, shame, and fear. He might have the same blood as her, but judging by her reactions, I think it's safe to say there's no love there."

I rub my hand over my face. Thinking back and looking past my own shock, I realize he's right.

"Do any of you really think she's a danger to the kids?"

I close my eyes and blow out my breath before answering. "No."

"Then can we please stop acting like fucking Neanderthals? She helped Avery escape, and she kept all these kids safe and calm. She could have run at any point, but she didn't. I think being here with all of us is confusing her. It's obvious she's never experienced anything like us."

"We're mercenaries, Zig, that's not surprising."

"Right now, Oz, you're just being a dick. I'm talking about family."

Oz shuts his mouth at that.

I look at Creed but can't get a read on what he's thinking.

Zig's words are starting to penetrate, though. We just pounced on her and treated her like shit. Why the fuck would she trust us and tell us her secret? If it were me, I would have left and never looked back.

My gaze moves to the kids before I curse. Walking away isn't an option when everyone she cares about is right here.

"I see you're getting it now." Zig sighs.

"Look, we've all fucked up. Some of us worse than others,"

Hawk starts, and I flip him off. "But that doesn't mean you can't make it right."

"She's seventeen."

"So you can't be her friend?"

"My dick doesn't want to be friends with her," I fire back.

"Well, if it helps, I think any shot you might have had with her is long gone." Oz grins. The prick.

"Jesus Christ, you make me glad I had a son, not a daughter. I'll go talk to her." Zig starts walking toward the door, but the thought of him alone with Lara makes something inside me snap. I don't give a fuck if he's with Salem or not.

"I'll go," I call out, stopping him.

"Not sure that's a good idea," Crew mutters, which doesn't surprise me. He knows how much I want her.

"It'll be fine. I just need to clear some things up. You wanna come?"

"No, I need some air." He turns and leaves in the other direction.

I walk over to Zig, who glares at me. Eventually, he sighs and nods. "Fine, but don't be a dick. I'd hate to have to kick your ass."

"Ask her what her gift is," Oz calls out. I don't even look at him as I head out.

I jog over to her place before I can change my mind. When I get there, I take a deep breath and knock. When she doesn't answer, I knock again, louder this time.

I tense before moving to look through the window, hoping she's just ignoring me and hasn't left. The thought of her leaving makes my stomach knot, even though I know she wouldn't go and leave the kids behind, especially not without saying goodbye.

I can't see her, so I head over to Greg's, hoping Lara told him where she was going. I pound on the door and wait impatiently for him to answer. When he finally does, I'm about ready to rip my hair out.

"Yes?"

"Do you know where Lara went? I can't find her."

"Why do you want to know where she is?"

"I just want to talk to her."

"I think you've said enough for now, Wilder. Don't you?"

"Dammit, Greg, now is not the time to piss me off. Do you know where she is or not?"

"I do. And no, she doesn't want to see you or anyone else."

I close my eyes and count to ten, reminding myself that he's recovering from a gunshot wound and that it would be shitty of me to punch him in the face.

Chapter Three

Lara

I sit on the edge of the bed as Greg answers the door. I knew they'd send someone to find me. I might be a coward for hiding away, but I'm not ready to talk to anyone yet. They didn't want to listen to me before, so now they can damn well wait. Yes, I know I sound like the child they think I am, but I don't care.

A child. Me. I snort at the idea. If a child is defined by their age, then sure, I guess for another few days, I'm a child. But if being a child is defined by their experiences, then I am positively ancient.

I lie back with a huff. I can hear the muffled voices, but I can't make out what's being said. Part of me is tempted to creep closer and listen in, but the other part doesn't want to know. I've found out the hard way that listening in on someone's conversation can cause more harm than good.

"She's defective. How does someone with a gift as strong as

mine produce a dud? I don't understand. Are you sure she's mine? Perhaps there was a mix-up with the samples used." I hear my father's voice and feel my heart break.

At ten, I'm already well aware that he is nothing like the fathers I see on TV. To him, I'm more of an inconvenience than anything else—someone who's easier to ignore than interact with. Still, deep down inside, there was a part of me that thought he might love me in his own way.

And now I know differently.

I stare at the ceiling as the memory drifts away, wondering where I go from here. Technically, I'm a minor. If I ran and was caught, I'd be returned to my father. If I stayed, these guys could be brought up on kidnapping charges. However, with the younger kids here, they must have considered that already.

It's not as easy as going to the police and filing a missing person report or pursuing kidnapping charges when my father would have to explain who these children were and why he had them in the first place. It's more complicated for me. There's a record of the others. They were all born in hospitals that would have registered their births. Which means they'll all have birth certificates. I have nothing. Not a birth certificate. Not a social security number. There is no record of my birth now that the lab has been blown up. I'm not sure if that's a blessing or a curse.

If people don't know about me, they can't hunt me down. But how do you live in a world that doesn't know you exist? How do you make connections, get a job, or buy a house? How would you get married?

I feel the tendrils of panic start to set in. Running away isn't an option. I can't survive without using my gift and doing that isn't something I'm comfortable with. I don't want to end up like my father.

I jolt at the sound of knocking on my door and lift up onto my elbows before it's pushed open a little, and Greg pokes his head in.

"It was Wilder. He wanted to talk to you, but I told him you didn't want to see him. He's gone now, but he'll be back. Won't hurt them all to stew a little," he tells me as I sit all the way up, thankful that he took care of Wilder for the time being.

"Are you doing okay?"

I nod before shaking my head, feeling tears fill my eyes.

"Oh, sweetheart," he says as he rushes over to me and sits on the bed next to me, grimacing in pain, but that doesn't stop him from wrapping his arm around me. "It might seem hopeless right now, but things have a way of figuring themselves out."

I lay my head on his shoulder and let the tears fall, trying to remember the last time I was held by someone. I draw a complete blank. How pathetic am I? I'm on the verge of adulthood, and where other girls my age are barely able to keep their hands to themselves, I'm touch-starved.

"You've had a lot happen in the last week. And well, I can only imagine what life was like for you before. I just want you to know I'm here for you if you need me. No strings attached. You just look like you could use a friend. And lucky for you, I happen to be a pretty damn good one."

"I don't have a very good track record with friends."

"I find that hard to believe, Lara."

I smile through my tears. "It's hard to make friends when the people you come into contact with never stick around."

"What about school or boyfriends?"

I lift my head and look at him, wiping my cheeks. "I didn't go to school. I had tutors, and I sure as heck wasn't allowed to be alone with any boys."

He turns to look at me and frowns. "You were homeschooled?"

"Homeschooled implies there was a home involved. I was born and raised at the Division, Greg," I tell him softly.

His sharp inhale of breath has me reaching over and squeezing his hands.

"I was alone sometimes. Sometimes there were other kids, but most were either much older or younger than me."

The look on his face has me snapping my mouth shut.

"What about your mother?"

I dip my head and bite my lip.

God, when I was little, how I used to pray for one of those. As I got older, though, I found, in a strange way, that I was grateful not to have one. No mother meant I had one less person to manipulate and use me. One less person to lose, one less person to make me feel completely expendable.

"I never had one in the truest sense of the word. An egg was harvested from a gifted one. It was fertilized in a test tube with my father's sperm and then placed inside a surrogate. I was born in the medical ward there, and the rest is, well, history." I shrug.

He looks dumbfounded and, if I'm honest, a little sad too.

"I'm okay, Greg. I'm here, safe and sound. I made it out alive and relatively unscathed. Not everyone was as lucky as I was."

"Only you would consider that lucky." He pulls me to him again. This time, I sense that it's more for his sake than mine. What I said has upset him, but I don't understand why.

"How about we head over to your place and grab some of your things? Tomorrow, I'll take you into town for breakfast. After that, we'll pick up some things to girly this place up a little and maybe get you some books or something. Girls like books, right?"

I feel myself getting choked up once more. "This girl does," I whisper. Books have, at times, been my only solace.

"Then that's what we'll do."

"Okay, but I'll go get my things. You need to rest for a little while."

He brushes me off. "Oh, I'll be fine."

I look up into his eyes. "Right now, you're the only friend I've got. Please. Even if you just do it for me."

He narrows his eyes at me. "Hmm... You're gonna be trouble, I can tell. Next thing I know, you'll be making me eat healthy crap and insist I take my medicine."

I smile. "Maybe."

Given that I only have the items that were purchased for me since I arrived here, it takes me next to no time to shove everything into a plastic bag.

I glance at the pink bunny lying on the pillow next to mine and picture Delaney's hair spread out on the pillow, snuggling with it. She doesn't sleep well alone, so she's been sleeping with me. I hope she'll be okay with the others.

Picking up the bunny, I hold it to my nose and breathe it in, ignoring the pang in my chest. I've never lived with a family before, yet I've never felt lonelier.

I place the bunny back on the bed, grab my bag, and walk out of the room and down the hall to the next one. Standing in the doorway, I look inside. The room has two beds sitting side by side, separated by a small table between them with a lamp set upon it. Each bed has blue bedding. One is meticulously made, and the other a balled-up mess.

Noah and Alfie couldn't be more different, but Alfie is protective of Noah and has taken him under his wing. I hope that it will continue in my absence.

At the Division, gifted people were so often seen as commodities at best and monsters at worst, but we were all simply human. As children, before everything had been beaten out of us and stripped away, our humanity was our greatest gift. They didn't seem to understand that we were not born monsters. We became what they forced us to be.

I stare around the small cabin that had felt more like home than the Division ever did and close my eyes against the onslaught of emotion and unshed tears.

It takes me far longer than I hoped to calm myself down. Longer still to bury my resentment and anger. I try not to let negative feelings like that consume me, but I'll admit that some days it's so much harder than others.

Taking a deep breath, I open my eyes and head for the front door. It's silly to mourn for something that doesn't have a heartbeat. But then, I suppose, in a roundabout way, homes do have heartbeats because they hold the people we love. And now, this place is nothing more than an empty shell, holding only tiny fragments of memories that, for a moment, made the biggest impression.

Chapter Four

Crew

Sweat coats my skin, making my T-shirt stick to me as I finish my run. Running has always allowed me to clear my mind and help me focus, but since Lara arrived, it's all been shot to shit.

Every time I try to push her from my mind, I see her face as we turned on her—the pain in her eyes before she could mask it.

I saw no guilt. Honestly, if I had to put money on it, I'd say Lara is as innocent as she's claiming to be. But I've been wrong before—an image of Cooper flashes through my mind—and I won't risk everyone here because my dick salutes every time she walks past me.

I shake my head, reminding myself that she's seventeen. Seven-fucking-teen. What kind of man gets hard for a girl half his age, one that's not even an adult yet?

I grimace. If anyone should feel guilty, it's me.

As I run past Hawk and Creed's place, I slow down when I spot Avery sitting on the deck with a mug in her hand. Her gaze is on the mountains in the distance, but something tells me she's not seeing them right now.

"Hey, Avery, you okay?" I stop and wait until she turns to look at me. She looks tired and anxious.

"I guess. I just have a lot on my mind."

"You talk to your men about it?"

"They're busy getting everything packed up so we can move into Luna's old place. With Ev and Bella and the baby on the way, we need the room."

"Makes sense." I sit on the bottom step, keeping a little space between us so I don't crowd her.

"If you need someone to talk to, I'm a pretty good listener," I offer.

She shakes her head and huffs out a little laugh before lifting her mug to her lips.

"Should you be drinking coffee in your condition?" I ask.

"It's decaf," she says before taking a drink.

"Oh."

Judging by her grimace, it's not good.

"Anyway, thanks for the offer, but I'm not sure you, of all people, can help me right now."

I frown. "What's that supposed to mean?"

She looks at me and lifts an eyebrow as if to say, really?

I blow out a breath. "Lara."

"She's all I can think about. I fucked up. I let her down when she needed me, and I don't think she'll let me back in again."

I roll my eyes. "You didn't do anything wrong."

"I didn't defend her. When everyone attacked her, I didn't step in."

"We were protecting our family," I say defensively.

"She might not be family to us yet, but to those kids, she's mom and dad all rolled into one. And we took her from them."

I don't know what to do with that, so I keep my mouth shut. The truth is, Lara is probably all they know, but that doesn't necessarily make her the best person to look after them.

"What we went through... How she kept a cool head and made sure all those kids were safe..." She shakes her head and blows out a breath. "She helped me get home. Shouldn't that make her my friend?"

I shrug. "Escaping a madman doesn't make you friends. She is a kid, though. Maybe we are being hard on her, given her age."

Now it's Avery's turn to frown. "I'd hardly call her a kid. I don't know what your life was like at that age, but mine, Astrid's, and Salem's were anything but easy. She's not a normal teenager. She's seen too much, and I bet she's been asked to do things she didn't want to. If our experiences determined our age, I'd say she's far more mature than you and Wilder put together."

I cross my arms, trying to figure out if that's a compliment to Lara or an insult to me.

"Bella refused to stay here last night. She wanted to stay with Delaney and the boys."

"She's a kid. Of course she'd want that."

"I think it was more than that. She's mad at me for the way everything went down yesterday. And I worry that, as a result, she'll be reluctant to tell me about her visions in the future in case they upset anyone."

I run my fingers through my hair and sigh. "I think you should talk to her. Tell her you're not mad. I'm sure she'll forgive you."

"I wasn't mad to begin with. I was shocked and, if anything, pissed at myself for not figuring it out sooner."

"How could you? If Bella hadn't let it slip, none of us would have known. What pisses me off is that she didn't tell us herself. That she was going to hide it from us."

"Was she? You seem to know an awful lot about the thought process of a girl you've known for a week." She gives me a knowing look, and I open my mouth, not sure what I'm about to say, when her face falls, and she sighs. "I've been thinking about what I would have done if Penn were my dad, and I can honestly say I wouldn't have said anything either. Not until I was sure I could trust you. Hell, I didn't tell you all I had a gift, and I considered you my family."

"You're right, Avery. I don't know her, neither of us do, and maybe that will change, but in the meantime, it would be wise to be cautious."

"Then don't expect her not to act the same way."

I look away, not sure I like that idea. If she's overly cautious, we won't get the information out of her that we need.

Avery laughs. "You can't have it both ways, Crew. You want to treat her with suspicion, then be prepared for her to return the favor."

Hmm... unless I can get her to lower her guard enough to let us in. I doubt she has much experience with men. Maybe her inexperience will come in handy. If we can get her to like us, then maybe she'll share. And if she does and exposes herself as a plant for her father, we'll be ready. If it turns out she's innocent, then she'll eventually understand our motives. After all, she told us herself that the most important thing is to keep the kids safe. And right now, this is the only way I can think to do it.

I stand up and look at Avery.

"Everything is a little fresh right now, but Bella will come around, and so will Lara. I'm going to go finish my run and grab a shower. I have my own apology to give."

She frowns at me for a moment before her expression changes, and I realize she's using her gift to tell if I'm lying. Fuck, I'm going to have to be careful how I word things.

"You're serious. I thought you were still insisting she wasn't trustworthy."

"I never said she wasn't trustworthy, just that I was wary of her, that's all. But you made me realize I'm being a bit of a dick."

She stares at me in shock, and I can't say I blame her. This is a complete one-eighty from when I sat down. But what I said was true. I never said she wasn't trustworthy. And I am a dick. I just don't think sharing my plan with her will make me very popular, so I need to make it believable. The fewer people that know, the better.

I finish my run, take a shower, and get dressed in a pair of black jeans and a gray T-shirt.

When I head out to the living area, I find Wilder at the kitchen island with a coffee in front of him.

"Hey, where were you this morning so early?"

"Couldn't sleep. I patrolled the perimeter before heading over to the main house."

I take in his expression. "Something wrong?"

He looks up at me and sighs. "No. Everything looked fine. I just have this weird feeling, that's all. I went over to see Zig."

"Because he seems to have a sixth sense when it comes to weird feelings."

"Yeah. I figured if he hadn't sensed anything wrong, then it was probably just in my head."

"And, what did he say?"

"Not much. Just told me to keep an eye out and my ear to the ground."

"Fuck. So he senses something off, too, huh?"

"That's my take on it. Though, to be fair, he was a little preoccupied when I saw him. One of the kids couldn't sleep. She spent most of the night crying for Lara."

An uncomfortable feeling swells inside me. It was my suggestion that we separate the kids from Lara to begin with.

"Do you think it's linked to Lara?"

"What? The odd feeling?"

I nod, reaching into the cupboard for a glass before filling it with water.

"I don't see how. She's had no contact with anyone outside Apex. She has no cell phone, laptop, or tablet, so she has no access to the internet or to email."

I nod, taking a drink of my water.

"Can I ask you something?"

I nod. "Sure."

"What do you want to do about Lara? I know we've backed off because of her age and who her father is. But she won't be seventeen forever, like everyone keeps reminding us."

I groan and take the seat beside him. "I feel like a fucking pervert. I knew she was young, but I thought she was like twenty-one. She doesn't act like any seventeen-year-old I know, and she sure as hell doesn't look like one. Not with all those curves. She looks more like a Victoria Secret model than a high school aged teenager

"Know many teenagers, do you?"

"No, but..." I rub my hand down my face.

He doesn't say anything while he waits for me to answer his original question.

"Fucking hell, Wilder. What do you want me to say? Do I still want her? Of course I do, she's a fucking goddess, a dream, but that's all it will ever be. She's half our fucking age."

"You know there's an age gap between all the women and their men here, right? But I'm not talking about doing anything while she is still seventeen. I'm talking about afterward," he says before he sighs. "But we don't know if we can trust her yet."

"We don't know that we can't." I play devil's advocate. "Anyway, this brings me to what I wanted to talk to you about. I was talking to Avery this morning, and it got me thinking."

"Why do I feel like I'm not going to like this?"

"Probably because you won't." I brace myself but push on. "Avery made a point earlier about how Lara will probably keep herself guarded now."

"Can't blame her for that. Trust goes both ways, right?"

"I know, and I get it, but we don't have the time to build it just so we can unearth the answers she is hiding."

His eyes widen. "The answers she's hiding? What the fuck does that mean?"

"She worked for the Division. I'm not saying she'd willingly put those kids in danger, far from it, but that doesn't mean she doesn't know something that she might keep to herself to protect her father."

"Shit."

"I'm not saying they have a perfect father-daughter relationship. She wouldn't have run with the kids if that was the case. But that doesn't mean she doesn't care for the man. You know how complicated families can be."

He nods. "So, what's your plan? Clearly, you have one."

"I think we need to get close to her. Just as friends for now, though I think she has a crush on us. So, a little flirting wouldn't hurt. Once we've gained her trust, I'm sure she'll tell us everything we need to know."

He frowns. "And then what?"

"Then we can back off."

"Jesus, Crew. I'm not that much of a dick. I'm not going to play with this girl's emotions like that. Besides, I don't know if, when all is said and done, I'll be able to walk away."

I look at him for a second, wishing things could've been different.

"Depending on what we find out, you might just have to."

Chapter Five

Lara

I turn away from the open window and cover my mouth with my hand so nothing comes out.

I thought a walk would clear my mind, but I had no idea that I would hear my name when I was walking past their window. I should have kept going. I know better than to listen in on conversations, but a part of me desperately wanted to know if there was even an ounce of regret in their actions.

Now I know I've been nothing but a fool. Tears prick my eyes, but I refuse to let them fall. Fuck them. I don't deserve this. I did nothing wrong, unless you count being born.

I hurry away before someone sees me and head back to Greg's place. Blowing out a deep breath, I make sure I'm composed before knocking on the door.

When Greg opens it, he frowns before cursing. "I can't believe I forgot to give you a key."

"It's okay. I didn't want to wake you. I just went for a walk."

"Well, now that we're both up and dressed, how about that ride into town?"

My first instinct is to say no and hide away in my room, but that's all I've ever done. Hide away from the world and watch life pass me by.

"Yeah, I'd like that, Greg. Thank you. I promise that when it's safe, I'll get a job and pay you back for everything."

"No, you won't. This is my gift to you. I don't have any kids or grandkids to give it to—something that hit home when I was shot. I can't take it with me when I go, so let me do what I want with it while I still can."

"Wow, and you said I was trouble. But you, sir, are the master of guilt."

He grins. "Thank you. I've been training my whole life for this moment."

I can't help it—I laugh. It's impossible not to like Greg.

"I'm going to head over to the main house and let the others know where we're going. I'll meet you over there."

"How about I meet you at the car?"

"I'll meet you at the main house. You've done nothing to be ashamed of. Don't let those assholes treat you like you have."

I bite my lip, giving in. "Okay, I'll meet you over there in ten minutes. I want to freshen up."

"Take as long as you need. I won't leave without you."

I swallow around the sudden lump in my throat, unsure where it came from. No, that's not true. It was Greg's comment about not leaving me. It's a sweet thing to say. No one has ever waited for me. I've always been an afterthought, always left alone. If life has taught me anything, saying and doing are two different things.

Freedom has always been a fairy tale to me, something unattainable, but loneliness has always been my constant companion. I could be standing in a room full of people, but I'll always be alone.

"I won't be long," I reiterate. I won't keep him waiting. I don't want to risk him changing his mind. And getting out of this place, even for just a little while, sounds like heaven.

I wait for Greg to leave before I head to the bathroom. Taking a deep breath, I wash my face and finger-comb my hair up into a messy bun. Staring at my reflection, I briefly wonder if it's worth getting up each morning and putting on the act I've been forced to play—the one where I meet everyone's expectations and don't rock the boat. I don't draw attention to myself or ask questions when I know it's better to keep my mouth shut.

It would be so much easier to go to sleep and never wake up. There'd be no more fear, no more pain, no more hiding who I am and where I came from. No more hiding what I can do.

But every time those dark thoughts creep in, I see Alfie in my mind—his too-serious face that's just one more loss away from crumbling. I picture Delaney crying for me at night and Noah withdrawing further. I shudder at the thought of Bella watching it all play out in a vision. No matter what, I won't do that to them. My pain is no greater than theirs. They have endured more than me, and they're still here, still holding on. If they can do it, so can I.

Standing straight, I turn away from the mirror and head out to meet Greg.

I don't pass anyone on my way, thankfully. But as I get closer, I can see through the windows that there are a few people already inside. I had hoped to avoid as many of them as I could for as long as possible, but I guess that was wishful thinking.

I pull the door open and freeze when the conversation grinds to a halt and all eyes turn my way. I stay where I am, my pulse racing, unsure if I should stay or turn around and run.

Greg takes the choice out of my hands. "Ah, there you are. Let's get this show on the road. You're going to have to drive, thanks to my stupid injury. Do you drive stick?"

I bite my lip, my head dipping with embarrassment. "I can't drive. I don't have a license."

More silence before I hear Oz speak. "You can't drive because you don't have a license, or you don't have a license because you can't drive?"

I lift my head, meeting his gaze. "Both."

He frowns at me, confused, and the truth spills out. "I can't get a license without a birth certificate, and even if I had one, there was never anyone to teach me."

He growls. "I'll teach you."

I jolt at the unexpected offer. "Did you forget that you hate me?"

He rolls his eyes. "I don't hate you. I'm an asshole, but I'm an asshole to everyone. Don't take it personally. I'm not saying I trust you, but I'm sure I'll get there."

I swallow and take a step forward. It's not the worst apology I've ever heard, but it's far from the best. Yet, it might just be the most genuine.

"Thank you, Oz, I'd like that," I tell him softly.

* * *

I take in the scenery as it speeds by. Everything is so big and bright.

"You okay back there?"

I look at Greg, who is peering over his shoulder at me from the front seat.

"Yeah. It's just really pretty here. I've never seen anything like it."

"You should see it in the fall. All the colors. I think it might be my favorite season. What about you?"

I shrug. "I never really got to appreciate the seasons in the city. Everything was just cold and gray, wet and gray, then warm and gray."

Oz snorts before taking a left turn. "You've never been to the country before?"

"I've never been anywhere before." I turn to look back out the window, not wanting to miss anything.

"Remind me to take you to see the ocean one day."

I whip my head around. "Really?" My voice comes out barely above a whisper.

I see him frown at me in the rearview mirror. "Of course."

I settle back in my seat, a soft smile playing on my lips at the thought. It might not seem like much to those who take it for granted, but seeing the ocean—dipping my feet in the cool water and leaving my footprints on the warm sand—has always been on my to-do list.

When I was younger, I watched a movie about a woman who found a message in a bottle. Something about it struck a chord with me. So few people knew I existed. I wanted to write a note and pour my heart out in it, but knowing my luck, it would probably end up on the ocean floor.

The dreamer in me, however, always loved the idea that one

day, maybe long after I'd gone, someone would read those words and know I lived. That I laughed and cried, had hope, and despaired. That I was more than my gift.

When the car stops, I realize I've gotten lost in my thoughts.

"We're here?"

"We are. I hope you're hungry. This diner makes amazing pancakes."

I grin as excited as a kid about to enter a toy store and hurriedly unbuckle my seat belt. I open my door and climb out before opening Greg's for him and offering him my hand.

He grumbles but takes it. "It should be me holding the door open for you."

"I'm a big girl. I've been opening doors on my own my whole life."

"Smart ass."

Smiling, I wait for him to step away from the door before I close it. Oz is ready and waiting for us on the sidewalk.

"You're coming with us?" Greg asks, surprised.

"Did you not hear me mention the pancakes here?"

I bite my lip as I step up next to Oz, and he looks down at me.

"That okay with you?"

"Are you going to be mean to me? Are you going to make me cry?" I let my lip wobble and hold back a smirk as his eyes widen.

"Fuck, no. Please don't cry. I'll get you a stack of pancakes if you don't cry."

"With bacon?"

"Of course."

"And syrup?"

His eyes narrow. "You little faker," he says, and I can't help but burst out laughing. He wraps his arm around my shoulders, shaking his head, and leads me toward the door. "And yes, syrup too. How can you possibly have pancakes without syrup? Come on, old man, keep up," he calls to Greg over his shoulder.

"Call me old again, and I'll shove my foot so far up your ass you'll be able to lick my toes," Greg mutters, making me giggle.

"Sounds kinky." Oz smirks.

"Remember, there is a child present," I tease, making Oz look down at me apologetically until he gets a look at the look on my face.

"Oh, I see how it is. I knew you were going to be trouble." I tense at his words, my mind flashing back to Wilder and Crew's disdain.

"Don't worry. I know all about trouble. Trouble is my middle name," he boasts, holding the door open for Greg and me.

"Liar. Your middle name is Zephyr," Greg says with a smirk.

I choke down a laugh. "Your name is Oz Zephyr?"

"It's Cosmic Zephyr, actually." Greg laughs as Oz glares at him.

"Cosmic Zephyr? Did your parents hate you? Did you break your mother's vagina with your giant head or something?"

"One, I do not have a giant head, and two, never mention my mother and her vagina in the same sentence again," he bellows as the waitress approaches us.

She stops, a surprised look on her face, before she spins on her heel and takes off. Oz looks at her retreating form with confusion, which has me cracking up.

"You never learned to use your indoor voice, did you?"

He rolls his eyes and walks between me and Greg to get to a

booth in the back. He slides in on one side, so I sit on the opposite side and scooch over so that Greg can ease in beside me.

I look around the place and smile. The vinyl booths, the long counter edged with chrome, and the large jukebox in the corner make me feel like I'm on the set of a movie.

"I love it here already," I announce.

Greg looks around and smiles.

"Yeah, they renovated after Avery was shot. Took it back to its retro roots."

"Avery was shot here?" I gasp. I knew she had hidden something from us, but I thought it was because she wanted to keep my and Bella's involvement to a minimum.

"You didn't know?" Oz asks, frowning, as he hands me one of the plastic-coated menus.

"No. I didn't. She called and said things hadn't gone as planned, but she didn't say anything about getting shot."

"She probably didn't want to worry you," Greg says, placing his hand on my knee.

"Yeah, probably," I say softly, but I'm not sure that's the truth. Did she ever really care about us, or were we just a job to her, a burden? Either way, if James hadn't kidnapped her, would she have returned?

My appetite disappears at the idea of being nothing more than an afterthought.

"You know what you want?" Greg asks Oz as my mind drifts.

I dwell on the fact that Avery could have died, my mind spinning with what-ifs.

"Lara."

I snap out of my thoughts and look at Oz, who watches me intensely.

"Still want pancakes?"

Pancakes. Something I've seen a million times but never actually had. All my meals were made for me. Each calorie counted and deemed healthy, so definitely no pancakes.

"Sure, Oz, pancakes sound good."

Chapter Six

Wilder

I contemplate Crew's words, and no matter how many times I go over them in my head, I can't picture a single scenario that will allow us to walk away without someone getting hurt.

"Is everything okay, Wilder?"

I look over at Salem as she walks towards me and offer her a smile.

"Yeah, I'm good."

"Really? Because I've been saying your name for the last five minutes."

I sigh as she sits down beside me and rests her head on my arm.

"I'm thinking about Lara," I admit.

"So you guys realized you were being assholes and apologized?"

"Rome wasn't built in a day, honey."

"No, but it burned in one. Look, if you don't fix this now, it'll get worse, and by the time you finally man up and find the balls to apologize, she won't listen to a word you say."

"Being a mom has made you mean."

"Being a mom brings out all these protective instincts in me. Lara might not be my daughter, but she is my sister. And I'm disgusted at how quickly a group of adults turned on her in a moment based on her DNA. You're all lucky I didn't kick your asses."

"None of us were acting rationally, Salem. It's been a rough few months. You were attacked, we almost lost Astrid, Avery was shot and kidnapped, James is dead, and Greg almost joined him. And it's all because of the Division and that motherfucker Penn. Everyone is just being cautious."

"I understand, but that doesn't make it right. Even Oz realized he was a dick, and let's be honest, self-awareness is not his strong point. He drove Greg and Lara into town earlier. Judging by the time, I'd say he decided to stick around, not because he doesn't trust her with Greg, but because he feels bad for what he said and wants a second chance."

"But we *don't* know if we can trust her yet."

"We didn't know if we could trust her before we found out her father is Penn, but that didn't stop you from wanting her. Now you're acting like she's guilty of something because he's her father. Are you really going to crucify the child for his sins? If so, then remember, he might be my father, too. Are you going to suddenly question my loyalty?"

"You know it's not the same."

"What I know is that a seventeen-year-old girl risked her life for a woman she hardly knows and a group of children who think

Candice Wright

the sun rises and sets with her. At seventeen, I was still figuring out how to look after myself, and here she is acting as a mother to a group of traumatized children. And she's doing it with such grace, having very likely gone through a lot of trauma herself."

I tap my fingers against my thigh, not liking the thought of that at all.

"Give her a chance, Wilder. If she's working against us, then we'll figure it out eventually. Really, there's not much she can do to hurt us. Oz and Zig have this place on high alert, and nobody leaves Apex unarmed."

"Oz is packing?"

"Yeah, and so is Greg. Even in his state, Greg's still a crackshot and able to protect Lara better than most men half his age."

I grin because she's right. We wind Greg up because he's the oldest one here and has naturally become a father figure to us all, especially to our women. But we don't tease him because we think he's weak. Anyone who assumes otherwise is an idiot.

"Where's Crew? He dropped in just after Lara, Greg, and Oz left, but I haven't seen him since."

If I had to guess, I'd say he's following them, keeping an eye on the trio from a distance. After all, recon is what me and Crew excel at. He'll want to observe Lara without her knowing she's being watched.

"Not sure," I lie. "He did mention maybe going for a run."

"You boys and your running," Salem mutters.

"We've gotta stay fit."

She snorts. "I've never sprained my knee eating a doughnut."

I slide my T-shirt up my stomach and reveal my hard-earned six-pack. "I've gotta run off those doughnuts if I want abs like these."

"Give me one good reason why I shouldn't slice you open and choke you with your intestines."

We both look over our shoulders and find Zig standing behind the sofa with a sleeping Aries in his arms.

"Because it would wake the baby." I press a kiss on Salem's cheek to piss off the boss and jump up out of reach.

"I'm going to look for Ev and see if he's found anything on that flash drive yet."

"You really can't sit still for long, can you?" Salem asks, leaning toward her sleeping son, kissing his head gently when Zig sits beside her.

"I like to be busy, that's all. Thanks for the chat, Salem. I'll think about what you said." I tell her as I turn and walk out of the room.

"What exactly did you guys chat about?" I hear Zig's voice rumble as I move down the hallway with a grin on my face.

I head upstairs, my grin slipping when I enter Ev's office and find the multiple screens of his computer full of scrolling information.

"How does that shit not give you a headache?"

He doesn't jump when I ask. He might be focused on what he's doing, but nobody will ever be able to sneak up on him unnoticed.

"What the fuck is all this shit?"

"That's what I'm trying to figure out," Ev mutters, enlarging the information on one of the screens so that I can see it better. Not that I understand any of it.

"It's some kind of code. I asked Avery to look at it, but it wasn't something she's seen before. Don't worry, I'll crack it eventually. I have an algorithm running to see if there's anything similar out there, which is doubtful, but you never know. We may get lucky."

"You could ask Lara," I offer begrudgingly.

"Oh, I will when she gets back, but I don't think she'll know what this is either. Not if her main job was the day-to-day care of the kids."

"No harm in asking, though."

"Agreed, plus there are a few things here not written in code that I'd like her to elaborate on."

"Like what?"

"Like the kids' files, for instance."

I pull out the chair beside him and sit down. "Do you have all the kids' information? Anything we need to know about?"

"Oh yeah, but only because I think we should all be aware of the hell these kids have survived."

Ev clicks a few buttons, and the screen in front of me suddenly shows a list of files. There are no names, just subject numbers, and as the screen scrolls up, more and more files appear.

"Jesus, how many are there?"

"A lot. It looks like they go back decades."

"There any way to find out which file goes with which of the kids we have here?"

"Yeah, actually. The files are saved in order from the first to the current batch of kids."

Ev's fingers fly across the keys until only four files remain on the screen. With a click of the mouse, one of them opens.

Subject: 08789 D.O.B.: 01/30/2016 Sex: Male

"Noah."

I start reading, and my body becomes more tense the farther

through the file I get. By the time I'm done, my hands are fisted so tightly that my fingers cramp.

"They found him in a fucking dog cage?!" I all but roar.

"Calm down. I know how you feel, but he's here now, and he's safe."

I rub my hand over my face, feeling sick to my stomach. According to the file, Noah's parents sold him when he was four to a loan shark after they ran up a debt they couldn't pay. When the loan shark realized Noah had a knack for numbers, he treated him like a prize pet, part of which meant performing on demand and being kept in a fucking cage.

"He screamed so much that he had to have surgery on his throat. There is a report that says"—Ev trails off, scrolling back through the file to find the report—"that although the surgery was successful, the psychological toll would take longer to heal. At a critical learning age, Noah learned that crying, screaming, and begging got him exactly nothing except pain. Now he's quiet, partly out of self-preservation, partly because he knows being loud doesn't work."

I look at Ev and shake my head. "I think I'm going to be sick."

"It's worth noting that it wasn't the Division that did this to him. They effectively rescued him."

"Yeah, but instead of making sure he went to a loving home, they kept him for their own use."

"From what I've been able to find out, that's why the government created the Division—to help find and save gifted people. It wasn't until the higher-ups started to question how these people could be used to further humanity that it became corrupt, and the gifted people were exploited. That's when the chip was developed and the Penn Travis project started. It wasn't much later that they started their breeding program." He shakes his head.

"A corrupt blacklist government-funded group gone rogue? Imagine that," I mock. I wish I could say this was the first time I heard of something like this happening, but that would be a lie.

"Right?" He snorts.

"What about Lara's file?"

"I have no way of narrowing down the field other than by age and sex, and that still leaves over four hundred people who fit the parameters."

"They have four hundred seventeen-year-old girls?"

"Not quite. They've had four hundred girls who would be seventeen now. What the files don't say is when or if the girl left, died, or was relocated. Lara is going to have to be the one who shows me the correct file."

"I don't see that happening anytime soon."

"Can you blame her? I've only read a few of these files, and each one is worse than the last. We don't know Lara's history or how she ended up at the Division. Was she one of the kids rescued—"

I jump up before he can finish. I can honestly say it never occurred to me that Lara might have been a victim herself. It should have, of course. Especially after everything Avery told us about her time working for the Division.

"But her father..." I protest.

"Didn't exactly take Salem in. But if he'd been keeping an eye on her, like we think, then he knew her mom had died. And he would have known about the situation with the cartel."

"So the man won't be winning father of the year anytime soon.

But for his daughter to end up in the hands of a...a..." I stumble, not wanting to put the words out there in case it makes them true.

"It might be worth talking to Greg, see if she's said anything to him. Let's hope, for our sake, we're wrong about this."

"What do you mean, for our sake?" I frown in confusion.

"Imagine the worst things that could have happened to that girl at the hands of her father. And then think about what it would feel like to finally be rescued, only to have the rescuers turn on you and, worse, believe you were working with their abuser."

And that comment has me running for the trash can and throwing up.

Chapter Seven

Lara

I stare at the book in my hand and stroke my hand over the cover.

"Are you going to caress it all day, or are you going to let one of us buy it for you?" Oz's amused voice sounds from beside me.

"I'm just trying to decide which one I want. I've narrowed it down to three." I look at him in time to catch his grin.

"Why not take all three, then?"

I bite my lip. "I don't want to take advantage."

His grin falls from his face. "It's a few books, Lara. You're hardly asking for a Ferrari."

"Wait, is that an option?" I ask with a smile of my own for a man I wanted to punch just last night.

"Not today, I'm afraid," he answers drolly.

"Bummer. Okay, if you don't mind, I'll take these three books. I've wanted to read these forever."

"You didn't get to read much?" he asks absently, taking the book from my hand and the two others I'd stacked on the edge of the book-covered table in front of me.

"I read whatever was ever on hand, mainly textbooks that put me to sleep. There were a handful of romance books that I read so many times that I could probably recite them by heart. Still, I've never owned my own books before. I'm not even going to pretend I'm not internally jumping up and down right now."

He stops short on his way to the counter and turns to look back at me with a frown. "You've never owned a book before?"

I flush with embarrassment. "No."

His jaw locks and his eyes move back to the table. "Which ones were you interested in?"

"Oz, it's fine. Three is more than—"

"Which ones?" he interrupts.

When I don't answer, he starts grabbing books randomly. I plead for him to stop, but he doesn't listen. By the time he's done, he must have about a dozen books in his arms. With a satisfied look on his face, he heads toward the checkout, with me trailing behind him.

"There you are. I've been wandering around this place like I was lost in Narnia," Greg complains, standing beside me.

He looks from me to the back of Oz's head as the man in question sets the books on the counter.

"What's going on?"

Oz turns at the sound of Greg's question and folds his arms across his chest.

"She's never owned her own books. Did you know that? I don't really read, but even I own books."

Greg's eyes drop to the pile of books on the counter before he looks back up with a grin. "Just go with it. There's no use arguing with him when he's like this."

"It's too much, though. I don't know when I'll ever be able to pay you back."

"You don't need to pay me back. It's a gift," Oz tells me before he steps closer and slides his finger under my chin, tipping my head back.

"They're just books, Lara."

I swallow hard, both of us knowing it's so much more than that.

"Say, 'thank you, Oz.'"

I feel a tear run down my face as I throw myself into Oz's arms. "Thank you, Oz."

He hesitates for a second before he wraps his arms tightly around me.

"All the bitching you did about Luna over the years, and here you are, adopting another little sister." Greg chuckles as Oz releases me.

"Luna is a pain in my ass. Lara clearly sees me for the awesome brother I am, right?" he asks playfully.

My answer is said with nothing but sincerity. "Absolutely."

He gets a look on his face, something I'm not a hundred percent sure I understand. It looks and feels a lot like protectiveness, and lord knows I could use a little of that in my life.

The cashier coughs to get Oz's attention, and I turn back to Greg.

"Told you they'd come around, and Oz is one of the hardest

nuts to crack. He's the joker of the bunch, never seeming to take anything seriously, but nobody is more protective of his family and the people he loves than him."

"But I'm nobody. I—"

"You are somebody to us, somebody we care about. And that doesn't happen often, especially not this quickly. What does that tell you?"

"That you're both certifiable?"

He laughs. "Apart from that?"

When I struggle to answer, he sighs before flicking me on the forehead.

"Ow."

"That you're lovable. I can see I'm going to have my work cut out with you."

"What do you mean?"

"I suspect you've spent your life so far being treated as if you were less than you are. They put you in a little box that you never tried to break out of while they filled you with lies about how disappointing and worthless you are."

I bite my lip hard enough to taste blood.

"But you know what?"

"What?"

"They fucking lied. You are so much more than you realize, sweetheart. And I'm going to make it my life's mission to make you see that."

"Here you go." Oz turns back to us and hands me two bags that are freaking heavy.

"Okay, maybe it would be better if Greg and I carried them."

"Hey. Not all of us look like the Hulk's love child."

Greg laughs out loud as Oz's eyes sparkle with amusement.

"Just give them here, woman."

"Nope. I got it."

"I'll tell you what, let's drop them off at the car."

"Deal."

His lips twitch as he bites back a smirk, but he gestures for me to follow him, so I do.

Greg walks beside me, making idle chit-chat as I try to will my arms not to fall off.

By the time I have the books safely locked in the trunk of the car, my arms are like jelly.

"Where to next? We have clothes, toiletries, and books. What else?" Greg asks.

"I think that's enough for now."

Oz turns and looks down the street before he grunts. "What about shoes?"

"I have my sneakers. I'm good."

"But you bought a few pretty dresses. You'll need something else."

I giggle. I can't help it. "It's not like I'll be going anywhere, Oz."

Ignoring me, he marches toward the shoe store, and I look at Greg.

"The man is on a mission. I'll say it again, just go with it."

"But—"

"You might want to hurry, though, if I were you."

"Wh—"

"Do you really want Oz to pick out shoes for you?" He lifts one eyebrow challengingly.

Giving in, I hurry after him and spend the next thirty minutes talking the man down from five pairs of shoes to two—a pair of simple tan ballet flats and a pair of black ankle boots with a chunky low heel.

"Okay, what else?" he asks when he shoves the shoes in the trunk.

"Honestly, right now, I could use a nap. Who knew shopping could be so exhausting?"

His eyes narrow on me as if he's testing the validity of my words.

"I don't know when we'll be able to get you back here with everything going on. And I don't want you coming alone, and even though Greg is more than capable of kicking ass and taking names, he's only one man and an injured one at that. Now, are you sure there is nowhere else you want to go?"

Biting my lip, I look up and down the street, but I don't see what I want.

Something must show on my face because Greg nudges me. "Tell me what you're looking for, and I'll tell you if we have one."

"A toy store? I don't need anything else, but kids get bored and might need something to play with," I reply hesitantly.

Both men are quiet for a moment, and I worry I've overstepped. But then Oz pulls out his cell phone and looks at me while waiting for the person on the other end to pick up.

"I'm gonna need you to bring the truck and meet us at Toy Tower," he says before hanging up and shoving his phone back in his pocket.

"Let's get this show on the road. We can hit the drive-thru on the way. I'm starving."

I blink at him as he climbs into the driver's seat.

"How can he be hungry? He ate my body weight in food less than three hours ago."

"The man is a human garbage disposal."

I grab the door for Greg, which makes him grumble again, but he doesn't complain, which I'll take as a win. Once he's inside and the door's shut, I get in the back and buckle up.

"Can I ask you a question, Lara?"

"You just did," I tease. "But sure."

"What did you do for fun? You know, when you weren't working. And while we are on the subject, I know you've been the one looking after the kids. But before you were old enough to do it, who looked after them? More importantly, who looked after you?"

I look at Greg, but he keeps his eyes forward, clearly waiting to see if I'll answer.

"I didn't do anything for fun, Oz. That's not how the Division worked. As for who looked after me, there was always someone around to make sure I had something to eat—clean clothes, that kind of thing. I had tutors, too, when I was old enough."

I watch Oz's hands as they squeeze the steering wheel tightly. "What about playing or going to the park?"

"I don't know what you want me to say."

"I want you to tell me that the things I'm thinking are not true. That my imagination is just running away with me because I'm a paranoid bastard. I want you to tell me that you had a life outside of that fucking place, a life where you got to run and shout and be a goddamn kid."

His anger is palpable. But what shocks me is that it's not aimed at me, but for me. If this man isn't careful, he will find himself with a new best friend.

"I can't. But it wasn't all bad."

"Yes, it fucking was. How much time did you spend at that fucking place?"

I tilt my head, wondering if I should lie, but decide nothing good will come from that.

"I lived there, Oz. I always have. And I've only left a few times."

Absolute silence.

One minute we're moving, and the next, Oz has pulled over and climbed out, slamming the door behind him. He roars at the sky, and though the sound is muted inside the car, it still makes me jump.

"Is he okay??"

"He just needs a minute. He mostly grew up here at Apex with Zig and their sister Luna. They were raised by their grandfather after their parents died, and they were allowed to mostly run wild. He's processing how different it was for you. I don't think he truly grasped what your life was like before. We only had Avery as a point of reference. Obviously, though monitored, she was free to come and go of her own free will. That wasn't the case with you, was it?"

"No. But I didn't know any different. I didn't get to run wild and even if that was an option, I had nobody to run wild with. I didn't have friends. I don't remember even seeing another kid until I was around seven or eight. I was stunned. Of course the kid wanted nothing to do with me. Though looking back, I understand now that they were traumatized and scared. But back then..." I shake my head and watch Oz bend over and take deep, calming breaths.

Chapter Eight

Crew

I'd followed them around for the best part of the morning, keeping my distance as I watched her with two men I considered family.

So why did I have the sudden urge to rip their throats out?

The interactions between Lara and the guys surprised me. Maybe not Greg so much, but Oz can be a mean bastard when he wants to be. Last night, he seemed firmly on the cautious, if not hostile, side. Today, it's almost like he's had a personality transplant.

The scene of him roaring at the sky after pulling over plays on a continuous loop in my head. What the fuck happened to get such a reaction from him?

The question was left unanswered as he climbed back into the car and continued driving. I followed at a distance, staying out of sight. I'd been so focused on trailing them that I hadn't been paying attention to where we were going. So I'm shocked as hell when we turn into the parking lot of a giant toy store twenty minutes later.

I circle the lot as they park before finding my own spot a few rows over. Pulling my ball cap down over my eyes, I follow them inside and watch as they split up in different directions, surprised they left Lara alone.

A surge of annoyance races through me at their recklessness. They know damn well we have enemies who would look for any opportunity to grab her. Not to mention the possibility, of course, of her taking off on her own.

I grit my teeth and follow Lara. With how unaware of her surroundings she is, I could be standing right behind her, and she'd be oblivious. Naturally, this pisses me off too. It seems everything about this woman is destined to give me high blood pressure.

Child. I remind myself. Lara is just a child.

I watch as she picks up a stuffed toy, something purple and fluffy, before she brings it to her face and rubs her cheek against it. She smiles and tucks it under her arm as she walks a little farther down the aisle. I refuse to be charmed by her, even if she is kind of adorable right now.

She stops in front of the dolls and reaches almost reverently for one that's twice the size of the Barbies I used to steal from my sister so that Batman had someone to rescue. She picks it up and keeps walking. I look around, still not seeing Oz or Greg. She stops again, this time reaching for something on a higher shelf. With the two things already in one arm, she stretches as far as she can before giving up. Blowing out a breath, she places the doll and stuffed toy on the shelf in front of her and nearly gives me a motherfucking heart attack when she starts to climb the shelves.

I don't think, just act. And run over to her. Thank fuck I do because her foot slips as she reaches for whatever caught her eye, and she falls. She gasps as I catch her and yank her tightly to my chest.

I'm sure she can hear my heart pounding, but she doesn't say anything. Instead, she pushes against me and scowls at me like a pissed-off kitten.

I will not be charmed.

I repeat it over and over in my head while fighting the urge to chuckle at how adorable she is.

Ah, fuck. I'm so screwed.

"Put me down, you big ape," she curses. She doesn't yell, but she may as well have when I hear the sound of boots hurrying in our direction.

I lower her to her feet, then cross my arms over my chest and scowl down at her. "What the fuck were you thinking? You could have broken your neck."

She looks from me to the shelf and then back again. "I've fallen out of beds higher than that," she mocks.

A burst of laughter has me turning to find Oz and Greg with big-ass grins on their faces.

"And where the fuck were you two? If you'd stayed with her, she wouldn't have fallen."

Greg ignores me and looks at Lara. "You okay, sweetheart?"

"It's not the first time a crazy man has accosted me."

"I meant from the fall." He laughs, but my mind clings to her words.

"Who the fuck accosted you?"

Oz full-out laughs. And Lara rolls her eyes, making me itch to put her over my knee and spank her.

She's seventeen, I remind my dick. *Seventeen*. And like always, my dick ignores me and starts to get hard as she blinks at me innocently.

"It's irrelevant now. But since you're here, Gigantor, can you please grab that dinosaur for me?"

I narrow my eyes at her before reaching up and grabbing the toy she wants, pinning her to the shelves in the process. Her eyes widen a fraction when she feels my hard dick press against her.

I shove the toy into her hands before turning and walking away. I need to get the fuck away from her before I do something I'll regret.

I'm almost at the door when I hear Greg behind me. "Slow down, motherfucker, unless you want me to keel over and die. Mind you, I can think of worse places to kick the bucket than between the Lego version of the Millennium Falcon and Barbie's Dreamhouse."

Turning, I glare at him, but let it go when I see how pale he is.

"Fuck, Greg. You were told not to overdo it." I scan the area and spot the book section, complete with bean bag chairs.

I grab his arm before he can tell me to fuck off and drag him over to one of the bean bags before shoving him into the neon orange monstrosity.

"You're an asshole," he bellows, drawing the attention of a scowling woman who reaches over to cover her child's ears.

"Sorry," Greg mumbles before looking at the kid with his ears covered. "Stay in school, or you'll end up like this dickhead."

The mother huffs before grabbing her son's hand and dragging him away.

"Was it something I said?" Greg looks up at me and frowns.

I shake my head and chuckle. "Some people are just too sensitive."

"Speaking of sensitivity, what was that all about with Lara?"

I tense. "I don't know what you're talking about."

"The fuck you don't." He stares at me, waiting me out.

"She's a fucking child."

"Say it often enough, and you might just believe it. I've already said it, but she won't be seventeen forever. And before you open your mouth and say something else that makes me want to punch you, she might be many things, but a child is not one of them."

"Oh, please, you only have to look at her to know she's innocent."

"And don't try to fool an old man like me by pretending that's not one of the things that drew you to her."

I fist my hands so that I don't wrap them around his throat and choke him to death.

"Don't confuse innocence with being childish or immature."

I open my mouth to argue, but he gives me a look that shuts it and continues.

"She sees the world through innocent eyes filled with wonder. And the fact that she can still do that after everything she's gone through makes her a remarkable young woman."

He looks back toward the aisle we left Lara in, a pensive look on his face, before he adds, "She has zero life experience outside of the Division. Everything is fresh and new and full of hope for her. Don't shit all over that because you can't get past your own hang-ups."

"Hey, this has nothing to do with me and everything to do with Lara being a potential threat."

"Bullshit. I dare you to spend time with her and then tell me you think she's in any way involved."

"Do you ever think that maybe she's just a good actress?"

He looks me dead in the eye. "No. Not for a second."

I throw up my hands and growl.

When I hear laughter behind me, I turn and see Lara and Oz racing down one of the aisles on scooters.

"In your face, missy," Oz yells like the oh-so-gracious winner he is.

Lara's bottom lip starts to quiver, and Oz immediately stops and apologizes before Lara busts up laughing.

"Why you little—" He picks her up and tosses her over his shoulder, making her squeal.

I take two steps toward them, ready to rip her out of his arms, when Greg's voice stops me.

"He sees her as a little sister, and honestly, that girl needs a family more than anyone I've ever met."

I stop and watch them together and realize he's right. There is no sexual chemistry between them at all.

Still, watching her smile because of another man makes it feel like a hot poker has been shoved into my chest.

"I'm not sure Salem would feel the same way if she saw them like that."

"Then you're a fucking idiot."

I whirl around because that isn't Greg's voice. It's Zig's.

"Zig—"

He cuts me off with a glare before he walks past me, knocking his shoulder into mine.

"Fuck," I mutter. Nobody likes pissing off the boss. Not if it means we'll end up with the shitty jobs.

Greg looks at me and smirks.

"You don't have to look so fucking smug."

"Actually, I do." He leans back and puts his hands behind his head, like he's relaxing on the beach.

"You're a dick. Good luck getting out of that thing on your own."

I turn and walk out, leaving him cursing away behind me.

I head back to my car and climb in before taking a deep breath. I drive home, pissed at how that all played out. How I became the bad guy all of a sudden, I don't know. All I want to do is protect the people I love, and I can't do that when there is still so much mystery surrounding Lara.

Pulling into the ranch, I park in the garage and head inside the house. A couple of the kids are sitting at the table coloring, and the others are in front of the TV watching something to do with talking sea creatures.

I make my way to the kitchen just as Salem slides a tray of cupcakes onto a cooling rack, and as I reach for one, she slaps the back of my hand with a spatula.

"Ouch. I don't remember you being this violent when you first moved in."

"That's because I wasn't until you all drove me to the brink of insanity."

"I resent that, even if it is the truth."

She chuckles before turning around and grabbing a second tray from the oven.

"How was your run?"

"My run?"

"Yeah, when I asked Wilder where you went earlier, he said you were out running."

"Oh, right. It was good. It gave me time to think."

I look over at Bella and Delaney, who are coloring, before my attention drifts to the two boys. The youngest one, Noah, is asleep, resting his head on Alfie's thigh.

"Where is everyone else?"

"Zig took the truck to meet up with Oz, Greg, and Lara. Ev is upstairs in his office. Astrid is working on a new game and Avery is shopping online for clothes for all the kids who are in the library. Hawk and Creed are moving all their things into their new place, and I believe Astrid volunteered Slade and Jagger to help, though I wouldn't be surprised if they managed to slip away somehow."

"Can't say I blame them."

"I keep picturing that scene from *Friends*—you know, the one with the sofa? Pivot!" she says, smiling, and I can't help but laugh, remembering the scene.

"Where's Lara?"

We both turn at the sound of Alfie's voice. He gently lifts Noah's head and slips a cushion underneath it before heading our way. He doesn't get too close, though, his distrust clear in his eyes.

"She went shopping. She won't be long."

He looks at me for a second before he nods and pulls his headphones out of his back pocket. Before he slides them on, I move closer, making him freeze. I don't crowd him. I'm not sure what his story is, but I don't want to make him any more uncomfortable than I already am.

I crouch down in front of him so that I'm not towering over him. "Hey, I'm sorry we upset you last night. That wasn't our intention. We just worry about you all."

"You made Lara cry. She never cries, not unless one of The Lost Ones is hurt."

"The Lost Ones?" I ask.

He looks at the girls. "You know, like from Peter Pan, but with girls. Lara is our Wendy."

I swallow at his reference. "You've known Lara a long time, huh?"

He shrugs.

"She's good to you? Doesn't make you do anything you don't want to?"

"Crew," Salem snaps from behind me, but I keep my focus on Alfie.

"She protects us. Even if she gets hurt doing it. She loves us even though she isn't allowed to. If she were my mom and not just my Wendy, she would have kept me safe."

I want to reach out and hug him, but I know instinctively that it would be the wrong move.

"You're safe here, though. You know that, right? None of us would hurt you."

"I know. Lara wouldn't let you."

"Even when Lara isn't here, you're still safe."

He looks at me, his eyes staring into mine, and in that moment, I understand what Greg meant about age and maturity not being the same thing. Alfie has the haunted eyes of a man who has seen and heard too much. I know that look. I've seen it on the faces of the men I served with.

"I don't think you'll hurt me," he says, eventually making me release a breath I didn't realize I was holding. But his following words have me tensing all over again. "I just don't want you to hurt Lara."

"I wouldn't do that either. I promise."

"People promise things all the time, but they always lie. You made Lara cry," he tells me accusingly.

And ain't that just a kick in the dick.

"I didn't mean to. I'll tell her I'm sorry, okay?"

He shrugs. "Don't say it if you don't mean it. She might forgive and forget, but I won't. Then you'll always be just another liar to me."

I hear Salem gasp, but I nod and hold my hand for him to shake.

"I can't guarantee I won't hurt her feelings or make her cry again. I mess up a lot. I'm sure you mess up sometimes, too. But I can promise that I'll always say sorry when I'm wrong, and I won't say it unless I mean it."

He stares at my hand for what feels like an eternity before he tentatively reaches out and shakes it quickly. As soon as he's done, he wipes his hand on his pants and pulls his headphones over his ears, clearly reaching his limit. I watch as he goes back to the sofa to join Noah, a lump in my throat.

I clear my throat and stand up. Turning, I find Salem glaring at me.

"She's good to you? Doesn't make you do anything you don't want to? That was a dick move questioning him like that."

I don't argue because it was absolutely a dick move.

"I hope his words hit home because every time you step over the line, you'll find it harder and harder to find your way back."

I open my mouth to tell her I have everything under control, but she cuts me off.

"Penn was a good man once, at least to me. He changed my life by teaching me what he did. And I'm alive because of those lessons. I don't think he taught them because he had some plan for me one day. I think he was a good man, or maybe a man who had few morals but still knew the difference between right and wrong. But somewhere along the way, he crossed a line too. Then he crossed another and each time it became easier. And now, he can never go back to being the Penn I knew him to be. I would have loved for him to have told me he was my father back then because God knows I needed one. But now, that bridge has been burned. He will never know me as his daughter. He will never know his grandchildren, and there is every possibility that one of us will have to die for the other to stay alive."

I reach for her, but she backs away.

"This here, being with you all, my family, and the love I've found with Oz and Zig, it's as close to heaven as I can get without dying. For my father to achieve his goals, he will have to tear my world to shreds. The man I once knew would never do that. But that was then, and the man he is now wouldn't blink twice. I'm telling you this as a cautionary tale. Don't lose yourself in this by crossing lines you know are there for a reason. Don't become the very monsters hunting us. What's the point in fighting if they turn us into what they wanted all along?"

She turns away and wipes at her eyes. "Watch the kids for a second. I need to check on Aries."

She's gone before I can say anything, leaving me with a brick in my stomach and a wildfire of thoughts burning up my brain.

Chapter Nine

Lara

I climb out of Oz's car and open the door for Greg.

Oz walks over to Zig's truck and opens the tailgate. Zig joins him after getting out of the truck, and they immediately start arguing, which has me rolling my eyes and Greg laughing.

"And before you ask, yes, they are always like this."

"I figured that out at the toy store. You know, I only wanted to get a few things, not half the store. It's going to take me forever to pay them back."

"It will take longer than that because they won't take a penny from you."

"Stupid, stubborn ass men," I grumble.

"It's finally sinking in. Besides, after the chaos they caused, I think it's only fair the store was compensated."

I smile and shake my head, picturing Oz and Zig bouncing up and down the aisles on space hoppers, of all things.

"I've never seen anyone use those bouncy balls in real life before, let alone so competitively."

"They're twins, sweetheart. Everything is a competition with those two."

"Poor Salem," I sigh before I realize what I said.

Greg cracks up, drawing the attention of the two arguing fools.

"What's so funny?" Oz asks.

"You mean other than your face?" Greg fires back.

"At least I get laid on the regular. When was the last time you got—" Zig elbows him in the chest before nodding to me.

"Shit. Fuck. I forgot."

"I'm a big girl, Oz. I know what sex is. And even though I'm still a virgin, I even know what a cock is," I mock just as I feel a presence behind me.

Turning, I look up to find Wilder staring at me and feel my face flame. I must be the color of a fucking tomato.

"Uh...hi," I say lamely, praying for the ground to open up and swallow me whole. But alas, no such luck. So, I do what any self-respecting woman would do. I run. "Bye."

I ignore the sounds of laughter and head inside. I slow my steps once I reach the kitchen and stop when both Delaney and Bella look up from the table where they're sitting and coloring.

"Lara, you're back," Bella yells, jumping down from her chair and running over to throw herself at me.

I drop to my knees and wrap my arms around her, breathing her in before Delaney barrels into us. Pulling my arm free, I tug her in for a three-way hug before they both pull back and start questioning me.

70

"Where did you go?"

"Why didn't you take me with you?"

"Did you get us anything?"

They ask the questions so fast I can barely keep up, making me laugh.

I stand up when I see Alfie approach me. He's wearing his headphones, but he tugs them off when he's in front of me. I wait him out, knowing he hates to be pushed.

"You came back."

Unable to stop myself, I cup his chin, tilting his head back so that he can see the sincerity in my eyes. "I won't always be able to take you with me, but I will always come back to you."

"Everyone leaves, Lara," he whispers, his pain far heavier than anyone his age should carry.

"I know. But I've never loved anyone like I love you—like I love all of you. No matter how far I go or for how long, I will always come home to you."

"This is our home now?" he asks uncertainly.

Though I don't take my eyes off Alfie, I can sense there are others in the room with us now. Not sure what's going to happen—now or in the future—I pick my words carefully, knowing he won't forget them.

"My home is where you are, be it in a fancy house or a cardboard box."

He steps forward, wraps his arms around my stomach, and buries his head against my chest. I press a kiss to the crown of his head before he pulls back.

Tears fill my eyes, but I hold them back as he offers me a small smile and slips his headphones back on before moving back over to the sofa. As far as he's come, he will always be on the introverted side. His social energy drains faster than others because his brain works overtime.

I look around for the girls, but instead, I find both Wilder and Crew watching me with an intensity that makes me take a step back. I mentally curse myself for doing it, but I don't trust these guys. Worse, I don't trust myself around them.

"Do Oz and Zig need help bringing everything in?"

"No, we've got it. Just wanted to know where you wanted it all," Crew replies, his eyes dropping to my lips briefly.

"Here is good, I guess. If that's okay. The kids don't live with me anymore, remember, so I don't have any say in where they'll go." I don't manage to keep the bitterness or the hurt out of my voice.

"Lara—" Wilder starts, but I ignore him, looking down when a small hand slips into mine.

A sleepy Noah looks up at me before slipping his thumb into his mouth. I reach down and pick him up, sitting him on my hip, even though he's far too heavy for me to hold for long, but when he snuggles into me and releases a contented sigh, I know I'll find a way somehow. He might be eight, the same age as Delaney, but with how he was raised, he's mentally much younger. He has time to catch up, and I'll be damned if I let anyone push him just because they think he should be hitting milestones that other kids his age are. He had enough of that from father's team.

The fact that he is as kind and thoughtful and sweet as he is after the abuse he's known is a testament to the size of this small boy's heart.

"You've been napping, huh? After my day of shopping, I'm ready for a nap myself," I tell him.

He doesn't answer, but he slips his thumb free from his mouth so he can play with a strand of my hair.

"Laraaa," Bella drags out my name with more attitude in her tone than a six-year-old should be able to achieve.

"Did you get me a present? I've been really good."

"You have been good. You all have. And I am so extraordinarily proud of all of you, which is why I asked Oz and Greg if they would take me to the toy store."

I let my words sink in before she and Delaney start screeching, making poor Noah jolt in my arms.

Refusing to hide any longer, I look up and find Crew still watching me. Wilder is gone—probably letting Oz and Zig know where to bring the toys.

"Hey, Lara, are you hungry?"

I jump at the sound of Salem's voice, not realizing she was in the room. I spot her sitting on a chair at the island, feeding her son, who is cradled in her arms.

"I'm good, but thank you. We ate at the diner and again when Oz insisted on going through the drive-thru."

She rolls her eyes. "He never stops eating. I think he's making up for when we were stranded in the jungle."

What the fuck?

"And that's also why I'll never eat another mango in my life ever again." Oz shudders as he walks in, his arms full of toys.

"Oz! Are those toys for us?" Bella asks excitedly, and Noah lifts his head to see what's going on.

"They sure are. And there's a bunch more outside. So you might want to move out of the way so you don't get accidentally squished."

"You can't squish me, silly. I'm not a bug," she huffs, rolling her eyes.

"And here was me thinking you're a beautiful butterfly."

"Laying it on there a little thick there, aren't you, big guy?" Salem mumbles.

"I'm just making sure I'm her favorite."

Crew jumps in. "You can't buy her love, Oz."

"Yes, he can. You can, Oz. Next time, I think I'd like a pony."

"Bella," I scold gently.

"I'm just letting him know, Lara."

Before I can say anything else, Zig and Wilder, walk in with their arms filled with more toys.

"Whoa, is that all for us?" Delaney asks with a whole lot of wonder in her eyes.

"It sure is."

"Was there anything left in the store?" Salem asks.

"Lara picked out a few things for you, and well, we decided to just add to it. We might have gotten carried away," Zig admits, making me laugh.

"What did you choose for us, Lara?" Bella asks before Zig can reply.

I wait for the toys to be dropped on the table before I pick up the purple sparkly teddy and hand it to Bella.

She squeezes it tightly. "She's so pretty. I'm going to call her Mrs. Sparkly Pants."

I grin before grabbing the doll and handing it to Delaney.

"She's mine? Really?"

"Really."

"I don't have to give her back?"

I swallow and shake my head, ignoring the growl coming from Oz.

"Nope. She's all yours."

"Wow," she whispers, sitting down and crossing her legs with her doll in her lap.

Leaving her to play, I dig around until I find the dinosaur for Noah. I hand it to him, and he wraps his arm around it tightly.

Greg walks in and sees the kids with their toys and smiles.

"I've never seen so many happy faces before."

He sits down on the chair next to Salem as I look at Oz, who is watching me with a smile on his face. He's given me a lot today, and I'm not just talking about the toys and the books. There isn't much I can give him back to show him my gratitude, except my trust. There's only one thing here that matters to me, and that's my Lost Ones.

I whisper in Noah's ear, so he's prepared, as I walk over to Oz. Noah looks up at me, but he doesn't look scared, which is a relief. I'd never force him to do anything he doesn't want to. Well, except when he refuses to brush his teeth.

"Hey, Oz, can you hold Noah for me for a second? He's just woken up from a nap, and he likes to snuggle when he's still sleepy."

Oz, being the smart man he is, takes the gesture for what it is. His smile is brilliant and blinding.

"Of course. I love snuggles."

"Hey, Noah, want to snuggle with Uncle Oz for a minute?"

Oz sucks in a sharp breath when I call him uncle. Noah reaches his arms out for Oz, who takes him without hesitation. Noah tucks his head under Oz's chin.

"And pop goes the ovary." Salem sighs.

"I'm not sure that's how the song goes," Greg teases, but Salem just shakes her head.

"It is now."

I grab a couple things from the pile and walk over to the sofa where Alfie is sitting. I knew he wouldn't join us, even if he was curious. He wouldn't want to put himself in a position to be disappointed. He's learned to expect nothing, but that's not gonna fly with me.

I sit beside him and hand him the iPad and the brand-new set of earphones that are a serious upgrade on the ones he has. He might be ten, but he has little interest in toys. Now, books and music, however, are another thing altogether.

His head whips up when he sees what I've placed in his lap, a look of shock plastered on his face. "For me?"

"For you. And Zig has a gift card over there so that you can fill it up with books and music."

His jaw is hanging open.

I smile, but it slips off my face when tears run down his cheeks.

"It's really mine?"

I fight back tears of my own as hatred for the people who hurt him rushes through my veins. The kids might have been rescued by the Division, but they were still treated like commodities, not children. Like me, I don't think they ever got presents. If they did, it was to manipulate them. Then they'd be taken away as punishment just as quickly.

"It's all yours."

"Nobody's ever given me a gift before, and this is an iPad, Lara. It's a lot."

"You love it?"

He nods rapidly.

"Then it's priceless."

He still looks unsure as his hands smooth over the box.

"I get it, trust me. You should have seen my face when Oz bought me some books. I cried," I admit, elbowing him lightly. "There may have even been snot involved."

He laughs, making me smile as I wrap my arm around his shoulders and tug him close. "Zig says Ev will help you set it up. I'm going to expect you to read to me next time."

"Nuh-uh," he says. "Wendy is the one who does the reading. But I'll find a book for you."

"You sure? You have a beautiful voice."

He hesitates for a moment before answering. "I won't forget your stories. If something happens, I'll have a bunch of them in my head."

I squeeze his hand, knowing he's talking about being taken away. It doesn't matter how many times I've reassured him. The reasons for his doubt are valid.

My stomach churns at the thought of anything happening to these kids. So many have come into my life over the years, and each of them is lost to me now. I don't know where they went or if they're still alive. Every time they were sent away, a small piece of me went with them.

Bella, Noah, Delaney, and Alfie have been with me the longest. In the beginning, I tried to keep my distance, but it was impossible not to love them.

I stand up when Alfie's attention goes back to his new iPad and head toward the front door.

"Lara?" Greg calls. I wave him off, feeling myself start to unravel, needing to be alone so that I can cry and not be judged for it.

"I just need a minute," I tell him before hurrying outside, praying that nobody follows me.

I make it all the way back to Greg's and breathe a sigh of relief that I have a key now so that I can let myself in. I pull off my jacket and hang it up before walking to the room that's now mine for however long I stay.

I climb up onto the bed and curl into a ball, letting the tears I've been holding back fall. I cry for The Lost Ones, hoping and praying that life with me is nothing but sunshine and rainbows for them now. I cry for the younger version of myself. I wish I could go back and tell her to stop trying so hard to make people love her. Relationships might be hard, but love should be effortless. I know that now, even if I don't have it yet. Damn, I could have spared myself the heartache if I had figured it out sooner.

I thought if I was better, smarter, quieter—all things my father wanted from me—then he'd love me. But the one thing he wanted from me was power, and that's what I refused to give him.

As a low-grade telekinetic, people were astonished by my ability to float minor things from one side of the room to the other. Once the novelty had worn off, though, they realized it wasn't the most exciting gift. My gift was too weak to be considered defensive or offensive, so I was relegated to babysitting duties. If anyone had paid me more attention, they would have noticed why I'm so good with the kids. I might be a lousy telekinetic, but I'm a strong empath, maybe even stronger than my father. I hadn't been able to test that theory without giving myself away, though, so I kept that gift a secret and only used it when he wasn't around.

I sigh. If these guys knew what I could do, they'd kick me out for sure. But I can't help that I was born with a gift I never asked for. The gift doesn't make me good or bad. It's just a part of my

DNA. I'm so damn tired of being judged for every little thing. How ironic that back at the Division I was considered a dud, and here I'm considered a threat.

I roll over and stop at the sound of crinkling paper. I lift my head and find a folded piece of lined paper. I open it up and almost throw up all over my bed.

There, in my father's handwriting, is a message.

Time to come home, Lara.

Chapter Ten

Wilder

While the kids are playing with all their new stuff, the rest of us sit around the table talking.

"They've really never gotten presents before?" I can't wrap my head around it. Some of us have had shitty upbringings, but at least we've received a present or two.

"No. You should have seen Lara when I bought her those fucking books. You would have thought I'd handed her a slice of the moon," Oz exclaims.

"It makes sense, I guess, in a fucked-up way." Greg sighs.

"How the fuck does that make sense?"

"Giving gifts shows a level of caring. And building relationships in a place like the Division can be dangerous. Love can make people do crazy things, like protect people that don't deserve to be protected. Or sacrifice themselves when there is no other way out."

"Like Bella's mom?" Avery says quietly, remembering that the woman who helped her escape blew herself up as a distraction so her daughter could be free.

"Exactly."

"We don't know if there was ever any love between Lara and her father. Salem was saying that he used to be a good person."

"I said he was good to me, that he had good in him, not that he was a good person as such," Salem sighs..

"Be that as it may, Lara was born and raised in the Division. She's been isolated and deprived of love for seventeen fucking years. I don't know what kind of person he used to be, but he's never been a father to that girl," Greg states adamantly, his eyes moving to Crew's and mine.

"You can't still think she's working with him. You can't watch her with those kids and not know she'd fight to her last breath to protect them."

"I know," Crew admits. "There's a part of me that worries that she's just a good actress, and we're all being played. But those kids are smart. And they love and trust her, and there is nothing fake or forced about it."

"Should we move her back in with the kids?" Creed asks, looking around the table.

"I'm happy to have Lara with me. It's nice to have some company, and I get the feeling she's lonely."

"Keeping her away from the kids feels like a punishment, though," Oz admits.

"It's not a punishment, Oz. But I realized something last night when I was getting Delaney some water. Lara does this all on her own and has done it for—fuck knows how long. She's effectively a seventeen-year-old single mother of four. As much as I'd be happy to move them all back in together, I'm not sure it's the right move. Lara deserves to be free to do what she wants. Though I doubt she'd complain for a single second about taking care of those kids, I do think they're too dependent on each other. Maybe it will be good for all of them to spend a little time apart."

I rub my hands over my face.

"She isn't going to see it that way," I warn.

"I'll talk to her." Avery offers me a smile, but I can see the worry on her face.

"No offense, but I'm not sure she'd listen to you, Avery."

When Avery flinches, Hawk glares at me.

"I'm not saying that to be a dick. I'm saying I remember the way she looked at you last night. She felt betrayed by you. I'm not sitting here saying you did anything wrong. Hell, we said and did way worse than you, and I still believe in the reasons we did it. But she won't see it that way."

Hawk jumps in. "Avery wasn't trying to be a bitch, but finding out that dickhead was Lara's father was a shock to us all. How did she expect us to react?"

"With logic," Greg states. "You all turned on her because of who her father is, not because of anything she did. Because you know what she did do? She ran from the only home she's ever known, taking the kids she loves with her, not even knowing if they would end up in a worse place than they were, because she trusted Avery. Not to mention, she helped Avery get back home and gave her a flash drive with a fuck-ton of information on it."

He leans back, looking at us. Though he doesn't say it outright, he doesn't bother to hide his disappointment in us.

"She'll forgive you all in time. She's too nice not to. Hell, Oz is always a dick, and she forgave him. But the thing is, he manned up and apologized. Nothing is going to get fixed if you don't all at least start with 'I'm sorry.'"

"We get it, Greg, we're assholes," Crew grumbles.

"Good. The first step is admitting you have a problem. Spend time with her. You'll see that there isn't an evil cell in her body."

"What about what Zig suggests about keeping the kids separate from her?" Slade questions.

"Keeping them separate." Greg snorts. "You won't separate them, no matter what you do. But I can see what Zig means. And I agree, maybe it will be good for all of them to spend some time apart. But not because I think they're too dependent on each other, but because I think it's important they all learn, Lara included, to trust people outside their little group."

We're all quiet, considering his words, before Bella walks over to me and hands me a piece of paper.

"This for me?"

She nods, cuddling the purple stuffed bear Lara got for her. I look at the paper while the others watch on and find a drawing of three stick figures standing in front of an apple tree.

"This is really pretty. Thank you. Is that you?" I ask, pointing to the tallest figure, making Bella giggle.

"No, silly, that's you."

"Right, I can see it now. And what a handsome fella he is, too. What about this one?" I point to the one on the left, who is slightly shorter than the other two.

"That's Crew. He's grumpy."

Laughter breaks out around the table, and Bella takes a step closer, using me to shield her from them.

"Why is he grumpy?" I've gotta know what she thinks is causing it.

"He's grumpy because he loves Lara, but he doesn't want to love Lara. And Lara is in the middle so you can both protect her."

Silence fills the room as we all realize this isn't a regular picture.

"Who are we protecting Lara from, Bella? Do you know?"

She nods and presses herself against my leg. I lift my arm and gently put it around her shoulders.

"The bad man. He's mad at her."

"Why is he mad at her?"

"She belongs to him, but she didn't do what she was supposed to."

I run my hand gently up and down her back. "We won't let anything happen to Lara, Bella. I promise."

She looks up at me, her teeth biting into her bottom lip. "Even though you don't like her?"

"I like her. I do. I know it might not seem that way, but, well, it's complicated. I'm going to say sorry, though, and ask her if we can be friends. You think she'll forgive me?"

Bella nods frantically, her curls bouncing around all over the place. "She's really nice and pretty, and I think she likes you and Crew until you hurt her feelings and made her cry," she brutally replies before turning to look at Salem. "Can I have a cupcake now? I've been waiting forever," she asks with so much sass, it has all of us laughing and the mood instantly lightening.

"Sure, help yourself. There are strawberry and vanilla ones with vanilla and chocolate ones with chocolate frosting." Salem smiles at her.

Bella bites her lip in contemplation. "What if I don't like the one I pick?"

I frown at her. "You don't remember what kind of cupcakes you like?"

"I've never had cupcakes."

Slade jumps up and storms over to the counter. He grabs a plate and fills it with both flavors before walking around to Bella and handing them to her.

"Take them all. You'll figure it out," he tells her gruffly.

His eyes widen as she takes the plate from him. I half expect them to go toppling onto the floor, but she carries the plate to Delaney, who is sitting on the floor combing her doll's hair with the same care she would a grenade.

"What kind of kid has never had a cupcake?" snarls Jagger, who had been quiet up until now.

"The kind of kid who spent her life at the Division where all her dietary needs were taken care of for her. Of course, those needs didn't include treats or any kind of junk food," Greg replies.

"Jesus Christ. She's six years old. She's spent all her life there?" Jagger complains, but Greg is staring at me.

"I'm sure six years seems like a long time to us, but it would have felt like a blessing to Lara."

I open my mouth to ask him what he means when it hits me. "She was born at the Division. She's lived there her whole life, too, hasn't she?"

He nods as all the pieces fall together.

"No school, no friends... I..." I'm lost for words.

"How does someone come from that and still end up being so well-adjusted? I would have ended up feral." Oz places a kiss against Salem's neck, making her shiver.

"Hate to break it to you, Oz, but you are feral."

"Well, fuck."

Everyone laughs at him except for me and Crew. I can't find it in me. I look over at the girls, eating cupcakes, surrounded by a pile of toys, and picture a younger version of Lara in their place, her sad eyes looking up at me.

"I think we should just go talk to her. Apologize so we can work on getting back in her good books," Crew says so that only I can hear him.

"So we're not following through with your plan of getting close to her so we can get information from her?"

"I still want to know what she knows, but I don't want to fake anything. I think I'd like to be her friend."

"And when she's not seventeen anymore?"

"If I say no, I risk her finding someone else. And yeah, they might make her happy and give her the life she dreamed of, but I'm not noble enough to give her up. I thought I could. But I can't. Does she deserve better? Fuck yes, but I'm not going to let her go without a fight."

"Hey guys," Ev wanders in, his eyes briefly taking in the girls eating cupcakes.

Noah and Alfie are on the sofa on the far side of the room. Alfie is reading Noah a story by the looks of things.

"What's with all this?" he asks, looking at the pile of toys as he sits in the chair beside us with his iPad in his hand.

"We picked up a few things for the kids. Oh, that reminds me, we bought Alfie an iPad. You mind setting it up for him?"

"Sure, no problem. I'll grab it on my way back upstairs," he says as he takes his tablet and taps something on it before turning it around for us to see.

. . .

"I was searching through all the information I could find on the kids. There's a lot because there have been so many kids in and out over the years. I found Alfie, Noah, Bella, and Delaney easy enough because the files were in chronological order. Lara's has been harder to find. I've narrowed it down, but I'm hoping you can give me some more info on her so I can figure out which file is hers."

"It feels like an invasion of privacy—talking about her file without her permission," Avery tells him.

"I'm sorry, Avery, but we still don't know what her gift is and if it's dangerous. I'm not saying she'd hurt anyone, but is it something she has control over?"

Avery looks away, a flush of guilt on her face.

"Come on, Avery. I know you don't want to break her trust. I promise nobody here is going to say anything. She'll tell us when she's ready, and we'll just play dumb. But it's important that we know what she can do so we're prepared," Crew tells her.

Avery sighs and drops her head. "Her gift is telekinesis," she mumbles quietly.

"Are you serious? Holy fuck!" Oz exclaims, and Avery looks up at him.

"Yeah, it's pretty wild to see. Or at least, I think so."

"You make it sound like others aren't as impressed. Somehow, I find that hard to believe."

"She has the strength to move small objects from one side of the room to another, but anything larger than a stand mixer is a no-go. The division found that pretty underwhelming and told her that—repeatedly. I overheard some of the staff say that's why she was put in charge of the kids because she wasn't much use anywhere else."

I curse. "Not much use? What the fuck did they want, exactly?"

"I don't know—her to move a tank or something. But small objects don't really have the same impact."

I look around at others, who seem just as incredulous as I am.

"Well, I guess we can assume that it's not soldiers running the Division or any kind of ex-military." Zig leans back, crossing his arms over his chest.

Avery looks confused. "How did you get that from what I said?"

"Because a soldier would recognize just how useful moving smaller objects could be. Say, like, a grenade," he throws out, making Avery's mouth drop open as if the idea never occurred to her.

I look her in the eye so that she understands that Lara's gift shouldn't be taken lightly. "Or a bullet."

Chapter Eleven

Lara

I stare at the note as if it's a snake that's poised and ready to strike.

How the hell did he find me?

I'm not just talking about Apex. They may have known where this place is because of Cooper, or James given how they put a chip in him. But that doesn't explain how they knew I was staying here with Greg or that this was my room.

Is someone watching me? It seems like the most logical answer, but I don't think that's it. Even if they had somehow managed to sneak onsite without being spotted, they wouldn't have been able to hang around. None of the houses are hidden away. Though they're not right next door to each other, they're close enough that you can see each house when you look around outside.

No, if someone were lurking, they would have been noticed.

But if nobody's watching, then how does my father know where I am?

Wait, did they chip me too?

I grab my head, terror spiking through me, but I force myself to keep calm and use my brain.

I haven't had any surgeries or unexplained accidents that required me to be knocked out. I doubt they would risk sticking something in my head that might mess with my gift. But if not that, then what?

I cross my arms over my chest and pause, glancing down at my left arm.

A year ago, my father insisted on me having a contraceptive implant. I scoffed, knowing I'd rather die a virgin than let anyone at the Division touch me. He made a nasty comment about doing what I was told because he would select a viable partner when it was time to breed me.

My horror turned to amusement after I'd thrown up all over his shoes. But after he'd left, I decided that a contraceptive at least meant he couldn't force someone on me overnight. I'd have time to come up with an escape plan. *Hopefully.*

I open my eyes and curse. "That motherfucking motherfuck-er!" I'd bet a million dollars that it's a tracking chip in my arm, not a contraceptive implant. My father's gift doesn't work on me, though he's too stuck in his head to notice that. But that doesn't mean I'm immune to good, old-fashioned manipulation. He knew the thought of getting pregnant by a stranger would have me throw any objections I had about getting the implant out the window.

I let my eyes fall closed as despair hits me. It was me. I've led them right to Apex's front door. Everyone here said I couldn't be trusted. I had no idea they'd be right in the end.

I hurry to the kitchen and grab a knife from the knife block. I press it to my bicep but stop. If he already knows I'm here, removing the chip is pointless.

Tossing the knife, I grip my hair and fight the urge to scream. Just when I thought I was fucking free.

Well, fuck him. Fuck them all. Even if I went back, he'd still come after Salem and the kids and probably kill the others in the process. I can't let that happen.

I grip the counter and take a deep breath, trying to calm my racing heart. But it's impossible. Impossible because I know there is only one option left.

I need to run far away from this place and The Lost Ones so that the Division chases after me and leaves everyone here alone. Tears stream down my cheeks at the thought of going. I won't lie, the idea of being out there on my own is terrifying, but I won't stand around and watch as he kills the people I've come to care about and the kids that are more mine than anyone else's.

I don't wipe my tears away, knowing it's pointless—more will come. Instead, I make my way back to my bedroom and try to come up with a plan. How am I going to get out of here without being seen? I have no idea, but I have to try.

I'm not sure when the opportunity will arise, but I figure I should be ready to go at a moment's notice.

Hurrying to Greg's room, I search his closet for a bag and hit the jackpot when I find a backpack on the top shelf. I take it down and slip one of Greg's sweatshirts inside. I didn't pick many up when I went shopping, and I know I'll need something to keep me warm.

I take the backpack to my room and add my meager belongings, including my toiletries from the bathroom. Once I get my stuff from the car, I'll pack what I can and then wait for the right time to slip away.

Closing my eyes, I think of Alfie and what my leaving will do to him. I have to see him before I go. I have to make sure he knows how much I love him. God knows that if there was another way, I'd take it.

If it's possible to feel your heart break, then that's what I'm feeling right now. Trying to breathe is like inhaling a dozen tiny razor blades. The knowledge that I'm going to abandon them like every other adult in their life, even if it's for the right reasons, is torturous, and I know that it will eat away at my soul until I can see them again. Even then, there are no guarantees. Their hearts will heal slowly, and they'll move on. It won't matter that I'll carry them around with me like wounds. Maybe one day they'll scab over, leaving a scar where I had to cut them out, but I will never forget them like they'll forget me.

Maybe it's for the best. In my mission to keep them safe, it never occurred to me that I might be the one putting them in danger. I'm my father's property, even if I'm nothing but a giant disappointment. He won't just leave me in what he perceives to be the enemy's hands.

If I can draw him away and keep him busy hunting me, then maybe, just maybe, he'll leave the others alone. He already knows what a formidable team Apex is. He might have numbers on his side, but he can't afford the media exposure. It's bad enough, in his eyes, that Astrid has come out to the world and admitted what she can do. Sure, there are some who are skeptical. But having people come forward who Astrid has helped has swayed people's opinions of her. There is no fear, only curiosity. Of course, that wouldn't be the case with all of us. Some people have gifts that will always be considered too dangerous. If people knew what I could do, they'd be horrified. They'd lock me up and throw away the key.

No, some secrets are better taken to the grave.

I hide the bag under the bed, making sure it's hidden, before I make my way to the kitchen. I make half a dozen peanut butter and jelly sandwiches and grab some snacks that don't need refrigerating, along with a few bottles of water and a couple of cans of soda. It's going to make the bag heavy, but it's something I'll have to deal with, not knowing when and where I'll find my next meal.

As I head back to my bedroom, I pass the knife block and hesitate, but I don't take one, knowing Greg would notice right away. Instead, I rummage through the drawers until I find a small paring knife that will be easy to hide in my bag.

I carry everything back to my bedroom and lay it on the bed before dragging the bag out from under the bed and adding everything to it. There isn't a huge amount of space left, so I'm glad the backpack is one of the large hiking kinds designed to carry a sleeping bag and a tent.

That makes me pause. I wonder if Greg has a sleeping bag. There is every chance I'm going to have to be sleeping outside. I'll need something to protect me from the elements.

Shoving the bag back under the bed, I search Greg's room but don't find one. Disappointed, I'm about to give up when I check the closet where the towels and bedding are kept. And low and behold, there on the very top shelf is a sleeping bag.

It's heavy-duty and will definitely take up most of the remaining space in the bag, but I know it's something I can't afford to do without. I leave it there for now, not wanting Greg to notice it's missing. I head back to the kitchen, pouring myself a glass of juice as I try to decide the best time to leave.

It would be so easy to put it off for a few days, to delay leaving the people I love until the very last second, but every minute I stay brings them closer to danger.

A knock on the door has my head whipping around and panic washing over me. Do they know what I have planned? Did Bella *see* it? Shit, did I leave the bag out?

I set the glass down on the counter and hurry back to my bedroom, taking a relieved breath when I see that I didn't leave it out. I shove the note under my pillow and take a deep breath. I fix my hair and smooth down my top as I walk to the door.

Shoring up my defenses, I plaster on a fake-as-fuck smile and yank the door open.

The smile falls off my face the second I see who's there. Folding my arms over my chest, I look at Crew and Wilder warily.

"Yes?" Did they somehow know about the note? Shit, maybe Bella *saw* the note.

"We brought your things from the car, and we'd like to talk to you for a minute, if you don't mind," Wilder asks softly.

As much as I'd like to slam the door in their faces, I don't. I'm hurt by what they said to my face and feel betrayed by what I heard them say behind my back. But with me leaving, it doesn't matter anymore. I'll never be anything but a stupid little girl to them, one that will be the downfall of Apex. As much as I hate them for saying it, given what I know now, I can't deny it's the truth.

Maybe in another time and place, things could have been different.

I shake my head and step back. Wishful thinking like that will only end up crushing me in the end, so I shut down that line of thought.

They might not trust me and think that I'm too young, too dangerous, or whatever it is they think of me. But they don't know me, not one little bit. They have no idea the things I've seen or done or the things I've sacrificed. The truth hits me in the face as I let them in.

They're the ones who don't deserve me. I'm a good person, or I try to be. I treat everyone with kindness, and I don't judge people, knowing what it's like to be judged myself.

The realization boosts my confidence.

"Where do you want us to put this stuff? In your room?"

I absolutely do not want them in there, and it has nothing to do with the hidden bag and letter.

"Just put it on the floor over there."

They look at each other as if in silent conversation before doing as I ask.

I put some space between us and head to the kitchen. "Do either of you want something to drink?"

"I'll have a coffee," Crew calls out.

"Same," Wilder adds, making me sigh. Being polite sometimes sucks. Now I'll have to make conversation while they drink.

I fiddle with the expensive coffee machine, trying to remember how to use it. Greg gave me a crash course this morning, but this thing looks like it could launch a rocket.

"Here, let me."

I jump when Crew leans over me and takes over. I step out of the way, not wanting him to touch me. They might not be my favorite people, but that doesn't mean that their touch doesn't do something strange to my insides.

Before coming here, I'd never reacted to the opposite sex. I often wondered if I was broken or if my father's people had done something to me, but all that went out the window when I laid eyes on Crew and Wilder. At first, I'd been terrified. My body was reacting in ways it never had before, and I didn't like not being in control of it. I'd spent my whole life controlling my body's responses yet a part of me wanted to give in and let them take over.

"Do you want one?" He looks over his shoulder at me.

"Um, sure. A cappuccino would be great." I'm not about to admit that coffee is still new for me, so I've mostly stuck to the milky ones.

I pull out a chair at the table and place my hands in front of me as Wilder takes a seat. Silence fills the room, and there is nothing comfortable about it. By the time Crew places our coffees on the table, I'm ready to jump out of my skin.

"So, what did you want to talk to me about?" I ask, unable to wait any longer.

"We wanted to apologize," Wilder starts.

I look from him to Crew, and they both look genuine. I should feel relieved, but instead, I feel sad. If I hadn't heard what I did this morning, I might have been convinced they were truly remorseful. I hate that I can't trust my judgment when it comes to them. Their golden good looks must have short-circuited my brain. But it doesn't matter how appealing they are on the outside; their insides leave a lot to be desired.

Raised around liars and manipulators, I thought I could easily recognize them anywhere. I just never factored in my traitorous body.

"Apologies accepted," I lie, hoping they'll leave now.

Crew frowns, and Wilder looks like he is trying to figure me out. Good luck with that. I can't even figure myself out right now.

"We were out of line last night," Wilder adds, reaching across the table for my hands, but I move them and slip them into my lap.

"You were worried about your family. It's fine. I worry about mine all the time." I close my eyes and curse, realizing how that sounds. "I mean the kids, not my father. I don't care what happens to him."

"Hey, you don't need to explain. We get it. We reacted in the heat of the moment. But after thinking about it, we realized we were being dicks. You haven't done anything to deserve the way we treated you, and we've done nothing to earn your trust. Of course you weren't just going to come in and spill your guts out to us." Crew shakes his head.

"I'm sure our reaction was exactly why you held back."

"Maybe partly, but the other part of me just doesn't think of that man as my father. And he's never treated me like his daughter. Some of his DNA was used to make me, that's it. Otherwise, he's just another man I love to hate."

Wilder frowns at me. "Did he hurt you?"

I look at him and bite the inside of my cheek to stop myself from laughing. Is he joking right now?

"It's not really any of your business. Thank you for your apology, but saying sorry doesn't suddenly make us friends. It's not going to make me spill my secrets or open up to you about my childhood. Like you said, you haven't given me any reason to trust you. And I'll be damned if I give you my past to weaponize and use against me in the future."

"Fuck, Lara, that's not what this is." Crew runs his fingers through his hair, agitated. "We want to get to know you better, and maybe we can be friends."

I want to scream at him, but I'm too busy fighting back tears. I've been lied to a million times, so I have no idea why his lies hurt me so much more than the ones that came before. As resistant to the idea as I am, the harder I fight it, the more they're going to push. And that's only going to encourage them to hang around. That's the last thing I want right now. It's going to be hard enough as it is to sneak out of here, but it will be impossible if these guys are following me around trying to change my opinion of them.

"Okay, fine. We can be friends, but we need to take it slow. I'm not comfortable being around you both one-on-one right now."

Wilder looks as if I've hit him. "We would never hurt you."

"Physically, I know. But mentally..." I shake my head. "I've been through enough," I tell them, and it's the truth. "I'm trying to heal, trying to sift through all the negativity that has been thrown at me all my life and figure out my self-worth. And I can't do that around you." I hold up my hand to stop either of them from saying anything else.

"You know the saying: sticks and stones may break my bones, but words can never hurt me? Well, there have been many times I would rather have been punched in the face than belittled by someone who was supposed to care about me."

"We won't let anyone hurt you," Crew snarls.

I touch my temple and offer him a small smile that I know is full of sadness and regret. "They're in my head. Every time I close my eyes, I hear a dozen voices telling me how worthless I am. I need to learn how to make my voice louder so I can drown out my father's."

"We can help you with that," Wilder jumps in.

"I have to do it on my own. It's important to me."

"I get it," Wilder says softly.

Crew looks at him and blows out a breath. "I don't, but I've always had friends to lean on."

I flinch at that, making him curse.

"Fuck, that's not what I meant." He stands up and walks around the table before squatting down beside me and taking my hand in his. "What I meant was that I've never had the weight of the world placed solely on my shoulders. I've always had someone in my corner who could back me up if I needed it or pull me out if I got into trouble. You've only had yourself to rely on. That already makes you stronger than you think."

Part of me wants to believe him. I want to let his words soak into my skin and ease the constant ache. But I can't. I don't know how much of what he's saying is the truth and how much is just part of his plan to get closer to me to pump me for information.

I slip my hand free from his and offer him a quick smile. "Thank you," I say, and reach for my coffee so he can't grab my hand again and take a sip.

He watches me for a moment before sighing and standing back up and walking to his seat.

We're all quiet for a moment, lost in thought and unsure of what to say.

"You want to come back over and have dinner? Salem is making spaghetti and meatballs at Delaney's request. And let me tell you, they are fucking amazing."

I think about it. It will give me a chance to spend some time with the kids. I swallow around a lump in my throat and nod.

"Yeah, that sounds good. Can I meet you there? I want to take a shower and put my things away first."

"I mean, we're happy to wait—" Crew says, but I'm already shaking my head. No. Not just no, but hell no. There is no way I'm getting naked while those two are here.

"I really do need a moment. I had a lot of fun today with Oz and Greg, but I'm not used to it. I just need to have a little quiet time before I jump back into the chaos that is an Apex dinner."

Wilder chuckles. "That's fair. We'll let everyone know you're coming." He stands, Crew following suit.

"We'll take our coffees with us."

"Okay, well, thanks for stopping by and apologizing." As hard as it is for me to say, I am glad there is some sort of closure between us. This awkwardness is most likely all there will ever be between us, but it's better than the alternative. I know they'll all be mad when I run. Hell, I'm sure some of them will think I ran back to my father and filled him in on everything I know about Apex. There isn't anything I can do about that. I just don't want everyone to hate me. I feel pathetic even thinking about it. What does it matter, though? Heck, I might not even survive. Just because my father found a use for me before doesn't mean he will now. I left him and took the kids with me. He'll punish me for sure if he catches me. But will it stop at that? Or will he decide I'm more trouble than I'm worth and just get rid of me for good?

Knowing the risks doesn't change anything. If it keeps the kids safe, then I'm more than willing to be the sacrificial lamb. But that doesn't mean I'm going to make it easy for him.

"Lara?" Crew calls my name, making me jump.

"Sorry, I was thinking." I stand and follow them to the door.

Wilder opens it and steps outside. Crew moves to follow but pauses beside me. He turns and looks down at me before he dips his head and kisses my forehead.

"I know we have a lot to make up for, but thanks for giving us a chance."

I suck in a sharp breath and nod, managing to close the door behind them before the first tear falls.

It might all be an act, but my foolish heart doesn't care.

Chapter Twelve

Crew

"I can't put my finger on what it is, but something feels off with Lara."

"You mean something other than the fact she hates us?" Wilder asks, frustration evident in his voice.

"I don't think she hates us. I think we hurt her more than we realized."

"I'm not sure which is worse."

"If she didn't like us, we wouldn't have been able to hurt her at all. I'll take that over nothing any day. We'll just need to work hard to redeem ourselves. But we're going to have to listen to her and go slow. She looked tense, and I don't want to make things worse than they already are."

"I'm not sure we can make it worse." Wilder shakes his head as we walk into the main house.

"Oh, it could be a hell of a lot worse. She could refuse to talk to us at all. Stay away from us. Leave when we enter the room—"

"Fucking hell, I get it."

I grin at him and head into the kitchen, which is surprisingly quiet.

"Where is everyone?"

I look around with a frown.

"Even the kids are gone." I head up to Ev's room with Wilder right behind me because Ev will be able to find everyone faster than I can.

I swing his door open without knocking. After I've done it, I realize my mistake. I'm just thankful he's alone.

Ev spins around and glares at me as if knowing what I was thinking. "You ever come in here and catch Avery naked, I'll cut off your balls."

"Got it. I'm just so used to you being single that I didn't think about it until I'd already opened the door."

He turns back to the screens, and I walk over to sit in the chair beside him. A knock sounds at the open door.

I look over to find a grinning Wilder and flip him off. "Smart-ass."

"What can I do for you both? I get the feeling you're not here to help."

"We can if you need it."

Ev looks at me. And for a second, I think he'll ask, but he sighs and shakes his head. "No, it's fine." He sighs again. "It's stupid, but seeing all this shit... I feel like if it's just me looking, I'm not totally invading their privacy. But if I get all of you looking, it's a violation. It doesn't usually bother me this much. I'm not sure why it's bothering me now."

"Maybe because before, they were just numbers. Now those files are people—Noah, Alfie, Delaney, Bella, and Lara."

"And there's a good chance there's one on Avery, too," Wilder says gently.

"I'm good with computers, not humans. This is a lot," Ev admits.

"You're better with humans than you realize. Just ask Avery. I'm not sure she would have worked things out with Hawk and Creed without you."

"They would have figured it out eventually."

"Maybe, but there's no denying the Evander effect."

Ev looks at me and laughs, his shoulders relaxing a little. "Sorry, it's so easy to drown in this shit."

"I believe it. Anyway, we came to ask if you knew where everyone was, but now I think you need a break."

He looks at me, unsure.

"Come on, all this will still be here tomorrow."

"I know, but if we don't figure it out fast, we'll be sitting ducks."

"And if you don't take a break, you'll miss something that could be important. You're only one person, Ev. Take the rest of the day off. Wilder and I will help you out tomorrow. Our last case is finished, and the books are clear for now while we figure this shit out. So put us to work before we do something stupid."

I hold up my hand before he can say anything. "We'll steer clear of the subject files. You're right, it should just be you who sees them. If you find something you think will impact the rest of us, tell us. Otherwise, we don't need to know."

Ev blows out a breath. "Okay. You're right. If I carry on like this, I'm going to miss something."

"Good." Wilder slaps his shoulder. "Now, do you know where the others are? The kitchen is like a ghost town."

"Uh, yeah." Ev taps on the keyboard, making one of the camera feeds pop up. "A gift from Hendrix and Nash. They're sorry they can't be here, but they have their own shit going down."

I stare at the huge outdoor playset the guys are installing as the kids and women look on with excitement.

"Truthfully, I'm glad they're not here. If shit goes sideways, we have them on standby," I say, standing up.

"Yeah, but I don't think it'll be as easy as you think. They've been trying to pull out for months now, and something keeps pulling them back in. It shouldn't be taking this long."

"Russia is not a friendly place to be right now, with what's going on between them and Ukraine and now NATO... No wonder they're having a hard time pulling out. I've watched the news coverage." I shake my head, my hands balling into fists at the thought.

Wilder looks from me to Ev, eyeing him before crossing his arms. "You think it's more than just that, don't you?"

"Hendrix and Nash are good at what they do. That's why they were the ones stationed over there. We've severed our ties with our government after what happened to Salem, but that doesn't mean they don't know where Nash and Hendrix are."

"And you think they'll threaten to out them? Why?"

"To distract us maybe. Tensions are high over there right now. The last thing Hendrix and Nash want is to be considered traitors to our country. Or worse, spies."

"Fuck, we need to talk to Zig about this."

"We'll do it after the kids are down for the night. And if

anything is going to tire them out, it's going to be that monstrosity." Ev stands up.

"Well, let's help those fuckers finish putting it together then."

We turn toward the door. "Fuck, wait." Ev grabs something from his desk. "Can't forget Alfie's iPad."

"Yeah, that wouldn't go over well."

"Nope."

We leave and head downstairs, Ev stops us when we reach the bottom. "You two go on outside. I'm going to leave this in the den and meet you out there."

We both nod, and Wilder leads the way outside and around the back of what used to be Luna's place, which is now where Hawk, Ev, Avery, and Creed are living. It has a large open space behind it, which is perfect for a playground.

When we get there, the excitement among the kids is plain to see. Even Noah and Alfie look excited, though they are much more reserved.

"Hendrix and Nash don't know the meaning of the word subtle, do they?" I comment, making Oz laugh.

"Get over here and help before the kids spontaneously combust. Where's Lara?"

"She needed a little while to chill on her own. As a group, we can be a lot to handle."

"No shit." Oz chuckles before cursing and jumping to the side when Zig throws a hammer at him.

"There are children present, dickface."

I shake my head and chuckle as I watch the two of them.

"She's coming over to eat later. I tempted her with Salem's cooking, but if you'd rather order pizza or something, I don't think anyone would object."

Salem blows her hair away from her face, Aries cradled in her arms, as she steps closer.

"What do you say, little one? Want to cook or order in tonight?" Oz asks her, moving to press a kiss on his son's head.

"As much as I like cooking for you all, I won't say no to pizza. With the kids not sleeping well last night, I'm exhausted. How they still have so much energy is beyond me."

"Ah, to be young again. Here, give little man to me and go lie down for a while. We can keep an eye on all the kids."

"Are you sure?" she asks as I reach for Aries. She releases him, making sure I'm supporting his head as I cradle him in my arms, his little face scrunching in his sleep.

"Positive. Now shoo, woman."

She kisses Aries's head, then my cheek, ignoring Oz's disgruntled protests, and heads inside.

"Oh, would you look at that? My hands are full. I'm going to go sit with the women and kids."

"Hey, that's my kid. If anyone should sit out with him, it should be me," Oz protests, stepping closer.

I turn my back and walk away. "You snooze, you lose," I say, walking over to squeeze myself between Avery and Astrid.

"No, please have a seat," Astrid deadpans, rolling her eyes. They move over a little, giving me some space.

"I take it you sent Salem for a nap?" Avery asks, running her fingers over the top of Aries's head.

"Yep. I don't think she's had a full night's sleep since Aries made his appearance, but last night didn't help."

"Oz and Zig might be amazing at helping out, but until they grow boobs and start lactating, there's only so much they can do," Astrid says.

I grin. I like being one of the girls.

"What are you smirking about?" Wilder grumbles.

"Boobs."

He looks from me to Avery and Astrid before he pouts like he's missing out. He walks away with slumped shoulders, making Avery laugh.

"You are so bad. He looked like he was two seconds away from tackling you."

"He's just jealous he didn't think of offering to look after Aries before me. How's the move going?"

"Not bad. The guys wouldn't let me help because of the baby, so I spent the day shopping online." She smiles, and I can't help but chuckle. I have a feeling those three won't be letting her do much for the next nine months.

"How's Lara doing? I kind of expected her to come back with the two of you."

"She needed some time to herself after the day she had. All this is more than she's used to."

"The Division was always busy," Avery starts. "But I only remember seeing Lara with the kids. I don't think I can ever recall her interacting with another adult besides myself. It's weird now that I think about it. Everyone moved around her like she was invisible unless they needed her to deal with one of the kids."

"That's fucked up," I grunt.

"It's sad," Astrid adds. "And must have been incredibly lonely. I know what that feels like."

"I was too wrapped up in my own issues to notice when I was there. But now..." Avery sighs. "I've been a shitty friend."

"I get the feeling that if you had been better friends, it would have given the Division something else to use against you both. I feel like, after growing up there, she should have made more friends, even without trying. It makes me wonder if people kept their distance on purpose," Astrid says.

"You mean they were ordered to stay away?" I ask, disgusted. "Is that something they would do?" I look at Avery, who has a sad look on her face.

"Yeah, that sounds exactly like something they would do."

I glance over at the kids. They're sitting together, the girls giggling and laughing, the boys holding back a little more. But all of them are watching the playground being assembled.

"I can't get over how happy they all seem, considering what they've all gone through." I look at Avery, who smiles softly.

"It's the Lara touch. That's what we called it at the Division. She has this way with kids that helps them blossom even when all they've known is darkness. The boys are quieter and hold themselves back more, but them sitting there and allowing themselves to be a part of this is all Lara. You don't see the effect she has on them as much because they aren't as outgoing as Bella and Delaney. But if you knew the details of what those boys have been through, you'd wonder how the fuck they're still functioning at all. Lara is able to heal those broken parts. Not like Salem does. She's not a healer. I mean, somehow, the way she is with them, loving them unconditionally and accepting them no matter what, smooths away the rough edges of their memories. They still remember what happened to them and still hurt because of it. But the softened edges don't cause nearly as much pain as the sharp broken pieces do."

"I wish Lara had someone like that," Astrid says, leaning back on her elbows, her legs out straight in front of her. "We both grew up so isolated and cut off from love and yet somehow she managed to not only feel it but cultivate it in others. That's a gift all in itself, if you ask me."

We sit quietly for a moment watching the kids have fun.

"Wilder and I apologized, but I think it will take a lot more than that to earn forgiveness."

"You know what they say: actions speak louder than words."

Astrid looks at me and smiles. "Why do you look excited at the prospect?"

"Because I am. If Lara needs me to chase her, then that's what I'll do. After all, I'm an excellent hunter."

Her age is the only thing holding me back. But once she turns eighteen, all bets are off.

Chapter Thirteen

Lara

The main house is empty when I walk in, making me frown. Then I hear laughter from outside and realize they must have taken the kids out to stretch their legs for a bit.

I go to join them when I spot Alfie's iPad on the sofa. I hesitate for a second before I walk over to it and open it up. I find the Notes app, and after swallowing down a wave of pain, I write a letter to Alfie, expressing everything I won't be able to say to his face. By the time I'm done, tears are running down my cheeks and dripping off my chin.

I place the iPad back on the sofa and wipe my face, taking a few deep breaths. It doesn't stop my heart from feeling like it's being torn in two, but my breathing is under control, and I feel strong enough to make it through the next few hours. As long as I don't think about what I'll have to do, I'll be okay.

I make my way outside and follow the sound of Bella's laughter, the joyful sound making my lips twitch. Sometimes, I swear she's made up of sunshine to counteract all the darkness she sees.

For a minute, all I can do is watch, memorizing the perfection of the moment—something I know I'll pull up and remember in the future with tears in my eyes and heartbreak in my soul. The pain won't make it any less perfect. Instead, the hurt will make the memory sharper, each tiny detail etched into my brain with HD clarity. A fleeting moment in time that has *I was there*, written across it with invisible ink. And for this right here—Delaney's laugh, Bella's shrieks of joy, Noah's quiet giggle and Alfie's tentative smile—it will all be worth it.

A price must be paid to balance the scales. I took the kids and denied my father the future he had been striving to create. By taking them like I did and Apex thwarting them at every turn, the balance has been tipped too far in our favor.

I feel the sense of impending doom hanging over our heads like a pendulum reaching the apex of its curve before beginning its downward swing. The only thing stopping it from destroying what they've built here is for me to step in front of them and take the blow.

A sacrifice has to be made, and it's me that has to make it—my happiness for theirs. It's a price I'd willingly pay every single time.

"Hey, Lara. Come over here and hold this for me," Zig calls out when he spots me.

Heads turn in my direction, but I keep my eyes on Zig. I'm struggling to keep my emotions in check, and right now, I can only focus on so much before I fall apart.

"Hi," I offer when I reach him, hating how small my voice sounds. He looks at me, his eyes probing. And for a brief moment,

I'm almost convinced that he can see inside my mind. Just as the first tendrils of panic start to wrap themselves around my lungs and squeeze, he lowers his head and his voice so only I can hear him.

"I don't like those shadows in your eyes."

"I'm okay, Zig, I promise."

"Liar. But things will be different now. You'll see."

Tears prick my eyes, but I fight them back. "They already are. Look at this. Look at them. You're changing their whole world, and it's only been a week. Imagine what you can do in a month or a year."

I place my hand on his wrist. "Most of them are still young enough to be able to grow up without the past haunting them. You gave them that, and I'll never be able to repay you for it."

"You don't have to repay us, Lara. Jesus—"

"Accept my thank you, Zig," I interrupt him, my voice quiet but fierce. "Any other thanks you get will pale in comparison because, I swear to you, nobody will ever mean it more than I do right now."

"Anyone ever tell you you're intense when you're being all forceful and shit?"

A startled laugh escapes me. That sounded like something Oz would say.

"There she is," he murmurs, making me frown. Before I can ask what he means, he hands me a piece of wood. "I'm building the ladder, but I need an extra set of hands to hold shit in place while I screw it together."

"Okay, point me to where you want me."

He puts me to work. He's quiet, not feeling forced to fill the silence between us, and it settles something inside me. I've never mastered the art of small talk, not with so few people willing to have a conversation with me. Now, when people start talking, I feel overwhelmed. Zig has eased that. I know that when I leave, I'll need to work on it. For now, though, I can just be me.

We work in silence against a backdrop of talking and laughter. When we're finished, the kids run over, the leash on their patience snapping. We all stand back and watch the kids just be kids, and it's fucking glorious.

An arm wraps around my shoulders, and I look up and find Oz looking down at me with a smile on his face.

"I almost sweated my balls right off, but seeing them like this was worth it."

I slip my arm around his waist and lean my head against him. Any lingering doubts I might have had about leaving the kids here with these people evaporate. Here they have a chance at a real life, in a real home with people who will love them in spite of their gifts, not because of them.

"Alright, who wants pizza?" Wilder walks over, his eyes moving from Oz to me. I tense, expecting him to make a snide comment about Oz being someone else's man, though there is nothing like that between him and me. But Wilder surprises me by offering me a soft smile that almost seems like approval. But that can't be, right?

I swear being around him and Crew has fried more brain cells than any of the vigorous testing I've been through over the years.

"I want an extra-large meat lovers," Oz says.

"Same," Zig shouts from where he's standing.

I bite my lip, unsure because pizza isn't something I was ever permitted to have. I think of the commercials I've seen over the years and decide to keep it simple.

"I'll have a slice of pepperoni, if that's okay?"

Wilder scowls at me playfully. "It's illegal to order a single slice of pizza."

I raise my eyebrow. "Really?"

He grins. "No, but it should be. Cold pizza for breakfast the next day is even better than when it arrives piping hot."

I grimace. The thought of cold pizza does not sound appealing at all.

Wilder laughs. "Don't knock it until you try it. Trust me."

I press my lips together before I say anything else.

"I'll go see what the kids want." He hesitates before looking back at me. "Anything they can't have?"

"Not that I know of. But they're trying a lot of new things, so maybe just keep an eye on them."

"Don't worry. We have Salem if they have an allergic reaction to something." I look up at Zig as Oz and Wilder go still.

I feel like his admitting Salem's gift out loud is a monumental thing. I'm just unsure why.

"Thank you, but I'm sure they'll be fine."

The sound of crying catches our attention as Wilder walks over to the kids. I turn and see Astrid with Aries in her arms, and he's crying his heart out.

As if on instinct, Oz, Zig, and I rush over to them both.

Astrid looks up at us and smiles. "I don't think he's hungry. Salem fed him right before she went for her nap. Maybe he just likes Crew more than me."

"Where is Crew?" Zig asks as he reaches for Aries and pulls him to his chest, but the little guy keeps crying, his face rosy red.

"He had to use the bathroom."

"Maybe he's cutting a tooth. May I?" I hold my arms out for him and smile when Zig doesn't hesitate to hand him to me.

"Isn't he too young for that?" Zig asks.

I shrug. "Most babies won't teeth this early, but then some babies are born with a tooth or two. There are always exceptions."

As soon as Aries is in my arms, I place him so his head is resting on my shoulder and start rubbing his back. I gently soothe him, dampening the pain and sending calming waves his way. He stops crying almost immediately and falls asleep in my arms.

"Holy shit, she's a baby whisperer," Oz gasps, and I look at him with a grin. "You do know this means you can never leave, right?"

My smile turns brittle. Oz, just like his brother, is far too perceptive, so I look away.

"Now you know what it is, Salem will be able to heal him if it acts up again." I keep my voice even before burying my nose against Aries's head. I breathe him in with a sigh. "Why do babies always smell so good?" I murmur.

"Oh, trust me, this little stinker didn't smell good at six a.m. this morning," Zig says, making me chuckle.

I shift Aries to cradle him in my arms as I move to sit beside Astrid. Avery looks over at me and offers a tentative smile. I give her a small one in return. I'm trying not to be a petty bitch because I don't want to leave here on bad terms, but it's hard to forgive and forget. She was the only person here, except for the kids, that I expected to stand up for me. But when I needed her, she hesitated. Yeah, maybe I'm heaping all my past letdowns and hurts onto her, but I can't help how I feel. I'm not mad at her anymore. In some respects, I can even understand it, but that doesn't mean I'm not still hurt by it.

"You have a gift," Astrid states, making my head whip around to look at her, but she's staring down at Aries with a soft smile.

I look over at Avery. She's watching me with a frown. She knows I'm telekinetic, but has she put two and two together and figured out that I inherited my father's gift as well as my mother's?

Shit, I need a distraction.

"I thought we were all gifted here," I say with a smile. Though I can feel the strain of my words, I'm hoping the others don't notice.

"Well, the cool people are anyway." She winks at me as Oz whines.

"That was mean, and besides, I'm so fucking cool I don't need a gift. The world wouldn't be able to handle all this if I was gifted too." He waves his hand over his body, making Zig groan and cover his eyes.

"My brother, ladies and gentlemen. If he didn't look so much like me, I would have thought he was switched at birth."

I laugh, trying to keep my voice down so I don't wake Aries. "Hell, I'm not even cool with a gift, so I promise you're not missing out on anything."

Crew comes back just as I finish talking. He frowns and looks at Oz. "She really has no fucking clue, does she?"

"No clue about what?" I growl, not liking where this is going.

He looks at me, a smile playing on his lips. "You're fucking gorgeous, Lara."

I suck in a sharp breath and feel my cheeks flame. Holy crap, I had not been expecting that.

"You're loyal, brave, and kind. I don't know why you think there's nothing special about you when all I see is someone pretty fucking amazing."

"Close your mouth, hon," Astrid whispers in my ear.

My mouth snaps closed with an audible click, making her chuckle.

"Uncle Oz, Uncle Zig," Bella calls, making the two brothers turn to look at her. "Slade and Jagger said they can do the monkey bars faster than you."

I see the two men in question over by the monkey bars, smirking.

"Oh, it's on like Donkey Kong," Oz growls.

Crew sits beside me, chuckling, and I can't help myself. I lean into him and ask quietly, "What's Donkey Kong?"

He freezes, and I can picture the inside of his brain now flashing like a neon light. *She's seventeen, seventeen, seventeen.*

"Just kidding," I say.

He looks at me for a second before he sighs. "I deserved that."

"You really did." I smile, and he chuckles.

"What are the chances of me getting Aries back?"

"Not good. You left. He's mine now."

"Yeah, how dare I need to use the bathroom," he says with a snort.

"You'll know better for next time." I smile and pat his arm.

I turn back to the monkey bars when I hear whooping and hollering.

I can't help but laugh when Slade and Zig start whipping their T-shirts off. Greg walks over to them, waving his phone, and I realize he's going to time them.

I spot Ev and Hawk sitting at the top of the crow's nest, watching on with amusement while Creed gets into position to video it all.

"And to think I thought this was for the kids."

"The first thing you should know about living here, Lara, is that they are all big kids. I don't know how they survived before Salem came along," Astrid admits.

"Luna," Avery and Crew say at the same time, not taking their eyes off the action, and we both laugh before turning our attention back to Zig and Slade.

I smile as the crowd starts cheering, and both Slade and Zig take off like lightning.

"Holy crap." I watch, mesmerized, as they move seamlessly from one bar to the next. I'd be lying if I said I wasn't impressed.

Movement out of the corner of my eye catches my attention. I turn to look at the other side of the playset just as Bella, frustrated at being unable to see, decides to climb to the top of the second crow's nest, like Ev and Hawk, to get a better view.

My heart lodges in my throat as I watch her climb, but I don't shout out, worried I'll distract her and she'll slip. Then, as if my thoughts make it reality, she loses her grip and falls.

Her scream pierces the air as she plummets to the ground. Everyone turns, and all the men run toward her, but they won't make it in time.

I don't stop to think. I act on instinct, throwing my free arm out and pushing as much force as I can out of it. If I had time to worry, I'd panic that she was too far away. But there is no time for panic now, which shuts out the voice of doubt in my brain.

Bella freezes in the air a few inches from the ground. The pressure of taking her weight rocks me forward. I hold Aries tightly and focus on holding Bella still. I catch my breath and gently lower her to the ground.

As soon as I release her, I feel the telltale warmth of blood running from my nose over my lips. I lift my hand to swipe my face and freeze when I realize everyone's eyes are on me.

Chapter Fourteen

Wilder

I stand there with a stack of pizza boxes burning my hands and watch as Lara dips her head, trying to hide.

I look over at Bella as Crew and the guys reach her. They check to make sure she's okay, but she laughs and runs off to play.

Jagger looks at me in shock as I turn to look back at Lara, who is carefully handing Aries over to Astrid. I know as soon as he's out of her arms, she's going to run.

I hurry over to her, slowing only to shove the pizzas at Greg. My eyes don't leave Lara as she gets to her feet and moves towards the house. Before she can take another step, I sweep her up and pull her to my chest. She's stiff as a board in my arms, and I don't blame her. I've done nothing but give her mixed signals.

I feel the others approaching as I press a kiss to the crown of her head. "That was fucking amazing, Lara."

She jolts at my words, her head tipping back to look at me, trying to gauge my sincerity. She won't find anything but honesty on my face. "She could have broken her arm or leg or—heaven fucking forbid—her neck."

She swallows hard, her lip quivering. "I didn't think. I don't usually react like that, but I couldn't let her get hurt. I promise, I'm not a danger to anyone. I've never even lifted anything as heavy as Bella before," she rambles.

Zig steps closer, touching her shoulder lightly to grab her attention, making her jump. "You should be proud of yourself, Lara. None of us would have reached her in time. Yes, Salem could have healed her, but that wouldn't have spared either Bella or Salem the pain. What you did was incredible."

She stares at him before her eyes scan the rest of the people gathered around, each of them congratulating her or patting her on the back. She looks so adorably confused that I'm torn between kissing the frown away and going on a rampage to kill everyone who ever made her feel less than she is.

"I never thought I'd actually be able to do anything useful with it," she whispers.

"Those aren't your words, baby. Those are someone else's. I don't care who said them. They were talking shit. Seems to me, you could do anything you put your mind to." I swipe my thumb under her nose, wiping the blood away as best I can.

When her eyes start to well up, I pull her back to my chest, knowing instinctively that she won't want the others to see her cry. Everyone immediately understands, backing away to give her some space. All except Crew, who walks over and stands beside us both, his hand taking Lara's.

She doesn't fight or pull away from us. She stands there and lets us support her in the only way we can right now.

When she finally pulls back, she looks up at me before her eyes slip to Crew's.

"Thank you," she whispers. A part of me sighs as I see her mentally building her walls back up to shut us out.

"Let's get some pizza before everyone eats it all." With his hand still holding Lara's, Crew tugs her from my embrace and leads her to where everyone's gathered. I follow behind and wait for them to sit before I sit beside her.

Nobody says anything about what just happened, which makes Lara relax slightly. She takes the pizza box Greg offers her and sets it on her lap.

As everyone talks among themselves, I watch Lara lift a slice of pizza to her mouth and take a bite. When her eyes drift closed and a moan slips from her lips, I feel my cock go rock hard. When I look over her head at Crew, I can tell from the pained expression on his face that he's just as affected as I am.

I fight between pulling away and pushing closer. Reminding myself she's seventeen, which seems to have become my fucking mantra, I scrub my hand over my face and reach for my own slice of pizza.

I feel Lara's eyes on me, but I keep looking forward, needing a minute to get myself together. The fact that I can't control my dick around a teenage girl is messing with my head more than I want to admit.

Once my dick settles down, I stand up and make some excuse about grabbing a drink and head inside. I lean against the kitchen counter and take a deep breath, trying to figure out where to go from here. It all seemed so clear before. Enemies to friends, friends to lovers—once she's old enough to decide what she wants, of course.

The problem with that is that I seriously underestimated how my body would react to hers. I'm not sure I'm going to be able to pull off a friendship without it feeling strained, and Lara is way too perceptive not to pick up on it and question why. And what the fuck do I say to her? Sorry, but I can't stand beside you without wanting to shove my cock down your throat.

"Jesus, fuck," I growl and press my forehead against the cool marble.

"If Aries's first word is *fuck*, I will stab you in the balls, heal you, and then stab you all over again."

I lift my head at the sound of Salem's voice and grin at her sleepy face.

"Question: if you take on the injuries you heal, would you feel nothing or have phantom pain like some amputees have?" I ask curiously.

She looks at me like I'm from another planet. "What's wrong with you?"

I sigh and walk over to the table, yanking a chair out and dropping down onto it. "I ask myself that daily at the moment."

She walks over to the fridge and pulls out two cans of Coke, placing one in front of me before she sits down and pops hers open, taking a small sip as she waits me out.

"Bella fell from the playset—"

Salem jumps up, ready to run outside, but I reach out and gently grab her wrist. "She's fine. Lara caught her."

She slowly sits back down, her eyes staring into mine. "Why do I get the feeling there is more to it than that?"

"Because you aren't stupid. Lara caught her before she hit the ground, but she was sitting a good fifteen feet away with Aries sleeping in her arms."

"So how did she..." Her voice drifts off as she gets a knowing look in her eyes. "Right, telekinesis. Wow, I'm sorry I missed it. Everyone's okay, though, right?"

"Yeah, everyone's fine. Bella was off and playing again before most of the adults' heart rates had returned to normal."

Salem chuckles. "Kids are fearless. I'm sure they'll cause a lot of gray hairs."

I smile, thinking she might be right, before I feel it slip from my face. "I can't get her reaction out of my head."

"Who, Bella's? You said she was fine."

"No, Lara's. She was terrified."

"Why? Did she think we would be mad at her?"

"I don't know, maybe. She started babbling about never using it on anyone before, and she's never lifted anything as heavy as Bella before, but she calmed down when we all reassured her it was fine. It was after, when we were all praising her, that she fell apart."

"Don't forget what Avery said earlier. Lara was told she was useless her whole life because she couldn't move bigger objects."

"Yeah, well, hearing about it and seeing the damage it's caused are two different things altogether."

She reaches over and grabs my can, opening it before sliding it back to me. "We'll just have to keep reminding her how amazing she is. She'll learn, just like Astrid did. They're similar, you know. They were both starved of love and belittled. The difference is while Astrid shut herself off from the world, Lara was hidden from it."

I nod, thinking she might be on to something there. We are the sum of our experiences, but Lara has spent her life in a figurative cage. Her experiences have been so negative it's a wonder that she's turned out as well as she has.

"Those kids, they kept her going." It's a statement because I've seen the sadness in her eyes and how lost in her head she gets even in a crowded room.

"Kids are the greatest gift. You'd be amazed at what someone would be willing to do to protect one. Still, none of this explains why you're in here instead of out there with everyone else."

I take a sip of my soda and think about how to word it without coming off as a pervert. "I don't know how to be her friend and not..." I trail off because I can't think of anything PG to say.

Salem rolls her eyes. "God, spare me from testosterone-filled idiots. Oz and Zig were my friends before they were my lovers. Yes, what we went through was an unusual way to get to where we are now."

I snicker. "Yeah, I think crash-landing in a jungle and then having to survive for months together alone is more than unusual."

"My point is, I had to trust them. They became my sounding board and my shoulder to cry on. They helped carry my burdens, and they've never made me feel less than I am to make themselves feel better. We built a friendship before and alongside our physical relationship."

I stare at her, waiting for her to get to the point. When she rolls her eyes, I realize I missed the point entirely.

"You can date without having sex, Wilder," she snaps, making me grateful the fruit bowl in the middle of the table is empty as she eyes it. I have a feeling she would have thrown something at my head.

"I know that," I tell her. Though mentally, I'm wondering if she's on drugs. A relationship without fucking sounds exhausting. It would be different if Lara were injured, or... wait, that's it. I could pretend she has an injury or a disease preventing me from sleeping with her.

"I do not like that dumb look on your face." Salem sighs as I stand up and smile.

"No, what you said makes perfect sense. Thanks. You helped me put things into perspective."

"Wait, really?"

"Yep. I'm just going to pretend she's sick or has a disease or something, so I can't fu— be intimate with her," I correct myself as she glares at me. "That way, I won't feel like I'm missing out. I'll feel like I'm doing the right thing, waiting for her to heal."

Salem presses her fingers to her temples. "I don't know what worries me more, your twelve-year-old boy logic or the fact that I understood it. So what you're saying is, you're going to pretend that girl out there is sick in order to keep your dick under control?"

"Exactly."

Salem stands and rests her hands on the table, taking a deep breath as if trying to find strength. "Why don't you just remind yourself she's only seventeen instead of jinxing her with an illness?" she asks slowly, as if addressing a child.

"Because I don't want to hurt her. Imagining she's sick will stop me from touching her. Telling myself she's only seventeen isn't enough, no matter how many times I remind myself."

She's quiet for a moment before she shakes her head. "I give up trying to understand men. Do what you have to do, but don't fuck with her head, Wilder. She deserves better than that."

"You said fuck."

"I'm exempt from the rule."

"That's not fair."

"Yeah, well, when you've squeezed a whole ass human out of you, then you can complain. Right now, everything is measured by a unit of fuck. Fuck me, fuck this shit, what the fuck, fuck off, and my personal favorite, fuck you."

I stare at the tiny, angry woman and slowly back up. "Well, thanks for the chat. I'm going to head out and think about everything."

"You do that. And tell Oz and Zig they better have saved me some pizza."

"I'll get right on that." I grin, leaving her to it for a moment.

I head out and see Crew talking to Lara, who looks like she'd rather be anywhere else.

The sight makes me laugh. I can't help it.

"Salem's awake, and she said you'd better have saved her some pizza," I yell to Oz.

"We hid a box from the kids. They're like tiny human garbage disposals."

I laugh, knowing that, kids or not, nobody puts away as much food as he does.

Looking back over at Lara, I see her look away as soon as my attention is on her. I sigh, knowing it's my own damn fault. For all the times I've reminded myself she's just a teenager, only one of us here is acting like a kid. And it's not her.

I sit back down beside Lara and turn to look at her. "Sorry about that. I got caught up talking to Salem."

Lara turns to look at me and offers me a nod. I can't tell if she believes my excuse or not. And that's all it is—an excuse. I stayed to chat with Salem, sure, but that's not the reason I left in the first place. And Lara knows it.

"It's fine. Crew's been talking my ear off anyway," she says with a small smile.

"I told you I wanted to be friends, and friends talk, right?" he asks sincerely.

Lara's smile looks strained as she gets to her feet and brushes the grass off her jeans. "I'm just going to spend a little time with the kids before bed."

I almost ask her if she wants company, but something tells me she'll make an excuse and bolt. I groan as I watch her leave.

"Well, that went well." Crew sighs. "What the hell was wrong with you? One minute, you're talking to Lara, and the next, you're gone."

"I just needed a minute, that's all. What were you guys talking about?"

"Not much. She's a prickly little thing. I see her let her guard down a little when she's talking to the others or with the kids, but as soon as I try to talk to her, she slams that door between us. It's frustrating as fuck."

"Yeah, I've noticed it too." I sigh. "We did hurt her. We accused her of a bunch of shit, and now we're telling her we want to be her friends. I'm not sure I'd believe her either if the roles were reversed."

He shakes his head. "I was so sure that when we found our woman, we wouldn't fuck it up like the others did."

"At this point, I'm thinking it's a rite of passage. Everyone here had to fight tooth and nail to make their relationships work. If the most we have to do is beg for forgiveness, then we got off pretty fucking lucky."

Chapter Fifteen

Lara

I spend the rest of the evening chasing the kids around the playground, plastering a grin on my face even though my heart breaks with each fake smile.

"Alright, kids, I think it's time for a bath and then bed," Salem calls out.

Bella complains loudly, but the others stop playing right away, still too used to harsh consequences for rule-breaking.

"You can play out here again tomorrow, I promise," Salem vows, and Bella reluctantly agrees and climbs down.

I look at my watch and see that it's past their bedtime. With all the excitement of the day, I'm sure they'll be out cold the second their heads hit the pillow.

"Well, I'm going to go to bed myself. I'm exhausted, so come hug me first." I crouch down as my voice cracks, but thankfully nobody seems to notice.

Delaney's first. She throws herself into my arms and plants a kiss on my cheek before pulling back.

"Night, Lara."

"Night," I whisper as she runs into the house. Bella's next to hug me. I squeeze her tightly before pulling back, willing myself to keep it the fuck together until I'm alone.

"Love you, Lara."

"I love you too, pretty girl."

She gives me a quick kiss and a huge grin before she skips off after Delaney. Noah walks over to me slowly, waiting for me to open my arms before he steps into them. I breathe him in, but I don't say anything. I can't speak around the lump in my throat.

We stay like that for a few moments, with him drawing comfort from me as I etch this memory into my brain so I never lose it. Once he's done, he lets go of me and walks over to Slade, of all people, and stands beside him, looking up.

I watch as Slade holds out his hand to him. When Noah slips his tiny hand into Slade's, I have to bite my lip to hold back my sob. I get to my feet and look at Alfie, who has waited for everyone else to have their turn.

There are so many things I want to say, but I swallow them down and close the distance between us. I wrap him in my arms and hold him to me as he rests his head against my chest.

It's true what they say about never knowing how strong you are until being strong is all you have left. I might be running as far as I can from this place tonight, but my heart will stay in the hands of this boy until I can come back and get it.

I pull back and cup his jaw, my thumb sliding over the apple of his cheek. "Thank you for being you. You show me every day what it means to be strong. Thank you for loving me and letting me love you back."

He swallows hard, too choked up to say anything, but that's okay. I don't need to hear his words. Everything he wants to say is right there in his eyes.

I kiss his forehead, my lips lingering for a second against his skin. "Keep an eye on the girls. You know what kind of trouble they can get into."

He huffs out an exasperated laugh, making me grin. "Night, Lara," he says quietly before slipping his headphones on and walking away.

"Bye, Alfie," I whisper.

"Are you okay?" I jump and turn at the sound of Astrid's voice.

She's standing next to Jagger, who watches me in that quiet way of his.

"Yeah, just tired."

"Are you sure?"

"I'm sure." I nod.

"We're all going to watch a movie. You want to come?"

"No. I'm going to head back to Greg's and get some sleep. But thanks," I tack on. She offers me an unsure smile before Jagger wraps his arm around her shoulders and leads her inside.

"We'll walk you back." I spin around and find Crew and Wilder behind me.

"Oh no, that's okay, but thank you."

"We insist." Crew smiles, linking our fingers.

Wilder takes my free hand, and before I can object further, they start leading me toward Greg's. On our way, we run into the man himself. He looks from me to the guys, his eyebrow cocked in question. There is no teasing or innuendo. He's genuinely asking me if I'm okay. I give him a slight nod and what I hope is a reassuring smile.

"Well, I'm heading in to watch a movie with the rest of the gang, but I won't be too late. You know where I am if you need me," he says the last part with his gaze locked on the guys, his warning clear.

Suddenly, I know I can't leave without hugging him, so that's what I do. I pull free from Crew and Wilder and walk right up to Greg before wrapping my arms around him. There is no hesitation as he wraps his arms around me and squeezes me.

"Thank you" is all I can get out, but I know, for now, at least, it has to be enough.

"I was never blessed enough to have children, but I always dreamed of one day living on a ranch with a bunch of daughters to hover over me with their overbearing ways and need to look after me."

I suck in a sharp breath as he smiles at me. "Now I've got four. The man upstairs really does work in mysterious ways."

This time, I have no chance of holding back my tears.

All my life, I've been a disappointment, the daughter of a neglectful tyrant who ruled over our little kingdom with an iron fist. All I ever dreamed about was being free. To be loved like a daughter should be.

And now here's Greg. A man I don't share blood with. We have no history binding us together. He's just a good man who could love me like a daughter should be loved. As long as he can find it in his heart one day to forgive me for what I'm about to do.

"Now, off you go. Get some sleep, and tomorrow, I'll take you down and show you the orchards and Oz said he'd give you your first driving lesson."

"Okay," I choke out, wanting more than anything to do just that.

I watch him leave before continuing on to the cabin with Crew and Wilder on either side of me. They must know I'm not in the mood to talk right now because they don't ask me any questions. They walk quietly beside me like guards keeping watch.

Part of me wants to scream at them to go away. To tell them they're just making everything so much more complicated.

The other part, though, needs these last few moments to tide me over. I might be nothing more than just a girl to them, but they are the first men ever to make me feel anything. Maybe I am just a kid, and this is nothing more than a crush, but if what we have right now is all it will ever be, it's still something I'll cherish. Because for a few fleeting moments, they made me feel like a normal girl and not like Frankenstein's first attempt at a monster.

I unlock the door and open it, turning in the doorway so they don't follow me inside. I stare at them both, having so much to say. But not a single word passes my lips because nothing feels adequate.

"Are you sure you're okay?" Crew questions, his frown deepening as his eyes rove over my face for the truth.

"Yeah, I'm okay. It's just still a lot for me to get used to. I spent a lot of time being invisible to everyone but the kids, and now it feels like all eyes are on me."

"You're the new kid," Wilder says, making me wince at the term *kid*. "The novelty will wear off eventually."

"I guess. After last night..." I bite my lip, trying to find the right words without sounding like a bitch.

"When we acted like assholes?" Crew offers, making me smile.

"Yeah. After that, everyone's been super nice. I didn't expect that. I half expected to wake up and find myself being kicked out. But when Oz apologized... It was like everyone acknowledged that they had overreacted. I'm not sure what to do with that. I'm so used to waiting for the other shoe to drop that I feel a little off balance. And then the incident with Bella—"

"We knew you were telekinetic," Wilder tells me gently.

"How?" I ask, confused.

"It was in your file."

I swallow and cross my arms over my chest protectively. "What else did this file say?"

Wilder shrugs. "Ev won't let anyone read the files except him. Said it's an invasion of privacy. So we don't know, and he won't tell any of us unless it's absolutely necessary."

I drop my arms and nod, relaxing a bit.

We all stand there, quiet, looking at each other for a few minutes. Wilder looks like he wants to say something, but it's Crew that breaks the silence.

"You sure you don't want to come watch the movie with us? We can make some popcorn, raid Slade's not-so-secret stash of snacks."

I shake my head, knowing I need to end this thing between us here and now. A clean break, and then a prayer that the edges are smooth and not jagged because my insides already feel like they are being torn apart.

"I think I'm going to take a nice long soak in the tub and read for a little while. I have all those new books Oz bought me." I force a grin and hope they buy it.

I can see that they don't want to leave. I'm not sure why. Maybe they can feel the angry static around us that's pulsing with a warning.

Knowing they want to push harder, I step forward and wrap an arm around each of them, drawing just the smallest amount of their energy from them and replacing it with something much calmer and more soothing. I don't press my suggestions on them. That's something I just won't do, but I can gloss over their crazy need to stay with me enough to make them leave.

When I pull back, and they're both leaning down over me, I summon all my courage and kiss Wilder. Nothing more than a brief press of my lips on his before doing the same with Crew.

They'll never know they were my first kiss. And if my father wins, they might just be my last.

They both look stunned for a minute. Before they can tell me they regret it or that nothing can happen because of my age, I simply whisper goodbye and close the door in their faces.

I rest my head against the cool wood, my fingertips pressing into the door as if I could reach through and touch them. But I can't. I stand firm, holding my ground, until I hear them mumble something and walk away. Only when I'm sure I'm alone do I allow the dam to break. Collapsing to the floor, I wrap my arms around my legs and sob my fucking heart out.

I was so close to having it all, and now, thanks to my father, it's once again just beyond my reach. I wipe my tears, anger flooding my system, drowning out the sorrow.

If I can't have Apex, then neither can my father, even if that means I have to make him chase me all over the world. I harden my heart as I pull myself up to my feet and make a promise to myself. He will never cage me again. I would rather rip off my own wings and throw myself from the highest of heights than be trapped in a life I hate.

Knowing I can't leave just yet, I head to the bathroom and run a bath. It might have initially been a lie, part of the cover story I told Crew and Wilder, but it makes sense. I have no idea when I might be able to soak in a tub again.

I don't bother with one of the books, knowing I won't be able to concentrate. Instead, I slip under the water and go over the plan in my head once more. Not that it's much of a plan. Get out, get far away, and don't get caught are as detailed as my plans get.

Still, as luck would have it, I overheard Ev telling Zig that he's taking the night off. That means that the cameras might catch me, but nobody will be monitoring them.

I lie in the tub for a while, but it does nothing to relax me. My mind is too busy turning everything over in my head.

Draining the water, I climb out and get dressed. I pull on a pair of black leggings and a long-sleeved black T-shirt, then pull my hair into a braid. Once I'm dressed, I lay a black hoodie and jacket on the chair for later, with my sneakers sitting on the floor beside them, ready for me to step into.

I check to make sure I'm still alone and grab the sleeping bag. I add it to my backpack with a couple more changes of clothes before it's full. I look longingly at the books, but I know I can't take them with me.

I run my fingers over the cover of the top one and close my eyes before bringing it to my nose and breathing it in. There is something magical about the smell of a book. It's both calming and enticing. My only hope is that someone else here will find some joy in them.

I stack the books neatly on the table beside the bed and put away the rest of my things. A voice I try to ignore whispers that it's so I might be able to come back home at some point. But the cynic in me hopes it will buy me some time. Hopefully, when they find my room empty, they'll assume I've gone for a walk.

With nothing else to do, I lie down on the bed and pull the soft throw blanket over my body. I close my eyes and let my tears fall once more. I might as well get it out of my system. There won't be time for tears once I'm gone.

I must cry myself to sleep because when I open my eyes, it's eerily quiet and pitch-black. It never gets this dark in the city, even on the outskirts. There are too many lights for it ever to be truly dark. But here, it's like a veil has been placed over everything, snuffing out the light completely.

I sit up and look at the clock on the bedside table. The time shows that it's two a.m. I get to my feet and creep out of my room. I head down the hall toward Greg's room and pause halfway when I hear him snoring. Turning back, I walk to the chair and sit down, slipping on my sneakers and lacing them up. I tug the hoodie over my head before pulling on the waterproof coat. I slowly drag the backpack out from under the bed and heave it onto my back.

Blowing out a deep breath, I quietly head to the front door. The panel on the wall is lit up, showing me the alarm is on. I type in the code and freeze when a low beep sounds. I wait, listening for Greg. When I don't hear anything, I carefully twist the handle and open the door.

The cool night air hits me in the face, wiping away any trace of my sleepiness that remained. With one final look behind me, I close the door and head around the back of the building, keeping to the shadows. I take it slow, avoiding the buildings so that I stay undetected. When I reach the driveway, I look over at the garage, wishing I could drive so I could take one of the cars. I'm sure they would find it if I left it somewhere they could pick it up later. I'd be shocked as heck if they didn't have some kind of tracking device on the cars. But alas, a car is out of the question.

I keep walking with light steps and a heavy heart, pausing only when I reach the Apex sign. I look back at the main house and picture all the kids inside fast asleep after tiring themselves out from playing outside all evening. I smile, bittersweet as it is. I might not be their actual mother, but that doesn't mean I wouldn't give up everything to make sure they're safe and happy.

Well, they'll be safe here without me, safer than anywhere else in the world. Happiness will be a more gradual thing. But for the first time in forever, they all have a shot at a bright future, and I'll be damned if I let my father take that away from them.

And with that thought, my sense of purpose becomes my shield. I hurry away, knowing I'll take as many hits as necessary if it means they remain free.

Chapter Sixteen

Crew

Sweat drips down my back as I stop to catch my breath.

After a restless night's sleep, I eventually gave up at five a.m. and crawled out of bed. I got dressed in a pair of shorts and decided to outrun my demons instead.

I wipe my face with the bottom of my T-shirt and head home to take a shower. It's still quiet when I enter, but then Wilder never gets up early unless he's on perimeter duty.

I strip out of my clothes as I walk to the shower, climbing in before the water even has a chance to get hot. I wash myself and stand under the water for a minute, my mind flashing back to Lara.

She kissed us. Both of us. Sure, it was nothing more than a peck, but Lara doesn't strike me as someone who takes the initiative very often. It might have been barely a brush—the most innocent kiss—but that didn't stop my dick from standing up and paying attention. Before I could make the blood flow back to my brain and remind us both of all the reasons things couldn't happen between us yet, she closed the door between us.

Neither Wilder nor I were up for movie night after that. Instead, we opted for cold showers and an early night.

I reach down and grab my cock, giving it a firm stroke. Lara's pouty lips flash in my head, and goddammit, I stroke my cock faster as I think of slipping it between her lips and having her suck me hard and deep.

I try to change the image of Lara to someone more generic, but my brain refuses, and my dick is a slave to its urges. I give in, knowing I'll hate myself afterward, but not giving a fuck right now. I keep stroking, tightening my grip as I thrust into my fist and imagine Lara's tight, wet pussy wrapped around me.

It's more than I can bear. I come with a growl, spraying the tiles as I swallow Lara's name.

Angry and still frustrated, I rinse off and climb out of the shower. I wrap a towel around my waist before stomping into the bedroom for clean clothes. Something's gotta give. The run should have helped, but it didn't. I need some kind of release, or I'm going to end up throwing my morals out the fucking window.

By the time I'm dressed and have semi-calmed down, I head to the main house to see if anyone else is up. I need something to do before I lose my damn mind.

When I walk in, I find Salem passed out on the sofa with Aries asleep in his little bounce chair on the floor beside her. I tug the blanket off the back of the sofa and lay it over her before making my way into the kitchen. I avoid the coffee machine, not wanting to wake either of them, and instead pour myself a glass of orange juice from the fridge.

With nobody else around, I head outside, stopping when I spot

Alfie sitting in the crow's nest. I take a sip of my juice and place it on the top step of the deck before walking over to the playground. I climb up to him. When I reach the top, I wait for him to acknowledge me. He's not wearing his headphones, so I know he heard me coming as he stares down at his iPad.

Eventually, he lifts his head, his red-rimmed eyes colliding with mine.

"Hey, what's wrong?" I ask.

He doesn't answer, his eyes dropping back down to his iPad, so I edge closer. "I'm going to sit down next to you, okay? And whenever you're ready, you can tell me what's wrong. There's no rush. I have no other place to be than here with you."

He doesn't say anything to let me know if I'm welcome, but he also doesn't scream at me to leave, so I'm counting that as a win. I sit next to him, both our legs hanging over the edge, close but not touching.

Even though he's not speaking, I know whatever's troubling him is bad. He's gripping the iPad hard enough to crack it.

"Do you want me to get Lara?"

He sniffs and looks up at me. There is so much sorrow in his gaze it breaks my fucking heart.

"Jesus, kid, you're killing me. Tell me what's wrong."

He leans his head against my arm, and I have to suck in a sharp breath to stop myself from squeezing him tightly. He's not the kid for that. He tolerates the women here who ruffle his hair or nudge him playfully, but even they know not to push too much. The only person he is one hundred percent comfortable with is Lara. Yet here he is, seeking comfort from an asshole like me.

With a shaky hand, he passes me his iPad, the Notes app open.

"You want me to read what you wrote?"

142

"I didn't write it. I remember everything. I don't need to write notes."

"Well, if you didn't write it, who did?"

He looks at me again, and I know what he's going to say before he opens his mouth.

"Lara did."

I swallow the sudden urge to puke. I know it could be an innocent thing, something sweet for Alfie to find that would make his day, but my gut tells me it's not. Whatever she wrote is bad. And as much as I want to know what the fuck is going on; I can't help but hesitate.

I close my eyes for a moment and will my fucking heart to calm down before I keel over and have a heart attack, scaring the boy beside me more than he already is. Releasing a deep breath, I open my eyes and start to read.

Alfie,

By the time you read this, I'll be gone. I never thought I'd ever say those words, least of all to you, but it's the only way I know to keep you safe. I know you won't understand, and you have every right to be upset and angry with me, but please don't hate me. I think I could survive just about anything but that.

I can't tell you the reason I have to go, just know I would have stayed if I could. If I was given the choice, I'd spend a thousand lifetimes with you and the rest of The Lost Ones. All my favorite memories are filled with you, Noah, Bella, and Delaney. You are what gets me up in the morning and what makes me smile when I lay my head down at night. I know none of this makes sense, and I'm sorry for that, but I promise I'll explain one day when I know it's okay for me to come back.

Know I love you to the moon and back, and if it ever becomes too much, look for me in the stars. I guarantee I'll be looking up thinking of you all, and there's comfort in knowing it's the same sky above us both.

Love always,

Lara

I read the note a second time, numbness settling inside me before everything comes rushing back into focus.

"Can I borrow this?"

He nods.

I reach out and, oh so slowly, cup his jaw and tilt his head back. "I'll find her, Alfie. I swear on my life, I won't stop until she's back home."

He's so tense he looks like he is moments away from breaking. I let go of him and jump off the playset, running to Greg's place first.

I pound on his door and don't stop until a pissed-off, half-asleep Greg answers it.

"What the fuck is your problem?" he bellows.

I ignore him, shoving past and heading for Lara's room. I push the door open and find the room empty and the bed made.

"I swear to God, Crew, I'm going to kick your— Where's Lara?"

I turn to look at Greg, who's staring into Lara's empty room over my shoulder.

144

"She's gone." I leave him standing there and head for the door.

"What do you mean, she's gone?" he roars.

I'm out the door before I can answer and running to Ev's place. I pound on the door the same way I did at Greg's. Hawk must have already been up because he answers almost immediately.

He takes in the expression on my face and gestures for me to come in. "What's wrong?"

"I need Ev."

"Alright, I'll get him. But you need to tell me what's happening first."

"Lara's gone. I need him to find her for me."

"Oh, fuck. Alright, I'll wake him up and gather everyone else. We'll meet you at the main house in five."

I nod before walking out and heading home, knowing I need to be the one to tell Wilder.

Nothing makes sense. I'm trained to deal with situations like this, but none of them have ever involved my heart before. And I'm finding it harder to separate my emotions from the cold, hard facts than I should.

I make it home and walk straight into Wilder's room without knocking to find him pulling a T-shirt on over his head.

"No, please do come in," he jokes until he gets a good look at me. "What's happened?"

"Lara's gone. Family meeting at the main house in five."

"Gone? What do you mean, she's gone?"

I stare at him before rubbing my hands over my face, suddenly feeling exhausted. "I mean, she left a goodbye note for Alfie and disappeared without a fucking word to anyone."

Chapter Seventeen

Lara

I hitched a ride with a nun. There's something I never thought I'd say in my life, but there you have it. After leaving Apex and walking for a few hours, I decided the only option I had if I wanted to put some distance between me and those I loved was to hitch a ride.

I took the knife I'd stashed in my bag, eased it into the front pocket of my hoodie, and stuck my thumb out like I'd seen people do in the movies.

I started to lose faith in my plan when hardly any cars had passed me for most of the night. So, imagine my surprise when an old-fashioned station wagon pulled up beside me with a habit-wearing nun behind the wheel. It had to be a joke.

Yet here I am, waving goodbye to Sister Mary Dorothea after driving for the last twelve hours with her as she heads to her convent. I look up at the shelter she insisted on taking me to and blow out a nervous breath.

I've heard horror stories about what can happen in these places. But Sister Mary had promised that this was a good one that only allowed entrance to women. I'm not stupid. I know a woman could just as easily shove a knife in my stomach and steal my things, but she'd be unable to steal the one thing a man could take from me.

I head through the door before I can talk myself out of it and find a woman behind a high counter with a protective screen in front of her. I'm not sure if it's for her safety or something left over from COVID, but it makes me feel like I'm a criminal walking into a police station.

"Can I help you?"

"Hi, I was wondering if you had a bed for the night."

The woman removes her glasses and looks me up and down. "How old are you, dear?"

"Eighteen." She looks at me with suspicion which is unusual. Most people think I look older.

"It was my birthday a few days ago. I ran as soon as I knew I couldn't be dragged back. Sister Mary Dorothea told me to come here."

I layer the lie with the truth and hope she buys it. I can make her feel any number of things, but I don't want to use my gift unless I have to.

"Oh, Sister Mary is a sweetheart. Well, come on in. You'll catch a chill standing there."

I offer her a relieved smile. "Thank you. I didn't know where else to go."

"Well, we'll look after you here. I need to ask, though, for the safety of the others: is anyone likely to turn up here looking for you?"

I want to say no, but I know my father will be tracking me. "Maybe. But by then, I'll be long gone."

"Are you in trouble?"

"Yes, but I promise to leave before any one comes for me."

She doesn't say anything to that, but gestures for me to follow her. She leads me through to one of the rooms and opens the door, revealing a single bed and a set of bunk beds.

"This is the family room. You can use it for tonight. There is a lock on the door and an intercom beside it. If anyone needs you, we'll buzz you, okay? Nobody is getting in without your permission."

"Wow, that's so much more than I expected," I tell her as I follow her into the room.

"A family moved out this morning, and the next one isn't moving in until tomorrow. There's no point in leaving it empty. We're quiet tonight anyway. I hope I didn't just jinx us by saying that."

I smile at her, thankful for her generosity.

"You want something to eat?"

"I have a few peanut butter and jelly sandwiches in my bag."

"They'll keep. I'll bring you some stew. It's hearty and will warm you up." She heads to the door but stops, turning to me before she leaves. "There are people that can help you. Whatever it is you're going through, you don't have to do it alone."

"The man after me is my father, and he's a really bad man. But he's powerful and connected. He has friends that—"

She holds up her hand to stop me. "Say no more. I wish I could tell you that the police can protect you, but we both know that isn't always true. And you wouldn't be here if you thought they could. Tell me something about him."

I jolt at her words and wonder why the hell she wants to know that.

"So many women come through those doors because we are their last resort. Because when they finally found the courage to tell their story, not everyone believed them. Tell me one thing you wish the world knew, and I'll believe you."

I swallow hard and feel tears prick the backs of my eyes. "He's a human trafficker. Men, women, but mostly children. And he works for the government," I finish in a whisper.

"Oh, child," she murmurs before rushing over and tugging me in for a surprising hug. "I believe you. God knows, I wish you were lying, but I know you're not."

She pulls back and looks down at me, weariness lining her face. I have a feeling she's heard a thousand stories like mine, and each one makes her lose a little more faith in humanity.

"You know what makes me smile, though? This big, bad, powerful man just got given the slip by a young lady he clearly underestimated. Keep going. Don't back down. Keep giving him hell. I have a feeling about you. I see an inner strength that few still have by the time they make it here. Surviving is hard. And when I say hard, I mean freaking exhausting. But every day you survive is a day you win. And if you're winning, then your father is losing."

I smile at that, knowing I'll need to remember this conversation someday to keep me going.

"Now, I'm going to get you some stew while you settle in for the night."

"Okay. And thank you again."

She waves me off. "You ever seen that movie *Pay It Forward*?"

"No, I've never seen it, but I understand the concept."

"Good. When the opportunity arises for you to help someone in need, take it, and then we can call it even."

She's gone before I can say anything else, closing the door behind her. I drop my bag and walk over to the door, locking it before leaning against it.

I look around the plain but clean room and send up a silent prayer of thanks. I know my journey won't always be an easy one, but tonight, at least, I'll have a roof over my head and a bed to sleep in.

Picking up my bag, I toss it onto the top bunk before climbing up. I shove the bag until it's pressed up against the wall, then make myself comfortable. I stare at the ceiling and try not to think about everyone at Apex. They'll know I'm gone by now. I don't want to think about what their reactions will be. Most will be hurt, and others will be angry. Maybe they'll think this was all part of some elaborate scheme. God, if only. I wish I could have told them the truth, but they would have just made me stay. They'd risk my father and his men coming to Apex so that I wasn't out here alone. I know that. But they don't know my dad like I do. If he couldn't get to me, he'd wipe Apex off the map. If he can't have me, nobody can. The chip in my arm is the only thing I have going for me right now. He'll follow me. He won't be able to help himself. And while he's focusing on me, he won't be looking at Apex.

I run my fingertips over the small bump in my arm I'd thought was a contraceptive implant and debate whether or not to cut it out and flush it away. A smile pulls at my lips as I imagine a team of my father's men wading through the sewer system, looking for me.

It wouldn't take him long, though, to figure out what I'd done.

Then he'd turn his attention back to Apex. No, for now, this is the best option.

A buzz on the intercom has me climbing off the bed and hitting the button beside the speaker. "Yes?"

"Dinner."

I smile and open the door, my stomach rumbling at the smell.

"You are more than welcome to come and eat out here, but a couple more people have shown up. If you don't want people to remember you, it might be better to stay in here."

"Yeah, I'll eat in here. I don't want to drag anyone else into my mess."

She places the tray on the small table at the side of the room. There is a large bowl of stew on it, along with a couple of dinner rolls and a bottle of water. Next to the bowl is a cell phone.

I look up at her, and she crosses her arms over her chest, daring me to argue. "We keep a couple extra here. The truth is, we have wives running from husbands who are cops and judges. And nobody wants to believe they're capable of such acts. More often than not, the wife is called a liar. Those cases are the worst, and our hands here are tied. There is only so much we can do because those assholes wouldn't think twice about calling in a few favors and having this place shut down."

"You might not be able to help everyone, but you help some."

"It never feels like enough, though," she admits. "Take the phone. It's prepaid. It has fifty dollars on it, and the number is on the back of the phone for you to memorize. I don't know it, and I don't want to. The less I know, the less anyone can get out of me."

"I can't take this. Someone else might need it more."

She wraps her hand around my wrist. "A young woman alone needs a damn phone, even if you only use it for emergencies. Find a library. They'll usually let you charge it there for free. Other places, like bus terminals, trains, and internet cafés, also have charging stations. Hell, even most hospital waiting rooms have them now, which I always found odd when they insist you turn the damn things off. Anyway, keep it charged. A smart girl like you will figure it out. One day, when the coast is clear, come back and let me know you're okay."

"Thank you..." I pause, realizing I don't know her name.

"Mallory. Don't tell me yours. Like I said, the less I know, the better. But you might want to start going by an alias."

I nod, knowing she's right. It's just more proof of how willfully unprepared I am.

"When you're done, just leave your tray outside the door, and I'll come and collect it. If I don't see you before you leave, good luck and be safe." She gives me a smile and turns and leaves as I choke down the emotion she's triggered by her unexpected kindness.

Sitting at the table, I eat the stew even though I've lost my appetite because I know that for every good day I have, I'll have plenty more bad ones.

Once I've finished everything on the tray, I leave it outside the door and grab my bag before heading into the tiny en-suite bathroom.

The shower has virtually no water pressure, but it's warm, and there are toiletries and clean towels. I wash away the day's grime and re-braid my hair after drying off.

I'd love nothing more than to put on a cozy pair of pajamas and snuggle up with a book, but unfortunately, that's not meant to be. I can't afford to let my guard down now.

I pull on clean underwear and get dressed in the same outfit as before. Then, I wash my panties, socks, and bra and hang them on the heated towel rack. They shouldn't take long to dry. While they do, I rummage through the front pocket of my bag and grab the map and pen Sister Mary gave me.

She looked like she wanted to roll her eyes at me when I admitted that I'd never seen a paper map before, but she was far too disciplined for that.

I spread the map out on the table and circle the area where I started before tracing my way to where I am now. I don't have a destination in mind. My only thoughts are to stay as far away from the Division's headquarters as possible, which I angrily circle, and to try and stick mostly to cities and large towns where it's easier to get lost.

People will remember a stranger turning up in a small town, and by the end of the day, the whole damn town will know. Of course, hiding in a city will have its own problems. I might be a little safer from my dad, but I'll be an easy target for others.

Luckily, I have a weapon at my disposal that nobody can take away from me. It's both a comfort and a worry.

As much as I don't want to use my gift, I will if I'm in danger. It's the only thing stopping me from having a panic attack right now.

I refold the map and tuck it back into the front pocket with the pen. I throw the bag back on to the top bunk before climbing up and getting comfortable, pressing myself as close to the wall as possible. It would be just my luck if I fell off in the middle of the night and broke my arm, but I feel safe up here in the shadows.

I close my eyes, and with nothing else to do, I cry myself to sleep.

Chapter Eighteen

Wilder

The search around town and the bus station turned up nothing. We returned home, hoping the others had better news. As they started trickling in, it became apparent from their moods that they weren't successful either.

I lean on the island, trying to control my breathing. I'm too worked up to think about anything beyond the danger that Lara has put herself in. With a roar, I swipe my arm out, flinging everything off the counter and making it crash to the floor. Jagger comes up to me and grabs my arms, pinning me in place.

"That's enough," he says quietly.

My eyes are burning. "It's far from enough. Lara is out there. God knows where, and—"

"And she's smart. I know how you feel because Astrid did the same thing."

I shrug him off. "It's not the same, Jagger, and you know it.

Astrid had a fuck-ton of money and a mansion to hide out in. Lara has nothing. Greg said she took his camping backpack and sleeping bag, and that one of the small kitchen knives is missing. But do you know what she didn't take? Money. Not one single cent is missing from Greg's wallet." My chest is heaving by the time I've finished yelling at him. It's not his fault, but he has no fucking clue what I'm feeling right now. None.

"I've got it." Ev comes running into the room.

Jagger lets me go as Crew steps up beside me. He's been quiet, deeply so, and nobody can seem to get through to him.

I take a quick look around and see that all the men are here. The women are still outside with the kids, though the shine of the playground has worn off with Lara's disappearance.

"What did you find?" Zig asks, taking the paper from his hand and scanning it over as Ev answers for the rest of us.

"I found Lara's file. When I found out what her gift was and that she'd been born and bred at the Division, I was able to narrow it down to just one file.

"We know who her father is, but he is only recorded as a number. Same with the mother. I'm trying to match her number to the other files, but that will take time. It doesn't matter, though, mom never carried Lara. A surrogate did. She's also referred to a number, but the file says she died due to complications during childbirth. It doesn't say specifically what went wrong, but given the circumstances, I don't think it would have mattered. She would have served her purpose, and Lara would have been the priority."

"Is there a point to all this? Because as fun as it is standing here listening to you talk, she's still out there, getting farther and farther away."

"Calm the fuck down and hear him out," Oz snarls at me.

I take a step toward him, but Crew yanks me back. "Enough," he says quietly.

I shrug him off, but I stay where I am and turn back to Ev.

"Her telekinetic powers manifested when she was three, but they never increased in strength, according to the multitude of tests and examinations. She was declared a dud. For the last five years, she was given a yearly physical, but that was it."

"It sounds like they wiped their hands of her," Creed says, and I notice Greg shaking his head, a look of disgust and sadness on his face.

"Not quite. There's a letter in the file that says she's to be entered into the breeding program once she turns eighteen. They hope she'll produce offspring stronger than she is."

The room goes silent at that. I'm not sure I'm even breathing.

"What the fuck?" Crew curses.

"There's more. A contraceptive implant was recommended when she turned sixteen."

"Well, they wouldn't want her to get pregnant by just anyone, now, would they?" Slade huffs in disgust.

"Yeah, well, maybe they decided to take that risk. The implant was scheduled but not inserted. A tracking device was placed in her arm a year ago instead."

"So not only does she think she's protected, but they also knew exactly where she was at all times?" I snap.

"Holy fuck, that's it." Greg stumbles.

"Whoa, easy there." Jagger grabs him before he loses his balance.

"What's it? What are you thinking?" Zig questions him.

"She figured it out. You didn't really think she'd just leave the kids, did you? There had to have been something huge happen to make her leave."

"Like the kids being in danger," Oz says.

"But why not just tell us about it? We could have had it removed, but she didn't—" I cut myself off with a curse. "She led them away. That fucking reckless girl," I growl, but I keep it together for the most part.

"She would have anticipated us removing it. And she knew the second we did; her father would have this place surrounded. So she did the only thing she thought she could," Zig says thoughtfully.

"But at what cost, Zig?" Crew grounds out. "Do you think she has any idea what her father has planned for her? And once he has her, there will be nothing stopping him from coming here."

"I'm not sure, Crew, but she's smart," Zig replies. "She's also bought us time to prepare ourselves for war. Let's not let her sacrifice be made in vain."

"So that's it. We're just going to let her dangle herself out there as bait?" I fist my hands at my sides.

"Fuck no. I'm sending you and Crew after her."

"You want them to bring her back?" Jagger asks. I'm about to punch the asshole when Zig shakes his head.

"Not until we're ready. But Crew and Wilder can protect Lara, and they know a thing or two about evading their enemies and causing chaos."

Something settles inside me at that. "Done. We'll leave now."

"You'll eat, spend time with the kids, and make sure you have all the supplies you need first. Use your fucking brain, soldier," he orders.

I stand down, knowing he's right.

"One more thing you should know," Ev starts again, looking from me to Crew. "According to her file, she turns eighteen in three days."

"And that makes her an even bigger target," Greg complains. But when Crew and I look at each other, I can see my thoughts reflected back at me.

"No, that means in three days, Lara is ours."

Oz looks like he wants to say something sarcastic, but he stops and frowns, cocking his head in thought.

"What is it?"

"Why now?"

"Because she'll be eighteen—"

"Not you, dumbass. Why did Lara wait until now to run? If she knew about the tracking device, she would have left days ago."

"Maybe she just figured it out?" Slade frowns. "But that makes no sense. No seventeen-year-old girl is going to wake up one day after having what she thought was the implant implanted and then, nearly a year later, think it's a tracking device."

Ev's head whips up. "Unless they somehow made contact."

We all freeze at the thought, but it makes sense.

"She had no phone and no access to the internet." I shake my head.

"What about Alfie's iPad?" Crew asks.

Ev shakes his head. "I've got it locked down tight."

Zig taps his chin. "Greg, take Wilder and check out her room at your place. Slade and Jagger, check the cabin she was originally staying in. And Crew, start getting together what you need to find our girl."

Greg heads for the door, and I follow after him. We don't

speak—both of us too consumed with worry, aware of the kind of danger she'll face out there.

He opens the door, and we head straight for her room. Greg pauses in the doorway, a shaky breath escaping as he looks at me over his shoulder. "She left her stuff here like she plans to come back. At first, I thought she just couldn't fit it all in her pack with the sleeping bag. But look at how neatly she has the books arranged and the way she made her bed. It's like—"

"It's her home. And she didn't want to run. She wants to be here. That's because of the kids and how Oz and Zig have accepted her as family. But it's also because of you, Greg. She adores you. We saw that yesterday when she..." My voice trails off as Greg sighs.

"When she hugged me, she was saying goodbye."

He walks into the room, and I follow. For a moment, we do nothing, not wanting to touch anything to disturb Lara's memory.

"Come on. The sooner we look, the sooner Crew and I can go find her."

So that's what we do. We quietly and methodically move around the room, checking all the places she might have hidden something. After an hour, I stand back and scan the room, frustrated as fuck.

"Anything?" I ask Greg, but he shakes his head.

"It would help if we thought like teenage girls."

"Well, then we're both fucked. I could ask one of the women to come look. Maybe they'd have an idea."

"Or maybe there just isn't anything here. Teenage girl, teenage girl," he mutters to himself as he looks around the room.

"I dated one girl all through high school, and the only thing I can remember her hiding was her lipstick in her bra and her diary under her pillow."

He turns and yanks the pillow off the bed. And there, as if by magic, is a fucking piece of paper.

"You're a fucking genius. What's it say?"

"Time to come home, Lara."

"How can one sentence cause so much trouble?"

He flips the paper over before lifting the pillow again. "There's no envelope, which means someone hand-delivered it."

"Fuck. That's why she ran."

He nods. "Yeah, looks that way."

"But how? How did someone hand-deliver it without being seen?"

"I'm not sure, but it looks like we have to face the fact that there's a fault in our security. Because someone walked into our fucking home and left again without being detected."

I rub my hand over my face. "We need to let the others know what's going on."

"Let's head back to the main house, the others are probably done by now."

This time, I lead but stop at the door when I see Greg wince. The man is trying to hide the fact that he's overdoing it, but he's not fooling me. Still, I know better than to tell him to sit down and rest. I'm not sure any of us will rest until Lara is back home.

"Do you need your painkillers?"

"I'm fine," he answers too quickly.

"How about you take a couple anyway, and I won't tell the others dick about you hurting? I know you want to be a part of this, but you'll break Lara's heart if she comes back to find you in the hospital."

He glares at me before stomping over to the kitchen. He yanks open one of the drawers and pulls out a bottle of prescription pills before swallowing a couple with a mouthful of water from the faucet.

"Happy?"

"Ecstatic."

He straightens his shoulders and walks toward me and out the door, leaving me to lock up.

I don't take his attitude personally. We've all been injured, and none of us make very good patients.

I follow behind him as we make our way back to the main house.

"Did you find anything?" Zig asks as soon as we walk through the doors.

Greg waves the paper at him, and Oz grabs it. "Found it under her pillow."

Zig leans over Oz and reads the words, his face turning red as he fights to keep his temper in check. "Some motherfucker came into our home?" he all but roars.

He spins and glares at Ev, who holds his hands up. "I'll go check the feeds again, see if I missed something," he jogs off before anyone can stop him.

"It's not Ev's fault," Creed starts. "He's just one person, and we ask too fucking much of him."

Zig runs his hands through his hair, frustrated. "I'm not blaming Ev. I just need to know where the problem is so we can fix it. They came into our home, Creed. Walked right into Lara's bedroom like they had every fucking right to. And if they hadn't left this note, we'd be none the wiser. What happens if they do it again, only this time they take Salem or one of the kids with them?"

A lot of angry growls fill the room now as they realize how much worse it could have been.

"We need to lock this place down."

"Me, Hawk, and Slade can do a supply run. I'll find the women and ask them what they want. If you guys need anything, write it fucking down because if it's not on the list, I won't remember," Creed orders.

"I'll take Oz and check the perimeter," Jagger volunteers, and Zig nods.

"Where's Crew?" I question Zig.

"Still getting your stuff together. You might want to pack a few more things for Lara, too. I'm not sure how long you guys will be gone for. I want you to check in every day. Your truck and phones are tagged so Ev can track you guys on our end. Hit the SOS, and we'll come to the rescue. Just because we're not with you doesn't mean you're alone."

"Thanks, Zig."

I turn to Greg, who's been quiet. "Can you help Ev? Crew and I were going to help him go through the files on the flash drive, but now..." I shake my head. "Anyway, he needs a second set of eyes. And we're also gonna need help finding Lara."

He nods, looking relieved to have something to do.

"Yeah, I can do that. Boy Wonder is getting a sidekick whether he likes it or not." He strolls out of the kitchen to catch up with Ev.

"He's hiding how much pain he's in. So while he helps Ev, one of you needs to watch him."

"Don't worry about shit here. We have it covered," Slade says, and the others nod.

"Good. I'm going to help Crew finish packing and fill him in on the note. Once we're done, we'll say our goodbyes so we can leave as soon as Ev has something for us to go on. The longer we take to leave, the farther away Lara gets."

Zig nods. "I get it, but going out there half-cocked won't help. You have no idea which way she went or if she has a destination in mind. Do what you need to do while Ev works his magic. It's better for you to leave later with a plan in place then to wing it now only to have to back up if Ev picks up her trail going in the opposite direction. I'll go talk to the women and fill them in. I am not looking forward to telling them they're being locked down again."

"Once they realize how easy it was for someone to get in and what that could mean for the kids, I think they'll understand. No, what I'd be worried about is them going mama bear on your ass and wanting to go into attack mode." I grin.

Jagger chuckles as Zig groans and looks to the ceiling as if he is sending up a silent prayer.

"Next time, I'm going to do the supply run, and someone else can go brief the coven."

"Coven? What coven?" I turn at the sound of Salem's voice. She's standing just inside the door with her arms crossed and her eyes glaring at Zig.

"Good luck with that, man." I slap him on the shoulder and take that as my cue to leave. The rest of the guys follow suit.

"Whatever happened to never leaving a man behind?" Zig mumbles to himself, making me laugh.

I head home to find Crew, bracing myself for his reaction to the note.

As scared as everyone is for the kids, it's the thought of

someone being in Lara's room, potentially while she was there, that's fucking with me. She could have been sleeping or showering or any number of things that weren't meant for anyone to see. She was supposed to be safe here. And yet, somehow, her father managed to find a way to get to her.

Logically speaking, nothing I could have said or done would have changed things. So why do I feel like somehow I've let her down?

Chapter Nineteen

Lara

I was sad to say goodbye to Mallory. But even staying one extra night was risky, at least until I'd put a little more distance between here and back home.

My main worry is how I'm going to make money. I can't exactly hold down a job if I'm not staying in one place for more than a few days.

The sun beats down on me as I contemplate my dilemma, making me stop for a minute. I take out a bottle of water from my bag and drink half of it before slipping it back into one of the side pockets.

I strip my hoodie off, tie it around my waist, and take a second to catch my breath. After leaving the shelter at first light, I hitched a ride with a man who looked older than Jesus, who was returning home after visiting his grandchildren.

He dropped me off outside his house about four hours from the shelter before inviting me in for a drink that I politely refused.

I've been walking for a couple of hours since then and I'm going to need to find somewhere to rest soon before my legs give out. My feet are throbbing, making me grateful that I chose to wear my sneakers instead of any of the new shoes Oz bought me; otherwise, my feet would be covered in blisters.

I check my pocket to make sure my knife is handy and heave my bag back on. I swear the damn thing gets heavier the farther I walk. I keep going, taking in the scenery as I pass. A children's park appears up ahead on my right, and the sight of it almost has me breaking down on the side of the damn street.

Every time I think I have come to terms with my decision, something triggers me, and my heart feels like it's been smashed all over again.

Before I question my actions, I head toward the park. There are children playing on the swings, and a squeal of laughter comes from a small red-haired boy as he slides down the slide so fast that he goes shooting off the end. Thankfully, Dad is there to catch him. Judging from the boy's continuous laughter, that was part of the fun.

I keep walking, heading for the large picnic area filled with mostly empty benches. I pick the one farthest from the playgrounds and sit down with a groan. I think my feet hurt worse now that I've stopped.

Taking my backpack off, I put it down next to me and look around. When I see nobody's paying attention to me, I use the bag as a pillow, lie down on the bench, and close my eyes.

The sound of the children playing lulls me. As my mind drifts,

I can almost convince myself I'm back home, listening to The Lost Ones running around.

I don't intend to fall asleep, but I must have because when something wet touches my arm, I wake up with a squeal.

My pulse races frantically as my heart threatens to beat out of my chest. I'm reaching for my knife when I see a dog sitting in front of me with his head cocked to the side.

"I can see you judging me."

He barks once, making me shake my head at him.

"I'll have you know I'm a ninja. I'm just trying to blend in with the common folk. Which means I should probably stop talking to dogs, huh?"

I reach out and pet his head. He leans into it, his tongue hanging out as he pants.

I look around to see who he belongs to, but the park is empty now. "Jesus, how long have I been here?"

The dog doesn't answer me, obviously, so I check my watch.

"Four o'clock. Fuck." I stand up and stretch. Two hours spent in the park means I've missed out on two hours of looking for somewhere to stay tonight.

Untying the hoodie from around my waist, I pull it back on before digging around in my bag for one of my peanut butter and jelly sandwiches. It's a little squished, but otherwise, it's still good. I eat the sandwich as the dog watches me.

"Sorry, doggy. You can't have this. I don't want to make you sick."

He looks at me with big, sad eyes, and I sigh, reaching inside my bag for the pack of crackers I took from an empty table I passed outside a coffee shop earlier. I open them up and offer one to the dog, who happily wolfs it down. I'm tempted to eat one myself, but

I decide against it and pull out my water bottle instead to take a drink.

I give him another cracker as I stand up and stretch. Bending down, I check his collar for a tag, but if he had one, it's not there now.

"Do you know your way home, boy?" I look around, wondering if someone is looking for him. I don't want to leave him out here alone.

"Alright, why don't you come and wander with me for a little while? We'll see if you can find your owner."

He follows close behind me as I walk across the picnic area toward the little wooden playhouses I can see in the distance.

As I get closer, I see that they're really small, most likely designed for preschool kids. But if I curl up, I should be okay. I've got a couple of hours before it gets dark, so I figure I'll explore the area a little bit. If I can't find anywhere better, I'll sleep here. It's not exactly cozy, but it is a shelter, and if it rains, I'm going to need it. Hopefully, Greg's sleeping bag will keep me warm.

"Come on, boy. Let's see if we can find your owner."

He lets out a bark, like he understands what I'm saying. I smile at him. He really is adorable. I have no idea what kind of dog he is. He's big, standing hip-height to me, with pointy ears and a fluffy tail. I think he's some kind of mixed breed. He has the coat and ears of a German shepherd but the coloring of a Doberman.

We cross the park towards a housing development.

"This where you from, boy?"

He doesn't seem overly excited, but I head that way anyway. The farther I walk, the bigger the houses become before I reach a gated community. There is a guardhouse on one side with a man stationed inside reading the newspaper.

"Excuse me, hi."

He turns to look at me, his eyes moving from me to the dog.

"Can I help you, miss?"

"I hope so. I found this guy at the park. His tag seems to have fallen off his collar, and I couldn't find anyone around. I don't suppose you recognize him, do you?"

He shakes his head with a chuckle.

"He's a good-looking dog. But on the other side of those gates, you'll only find dogs that fit in handbags."

I sigh. "Right." I turn around and look at the other houses, the immaculate lawns, and the pretty flower beds. None of them look like a dog might live there.

"Is there anyone on this side of the gate that he might belong to?"

"I don't know. People tend to keep to themselves around here. Can't say I remember anyone walking a dog. I can ask around, though."

"That would be nice. Thank you. I'm not here for long, but I can come back tomorrow and see if you've had any luck. I don't want him to end up at the pound."

"A nice-looking dog like that shouldn't have any problem getting adopted."

"Unless people want a handbag dog," I answer wryly.

"Right. Well, he seems to like you. Might find that he isn't lost at all but found."

I jolt at his words and look down at the dog, who is leaning against my leg, looking up at me.

"As much as I'd love to keep him, my life isn't exactly conducive for looking after a pet right now. Hell, I can hardly look after myself."

"I hear that."

The sound of an approaching car steals his attention.

"I'll be back tomorrow. Thanks for your help."

I walk through the housing development, spotting a couple of joggers.

"Excuse me, do either of you recognize this dog?"

"No, sorry," one of them huffs out, not breaking their stride as they pass me. The other jogger doesn't even acknowledge my existence.

"I bet he's the kind of jogger that finds a body while running in the park and doesn't report it because it will interfere with his schedule."

"I bet you'd report it, though." I look down at the dog and grin. "You're a pretty good listener, you know that?"

We make it through the development without running into anyone else. With a frustrated sigh, I turn around and head back to the park. It's getting dark, and I don't think I'm going to find somewhere better to sleep tonight.

"This is your fault, you know. You're lucky you're so cute," I grumble.

I pick the playhouse in the middle of the others. Opening the door, I look inside and sigh. It will have to do. I tug out the sleeping bag and toe off my sneakers, putting them inside my backpack so nothing can crawl inside them while I sleep. I toss the bag into the house before I crawl inside and unroll the sleeping bag, closing the small door behind me. It's a little tight in here, but at least I have a roof over my head.

I unzip the sleeping bag, and I'm about to lie down when the dog starts whining from outside.

"There isn't much room in here, doggie. And I don't want to squish you."

He keeps whining until I open the door. He bounds in, almost knocking me flying.

"Alright, calm down."

I lie back down and zip the bag up. I keep the backpack beside me, the knife in the front pocket in case I need it.

I move around until I'm comfortable, giggling when a furry head rests on my thigh. "Ahh, it's like that, is it?"

He snuggles closer, and my heart melts a little more for him.

"Dammit, doggie, I've said enough goodbyes to last me a lifetime. I can't take you with me. You understand that, right?"

He rests his paw on my thigh next to his head, and I give up trying to reason with him.

Reason with him? He's a freaking dog, Lara. You're losing your damn mind.

With a sigh, I burrow deeper into the sleeping bag and drift off, happy for the company even if I'll be sad to say goodbye to him tomorrow.

The wind picks up during the night, making it difficult to get much sleep, though the sleeping bag did a good job keeping me warm. By the time the sun's up, I'm exhausted. My body aches from all the walking yesterday, and I can't say I'm looking forward to doing more today, but I'll push through. There will be time for rest later.

"Thanks for keeping me company." I rub the spot behind the dog's ear, which he seems to like so much, before checking the time.

Six a.m. I've never been a fan of getting up this early, but it does have its benefits. Now would be a good time to head downtown because it will be quieter at this hour than usual.

I drink some water but don't bother eating anything. I'm not hungry just yet, and if I eat too early, I'll have to wait longer until I can eat again.

Sighing, I grab my backpack and take out my sneakers, sliding them back on my feet before rolling up the sleeping bag and shoving it back into my bag. With that done, I quickly drag a brush through my hair and pull it up into a messy bun.

I open the little door to the playhouse and climb out. There's a chill in the air this morning, so I pull the raincoat on over my hoodie, hoping to ward off the worst of it.

Throwing my backpack over my shoulder, I take a deep breath and look down at the dog. "Come on. Let's go stretch our legs."

We walk through the park, past the playground, and head downtown. There are a few cars on the road, but the streets themselves are quiet. We pass a couple walking their dog and a row of houses with the curtains closed, and I can't help wishing I could trade places with the people inside.

As if sensing my mood, the dog presses against my leg. I run my hand through his fur. "I'm okay. A little sad, but that's to be expected. It will get better, though, right?"

By the time we get to town, there are a lot more cars on the road. Some of the stores are open, while others are preparing for the morning rush.

I see a coffee shop on the corner, and a woman inside flipping the closed sign to open. People are going about their business, living their lives, completely unaware of the void inside me threatening to consume me any minute.

I shake off my negative thoughts and keep my head down as we continue on. When we walk past a building site, I notice the corner of a large tarp fluttering in the wind. I move toward it and see that it's being used to cover a pile of bricks. The rope holding down the one side hasn't been tied off properly and has come undone.

I stare at it for a second before I work on loosening the knot at the other end. Once it gives, I slip it free.

"Well, this might work."

I fashion a large loop at one end and thread the other end through the dog's collar, knotting it tight, creating a sort of leash.

"There we go. As good as you are, I'd hate for someone to see you wandering around without one and call animal control. Wait, is that a real thing? I swear I've watched one too many animated movies," I mutter, more to myself than the dog.

We walk around the center of town, taking in the sights and sounds. It doesn't take long, though, so after passing the same coffee shop for the second time, I stop and check the time. It's nine-thirty. I can't stay here any longer. I have to keep moving. But what about this dog?

"What to do?" I blow out a breath. My thoughts are all over the place. I feel so out of my depth it's not even funny. With my thoughts taking on a panicked edge, I start humming. It's impossible to feel sad when singing a Disney song. I'm not sure if that's true, but I'll go with it. After a few minutes and a couple of songs, I've calmed down enough to make a decision.

"Alright, doggie. Let's head back to the guard and see if he has any news about your owners. We can eat in the park again, but then I've got to get back on the road."

I continue to hum as we walk, and by the time we make it back to the guardhouse, I've worked my way through ten Disney classics, gradually moving into the more modern stuff.

"Hey, you're back," the guard from yesterday says, looking surprised.

"I said I would be."

"I described your canine friend here to a few people and asked if they knew anyone with that kind of dog, but none of them said it sounded familiar. Sorry."

"It's okay. Thanks for asking anyway. I knew it was a long shot."

"Honestly, if the leash had broken or the dog had run off, the owners would have kept looking. But if there was nobody in the park, I'd say it's more likely the dog was dumped."

"Dumped?"

"Yeah, it happens. People like the idea of having a pet, but actually having one is a lot different. Not to mention, vet fees can be brutal."

"So they just threw him away?" I ask, outraged.

"Maybe."

"Shit. I don't know how I'm going to leave him here now."

"Where are you heading?"

"Anywhere west of here. I don't care. I just need to get away."

He looks me over, flicking his tongue between his teeth in thought.

"I'm only working until twelve. It's supposed to be my weekend off, but me and another guy are covering for someone. If you can wait, I've got a truck. You and the dog are welcome to catch a ride. I'm supposed to be meeting up with my brothers for a fishing weekend, so I can take you as far as Denver."

"Are you serious?"

"Yeah. With the dog, the bus is out of the question, and I don't want to see him in the pound any more than you do. What will happen to him if no one wants him? Will they put him down? Nah, I can't live with that on my conscience. Besides, I think he'd make a good protector."

I look at the dog sitting at my feet. "You think?"

"He sure seems protective of you. So, what do you say? Want to hitch a ride with me?"

"Yes, thank you. That would be awesome, truly."

"Great. Meet you back here at twelvish. Now, all you have to do is think of a name for your new best friend."

"A name, hmm..." I need to think about it. It needs to be just right. "I know. I'll call you Rufio." I rub his head, and I swear for a minute, he smiles at me.

"Rufio? Never heard that one before," the guard muses as he turns away.

Guess he's never seen the movie *Hook*. It might be an odd name for a dog, but in a way, it makes me feel a little closer to my Lost Ones.

Chapter Twenty

Crew

After packing the last of our things into the back of the truck, I pull the cover over everything and hook it in place so the wind doesn't catch it.

"I think that's everything"

I turn at the sound of Wilder's voice as he shoves a bedroll in the back seat along with another couple of sleeping bags.

"Yeah, anything else we can just buy if we need to."

"I'm going to run inside and grab the drinks and food Salem packed for us."

"Better you than me. They were all crying when they found out we were leaving. You'd think we were going off to war or something."

"There are worse things in life than having someone at home who cares about you."

"I know, but I've never been good with tears. And those kids... fuck me."

"They just want us to bring Lara home, but you can see just how scared they are."

"They've lived through things none of us will ever understand. Notice how they're upset that Lara's gone, but they're not angry about it? They know she didn't abandon them because they know her. They know the only reason she would leave would be to protect them. That fear you saw wasn't for what might happen to them, but for what might happen to Lara."

"I know. That's why I just want to go already. I've got a really bad feeling about this whole thing."

"You and me both, but Zig's right. We can't just rush off and hope for the best. While I'm grabbing the food, go see if Ev managed to find us anything to point us in the right direction."

I nod and head inside, bypassing the kitchen and heading up to see Ev. The door is open, and he and Greg are looking at the screens when I knock. They both turn as I enter and point to the seat beside Ev.

"Alright, first things first. I want to show you this before I call a meeting with the others because I know you need to get on the road." He changes the image on the screen to a figure dressed from head to toe in black, just outside the back of the main house. "This is the intruder. I can't clean it up anymore, and they weren't caught on any other camera."

"How was that possible? I mean, not only did they break in without setting any of the alarms off, but to avoid almost all the cameras when they got here? It's like he knew where they were."

I look at Evander and then Greg when he doesn't say anything.

"Tell me you don't think we have a traitor."

If either of them says they thinks it's Lara, I'm going to puke.

"No, I think they dragged the information out of James."

"Shit." I run my hands through my hair.

"I'm going to have all the cameras relocated and adapt the sensors to pick up everything, even if that means an animal sets it off every two minutes. I don't give a fuck."

"Yeah, I don't think there's any such thing as being too cautious right now," I tell him, and he nods.

"Right. Now, on to Lara. I found the video of her leaving." He pushes a few keys and pulls it up for me.

I watch as she moves across the property. When she reaches the Apex sign, she pauses and looks back at the house. I swear, I can feel her pain through the screen. I continue to watch until she disappears from view, and Greg starts hitting the keys.

"I picked her up here, hitching a ride. I saw her getting into a car with—" Greg starts, but I cut him off.

"She hitched a fucking ride?" I yell. "Doesn't she know how dangerous that is? I've seen this movie, and it doesn't end well."

"With a nun," he finishes with a grin.

"Wait, what?"

"I ran the plates. The car is registered to Sister Mary Dorothea."

"Okay, there was that one movie with the nun, but this is fine, right?"

He ignores me, printing out something and handing it over. "I had to do a little process of elimination, because I could only track the car so far. That's what's taken me so long. My best guess is that Lara got out here. There is a shelter on that same street. I saw that Sister Mary drives past there a lot when she's in the area. It seems to be a good starting point. I'll keep looking and send you anything else I find."

"You are a fucking genius, Greg. Thank you."

"It was a team effort," he chuckles. "Just find her and keep her safe. Those kids are the most resilient kids I've ever met, but I don't think any of them would recover if something bad happened to Lara."

"I won't let that happen to her. I'll check in and keep you updated."

"Just be careful. If her father is tracking her, you'll need to watch each other's backs because he won't hesitate to take you out. Or worse, use you to manipulate her." Ev warns me

I nod and slap him on the shoulder as I stand up.

"Any news on Nash and Hendrix?"

"No. There's complete radio silence, and I don't have any contacts currently in the area to check on them. I'll keep trying to reach them and let you know what's going on."

"Appreciated."

I head downstairs and outside with the printout in my hand. Wilder is already behind the wheel waiting for me, so I jump in the passenger seat and show him what Greg gave me.

He hisses. "She hitched a ride?"

"With a nun." I wave him off as if I hadn't reacted the same way.

"I've seen that movie. Nuns can be evil too, you know."

I chuckle. "I'm starting to think we spend way too much time together."

"Yeah, well, we're going to be spending a hell of a lot more time together."

He types the coordinates into the GPS and sighs. "Looks like we'll be driving through the night. You might as well get some sleep. I'll wake you up in six hours, and we can switch."

"Okay."

* * *

"Crew, wake up." A finger jabbed in my ribs makes me throw my arm out and punch him.

I hear the oomph and a groan before opening my eyes to see Wilder rubbing his side. I probably bruised his ribs. Good. That's what he gets.

"Why must you always choose violence?"

"What can I say? You bring out the best in me."

"Jackass. I'm going to stop to get gas, then we can swap."

"Okay. I need to stretch my legs for a bit, anyway." We've been driving for hours, and this will be the third time we've stopped to switch drivers.

I look around and see we're pulling into a well-lit gas station with a diner attached.

"You wanna grab something to eat while we're here?"

"Yeah, but get it to go. We're making good time, and the sooner we get to Lara, the better."

I nod in agreement. When the truck stops, I jump out and head over to the diner while Wilder fills the tank. A little bell above the door signals my arrival to the lone waitress behind the counter and the two truckers eating in the far booth.

"Give me a second, love, and I'll be right with you," the waitress says without looking as she moves to the hatch between the dining room and the kitchen.

180

As she walks over to me, she tugs her notepad and pen from the little pocket of her apron.

"What can I get for ya?"

"Can I get a couple of burgers to go?"

"Sure can. What do you want on them?"

"Everything, but no onions on the one. Can I also get two orders of fries and two Cokes? And an order of onion rings."

"You got it. Shouldn't be long. You can sit at the counter while you wait." She offers me a tired smile as she rips off the page in her notepad and hands it to someone in the kitchen.

I pull out my phone and text Ev, telling him where we are. Though, thanks to the tracker, he already knows. I ask him if he's found anything else useful.

I see the bubbles appear, indicating that he's messaging me back.

I glance out the window and watch Wilder head inside the gas station to pay, just as my phone dings.

I've been looking at the cameras in the same area as the shelter and saw her hitch another ride a few hours away, before she set out on foot.

What the fuck? She's going to give me a heart attack. Bubbles appear, and I wait to see what else Ev has to say.

I followed her to a park. She appears to have picked up a companion.

What? Who? I text back.

A dog. Are you really surprised?

I sigh.

No. Alright, we'll deal with it. Thanks for the update.

. . .

I tap my phone on the counter, ready to get back on the road. The update makes her seem so much closer when, in actuality, she's still miles away. At least we know she's okay, though. Ev would have said if she looked injured.

When the bell jingles above the door, I turn and see Wilder walking inside and heading my way.

"I'll be with you in a second," the waitress calls as she pours coffee for one of the truckers.

"That's okay, I'm with him," Wilder tells her, pointing at me when she looks up.

"Alright, no problem. Food won't be long."

He thanks her and sits on the stool beside me.

"Got an update from Ev. He says Lara has been spotted in a park a few hours from the shelter with a dog."

"Huh?"

I chuckle. "Apparently, she has a dog. Or had a dog. I don't know, but this is Lara we're talking about."

"True. So are we heading to where she was last spotted first or to the shelter?"

"The shelter. They might be able to give us an idea of where she's going."

"It's a long shot. Those places tend to be tight-lipped, though, and for a very good reason."

"We've got nothing to lose by asking."

"I guess." He sighs.

"Besides, she's hardly still going to be in the same spot."

"Here you go. That will be $35."

I look over at the waitress with a smile as she places a brown bag in front of me. Pulling out my wallet, I hand her a fifty. "Thanks. Have a good day."

"You too. Come back anytime."

I grab the food, and we head outside to the truck, the smell coming from the bag making my mouth water. I open the door on the driver's side and climb in before opening the bag and pulling out the food and drinks. When Wilder settles into the passenger seat, I hand him his food. We dig in, neither of us talking, as we devour one of the best burgers I've ever had.

"Damn, that was good. I think I'd drive all this way again just for another one of those."

Wilder laughs as he wipes his hands with one of the paper napkins from the bag and gathers all the trash before taking it to the trash can.

I start the truck and find a radio station to listen to while I wait for Wilder to get back.

When the door opens, I look over at him. "You good?"

"Oh yeah, I'm about to slip into a food coma. Wake me when we get there."

"You got it."

I turn the music down and settle in for the drive. I don't mind driving at night. I find it peaceful, and most of the idiots are home in bed waiting to cause chaos during the day.

As the miles stretch endlessly in front of me and Wilder snores lightly beside me, I can't help but wonder what Lara's reaction to us turning up is going to be. And if that shocks her, she's going to lose her mind when I finally give in to the need that's been gnawing away at me and fuck her over the hood of my truck.

I feel my cock harden at the thought. For the first time, I don't feel any guilt, just raw need.

I return my focus to the road and let the hours pass to the sound of soft rock and jazz. When my cell phone rings, Wilder jolts awake. I fumble in my pocket for it and toss it to Wilder to answer.

"It's Wilder. What's up?" he asks before putting the call on speaker.

"Uncle Wilder?" Bella's voice asks softly through the phone.

"Bella? What's wrong, little one?" He frowns, looking at me. The time on the dash says 5:50, which is way too early for a phone call.

"I took Avery's phone because I need to talk to you."

"Alright, well, you've got me and Uncle Crew. You're on speaker, so we can both hear you. What's wrong?"

"You need to hurry. Lara's gonna be hurt."

Wilder sits up straight in his seat. "Did you have a vision?"

Bella sniffs. Her voice cracking as she speaks. "Yes."

"I know this is hard, sweetheart, but I need you to be brave just a little while longer. Can you see where Lara is?"

"She'll be at the cemetery. The big sign says Sextown."

I frown at that. "All right, sweetheart, you're doing amazing. Now, I want you to wake Avery up and tell her what you saw. She'll help you make a little more sense of it. Give the phone to Creed or Hawk and have them call me back, okay?"

"Okay, Uncle Wilder."

She hangs up as Wilder leans over to type in the name of the cemetery into the GPS.

"There is no fucking Sex Town Cemetery," he curses. "Oh, wait, there's a Saxton Memorial Garden Cemetery. It's eleven hours from here."

"Fuck. Should we call the cops?"

"We don't know what kind of trouble Lara is in yet. If we call them, her father will find her in a heartbeat. Besides, Bella's vision might not have happened yet. She doesn't see what's happening, but what *will* happen."

"What the fuck is she doing at a cemetery?"

"I don't know, but I'll be sure to ask once we find her."

Chapter Twenty-One

Lara

We killed time in the park, Rufio and I watching the kids run around like chickens with their heads cut off while their parents half-watch from the benches scattered around the playground.

I finish another sandwich and give Rufio a cereal bar and some water before we make our way back to the guardhouse. We're a little early, so we have to wait until the other guard arrives to swap shifts. When the other guard arrived, he nodded his head at me in greeting before talking quietly to my guard.

Once they're finished, they shake hands, and my guard walks over to me.

"I just realized I never told you my name. I'm Giles." He holds his hand out, and I shake it, opening my mouth to tell him my name before remembering I need an alias.

"Wendy. Thanks for helping like this."

"No problem, honestly. It will be nice to have company. Here, follow me. My truck is parked around the back. The folks don't like worker vehicles spoiling their view."

"Heaven forbid." I laugh as I follow him around to the parking lot. He has an old Ford pickup. When we reach it, he opens the door for me and holds it as I climb in, Rufio jumping in beside me.

"Good job, buddy." I snort before looking back at Giles.

"Good thing you have a bench seat." I say as Giles closes the door, and Rufio makes himself comfortable beside me before licking the side of my face.

"You're lucky you're cute," I tell him as Giles climbs into the driver's seat.

"I need to head home first to change and grab my camping gear, if that's alright."

"Of course."

I sit quietly as he drives, still not sure how to make small talk with someone I barely know. Suddenly, all my insecurities about being socially awkward make their way to the forefront. I have to look out the window so he doesn't question the tears in my eyes.

"You mind if I put some music on?"

"No, please go ahead. Just don't be surprised if I doze off. I didn't sleep well last night."

Which isn't entirely untrue. It was windy, which kept waking me up, thanks to the lack of glass in windows of the little playhouse.

"Do what you need to do. I'm just going to be loading up the truck anyway. One of us might as well get some sleep," he jokes.

I relax and close my eyes, but I don't sleep. I'm not sleeping in a car with a man I don't know. But faking it, no matter how pathetic that makes me, means I can avoid small talk. I'd feel embarrassed if I wasn't so goddamn relieved.

When we stop, I crack my eyes and see we've pulled up outside an apartment complex. Giles jumps out of the truck and closes the door softly, clicking the locks. I flinch at the sound, though he probably only did it because he thinks I'm asleep and doesn't want anyone to bother me. Still, the last thing a woman feels is safe when someone locks them in somewhere. Tension thrums in my veins as I watch him walk toward the apartment without looking back.

He hasn't set off my alarm bells, but that doesn't mean I'm going to let my guard down. I reach into the pocket of the backpack and pull out the phone and my knife. I'd put them there earlier, not thinking I'd need them. But now... well, I'd rather be safe than sorry.

I go to put the phone in the back pocket of my jeans, but a little voice in my head tells me to be cautious. Instead, I slip it into one of my socks. The knife is harder to hide, so I slip it into the front pocket of my hoodie.

I run my hand over Rufio, who has his head resting on my shoulder. I turn a little and rest my head on top of his, closing my eyes and pretending to sleep once more. My nerves are already frayed.

It takes Giles twenty minutes to get changed and bring his things down. He loads up the back of his truck before opening his door and climbing back in. He closes the door loud enough to wake me if I were asleep, so I pretend to wake up. Jesus, when I think about my performances lately, I deserve an Oscar.

"Sorry about that. I'm ready to go now. Did you need to stop anywhere or let anyone know you're coming?"

I hesitate, unsure how to answer. "I'm going to surprise them. Besides, I don't have a phone." That might be a stupid thing to say, but for some reason, I don't want him to know I have one. I've kept the thing shut off since Mallory gave it to me, so it still has plenty of battery life.

"You don't have a phone?" He looks at me with a grin. "I've never met a woman who doesn't own a cell phone before."

"Oh, I own one. I just don't have one. I dropped the damn thing in the river, and I haven't had a chance to buy a new one yet, but I figured I can do that when I get to where I'm going."

"You're a strange woman, Wendy."

"Thanks."

He laughs at me, but he's quiet after that. I lean back and gaze out the window at the ever-changing scenery. Thankfully, this time, he doesn't try to make small talk. He just drives, looking more and more relaxed the farther we get from the city.

Despite my promise to myself not to fall asleep, the last few days catch up with me, and I fall into a light sleep.

We hit a bump, and I'm jolted awake. It takes me a while to realize we've turned off the road and are moving over bumpier terrain. I sit up and look around, noticing it's starting to get dark now.

"Where are we?" I ask, looking at the trees on either side of us.

Before he can answer, I see metal gates just in front of us. He slows the truck and lowers his window so he can type something into the keypad before the gates swing open with an ominous creak. I don't get a chance to read the name atop the gates, but I don't need to. It doesn't take a rocket scientist to figure out that we're entering a cemetery.

"And we're in a cemetery because...? Oh shit, your name is

Giles, isn't it? Please tell me this isn't the part where you claim I'm The Chosen One, and we're going to wait at a freshly dug grave for a vampire to rise."

He full-out laughs at that but keeps driving until the road narrows.

"You mean like that one?" He points, and I follow his finger to see a mound of dirt.

I swallow hard. "I'm not the girl you're looking for."

He chuckles again. "You're hilarious. And no, I'm not here to tell you you're the slayer. My cousin works here. We're picking her up."

"I thought it was a fishing weekend with your brothers?" I ask, secretly relieved that it's a woman we're picking up and not a man. Being in the car with one strange man is one thing, but two is asking for trouble. Trouble I wouldn't be able to get myself out of with a stupid paring knife.

"Lisa grew up with me and my brothers. As far as she's concerned, she is one of us, and none of us have been able to tell her any different. Come on, might as well stretch your legs. Better leave the dog in the truck, though. I don't think we want him digging up bones here."

I gag, and one hundred percent agree. I give Rufio a pat on the head and climb out, closing the door behind me. He presses his paws against the window and barks, making me feel like a bitch. But then I think about him coming up to me with a femur in his mouth and decide we can let him out in a little while, somewhere where buried bodies aren't an issue.

There's a chill in the air, making me thankful I'm wearing the hoodie. I look around to see who else might be here, but it looks deserted. Mind you, the place is huge.

"This way," Giles says, catching my attention before heading down the narrow path, past some trees, and toward the new grave. I shiver, which he sees when he looks back over his shoulder.

He shakes his head, a smile playing on his lips. "I promise, no vampires. The groundskeeper's cottage is at the top of the hill."

"It's really quiet here," I say, trying to make conversation and wince. "Of course it's quiet," I mutter as I follow him up a sharp incline.

Just when I'm about to call it quits because my thighs are on fire, I see the cottage.

"Does your cousin live here?"

"Yeah, it's a perk of the job."

"Strange perk. I'm not sure I could live at the edge of a cemetery."

"I don't know, there's a peacefulness here. No bullshit, rich bitches trying to suck my dick while their husbands are at work. No pricks looking down at me like I'm nothing."

I tense at his words, his hate for his job feeding his anger and making me nervous.

"Why do you work there if you hate it?"

"Because I meet some interesting people." He looks at me, and for the first time, I see the flair of interest in his eyes as he takes me in.

Crap.

"So your cousin, she's expecting us, right?" I ask as we reach the door.

There is a wheelbarrow propped up against the side of the place, but otherwise, it's neat and tidy and kinda cute. You know, for a creepy-ass house that's surrounded by potential vampires and zombies.

Giles grabs the knob and turns it, pushing the door open. I walk inside after he gestures for me to enter.

"Hello?" I call out. When I don't get an answer, I turn around and look at Giles. "I don't think she's here."

He closes and locks the door before turning and grinning at me. There is something off about that smile. I swallow and take a step back as he looks at me. Suddenly, a dozen alarm bells start blaring.

"Where's your cousin, Giles?"

"Oh, he's already left."

"What? Wait, you said your cousin was a girl." I take another step back, my body making the connections my brain hasn't.

He laughs, but it's nothing like the light, friendly sound from before.

"You're all the same. So fucking easy."

I back up until I'm pressed against the wall. He slowly comes closer, making my head thud with each step.

"Every year, we bring a girl camping. We like something fun to hunt and fuck." And somehow, I know the person they fuck is the same person they hunt.

"This time it's my turn. I had someone else in mind, but then, like fate, you landed in my lap."

"Okay, whatever kind of joke this is, it's not funny. I want to leave now."

"Oh, we'll be leaving soon enough. But I've decided I want a taste first before the others tear you up. I hate secondhand pussy."

He moves closer, my shock rendering me frozen for a moment. The mistake proves costly when he backhands me across the face. I fall to the floor, my cheek feeling like it's going to explode.

"Fuck around, and I'll make it hurt so fucking bad you'll pray for death." He unbuckles his belt and pulls out his hard cock, giving it a stroke. "But you be good to me, and I can make it good for you too."

He lifts his leg and kicks me, his foot connecting just under my chin. Not hard enough to knock me out, but enough for my head to fly back and smack into the wall behind me. I can taste blood in my mouth. It's trickling down my chin, where my teeth have sliced into my lip.

He reaches down and runs his thumb across my chin, gathering some of my blood before sucking it into his mouth.

"Hmm...my favorite kind of lube. Now open your mouth. And if you even think about biting me, I'll rip your teeth out and feed them to you one by one."

With no other option—my brain too fuzzy to think clearly—I let down my barriers and allow myself to taste his emotions.

I almost puke at how excited he is. He wants to hurt me in the worst possible way. He's already so close to the edge that there will be no way to pull him back if he gives in to it.

I quickly suppress his lust and turn on his fear.

He stumbles, looking over his shoulder like he heard something, and it spooked him. He shakes his head and looks back at me, but fear wafts off him now, making him paranoid and uncertain.

His dick goes soft, making him snarl as he starts stroking it again. I keep pushing the pleasure back down, adding a spike of pain to the mix.

He grabs my hair, making me scream. "You did this. Fix it. Suck me off now, bitch."

I press on his guilt. There isn't much there to work with, but I coax it higher and higher until he releases me. He can't look at me anymore. He quickly shoves his cock in his pants before pulling his hair.

"What did I do? What did I do?"

It's a rhetorical question, so I don't answer. But as I slowly get to my feet, I ask my own question. My anger overrides everything else—my pain, my sense of self-preservation, and my promise not to use my powers unless it was life and death, which I guess it is. I could get away now. I could have him crying in the corner as I leave. But if I do, he'll eventually get over this and find another girl. A girl who won't have the gifts I do to help her escape. I can't live with someone else's death on my conscience. Not again.

"How many times have you done this?"

"Lots of times. It's easy. Pick someone who nobody would miss."

I hiss at him, knowing there are people out there who miss me a lot. "And after you hunt and rape them, then what?"

I turn up his guilt and poke at his conscience, making him want to spill his guts in hopes of finding some kind of absolution. He won't find that here.

"If they are still alive by the time we've finished with them, we kill them. After we bring them here, nobody ever looks for an extra body in a grave."

"That's why there's an open grave."

"Nobody comes here. It's private property and only open to the public on Tuesdays and Thursdays."

I turn up his self-loathing and get sick satisfaction out of making him cry.

"You were going to do that to me—hunt me, rape me, and then kill me?"

"No, I like you. I wanted you just for me. I wasn't going to let them hunt you, not really," he babbles, his mind fracturing at my onslaught.

"You were just going to rape and kill me. And what, toss me in a coffin and throw me in that hole before covering me up like I never existed?"

"There's already a coffin in there. You wouldn't have been alone." He laughs, the sound jarring as his emotions attack him. His nose and ears start to bleed as I scramble his brain like an egg.

I pull the knife from my pocket and use my telekinesis to float it in front of me. He sees it and freezes, his fear now becoming so palpable I can taste it.

"What are you?" he chokes out. Now he's the one backing up, except he forgot he locked us in.

"I'm the kind of girl you don't take home to meet your brothers." I shove forward and watch as the knife embeds itself in his throat.

His eyes go wide as I walk right up to him. He reaches for the handle and yanks it out.

Everyone knows that that's the worst thing you can do. Now there's nothing to stop the blood from gushing from the wound, spraying me in the process. He staggers forward, his face a mask of shock, fury, and terror, but he drops to his knees before he can grab me. He falls to the side, rolling onto his back. He stares up at the ceiling, tiny gasps escaping his mouth, accompanied by a wet sucking sound.

"That's for all the girls who came before me," I whisper, walking over to him.

As I stand here watching, the adrenaline begins to wear off, and the pain in my head and face intensifies until I want to puke. I touch the back of my head and realize I'm bleeding. I wonder if I have a concussion.

When no more sound comes from Giles, I drop to the floor, pulling my knees under my chin, and cry like a baby.

Using my powers has left me feeling drained, but my emotions are running wild. Knowing what almost happened to me has my guilt and righteousness fighting for dominance.

And now I'm at a loss. I can't call the cops, and it's not like I can just get rid of the body. I—

The sound of muffled voices outside has me freezing. I scramble back and try to hide in the shadows as the door opens. I hear a voice that would bring me to my knees if I wasn't already on the floor.

"Lara?"

Chapter Twenty-Two

Wilder

The sight that greets me is one I won't forget as long as I live.

A man lies sprawled out on the floor, blood pooling under him as he stares lifelessly at the ceiling.

"Lara?"

I turn my head when I hear a whimper, and there she is in the corner, her arms wrapped tight around her knees.

"Jesus Christ," Crew curses, hurrying past me. He drops to his knees in front of her and pulls her into his arms. "It's okay, Lara, we've got you. Nothing's going to happen to you now."

The sound of her crying breaks my heart and makes me want to stomp on the dead guy's face until there is nothing left but pulp. An overreaction, maybe, but I have no doubt he deserves it.

I move around the body and crouch down next to them. "Let's get you out of here."

She reaches out and grabs a handful of my T-shirt before lifting her tear-stained face to look at me. "He was going to rape and kill me."

"Shhh." I run my fingers down her cheek gently, seeing the damage that motherfucker has done to her. "We'll take care of it, Lara, but we need to get you out of here."

"Wait," she protests when Crew moves to lift her.

He pauses, pulling back so he can see her better.

"This place is closed to the public until Tuesday. His cousin, if he was telling the truth, works here. He was supposed to take me to where his brothers are camping. I don't know if he means biological brothers or frat or whatever," she babbles, clearly in shock. "They were going to hunt me," she whispers.

She doesn't need to say anymore. Both Crew and I know exactly what would have happened next.

"There's an open...grave out there...with a...casket already... inside. They were going to bring me here...after...they were...done. Nobody checks coffins for bodies, right? They were going to...to... add me to it. But Giles got excited. He wanted me for himself first. He came straight here to...to..."

I press a kiss against her temple. "We get it. You don't need to tell us anything else, at least not right now. But please let us get you out of here, just to the truck, so we can get a better look at you. And then we'll take care of everything."

"Okay." She nods, wrapping her arms around Crew's neck when he lifts her.

They leave the cottage, and I follow them out and down the path, pausing next to the mound of dirt with a hole beside it. Sure enough, there's an oak coffin lying inside.

"There's a special place in hell for this bastard."

I jog to catch up with Crew, who is almost at the truck. A snarl catches my attention. I look at the old pickup parked in front of us and see a dog going nuts inside, trying to get out.

"Rufio," Lara gasps, lifting her head at the sound of the dog barking.

"Let's clean you up a little first, or you'll get blood on the dog's fur," I tell her.

She nods jerkily as I move around them and drop the tailgate on the back of the truck. Crew gently lowers Lara before pulling back. He whips off his sweatshirt, which has blood on it, and looks at me.

"Grab a couple of bottles of water out of the truck."

I run around and grab them before walking back to where Crew is coaxing Lara out of her hoodie.

"It's covered in blood, Lara. I need to clean you up and get you into something else. I promise I won't even look."

She nods, and so I wait as Crew helps her out of it. I use the sleeve of his sweatshirt, pouring water onto the material, to clean her up the best I can.

She's wearing a basic white bra. Though her skin is pale, she doesn't seem to be sporting bruises anywhere other than her face.

"Are you hurt anywhere other than your face, Lara?" I ask her softly.

She shakes her head before she lifts her hand to the back of it and groans. "I hit my head."

I reach behind her and search until I find a bump and what feels like blood. "What's your vision like? Have you been sick?"

"No, I'm okay. I have a headache, but that's not surprising."

She offers me a small smile, reassuring me, when I'm the one who should be comforting her.

"Alright. Your face took the brunt of it. We'll need to ice it, but for now, I have some painkillers I want you to take."

She nods.

"I'll get them," Crew offers gruffly as I pull Lara gently to me and hold her, reassuring myself that she's fine. But I know the sight of her covered in blood will have me on edge for a while, and I can tell Crew's feeling the same.

He pulls a duffle bag out from under the cover and rummages through it. Finding a couple of long-sleeved T-shirts, he hands one to me before he tugs the other over his head and walks away to grab the painkillers.

"Let's put this on you." I help Lara slip it on. It's big on her, but it's better than nothing.

"Can we let Rufio out now?"

The dog is going crazy. I'm not sure if he'll be friendly or attack us.

As if sensing where my thoughts have gone, Lara reaches out and squeezes my arm. "He's friendly. I think he knows something's wrong, though, and that's why he's freaking out."

"Might be better if you're the one to let him out. He knows you." I lift her down and link her fingers through mine. He might not attack, but I'm not letting her go alone, just in case. I don't want to hurt him, but I won't let him hurt Lara, either.

We round the side of the truck and spot Crew, who is standing there, gripping the side of the truck, his jaw tight as he works to rein in his anger.

I don't say anything, knowing he needs a moment or two so he doesn't lose it. Lara and I pass him and walk to the pickup.

Once the dog spots Lara, he calms down a little. I stand back as Lara reaches for the door and opens it. The dog jumps out of the truck and immediately rubs his head against her legs, like he's checking for himself that she's okay.

"Hey, Rufio. You missed me, huh?" She bends down and scratches behind his ear.

Looking up at me, she smiles the first genuine smile since we got here. "Come down here, and I'll introduce you."

I crouch down next to her and hold out my hand. She takes it and moves it to the dog's nose. "Wilder, this is Rufio. He's my friend. Rufio, this is Wilder. He's my—"

I cut her off. "Man. I'm her man."

"What?" She looks at me, confused.

"We'll talk about it later."

Her mouth hangs open, so I slip my finger under her jaw and gently close it before pressing a soft kiss against her lips. The dog, not to be outdone, jumps between us and licks her face, making her giggle. For that alone, I'm going to buy him a big, juicy steak the first chance I get.

"Where did you find him? He's a beauty."

"I didn't. He found me. I tried to see who he might belong to, but Giles—" She swallows before pushing on. "He thought that Rufio might have been dumped at the park."

"Well, their loss is your gain." I stand up and help Lara to her feet as Crew approaches.

He walks up to the dog and scratches his ear. "You draw lost souls to you like flies to honey."

She huffs and shakes her head. But I see the smile on her lips until she turns her head and looks back up the hill toward the cottage.

"What are we going to do?"

"You are going to take these painkillers and get your cute ass into the truck and snuggle up with Rufio while we take care of the problem," he tells her, handing her a couple of pills and a bottle of water.

"But I—"

"Let us do this for you. Trust us," Crew whispers.

Her eyes flutter closed before she sighs and gives in with a nod. "Alright."

"Good girl." He kisses her temple and walks back to the truck, opening the rear passenger door for her.

"Lay down and get some rest. We'll be back before you know it. There are some sleeping bags in there. Drag one over you to keep yourself warm. I'm worried about you going into shock."

"I'm okay now that you're both here. I don't know why or how you found me, but I'm thankful anyway."

"We can talk about that afterward too. For now, just rest," I tell her.

"Oh wait, my bag is in his truck."

"I'll grab it for you." I leave her with Crew, who helps her into the back seat.

I grab Lara's backpack from the front passenger footwell. I take it back to the truck and shove it in the back with the rest of our things.

Crew walks around to join me as we step away so that Lara can't hear us. "Plan?"

"First, get rid of the body. I figure it would be a shame for him to go to all this trouble..."

He looks at me with understanding, his lips pulling up into a wicked grin. "You want to stick him in the grave."

202

"Seems poetic to me."

He nods in agreement.

"We got anything back there we can wrap him in?" I ask since Crew was the one to pack the truck.

"No, but since it's his plan, he might."

We walk to the pickup truck and drop the tailgate. I hop up to take a look and find plastic sheeting and rope.

I give Crew a dark look before passing them to him.

"Anything else in there that might be useful?"

"Couple of guns, ammo, and a wicked-looking hunting knife. He's got a bunch of camping shit too."

He nods, running his hand over his mouth.

"Alright. We'll need to get rid of his truck. But let's take his supplies. If we have a run-in with her father, it'll be nice for the police to find the bullets fired from guns registered to this Giles guy."

"*If* they're registered," I say as I jump out of the truck.

"Oh, he'll have them registered, I guarantee it. If he's out there with his buddies hunting women, he won't risk getting pulled over and getting caught with unregistered guns. No, I'd say he's a model citizen—a nice guy who plays by the rules. He wouldn't want anyone to suspect otherwise."

I'd like to think this is just Crew's obsession with crime shows talking, but the truth is we've seen this shit before. And it's always the average Joes and good Samaritans, who blend in seamlessly, that make the most ruthless killers.

"Take this"—Crew hands me the plastic and rope—"I'm going to go get the jerry can. There's too much blood in the cottage. We'll need to burn it."

203

"Fine. Let's just get this over with. I want to put some miles between us and this place."

I head up to the cottage. Crew catches up with me with the jerry can in his hand just as I reach the door. When we walk in, the air is thick with that copper tang of blood and the unmissable scent of death.

We stare at the bloody scene before us for a moment before Crew speaks. "I'll check his pockets. You spread out the plastic, and then we can roll him onto it," he tells me, putting the jerry can down.

I push the few pieces of furniture out of the way and do just that, spreading the plastic out so we can wrap him up like a human burrito.

"Got his wallet. The guy's name is Giles Walker. Age twenty-nine. I'll take a picture and send it to Ev, see what he can dig up." His voice is stone-cold, making me look up. I half expect him to stomp on the fucker's face, but he keeps his cool. *Just barely.*

He pulls out his phone and takes a picture of the guy's driver's license before returning it to his wallet and shoving it in his pocket. "Okay, you grab his feet."

I'm careful not to walk through the blood and grab Giles by the ankles. Between us, we lift him onto the plastic and roll him up.

"He's fucking heavy."

"Hold that thought. Pretty sure I saw a wheelbarrow outside."

I walk out the door and move around the edge of the building. There, against the wall, is a large wheelbarrow. Can't say I've seen one of these at a cemetery before, and I've been to more than a few funerals in my lifetime. Which begs the question: just how many bodies have been inside this thing?

I wheel it to the door and whistle for Crew. He pokes his head out and nods before disappearing inside. I hear the crinkle of plastic and a grunt before Crew appears with the dead body over his shoulder, whistling a merry tune.

"Your psycho is showing."

He bares his teeth at me, making me laugh as he tosses the body into the wheelbarrow.

"If you think the whistling's too much, you really won't like it when I dance on his grave."

I shake my head at the lunatic.

"No. For what he tried to do to our girl..." he trails off, his fists clenching at his sides. "He's lucky he's dead because I would have fucking killed him."

He's right. The thought is sobering. We could have lost our girl before we had a chance with her because of this motherfucker.

"Let's get this show on the road."

I push the wheelbarrow down the hill, making sure my grip is tight. The last thing I want is a *Weekend at Bernie's* incident with a body rolling away from us down the hill.

Once we get to the grave, Crew jumps down into the hole and pops open the coffin inside. The smell that escapes makes me gag, but I manage to stop myself from throwing up.

"Jesus, he's ripe. Help me out."

I reach down, grab Crew's hand, and help him out.

"Alright, let's get this asshole in."

It takes a little time maneuvering him, but we manage to squeeze him into the coffin. I smile at the thought of him spending eternity in there. The image of Crew jumping on the coffin to get the lid closed, followed by a little dance, is one I could have lived without, though.

Bent over with his hands on his knees, he catches his breath. I pick up one of the two shovels from next to the mound of dirt and start scooping it back into the hole. The soil hitting the oak box makes a satisfying thud.

Crew picks up the second shovel and starts shoveling the dirt into the hole as well. After half an hour, we're done.

"I have a whole new respect for people who do this for a living," I admit, wiping the sweat from my forehead.

"Agreed. Now, let's torch the cottage and get the fuck out of here. I need a shower and a cold beer."

"Don't tease me with a good time."

"I don't share beer."

"But you'll share your shower?" I laugh.

Crew chuckles, some of the tension finally easing from him now that the asshole is buried.

"If Lara was between us, fuck yeah."

"It's really fucking inappropriate to get a hard-on in a graveyard."

"There are worse places."

"Oh yeah? Name one."

He opens his mouth to reply, but I hold up my hand to stop him.

"Forget it. I changed my mind. I just know I don't want to hear whatever it is you're going to say."

He shrugs, his loss, and we head back to the cottage.

Without the body stealing my focus, I spot the knife on the floor and pick it up. I could leave it, but it's never a good idea to leave the murder weapon at the crime scene. Besides, Lara has proven she knows how to use a blade. She should keep it in case she ever needs it again. As much as I'd like to say nothing will happen to her now that me and Crew are with her, the truth is, we aren't bulletproof. And if we are taken out first, we'll leave Lara vulnerable. A knife, no matter what, at least gives her a fighting chance. This cottage with the blood-stained floor is proof of that.

Chapter Twenty-Three

Lara

The vibrations of the truck are the first thing I feel when I wake up. The second is the throbbing headache. The third is the wet nose pressed against my cheek.

I open my eyes and find Rufio asleep beside me. I twist a little and wince. Sitting up, I look around. It's dark outside now, and all I can see are trees. Rufio uses my distraction to his advantage and licks my face. I can't help but chuckle.

"Hey, how you feeling?" Wilder asks.

"Sore," I say, settling on the truth.

"I can imagine," he replies as I look over and notice the passenger seat is empty, and there's a weird smell in the truck.

"Is something burning? And where's Crew?" I ask as I slide across the seat and strap myself in.

"Crew's dumping the other truck."

"Oh," I say softly, not sure what else to say to that. He said they would take care of everything. I should have realized what that meant.

"I'm sorry about all this," I blurt out after a few minutes of silence. "I should have known better. I should have—"

"Shoulda, woulda, coulda. You think his other victims didn't think the same thoughts? There is nothing, and I mean nothing, a woman can do to deserve being raped and murdered. You know that, right? You could have stripped naked and given him a lap dance, and 'no' still would have meant no. Once he set his sights on you, there was nothing you could have done to change his mind. Maybe you shouldn't have gotten in his truck. Maybe he would have hit you over the head and taken you anyway."

I swallow. Even though I know he's right, part of me is beating myself up. I need to make smarter choices. But how do I do that when all my choices are so damn limited? Every action has a consequence. But I'm so tied up in knots that I can't see the consequences until the rope I'll eventually hang myself with unravels.

Wilder's cell phone rings. "It's Crew," he tells me as he answers. "Yeah. You're on speaker, by the way."

"I'm done. Can you track my phone to find me?"

"Yeah, be there soon."

He hangs up and fiddles with his phone before placing it in the holder in front of him.

The truck starts to move, and I can't help but close my eyes and grit my teeth as Wilder hits every bump. Eventually, I open my eyes as he pulls out of the trees and onto the paved road, and I take a shaky breath. We drive for about twenty minutes, my head still pounding, making me feel like I'm going to puke. I take another deep breath, and before I can close my eyes again, the headlights flash, and I see Crew on the side of the road. Wilder slows down and pulls over.

My door opens, and there's Crew looking at me with worried eyes. "What's wrong?"

"I feel a little sick, and my head is killing me."

"It's only been a couple hours since your last dose of painkillers." He looks into my eyes before gently rubbing my temples.

"Okay," I blow out.

"Can we let Rufio out for a bit? He's been cooped up and probably needs to pee."

"Sure. You want to walk around a little too?"

"Yeah, I think the fresh air will help."

I let him help me out of the truck and then call Rufio, who jumps out behind me. He runs off to explore but looks back to make sure I'm still in sight.

"You sure have a bond with him, considering you just met."

"Sounds familiar," Wilder says as he walks around to join us with a flashlight in his hand.

I don't know what to say to that, so I don't say anything. I follow Rufio as Wilder and Crew, walk beside me.

When Crew's cell chimes, I jump. Wilder's hand finds the small of my back, offering me comfort.

"It's Ev. He's found a dog-friendly motel nearby and a pet store for supplies."

My cheeks flush with shame. I have no right picking up a pet when I don't have the money to take care of him. Hell, I don't have the money to take care of myself.

"Don't," Crew snaps.

I look away, but he stands in front of me and cups the side of my face, gently turning my head to look at him.

"Forget about the money. We just want to look after you. And Lara, you're going to let us."

"You don't understand. Look, I appreciate you guys coming more than you'll ever know, but I can't come home."

"We know. We're not here to take you back."

Fuck me, why did that feel like a knife to the heart?

"Oh. Umm... okay."

"No, you misunderstand. We're not taking you back, but we are here for you. And we're staying until your father is no longer a threat," Wilder adds.

"What?" I whisper. "But that could take forever."

"Then so be it."

"You don't mean that. You don't know what he is capable of or what he'll do. I'll—"

"Fuck it," Crew says a second before his mouth is on mine. This kiss is anything but soft and gentle. It's demanding and filled with promises I never thought he'd make.

Crew pulls away, and Wilder takes his place. His kiss is more coaxing, a tease of what he can and will do to me if I let him. I want to, dear God, I do, but they don't understand.

I rip my mouth free and try to catch my breath. They watch me like I'm a wild animal that might lash out at any moment. And hell, maybe they're right. Part of me wants to yell at them. I remember the words I overheard. Is that what this is? Only that doesn't make sense. I had already left. I wasn't a danger to them anymore. So why come after me? Oh, my fragile heart wants it to be because they feel even a sliver of what I feel for them. But I'm scared. I don't know if I can trust my instincts when it comes to them.

"We won't push you for more than you're willing to give us," Crew says gently.

"We're willing to put in the work because we think you're worth it."

"What changed?"

"You left, and we realized we couldn't let you go."

I bite my lip, wincing a little, unsure what to say.

"Tell me you don't feel anything for us, and we'll back off. We'll still stay to keep you safe. This is not an either-or deal. We want you so fucking bad. But we want you to want us back and not because you feel obligated."

I walk away from them, my head spinning. I need a moment. Thankfully, they don't follow, giving me space to breathe.

I watch Rufio sniff his way along the bushes before he stops to mark his territory. Is that what Wilder and Crew are doing? Marking their territory? They want me, then they don't, and then they want me again. I'm getting whiplash from how fast they change their minds.

"God, I don't understand men," I grumble to myself.

Wilder and Crew appear beside me, scaring me half to death. Of course, they didn't let me wander off alone.

"We pushed too hard, too fast, didn't we?"

"I don't have the experience you guys do. And I admit, what I felt for you was new and confusing for me. Perhaps I let myself feel too much, but I'm not sure I have it in me to do it all over again."

They're quiet as they absorb my words. Maybe now they see that they did more damage than they realized.

"Do you have any idea how humiliating it was to stand there alone and have everyone look at me like I was scum over something I had no control of?"

They both look remorseful, but is it real or just an act?

"Part of me wants to just walk away. I'm so damn tired of people hurting me, and I let them. Every time I stay, every time I back down and make an excuse. Every time I make myself small, I give them permission to treat me like crap again and again. And I hate myself for it a little more each time. I'm sick and tired of begging for scraps of affection."

I'm not just talking about them anymore but about my father—the man who taught me that love comes with conditions.

I look at them, my heart in my throat, as I choke out my next words. "But you got rid of the body. You made yourself accomplices. Why'd you do that? Why'd you stay?"

They both step toward me, each of them pulling me in for a three-way hug.

"Walking away isn't an option, Lara. We're in too deep," Wilder says gently.

I blow out a shuddering breath and hold them to me. "Please don't hurt me."

Their arms tighten around me, reassuring me without words.

As scared as I am, I don't want fear to rule my life anymore. It's held me back for so long. At my age, I'm supposed to be taking chances and being reckless. That might not be in the cards for me, but that doesn't mean I should give up altogether, either. There is doing something for the good of others, and then there is becoming a martyr.

I'll give them a chance, and it might turn out to be the biggest mistake I'll ever make, but it's my mistake to make.

As I pull back and look up at them, I hold on to the glimmer of the girl my father tried to snuff out and let myself feel hope. This could all fall at the first hurdle. But what if we don't fall? What if we fly?

"Okay, let's see where this takes us. But you should know that my father won't like it. He'll do everything in his power to tear us apart. And if the cost of having you is your life, then I'll let him."

"We know what we're up against, Lara. You've gotta trust us," Crew growls.

"You think you know what you're up against, but you have no idea. Not really."

I sigh and whistle for Rufio. "Come on, boy. Time to go."

I look at Crew and frown. "How the heck did you get the truck out here anyway?"

"Easy, I drove it into the lake."

"You drove it into the lake?" I scan his clothes, but he looks dry enough to me.

"Naturally, I jumped out first."

"Naturally," I reply as flippantly as he does.

"Just go with it, Lara. The man's a little bit nuts." Wilder grins as he wraps his arm around my shoulders and starts walking us back to the truck, an excited Rufio following behind.

The ride to the motel is mostly quiet. It's not forced or filled with tension, though. It's as if we all need a few minutes to process what happened today. At least that's true for me.

Rufio's head rests in my lap, so I pet him absently as I think about how Wilder and Crew's arrival has changed things. As much as I worry, I can't deny the comfort it gives me to have them here. I've always been a loner, through no fault of my own. But I never understood what loneliness was. I was always so busy keeping my head down and looking after the various kids that came in and out of the Division.

Leaving Apex, though, a place that showed me exactly what a family should look like, left a hole in my chest that's done nothing but ache since I left.

I lean my head back and close my eyes. My head and face are throbbing. The movement of the truck isn't helping either.

By the time we pull up at the motel, I'm so ready to get out of the truck that I practically have the door open before it's even stopped. I gulp down a lungful of fresh air. Thankfully, it helps because the last thing I want to do is puke all over my feet. That would really set the mood.

"I'm going to check us in and grab some ice for your face," Crew says, climbing out.

He walks off before either Wilder or I can say anything.

"Do you have any more painkillers?"

"Yeah, hold on. Let me grab you a couple." Wilder leaves me leaning against the side of the truck with Rufio at my feet before returning moments later with a couple of painkillers and a bottle of water.

After he unscrews the cap for me, I take the pills and the bottle and drink half the tepid liquid before handing it back to him. "I need to get some stuff for Rufio. He'll need water. And fo—"

He places his finger to my lips.

"We'll get you settled first and then pick up everything Rufio might need."

I don't argue. I just rest my head against his chest and breathe him in. Maybe I could get used to relying on someone else for a change.

Maybe.

Chapter Twenty-Four

Crew

I got a double room for us at the far end of the building. If we get into trouble, it will be easier for us to get away.

Wilder is standing with Lara in his arms when I walk out. Five days ago, I would have questioned every little thing. But now, it just seems right.

"I got us a room, and there's an ice machine around the corner. Let's get you inside, and then I'll grab some," I tell Lara, who nods.

I walk to the room and unlock the door, opening it for them to enter. Rufio trots in behind Lara and moves around the room, sniffing everything before he curls up at the foot of the bed.

"I guess it passed his inspection." I chuckle. Lara doesn't say anything, her eyes fixed on the queen-sized bed.

"I...um... They only had one room?"

"If you think we're letting you out of our sight, you're insane." I walk over to her.

"I'm not going to run."

"I think you believe that, but what happens if you come back and find a note on your pillow threatening us?"

She flinches and looks away, knowing I'm right.

"I left because it was the right thing to do. And yes, I'd leave again if I thought it would keep you safe. Don't tell me you wouldn't do the same if the roles were reversed."

"We're used to working as a team. We are trained that having a partner to rely on is a blessing, not a curse. You don't get that yet, but you will."

"And how does watching over me translate into you sleeping with me?"

"Watching over you is our duty," I murmur, stepping closer until my front is pressed against hers. "Sleeping beside you is our privilege."

Her face flushes as she dips her head. I slip my finger under her chin and tip her head back so she has no choice but to look into my eyes.

"We want you. Every part of you."

"I thought my whole being seventeen was an issue."

I cock my head and grin. "At midnight, that won't be an issue, now, will it?"

"You know when my birthday is? Is that why you came, so you could to get laid?"

Before I can say anything, Wilder spins her around and tosses her over his shoulder, making her squeal. And he slaps her ass hard.

"You know better than that. Don't cheapen yourself or us by insinuating that this is all about getting a cheap fuck. We can get our dicks wet anywhere. But we don't want anyone else. We just want you."

He tosses her on the bed, making her yelp, before he climbs up beside her. I do the same on the other side.

"From now on, this is where you sleep. Between us."

"Do I get any say in this?" she huffs.

Wilder shakes his head. "No. It's a done deal. We've decided to keep you."

"Keep me? I'm not a freaking toy."

"I don't know about that. You sure are fun to play with," I tease, skating my lips down her neck, my hand moving to rest on her stomach just under the hem of her shirt.

She shivers under my touch, a soft moan escaping her lips. Wilder kisses her jaw, one of his legs pinning hers in place. I want nothing more than to watch him strip her bare and—

Shit. I thought I had a better handle on myself. I pull away and tug Wilder with me before we all get carried away.

"Midnight." I don't know if I'm reminding them or myself that we need to wait a little longer, but it seems to have the effect of a cold shower.

"Right. How about I get the ice and our bags? I need a second." He presses a kiss to Lara's lips before climbing off the bed and adjusting his cock with a grunt. He yanks the door open and stomps out, slamming it behind him.

Lara looks at me wide-eyed. "Did that just happen?" She slaps her hand over my mouth before I can answer.

I lick her palm, making her gasp, and drop her hand. "Make no mistake, Lara, we both want you badly. But we will wait until you're ready. Despite how irresistible you are."

"I don't want to wait. I've been waiting forever for my life to begin. If there is anything I've learned, it's that I can't keeping waiting around until my life is calm and easy before I start chasing my dreams. If I do that, my whole life will pass me by as I stand on the sidelines just watching."

"Life with you is always going to be chaotic, isn't it? What am I saying? Of course it is, with your group of hellions." I grin at her, her smile fragile.

"Are they okay?"

"Yeah, but they miss you. They know you well, by the way. They knew you only would have left them to keep them safe."

"Are they mad at me?" she whispers as I brush my thumb across her cheek.

"No. They're not mad. They just want you back safe and sound."

She buries her head against my shoulder.

"I want that too. I know most girls my age dream about leaving home, going to college, traveling, and a million other things that seem alien to me. But I just want to have a family. I want to be loved and to love people who don't care about my gift but who just care about me."

"You have that with Apex. And as soon as it's safe, we can go back."

She sighs and nods, but I'm not sure she sees an end in sight.

Wilder's voice breaks the moment. "Here we go. Ice and our bags."

I roll Lara off me and sit up. Wilder has dropped our bags by the door. He holds the bucket of ice out to me as he heads into the bathroom. He comes back with a small white towel. He fills the towel with ice, twists the ends, and gently places the homemade ice pack against the injured side of Lara's face.

"Ouch," she hisses.

"Yeah, that's going to hurt like a motherfucker tomorrow." He coughs when he realizes he cursed. "I mean, it will hurt like a—"

Lara holds up her hand.

"I'm a big girl. I can handle your dirty mouth. Besides, if what you guys are saying about me being yours at midnight is true, I might enjoy it." She wiggles her eyebrows at him, making me curse and a pained expression cross his face.

"She's doing this on purpose, isn't she?"

I glare at Lara and nod as she gives him her best innocent look.

"How about I take Rufio to the pet store and get him what he needs while you relax? Then we can order some food and come up with a plan."

"A plan?" Lara looks between me and Wilder.

"A plan," he confirms. "Running your father around in circles might work for now, but at some point, he's going to change his tactics. If he can't catch you, he'll try to draw you out. And what better way to do that than with bait?"

"The kids!" She jumps off the bed, dropping the ice pack. I grab her before she can get any farther.

"Apex is on lockdown. Nobody will get to the kids. But if there are other people out there, he'll use them."

She slumps in my arms, and I hold her tight. Rufio stands up and rubs his head against our legs.

"Come on, Rufio, let's go get you some food. Why don't you and Crew get cleaned up while I'm gone."

She grips my T-shirt as Rufio goes with Wilder. He pauses in the doorway, looking back at us. The dog must be happy with me looking after her because he follows Wilder out.

I let go of Lara and walk over to the door, locking it before walking back to her.

"Alright," I say, running my hands up and down her arms. "First things first. How about a shower?"

"That would be amazing." She smiles, making me smile.

"Okay, I'll run one for you. While I do that, why don't you go through the bags and find something comfortable to sleep in."

"Okay."

I place a chaste kiss on her lips and let her go before walking into the bathroom, happy to find it clean and tidy. I turn the shower on and note that they have little complimentary bottles of shampoo, conditioner, and body wash. That saves me from having to dig around for our stuff.

I walk back into the bedroom and see her standing there with her clothes in her hand. "There are towels and toiletries already in there, so we don't have to worry about any of that."

She nods, taking a step toward the bathroom.

I reach out and stop her. "Do you need a hand?"

She looks at me and blushes but shakes her head.

"Alright, but if that changes, call me. And leave the door open a crack, okay?" She looks at me, unsure. "I'm not going to watch you if that's what you're worried about. But you hurt your head today, and I'll feel better being able to hear you."

She bites her lip before agreeing and scurries off into the bathroom, leaving the door open a crack.

I sit on the end of the bed and take a deep breath. She's as skittish as a wild animal, but she said she wants more. She just doesn't know what more entails.

Fuck. I rub my hand down my face.

I'm not sure I've ever been with a virgin, and part of me is fucking terrified of hurting her. The other part of me, the side born with caveman instincts, is over the fucking moon that the only men to experience Lara's tight pussy will be me and Wilder.

My dick throbs at the thought. I look toward the crack in the door, and though I can't see anything, I have a pretty good imagination. In my head, I can picture the water sliding down her naked body as she lathers herself up. I groan and lean back. I need to get a fucking grip on myself and not on my dick like I really want.

Needing something to distract me, I go through our bags and take out what I think we might need for the night. I spot the little bag with Lara's toothbrush at the top of her backpack, so I don't go looking any further.

The last bag belonged to that dickhead Giles. I sit it on the bed and empty its contents. As much as I'd happily toss the clothes, you can't be too picky on the road. There isn't much else in there. A couple of books, snacks, some money, which is probably for emergencies, more ammo, and a handgun—a Smith and Wesson— that I check over and put on the table. Everything else I toss back in the bag for now.

I hear the shower shut off, so I grab the sweatpants I pulled from my bag, readying myself for the shower. I leave the books on the bed in case Lara wants to take a look and find a pen and notepad in the bedside drawer with the hotel's logo on it. I leave that with the books and the snacks.

A few minutes later, Lara comes out of the bathroom in one of my T-shirts, her hair wrapped in a towel on top of her head. My mouth immediately goes dry. I like to think I'm a good man, but Lara would test the morals of a saint. I don't think I've ever seen anything sexier than my girl wearing my shirt.

My girl. Fuck yeah, I like the sound of that.

I cough to clear my throat. "I'm going to jump in the shower now. I found some snacks and books and left them on the bed. I won't be long. I'll leave the door open a little in case you need me."

She smiles coyly. "I promise not to look."

"Lara, you can look at me any damn time you want. I'm all yours."

When her mouth drops open, I wink at her and walk into the bathroom with a smirk on my face.

Chapter Twenty-Five

Lara

I keep glancing at the bathroom door. Unfortunately, I can't see anything. I'm tempted to tiptoe over and take a peek, but I don't want to get caught and have him think I'm some kind of pervy creeper. But then he did say I could look anytime I wanted to, right?

Fuck it.

I get off the bed as quietly as I can and walk over to the door, pushing it open a tiny bit more. I can make out Crew's shape through the shower curtain. He's leaning with his head against the wall, and for a moment, I feel like I'm intruding. I'm about to back away when I see movement. It takes me a few seconds to realize I'm seeing his arm moving back and forth as he strokes his cock. I feel a spasm in my pussy, my eyes glued on the man that is unknowingly playing out one of my fantasies.

I slip my hand into my panties and dip my fingers between my legs, not surprised to find myself already wet. I stroke my clit lightly, my eyes feasting on the scene before me.

A hand covers my mouth, and a body presses up against me. I freeze, fear flooding my veins, until I feel lips whispering against my ear. "It's me, Lara."

I relax until I remember what Wilder has just caught me doing.

"See something you like, sweetheart?" His words rumble through me, softly spoken and full of intent.

"You make it so fucking hard to be good." As if to punctuate the word hard, he presses closer, and I can feel the hard column of his dick against my ass.

"I can't touch you until midnight, but that doesn't mean I can't feel you touch yourself, does it?"

His hand slips under the waistband of my panties and covers mine. I'm glad his hand is still over my mouth. I'm not sure I could be quiet, and I don't want to break whatever spell has been cast over us.

His finger moves over mine, encouraging me to stroke myself a little firmer. "You like watching Crew stroke his cock? Is it making you wet? Are you imagining it's your hand wrapped around him, or do you want him to do the stroking until he comes?"

I shudder at his words, making him moan softly.

"That one, huh? And where would you want him to come? Your stomach, your tits, your mouth? Or maybe you want him to come inside you?" My legs wobble at that. I'm glad he's holding me because I'm not sure I can hold myself up anymore.

My fingers move faster as Wilder's hand grips mine tighter. When Crew comes, his head thrown back as he harshly calls out my name, I come too, soaking my fingers and Wilder's.

Wilder picks me up and carries me to the bed, kissing me soundly before pulling back and sucking his wet fingers into his mouth.

My cheeks feel like they're on fire, but I don't regret what we did. As I look up at him, his eyes boring into mine, I'm hoping he doesn't either.

As if sensing my uncertainty, he gives me a wicked grin. "Delicious. I can't wait to taste it from the source."

My heart is beating so loudly that it's a wonder he can't hear it. I open my mouth to say something, but words fail me. What could I possibly say? Thanks for giving a hand? *Literally.*

Sensing my inner turmoil, Wilder backs off, though the smirk doesn't leave his face. "I got everything Rufio might need. I just have to bring it in."

I look around and realize I don't see my dog anywhere. I sit up. "Where is he?"

"I made the mistake of putting his new bed on the front seat, and now he's refusing to get out of the truck."

I laugh, imagining Wilder's face as he argues with the stubborn dog. "I'll see if he'll listen to me."

"I'd appreciate it. I'll grab the rest of the stuff. You might want to put some sweatpants on, though."

I look down at my bare legs. The hem of my T-shirt has ridden up to show my panties. Instead of being embarrassed, I glare at him. It's not like I'm going to walk outside like this.

"I'm good, but thanks." I climb off the bed and shove my feet into my sneakers before heading for the door.

As my hand grabs the knob, an arm wraps around my stomach, halting my movements.

"Nobody gets to see you like this but me and Crew."

226

"I'm wearing one of Crew's T-shirts. It covers more than some of the dresses Oz bought me and all of my swimsuits."

He growls, "We'll talk about those dresses in a minute. But for right now, I'm going to need you to back your cute ass up and put some sweatpants on."

"Why? What are you going to do? Finger fuck me against the door again?"

"What the fuck did you just say?" We freeze at the sound of Crew's voice, both of us too wrapped up in each other to hear him come in.

Wilder picks me up and turns us so we're both facing him. My brain misfires for a second when I see Crew standing in the bath-room doorway wearing nothing but a pair of gray sweatpants, his tanned, muscular chest and ripped stomach on display for me to drool over.

"What is she talking about?" Crew asks, his body tense as he looks from me to Wilder.

"Turns out our girl likes to watch," Wilder tells him as I wait for the ground to open up and swallow me whole. When Crew's eyes slowly move back to mine, I realize I'm much more likely to burst into flames than disappear.

I see understanding dawn. His eyes flare as he moves toward me with intent. With Wilder at my back, I have nowhere to go, so all I can do is wait to see what he'll do.

He reaches for my hand and then slowly brings it up to his face. He raises my fingers to his nose and inhales deeply.

I feel my legs shake and heat pool between my legs as he growls.

"And what did you do, Wilder?" Crew's voice is deeper now, like he's barely holding on.

"Nothing. I just held her hand. Isn't that right, Lara?"

He wants me to speak now? Does he not have any idea the effect either of them are having on me? I'm struggling to remember how to breathe, let alone form a coherent sentence.

"Lara?" Crew prompts.

"He didn't do anything to me," I manage to get out, not wanting to cause any kind of rift between the two. This room feels too small as it is with the three of us in here together. The last thing I need is to be caught in a game of tug-of-war.

"I'm going to get Rufio."

I pull free of them and head out while they are engaged in a stare-off. I hurry over to the truck and yank the door open.

Rufio looks up at me, and I swear, for a second, the dog smiles.

I lean in and scratch behind his ear. "You got spoiled, huh?" His bed is made of a dark gray fur and looks so cozy. I wonder if they make one in human size—it would be perfect for curling up in with a book.

"Come on, you can't stay in here forever. Besides, I need someone on my side in that room. I need my friend, okay?"

He might not understand my words, but something in my tone must give away my desperation because, when I step back, he jumps out with zero hesitation.

"Good boy, Rufio." I grab the large dog bed and use my butt to close the door before the bed is taken out of my hands, and Wilder's eyes are staring back at me.

"Sweatpants." He holds a pair out for me to take.

I ignore them and walk to the back of the truck, reaching inside for the bag of dog food. I feel my T-shirt ride up and know I'm flashing my panties. I don't rush to cover myself, though, knowing it will make Wilder lose his mind.

"You're playing with fire, little girl," Crew warns me. He steps up beside me, reaches for the bag of food, and slings it over his shoulder.

"I don't know what you're talking about," I tell him innocently. I reach for a shopping bag that looks like it's filled with dog toys and treats.

"Sure you don't." He laughs, taking the bag to the room. Rufio follows behind him.

I look for Wilder and find him heading back my way after taking the dog bed inside, the sweatpants still in his hand and a scowl on his face.

"You have two choices. Either you head back to the room and stay there, or you put these on."

"And if I don't?"

"I'll put you over my knee and spank your ass until it's so red you won't be able to sit down."

"If you try spanking me, I'll remove your dick from your body with my teeth."

He cocks his brow. "So you've thought about putting my dick in your mouth, huh?"

Instead of replying, I throw the bag at him and stomp back to the room. I ignore his laughter and slam the door closed behind me. Climbing onto the bed, I tuck my knees up under my T-shirt, grab one of the books from the end of the bed, and start reading.

All the words blur together, but when Wilder walks in moments later, I pretend to read, acting as if I'm completely engrossed in the book and oblivious to him.

Wilder steps up next to me and takes the book out of my hands before turning it the right way up and handing it back. "Might help if it was the right way."

"I hate you both," I mumble as Crew grins that grin of his that renders me stupid.

"I don't think you hate us, not even a little bit. I think you're embarrassed because you want us. What you don't seem to realize is that you have nothing to be embarrassed about. We told you we want you. We've wanted you from the start, and knowing you feel the same way is making it really fucking hard to resist you."

"I never said you had to resist me. That was all you. You're the two that imposed the age rule. I might understand it, but that doesn't mean that it doesn't piss me off."

"Lara—"

"No. You want me, but only at midnight and not a second before. Does that mean that I have until eleven fifty-nine to flirt with other boys?"

I don't even see him move, and yet I find myself pinned to the bed underneath Crew, who is seething with anger.

"There will be no flirting with anyone. You're not dealing with boys now, Lara. You're dealing with men. And if one even looks at you too long, I'll scoop out his eyes and use them as stress balls."

Before I can fire back at him, Wilder yanks him off.

"I think we should run out and get something to eat. Give Lara a chance to cool down."

"Me? I'm not the one who—" I shut up before Wilder can say anything about me touching myself as I spied on Crew in the shower.

Wilder looks at me with a grin, knowing exactly what I was just thinking about.

"Anything in particular you want?"

I shake my head. "I'll try anything." As much as I hate for him to be right, I could do with a little space now. A lot has happened in the last few days. And I don't think I've had a chance to deal with any of it.

"Alright, we won't be long," Wilder tells me before turning to Crew. "Put a T-shirt on. It's enough to put me off my food."

I bite my lip, not willing to admit that Crew's state of undress has the opposite effect on me. If I'm hungry for anything, it's—

A cell phone rings, cutting off my wayward thoughts. Crew reaches into his pocket and pulls it out, answering without looking to see who it is.

"Hey, everything okay?" He nods along to whatever is being said before his eyes meet mine. "Yeah, she's good. We won't let anything happen to her."

He hangs up. "That was Ev. I sent him a picture of Giles the prick's license, and he found some information."

"What kind of information?" I wrap my arms around myself, my brain flipping back to the image of Giles bleeding out on the floor.

"The kind of information that shows women often go missing after meeting him."

I shiver at the thought. All this with Wilder and Crew has distracted me from what I did. Not that I feel any guilt. I knew if I didn't do anything, there would be more women than there clearly already has been. I think I'm more concerned that I don't feel any remorse at all. Shouldn't I feel something after taking another man's life, even if he was a psycho? Maybe if I'd had more time to think about it, I would have felt worse.

"Have you guys been purposely distracting me?"

"I don't know what you're talking about. Anyway, Ev says he'll make sure Giles's boss receives a resignation letter and a request to send his final check to his parent's house in Tulsa. He's going to say something about meeting someone and wanting to see the world with them. So we're good for now, but he'll get reported as missing at some point. Ev is working on multiple things right now, so I'm not pushing him for more."

He looks at me before continuing. "He's been beefing up security measures. And he's still going through the files to see if there's anything in them that can help us bring the Division down."

"I should have spent some time with him, telling him all the little details I know. I'm not sure it would have helped since I wasn't involved with anything top secret, but I could name and point out key figures."

"I'll tell him he can talk to you if he has any questions. He's pretty good at figuring shit out on his own, though," Crew tells me as his fingers move over the screen of his phone.

"Okay, well, I'm here if he needs me."

Crew's cell phone pings with an incoming text message.

"He's working on something else right now, but when he's done, he'll call."

"What's more important than this?" Wilder asks what I was thinking.

Before Crew can say anything, his phone rings again. He looks at the screen and answers it. "Greg?" He listens for a minute before he speaks. "Hang on, let me put you on speaker." Crew pulls the phone from his ear and presses a button. "Okay, Greg, go ahead."

"The others didn't want to say anything, knowing it might turn out to be nothing. And because you have your hands full with Lara, who I hope knows how much we miss her."

"She knows," I whisper around the lump in my throat.

"Good. Now, I'm going to need you to look after my boys as much as I need them to look after you."

"What's going on, G? What is it the others don't want us to know?"

He sighs. "There's been an incident in Russia."

Crew curses, both men tensing as they lean closer to the phone.

"There was an explosion—" Greg continues, but he's cut off by Wilder.

"Are Hendrix and Nash okay?"

Greg says nothing for a moment, the weight of his silence weighing on us all.

"There is no word on them yet. As of right now, they're missing in action."

Chapter Twenty-Six

Wilder

We leave Rufio guarding Lara while we head across the street to the diner and order food. Crew and I questioned Greg for information, but he didn't have much more to give. Right now, all we can do is wait.

Part of me feels sick to my stomach at the thought of losing men I care about and consider family, even though they've spent most of their time halfway across the world. The other part of my brain knows better than to give up. We thought Oz and Zig were dead after they crashed in a fucking jungle, but they survived. If they can do it, then so can Nash and Hendrix.

"It will take more than a fucking explosion to take out Hendrix and Nash," Crew says.

"I hope so. What the fuck is going on over there? They were supposed to be pulling themselves out. Then something happened that they refused to talk about. Any time I've asked them when they're coming back, they've given an excuse."

"When Ev was crashing after being up for I don't know how many days straight, he said that he thought they were seeing someone."

"Something serious?"

"If it was stopping them from coming home, then yeah, I'd say it was serious. Men like Nash and Hendrix take their jobs very fucking seriously, especially over there. You do not want to be labeled a spy in Russia. They tend to end up with a little extra in their food."

"The kind of extra that makes you set off a Geiger counter?" He asks likely recalling the incident I am where a Russian dissident was poisoned in the UK with Polonium, a radioactive substance that was slipped into his cup of tea.

"Yeah. They wouldn't take risks unless they thought it absolutely necessary. Or if—"

"They'd found their version of Lara," I finish for him.

He's quiet, probably thinking the same thing I am. What wouldn't I do for Lara? I wouldn't hurt my family or the kids. But other than that, I doubt there is much I wouldn't do.

"I feel like we should be doing something."

"We are. We're keeping our girl safe. Right now, there is nothing else we can do. If Hendrix and Nash are okay, they'll find a way to let us know."

"And if they're not?"

"Then we find out what happened and avenge them." There's no point beating around the bush. If someone has taken them out, I'll kill them myself. And I won't lose a single second of sleep over it.

The waitress calls Crew's name, so we get up, grab our order, and leave. Stepping outside, the cool evening air is a shock against my skin after how warm it was in the diner.

"So what exactly went down with you and Lara before? And don't bullshit me." He looks at his watch. "We have three hours left until midnight, and we made a deal—"

"I didn't break the deal, but fucking hell, I wanted to," I admit. "The way she was watching you... Fuck. She was so into it that she didn't even hear me come back. She had no clue I was behind her until my hand was over her mouth, which was right around the time I realized her hand was in her underwear."

"Fuck," he grunts, as I feel my dick stir at the memory.

"You have no idea. It took every ounce of strength I had in me to stop myself from tossing her on the bed and fucking her into oblivion."

The memory of Lara with her hand in her panties stroking her clit as she watches him come has me groaning. "She was a sight to behold."

"I've never been jealous of you before, but right now, I have the strangest urge to punch you in your pretty-boy face."

"Aww, you think I'm pretty."

He opens the door, and the sight that greets us makes me want to thump my head against the wall.

Lara has fallen asleep in the center of the bed, on her stomach, her hair falling down her back in a riot of unruly curls. The T-shirt she's wearing has ridden up to her waist, revealing white cotton panties covering her pert ass.

"I always thought I was a leather and lace kind of guy," Crew admits, placing the bags on the table as Rufio lifts his head and dismisses us by lying back down. "How did I not see the appeal of basic cotton? It makes her more..."

"Virginal?" I drawl sarcastically.

He looks at me, but he doesn't deny it. "It's not lost on me that the thing that's held us back is also the thing that draws us in."

"Not sure if that makes us smart men or degenerates." I sigh.

"Probably both. But I've never been one to look a gift horse in the mouth. She's exquisite, and she's ours. She doesn't have any other experience to draw from. We have the perfect opportunity to show her just how good it can be. No fumbled backseat wham-bam-thank-you-ma'am fucks for Lara. We get her addicted to our cocks, and she'll never want to leave."

I chuckle at Crew. "I'm not sure it will be that easy, given how prone we are to fucking up."

He shrugs. "I'd be lying if I said some primal part of me doesn't get off on the fact that she'll be solely ours. And I know you feel it too. We'll be her first, her last, her everything."

I look at him and frown. "Did you just quote Barry White?"

He flips me off. "I'm a soldier, not a fucking poet, but you get what I mean. You can't tell me it doesn't make you hard as a rock, knowing she will only ever feel our hands on her body, our mouths on her tits, and our dicks inside her."

I adjust myself making him snigger.

"This is going to be the longest three hours of my life," I grumble as I take off my shirt.

"What are you doing?"

"What does it look like? I'm going to jump in the shower real quick and then go to bed. We can eat when we get up."

"Alright, I'll message Greg and see if they've heard anything else."

I nod and put my phone on the bedside table before I head into the bathroom and strip out of the rest of my clothes. I take a quick shower and dry off before walking back into the bedroom.

Crew is curled up behind Lara, his face buried in her hair. The man can fall asleep at the drop of a hat, something that both annoys and amuses me.

Using the light from the bathroom, I quietly search my bag for clean boxers. I slip them on before switching the light off and plunging the room into darkness.

I climb into bed beside Lara and gently pull her into my chest so I don't disturb either of them.

I breathe her in as she snuggles closer. With a contented sigh, I close my eyes and drift off.

I wake up disoriented, forgetting where I am for a moment. I grab my phone off the bedside table and see it's 1:15 a.m. Placing it back down, I roll over, wondering what it is that woke me. A soft moan grabs my attention.

I flick on the lamp and see Lara writhing in her sleep. There is no sign of Crew, but then I see the giant lump under the blankets between her legs, and I realize what's going on.

I pull back the blankets, and Crew looks up from where he's devouring Lara's pussy. My already hard cock turns to steel, especially when he lifts his head and I see how wet his mouth and jaw are from her arousal.

"It's after midnight," he reminds me, like he expects me to argue, the fucking idiot.

"She tastes fucking amazing," he whispers, telling me something I already know. He dips his head back down and carries on eating her out.

I slide the T-shirt up her body, revealing smooth, creamy skin. Her breasts are just big enough to fill my hands, which is what I do, cupping them both and flicking the nipples until they're erect. She tosses her head from side to side, her hips gyrating in her sleep as she chases her pleasure.

I dip my head and suck one of her nipples into my mouth, nipping it lightly with my teeth before soothing the sting with my tongue.

"Wilder?" Lara's uncertain voice makes me pause as I look up at her sleepy yet aroused face.

I take her mouth hard, knowing I need to back off but finding it impossible to do so. She's like a poison, and the antidote all rolled into one.

She kisses me back, tentatively at first, before relaxing into it. She grabs my hair with both hands and anchors me to her as I kiss her hard enough to leave us both breathless. I pull back as she releases my hair and grips the sheets instead.

"Oh God," she gasps as she comes, her eyes rolling into the back of her head.

When Crew climbs up beside her and kisses her, letting her taste herself on his lips, I know I can't hold back any longer. I get out of bed, grab a strip of condoms from my bag, and crawl up between her spread legs. I tear off a condom and roll it down my hard length before I glide it over her pussy, gathering her cream.

Crew tears his mouth from hers so he can watch, but my eyes are locked on Lara's.

"Are you sure you want this?"

She nods rapidly.

"Words, Lara. I need you to say them out loud."

"Fuck me, Wilder. Make me yours."

Her words snap something inside my brain, and I surge inside her.

In the back of my mind, a voice is screaming for me to calm the fuck down and take it easy. But the heat of her pussy and the feel of her nails scorching a blazing path down my back almost cause me to black out with blind need.

"Hurts," she whimpers, the words making me stop when nothing else penetrates.

"I know, baby, but you're doing so good taking Wilder like that. You stretch around him so fucking beautifully."

I hold still as she adjusts. I watch through hazy eyes as Crew moves down to focus his attention on her breasts. When I feel her relax underneath me, I ease back almost to the tip before thrusting inside her once more.

She groans, but the sound is now filled with more pleasure than pain.

I take that as my cue and fuck her in short, sharp strokes, working her back up into a frenzy before I push in deeper and harder.

"Wilder," she moans as I hit something inside her that makes her back arch and her eyes close.

"You can take it, Lara. You were built for taking our cocks. And one day, you'll take us both."

My words push her over the edge. She comes for a second time, dragging me over the edge with her—my cum so hot I swear it could burn through the condom.

I ease out of her and press a kiss to the top of her pussy before climbing off the bed and discarding the condom.

"Do you need to rest, or can you take me too?" I hear Crew ask.

I pause in the bathroom doorway and watch as she reaches for him.

"I can take you. I need to feel you too."

He doesn't need to be told twice. The condom is on, and he's between her legs in record time. Leaning down, he kisses her as he eases his way inside her. She's trembling, her body an overload of sensations. It's the most beautiful thing I've ever seen.

Crew pulls his lips from hers, and she holds him to her as he loses control, fucking her hard enough to leave bruises and deep enough that she'll feel him for days. She doesn't complain. She takes it like a good girl, lifting her hips to meet him thrust for thrust.

When she comes for the third time, it takes the last of her energy, and she passes out, missing when Crew pulls his cock from her swollen pussy. He yanks the condom off and strokes himself to completion, shooting his cum over her stomach and chest.

I walk back into the bathroom and wet a small towel before carrying it back into the bedroom. While Crew gets rid of his condom, I gently clean between her legs before wiping Crew's cum from her body.

She stirs, waking just as I'm finishing up.

"Wilder?"

"I'm here, Lara."

I toss the towel at Crew. He catches it and throws it into the bathroom before climbing in on the opposite side of Lara.

"Crew?"

"I'm here too, baby. How do you feel?"

"Like I was claimed." She smiles, my cock jerking at her words.

"We were rough," I admit.

"I liked it. Although I'll probably be sore tomorrow." She sighs. "I wish we had a tub."

"Hmm...leave it with me. I'll come up with something. Any regrets?"

I hear Crew suck in a breath as he waits for her response.

"Only that you made me wait so long."

I smile and kiss her temple as she drifts off once more.

"No more waiting," I whisper, before I lie down and fall asleep beside her.

Chapter Twenty-Seven

Lara

I'll admit, when Wilder suggested I use the motel pool to ease my aching muscles, I thought he'd lost his mind. But it turns out he knew what he was talking about.

Sure, I had to share it with a couple in their late-eighties and a few guys in their twenties who Crew kept side-eyeing, but it was exactly what I needed.

We had a pool onsite at the Division, but I didn't get to use it half as much as I would have liked because it was mostly used for rehabilitation purposes.

By the time I get out, my legs feel like noodles but the throb in my pussy has dulled to a more manageable ache.

Wilder goes back to the room to walk Rufio, while Crew guards the door to the changing room so I can strip out of my wet bathing suit and climb under the warm spray of the shower. Happy I packed the suit at the last minute, I tip my head back and close my eyes as the warm water beats down over my body, soothing more of the aches from last night's lovemaking.

I wash the chlorine out of my hair and use a strawberry-scented body wash to clean it from my skin. Once I'm done, I turn off the water and climb out, wrapping myself in a huge towel that brushes the tops of my feet.

A noise has me freezing before I slowly turn around. Nothing's there, and I strain my ears, but I don't hear anything else. With a sense of unease, I hurry to get dressed.

My still-damp skin makes getting dressed twice as hard, but eventually, I manage to maneuver myself into a pair of black leggings and a hoodie. Not wanting to waste time putting my sneakers on, I grab them in my free hand after shoving my towel and swimsuit into my bag. I hurry to the door, where I know Crew is waiting just outside.

I reach for the handle, almost convinced I've spooked myself, when a hand comes out of nowhere and covers my mouth, and I'm yanked back against a hard body.

"I don't want to hurt you. I just need you to answer some questions for me," the rough, unfamiliar voice says.

Fear is blanking my mind, making it almost impossible to think. When I kick out and my toes connect with the wall, the pain snaps me out of it. I wrap my gift around him like a blanket and gently push remorse into him.

He holds on, but I feel his aggressive stance loosen. When my breath hitches, I push empathy and panic into him. I'm turned around and pulled against his chest as the strange man tries to comfort me. Oddly bemused now that I have the upper hand, I pull back, happy he lets me. I frown when I stare up into the handsome but battered face of a man that's vaguely familiar, though I'm sure we've never met.

"Who are you, and what do you want?"

"Do Wilder and Crew know what you are?"

"How do you know Wilder and Crew?"

"I'm Apex."

"No, you're not. I've met everyone—" I suck in a sharp breath. "You're in the photos at the house. Hendrix?"

His expression shutters before his jaw locks, and he shakes his head.

"Nash," I whisper as I feel grief pouring out of him in a wave that threatens to drown us both.

I soothe him instinctively, smoothing out the jagged edges of his pain enough so that he can process it without it bringing him to his knees. He sucks in a ragged breath as I lift my hand and place it against his swollen cheek.

"We heard about the explosion. They haven't given up hope, but they've been so worried about you both. Everyone has."

I move to grab the door, but he stops me with his hand on my wrist.

"I can't," he grits out.

"I don't understand. Can't what? Crew's right outside the door. Let him help you."

"He can't help me. Not yet anyway. But you can."

"How? What happened? And where's Hendrix?"

His pain crashes into me again, making me stagger back. I reach for it and draw some of it away until I feel like my flesh is being stripped from my bones. I shake my head, knowing what he's going to say before he says it.

"Hendrix is dead."

I cover my mouth with my hand. I might not have met the man, but I know his death is going to destroy all the Apex members and their families.

"We were compromised. I didn't see it until it was too late. Hendrix was inside when the building blew. I had gone outside to —" He hesitates, his jaw tight, as he squeezes his hands into fists. "The blast threw me over a small stone wall, and it acted like a shield."

His face pales. For a second, I worry he's going to pass out, but he shakes the memory off and focuses back on me.

"I waited for the fire to burn out before searching for him. If anyone could have found a way to protect himself, it was Hendrix, you know? But there was nothing there. The fire burned too hot. It incinerated everything, leaving nothing behind but ash."

Barely refraining from throwing up, I look into his desolate eyes as his mind drifts between then and now.

"The fire... It was too hot and burned too fast. I can't explain it. I just know it wasn't right. It just felt... wrong." He gets frustrated, unable to explain it to me better, but ice starts forming in my veins at his words.

He must see something in my eyes because he nods solemnly. "Someone started that fire, did something to feed it until it was a ball of chaos and energy that exploded."

"You're not talking about an arsonist, are you?"

He shakes his head.

"You think a pyrokinetic started it," I whisper, my mind flashing back to a teenage boy I once knew. He had been fourteen, five years older than me, when he'd come to the Division. He'd been so fucking angry that being around him was almost painful. I'd tried to help him, but his anger was like his gift—a flame that never truly went out. I was able to dampen his rage for a while, but my gift was weaker back then. Eventually, his rage burned out of control. He'd been at the Division for six weeks before he disappeared. There was no panic over the missing child, so I assumed he'd been moved because of the damage he caused.

It looks like the Division found a way to take that hostile boy and use his anger to forge him into a formidable weapon.

"You know someone," he states.

"I knew someone a long time ago. His name was Jimmy. I don't know his last name. I'm sorry." I frown as I remember something else. "There was only one person he cared about, and that was his sister, Kate."

Nash freezes, not a single muscle moving. His breathing saws in and out of him like he can't get enough air. I thrust a wave of calm at him and see him relax a fraction.

"Was she gifted?" he asks through gritted teeth.

I nod slowly. "She was younger than him by three years. I can't remember the technical term for her gift, but they called her a siren. There was something about her that was alluring to men, and some women too. It was disturbing because she was only a child at the time, and it was obvious it was uncomfortable for her. Everyone wanted to talk to her and touch her. She left with Jimmy, and not because family means anything to the Division but because Kate acted as a sort of anchor to him. She was the only one who could rein him in. But even at nine, I knew it wouldn't last. It was like putting a Band-Aid on a bullet hole. Jimmy was destined to self-destruct and probably take his sister down with him."

"I think she had more control than you realized. Either that, or she grew into it."

"How do you know that?"

"Because Hendrix and I have been seeing a woman named Kate. She arranged for us to meet her brother on the day of the explosion. She was the reason I was outside instead of in the house with Hendrix. I'd gone after her because we'd argued. Only when I reached her, she was crying. She said she was sorry, that they were just following orders. That's when the house exploded, and I was knocked unconscious. By the time I came around, she was gone."

"Oh my God, Nash, I'm sorry. This is all my fault."

"No. We'd been seeing Kate for almost a year. We just had no idea she was gifted, but it's obvious now she was a plant."

"A sleeper agent," I murmur.

"What?"

"I've heard whispers that the Division works in similar ways to a terrorist organization. They have sleepers in place all over the world, working regular jobs, living in regular houses. Some have partners and families. But once activated, they do whatever they were ordered to do. Even if that means sacrificing themselves, though knowing the Division, they'd only do that as a last resort." Nobody wanted to lose valuable operatives if possible.

"We met her just after we got Oz and Zig back, when Salem came into our lives."

"And they triggered her and activated her brother because I defected." I swallow the bile in my throat.

"I told you; this isn't your fault. This is on me. I should have seen through her, should have figured it out somehow. If I had, Hendrix might still be alive."

"No. If it's not my fault, then it's not yours either. Let's put the blame where it deserves, on the Division."

He drops his head, his shoulders heavy, as he takes my words and brushes them away. It's still too fresh for him to feel anything other than guilt.

"I have to go. Don't tell the others you saw me."

"I have to tell them. They're worried sick."

"You can't. Not until I know for sure that we weren't sold out."

"Apex would never do that to you!" I say defensively.

"Once upon a time, I believed that too. But then Cooper betrayed us."

I shut my mouth. I knew who Cooper was and knew what he'd done, but my history with the man was different from theirs. To them, he was the teammate, friend, and brother who turned on them. In actuality, Cooper was part of the Division. The fact that he was able to feel those bonds was a miracle when most of his humanity had been hammered out of him. It was because of them that he met his wife, a woman he loved so much he blew his cover for her and sold out the very people he came to care about.

The last few times I'd seen Cooper, he had been a shell of himself. I think part of him had died with his wife's terminal cancer diagnosis.

"I'm really good at reading people's emotions if I let myself," I admit. "I'm telling you this because I'd trust everyone at Apex with my life, or I never would have left my kids there."

He considers my words before his voice cracks. "I hope to God you're right, but I have to be sure. Until then, I need you to promise me you'll stay quiet."

I don't want to lie to anyone, not when I know how worried they are.

"Have you told them what you can do?"

"They saw me save Bella when she fell from the playset you guys bought for the kids. They know."

He crowds closer to me. "I'm not talking about your telekinesis. I'm talking about the empathic gift you got from your daddy."

Everything in me revolts at the fact that he knows. "How is that possible? Nobody knows that, not even my father," I whisper, feeling myself start to shake.

"It's genetic isn't it? Still I wasn't one hundred percent sure until you started using it on me."

A tear runs down my face as my cheeks burn with shame.

He swipes the tear with his thumb, his expression tight. "You didn't hurt me. You helped me. I know that because I can breathe without it feeling like I'm inhaling shards of glass, and that's all I've felt since Hendrix died. But you could hurt me if you wanted to, couldn't you?" he asks me softly, tucking a strand of wet hair behind my ear.

"I would never hurt anyone unless they were hurting me or someone I care about."

"But you could."

Giving in, I nod.

"You kept it a secret from the Division? Not even your father knows?"

I shake my head. "I'll never let them turn me into a weapon. I won't become what he is."

He cocks his head, considering me. "You're right. You're nothing like him. You keep my secret, and I'll keep yours. I have a feeling that the fate of all of us might rest in your hands."

I stumble back when he lets me go and disappears around the

side of the lockers. By the time I right myself and follow him, he's gone. The only sign he was here at all is the open window.

I turn and head back to the door, swallowing around the boulder-sized lump in my throat. When the door opens, I jump a foot in the air.

Crew looks at me and smirks. "Jumpy little thing." His expression turns serious when he sees my face. "What's wrong?"

"Nothing. I'm just feeling a bit off, plus I have a headache."

"You're not coming down with something, are you?" He walks closer and places the back of his hand against my forehead.

"I'm probably just tired. It's been a rough few days, plus I miss the kids, you know?" I stick as much to the truth as I can because lying to them makes me feel like shit. It's bad enough that I'm hiding my true gift from them. If they find out I know about Nash and Hendrix, they'll never forgive me.

Chapter Twenty-Eight

Crew

I look over at her again as she sleeps soundly against Wilder's shoulder.

"Okay, spill. What's going on with you?"

I look up at Wilder and see him scowling at me.

"Something's off with Lara."

"She doesn't feel well. Of course, something is off with her."

"Yeah," I answer, focusing back on the road. I'd probably be sick of all this driving if it wasn't for Lara. Waking up with her sandwiched between us has made me look at things with rose-colored glasses. Yeah, this might not have been the way I pictured us being with her, but I'm not stupid enough to not seize the opportunity we've been given. The problem is something's wrong with Lara, and I don't think it has anything to do with her being tired or having a headache.

She was fine this morning, wasn't she? Or maybe I just saw

what I wanted to. Shit, did we hurt her? Scare her in some way? She said we didn't, but maybe she was just telling us what we wanted to hear. We tried to be gentle with her, wanting her first time to be memorable for all the right reasons, but maybe we made it memorable for all the wrong ones. I knew we'd gotten carried away. I underestimated the effect she'd have on me. I'd seen the lingering bruises on her body when I'd watched her in the pool. I'd felt oddly proud seeing them, like some primal part of my brain was relieved I'd marked her so every other man out there would recognize that she was mine.

Now, though, I'm questioning everything.

As if sensing where my thoughts have gone, he lowers his voice a fraction.

"You think we were too rough with her?"

"I don't know what I'm thinking. All I know is when I went into the changing room to get her, she didn't look ill. She looked upset and maybe a little afraid."

He's quiet for a minute.

"Of us? You think we did something last night that frightened her?"

"That's what I've been trying to figure out. On one hand, it makes sense, yet on the other, it doesn't quite fit. She isn't pulling away from us. If she was scared, I don't think she'd fall asleep on your shoulder."

We are both quiet, lost in thought over what could be wrong with our girl, when I spot a black SUV four cars behind ours. "We've got a tail."

"You sure?"

I nod. "Third time I've seen it now. How do you want to play this?"

"Keep the same speed, but let's outmaneuver these assholes."

"Alright. Stay on the freeway or get off?"

"See if you can put a few more cars between us without it looking obvious, and then take the next exit. As much as I'd like to think they won't do anything with so many witnesses, we know they have no regard for anyone but themselves. The last thing we want to do is get in a high-speed chase and cause an accident. At least if we get somewhere quieter, we can fire at them if necessary."

I keep driving, one eye on the road, one eye on the rearview mirror, watching the SUV. When I pass the car in front of us and change lanes to overtake the next, I notice them speed up behind me.

"Not sure putting distance between us is going to be an option unless we give up the pretense and speed up."

"Just keep going as you are for the minute," Wilder answers as he nudges Lara. "Lara, I need you to wake up for me."

She opens her eyes and takes a second to orientate herself before she turns to look up at Wilder. "Huh?"

Despite the situation, I chuckle. She really is adorable when she wakes up.

"We're being followed. I want you to climb into the back with Rufio, buckle yourself in, and keep your head down."

"Shit," she curses, the last traces of sleep vanishing in an instant.

I move my eyes back to the SUV to make sure they aren't any closer. Thankfully, they're not. The last thing we need is them ramming us while Lara has her seat belt off.

She wastes no time, leaving her questions for later. She flings herself over the seat and straps herself in next to Rufio, who sits next to her—awake and alert, like he senses the danger.

"Alright, I'm getting off the freeway. Hold onto Rufio, Lara, and keep your head down in case these assholes get trigger-happy."

She ducks down and grabs hold of the dog. I focus on the task at hand and, at the last minute, cut across two lanes to get off the road, ignoring the angry honking from behind us. I keep my eye on the SUV, but it looks like they weren't quick enough to take the same exit.

"Looks like we've lost them for now, but they'll just get off at the next exit. It won't give us a chance to get far."

"I'm chipped. My father had a tracking device implanted in my arm. They'll be able to find me anywhere," Lara tells us.

"We know, baby." I hear her sharp intake of breath.

"You know? How? I just found out. Wait. Did you know all along?"

"No. Ev found it in your file after you left."

"Oh."

"We just need to get far enough away—"

"What if, instead of being hunted, we hunt them for a change?" she says, cutting me off. "You only saw one car, right?

"Fuck that, Lara. Don't ask us to put you in danger because that'll never happen," I snap at her.

"I'm always in danger, Crew. Don't you get that? My father will keep coming for me."

"You're always saying he doesn't love you, but if that's the case, why come for you at all?"

Her eyes meet mine in the rearview mirror.

"It's not love. Don't get me wrong, he has the capacity to feel it.

He's not a psychopath. Though sometimes I think it would be easier if he were. As an empath, he is one of the strongest of the gifted people ever to be born. But imagine feeling everything all the time. Not just your own feelings, but everyone else's within a mile radius. Now imagine years of that—a relentless beating at your senses that takes and takes and gives nothing back—until, eventually, you're left with only a few options. You can crack and lose what's left of your mind, maybe find yourself in a padded cell muttering to yourself. Or you could make it stop. A bullet to the brain will stop it in an instant."

"That's it? A bullet or a straitjacket?" Wilder turns to look at Lara, but I'm still thinking over her words.

Her father is, without a doubt, an asshole. But even I can't help but feel a little sympathy for the man.

"The only way to stop hurting is to stop feeling."

"That doesn't just apply to empaths, Lara."

"No, but take every ounce of pain, grief, fear, and self-loathing you've ever felt and magnify it by a thousand," she says, and we're all quiet. I can't imagine what that's like.

After a few minutes, she sighs. "Being an empath isn't as rare as you think. A lot of people have low-level empathic gifts. Most will be completely oblivious to it because their gift lies in soothing the psyche of others. Some, though, are able to manifest their gifts in other ways."

"You're talking about influencing people."

"Yes. An empath can soothe the jagged edges of grief, ease the sting of heartbreak, and dull the embers of rage. My father can take that one step further and manipulate people to feel things he wants them to. So he can make a calm person angry or make a shy person get up on a table and dance."

Wilder nods his head.

Lara swallows. "Or he can make a preacher place a gun against a child's head and pull the trigger if he really wants to. It all depends on which emotions and suggestions he plays with."

"Fucking hell."

"And he'll never be found guilty, even if he's caught on video, because all anyone would see is someone else pulling the trigger."

"That's it, isn't it? That's what tipped him over the edge," Wilder says, making me wonder what I missed.

"That's my guess, yeah."

"What is? I ask confused.

"That once he realized that he could literally do anything and get away with it, he embraced it and did the worst thing an empath can do."

She looks out the window and absently strokes Rufio's fur. "He severed the thread."

"He what?" I look at Wilder to see if he gets what she's saying.

"He shut off his emotions?" Wilder guesses.

"Shutting something off implies it can be turned back on again," she says, looking back at us with a look I can't decipher before pursing her lips, like she's trying to think of how to explain.

"Imagine a piece of thread. Now, imagine that thread is pulled and yanked a million times. Sometimes it frays, sometimes it becomes knotted, but it's always there, and it never gives. Some might look at it as a lifeline, a tether to the here and now. But my father saw it as a chain, keeping him captive."

"So he broke it," I murmur.

"Yeah, but not the thread to his gift. His gift is a part of him. Its woven into his DNA. He would never stop being gifted unless he had a brain injury or disease affected it somehow. No, he didn't sever his gift, he blocked his ability to feel his own emotions. He dulls them down to nothing and feeds purely on the emotions of others."

"But isn't that what caused him to lose his mind to begin with?" Wilder frowns.

"He found a loophole. He manipulates people's feelings so he only feels what he wants to."

"So everyone around him is a puppet?" Jesus, that's fucked up.

"In a way, yeah, but the thing is, emotions are an integral part of our humanness, and humans weren't made to only feel certain ones. Pain, fear, love, heartbreak, shame, remorse, guilt—they teach us how to overcome, how to adapt and learn, how to thrive and survive. They teach us how to sympathize and empathize and how to forgive. By cutting off his ability to feel his true emotions he can't empathize anymore..." her voice trails off.

I suck in a deep breath as the implications become clear.

"What's an empath who doesn't feel empathy?"

"Very fucking dangerous."

"You said he wasn't a psychopath. But isn't the absence of empathy and remorse what defines a psychopath?"

"I don't think psychopath is a strong enough word for what my father is. He's shut down his emotions, but like I said, that doesn't stop him from playing with other people's. He thinks he's God, and the rest of us are merely his playthings."

She's quiet after the discussion about her dad. Sensing that she needs time to emotionally recover, Wilder and I don't bother her with the million questions we both have. We drive through the night, me and Wilder taking turns while Lara sleeps, on and off, before we finally decide to stop.

Ev sent the details for a rental property that belongs to an associate. It's just been cleaned after the previous tenants left, ready to go back on the rental market, but they are more than happy to let us use it for a few days.

As we pull up, Wilder lets out a pained noise. "A cornfield, really? Does Ev not watch horror movies? Nothing good ever happens when a cornfield's involved."

"What are you talking about? It's just a field." Lara laughs, and it's the first time she's relaxed since her swim.

Wilder counts using his fingers. "You say that now. But just you wait until we get attacked by a cult of demonic children, a scarecrow who comes back every twenty-three years, or a group of hostile aliens that leave crop circles to terrorize us."

I turn to look at him as Lara covers her mouth to smother her laughter. "I think you might want to stick to cartoons for a while."

"Oh, sure, laugh it up now. But don't come crying to me when Freddy and Jason come chasing after you."

"Freddy and Jason? Are they cats or something?" Lara asks innocently, but I catch her eye and know she's fucking with him. Now that she's eighteen and I'm not freaking out about her age so much, that doesn't mean lines like that don't make me feel old.

Wilder grabs his chest like he's been mortally wounded. "I don't even know who you are anymore," he grumbles before opening his door and climbing out.

As soon as he slams the door closed, Lara lets out the laugh she'd been holding back. "Is he serious?" she asks through her giggles.

I like seeing her like this after how down she's been. For that alone, I'd kiss the fuck out of Wilder if I swung that way.

"We all have our things."

She chuckles some more as she unfastens her seat belt. "I can't quite figure out if he likes horror movies or if he's scared of them."

"Honestly, I think it's a bit of both. He was teased as a kid for being scared of them, so he did a sort of exposure therapy. Now he can watch them without screaming like a girl. I think he even likes them to a degree. But I swear he's watched so many they've fried his brain." I get out and open Lara's door. Rufio jumps out first, and I offer Lara my hand, which she takes as she climbs out.

Wilder is standing a foot away from the cornfield with his hands on his hips, staring at nothing as the breeze stirs the field. We both walk over to him as Rufio sniffs around.

"Horror setting aside, it's kind of peaceful here," Lara says, looking across the field that stretches out before us.

Wilder lets out a long-suffering sigh, which has me looking over at Lara with a conspiratorial wink.

"I suppose it could always be worse," he agrees.

I nod and head toward the house. "Like a cabin in the woods."

"Or an underground bunker," Lara adds.

I look over my shoulder at her and grin as Wilder follows behind us.

"A haunted house," I throw out.

"An abandoned insane asylum." Lara grins.

"Ooh, that's a classic."

Wilder huffs, but he's not hiding his amusement. "You guys suck."

"Nah, that's a different kind of movie altogether," Lara jokes before she squeals and finds herself tossed over his shoulder.

"Put me down, you ass," she yells.

I look for the hidden key under the fake rock. With how out of the way the house is, I'm surprised they bothered to even lock it at all. Most people don't when they live in the middle of butt-fuck nowhere.

"Nope. I don't think I will. Not until I know you're sorry."

She's quiet for a moment. Too quiet.

I bite my lip, knowing Little Miss Troublemaker is far from remorseful.

"Fine."

"You're sorry?"

"Enough to sing for you."

I open the door with a cough to hide my amusement. "Really?" he asks.

"Yep. Are you ready?"

"Hit me with it," Wilder grins and looks smug as hell as he walks past me into the house.

Lara looks up at me with a grin before she starts singing, adopting a creepy little girl voice. *"One, two, Freddie's coming for you."*

He tosses her on the sofa, making her laugh as he stands over her. "You are evil," he complains before popping open the button on his jeans. Her laugh cuts off immediately.

"Fortunately, I have just the thing to keep you quiet."

Chapter Twenty-Nine

Lara

"Take your top off," Crew orders as I sit up.

I reach for the hem of my T-shirt and tug it up over my head and toss it aside.

"Bra, too," he orders as Wilder shoves his jeans down his thighs and strokes his cock.

"You going to let me fuck your mouth, Lara?" Wilder asks with a husky edge to his voice.

I nod, then remember his words from the other night. "Yes, I want to taste you."

He growls and steps forward, slipping one hand into my hair while the other guides his cock to my lips.

I open my mouth and let him in, relishing his groan of delight as I close my mouth around him.

"Fuck me, I fantasized about this a million times, but this is better than I imagined," he admits.

Crew steps closer so he can get a better look, but he doesn't touch me. He just watches as his best friend's cock slides in and out of my mouth.

I feel myself getting wet. Crew's eyes on us are only making things ten times hotter. I moan around Wilder, making him curse. His thrusts become more erratic, and his hand tightens in my hair to the point of pain, but not enough to aggravate the bump on the back of my head.

"I'm not gonna last much longer. It's too good. I feel like I've died and gone to heaven."

I hum in response, which seems to be his undoing.

"You going to swallow my cum, Lara?"

I nod my consent and feel him push forward and hold.

"Fuck, fuck." He shoots cum down my throat, and I won't lie, I have to focus on not gagging. It's not the most pleasant-tasting experience of my life. But it's not the worst, either. Besides, I like the way I feel when Wilder gives himself over to me.

When he pulls out, I suck in a deep breath and wipe my swollen lips.

"Thank you," he rumbles, bending down to kiss me gently before he's yanked away.

"Are you too sore to take me?" Crew asks as he strips out of his clothes and sits on the sofa beside me.

"I'm a little tender, but I can handle it." I don't know if that's the truth, but only an idiot would turn down a ride on Crew's pogo stick.

"Good. You just tell me if it's too much, and I'll stop."

I nod and get to my feet, moving to stand in front of him.

"Wilder, take the rest of her clothes off."

Wilder doesn't protest. He just drops to his knees behind me and eases my leggings and wet panties down over my hips. When they reach my ankles, I step out of them after kicking off my sneakers.

"I want you on top of me so you can set the pace."

I bite my lip. "I'm not sure what I'm doing," I warn him, placing my hands on his shoulders to steady myself as I straddle him. Once I'm ready, I take a deep breath and lower myself gingerly down his cock. Oh, God.

"Jesus fuck, you feel amazing. Just do what feels good."

"It all feels good," I admit. Even the twinge of pain from the pounding I took yesterday. Using my knees, I start to move, slowly bouncing up and down on his cock.

I jolt when I feel hands on me and tip my head. Wilder looks down at me with a fierce look of concentration as he tweaks one of my nipples with his left hand and strums my clit with the other.

"Oh my God, it's too much."

"You want to stop?" Crew asks, but I shake my head.

"No, God, don't stop. I just... I need..." Crap, I don't know what I need. Lucky for me, Wilder seems to know.

"I think she needs a helping hand."

Crew grins at me before grabbing my hips, helping to guide and steady my movements.

"Oh, Jesus. Oh, God."

"I never knew you were so religious," Wilder teases.

But I'm only vaguely aware of it as something coils tightly inside me. Suddenly, it bursts free, and I come, pleasure coursing through my body as my pussy squeezes Crew hard enough to make him curse.

"Oh fuck, condom," Crew groans before he pulls his cock from my still-spasming pussy and comes all over my stomach.

"That was close," he says, pushing a piece of my hair behind my ear. "You make me lose my damn mind."

I smile at his admission.

"I almost said, fuck it. I find I really like the idea of you round with my kid."

I bite my lip because I already have kids, and they need to be my priority for now.

"Someday?" he asks, sensing my hesitation.

I grin. "Someday."

I sit on the porch, looking out at the field, letting the peacefulness wash over me. Sometimes my life feels like one giant ball of chaos. If I didn't take the time to enjoy the simple things, I'd go insane. Or maybe I already have. The more I think about bringing the fight to me, the more I'm convinced it's the right move. I just don't know how to get the guys to agree.

Rufio lifts his head to look at me, like he can tell what I'm thinking.

"What do you think, boy? Should we keep running, or should we set a trap?"

He rests his head against my leg.

"You're the strong, silent type, huh?" I sigh and lean back.

I think about Nash and what he's doing. If he's safe or if he's going to get himself killed like Hendrix. If I tell Wilder and Crew about my gift, then Nash will have nothing to hold over me, and I can tell them he's alive, and—I shake my head. I can't tell them yet, not after explaining just how lethal my father is. They'd see me the same way, and they'd be right to. I'm every bit as deadly as he is, perhaps even more so. Unlike my father, my gift doesn't drain me. Not like when I use my telekinesis. Using my gift is as simple as breathing. Maybe it's because I've learned how to turn it off and on at will. All the things that caused my father's brain to crack under the stress are irrelevant to me because my brain's wired differently. I have the flow of emotions in and out, but I can turn them off when I need to as well, and that makes all the difference. The irony is that I probably picked up the ability by hiding my gift from him all these years.

I finish my drink, lost in thought, as I absently stroke Rufio's head.

I turn my head when I hear the door open behind me. I look over my shoulder as a sleep-ruffled Crew walks out and hands me his cell phone.

"It's for you."

Tentatively, I take it from him and hold it to my ear. "Hello?"

"You have some explaining to do, young lady," Oz's deep voice says down the phone. I don't know why it sets me off. Maybe it's the lack of anger in his voice or the memory of him buying me books, but I burst into tears, crying so hard I can't get my words out.

"What the fuck?" Crew grabs the phone from me and starts yelling into it. "What did you say to her?"

Crew looks at me before his shoulders slump. "No, I can't just tell her to stop crying. When in the history of women crying has that ever worked?"

He listens to whatever else Oz says before rubbing his temple. "No, Oz, you didn't break her."

More silence as I finally manage to get my tears under control.

"She misses you. She misses everyone. I think hearing your voice just—" He pauses. "Yeah."

He looks at me, tucking a strand of hair behind my ear. "You good to talk to him, or do you want me to get him to call you back?"

"I'm okay." My breath hitches in my chest, but I manage to keep myself together.

He hands me the phone and takes a seat beside me. Rufio, not liking that he's not the center of my attention anymore, walks over to Crew so he can pet him.

"Lara?" Oz's voice is softer this time.

"I'm here. I'm sorry." I blow out a breath before the tears can take hold of me again.

"What you did... I should shake some goddamn sense into you."

"I had to go, Oz. It was the only way for me to keep you all safe."

"I understand why you did what you did, Lara, but you're just as important as anyone else here. You're family too."

I swallow hard at his words and listen to him sigh.

"As mad as I am, I get it. I'm bone-headed enough to do some-thing just as stupid too," he admits, making me laugh. "That's better. I don't like making the ladies cry. I have a rep to protect, you know."

"You have a woman who loves you and a baby you adore. You have zero rep to protect."

"You're just as mean as your sister. I'll have you know it was my giant personality that won Salem over."

"Actually, it was his giant—" Salem's shouted words become muffled, like someone has covered her mouth.

I chuckle, missing them more than ever. But hearing them settles something inside me.

"Behave, woman," he growls, but I realize he's talking to Salem, not me.

"You guys remember I'm on the phone, right? I don't want to listen to you having sex."

There's some arguing and jostling, and then I hear a different voice on the line.

"Lara? Are you okay?"

I smile through my pain. "Yeah, Greg, I'm okay."

"Good, because when you get home, you are so fucking grounded."

I laugh. "I'm eighteen now, Greg. You can't ground me."

"Watch me. Young'ins today, with so much attitude." He sighs. "And so much courage," he adds quietly. "I hate that you felt you had to do this, but I get it. I can be pissed and proud at the same time, though. I just want you home safe."

He's quiet for a second before speaking again. "How are Crew and Wilder holding up with the news about Nash and Hendrix?"

The ball of guilt threatens to choke me, with the lie tasting like ash on my tongue.

"They're hanging in there, just waiting for news," I whisper. At that moment, I know I have to tell them the truth. I'm worried about Nash, and though he trusted me to stay quiet, I owe it to Wilder and Crew to put them first.

"Just be there for them. It's all you can do right now. The news coming in... well, it's not looking good."

"I'm sorry, Greg," I murmur. And I am, more than he'll ever know.

"I know. Me too. They're good men. We all know the risks.

What we do isn't for the faint of heart, but we sign up for the job with our eyes open. It's not the ones we lose, though, that have to deal with the fallout. It's the ones left behind. And fuck, I'm so sick of losing people."

"I know, but I won't be one of them. I'll come back." I make him a promise I have no business making, but it strengthens my resolve. I think part of me hadn't realized until now that I'd prepared myself for the worst-case scenario: that I wasn't surviving this. My father might not kill me, though with how much he's changed, there is no guarantee of that anymore. But I don't trust myself enough not to do something radical. I can't go back to being caged when I've only just gotten to taste freedom.

"How are The Lost Ones?"

"Missing you like crazy, but they know you're okay and that Crew and Wilder will keep you safe, he tells me softly.

"I miss them too. I couldn't risk my father getting anywhere near them. Not again. They're strong kids, but they've been through enough."

"You're a good mama, even if it's a job you should never have been given."

"They never felt like a job. I'm not forced to love them, Greg. I give them that freely, and I know they love me back."

"We all tend to find family in the most unlikely of places."

I hear grumbling in the background. "Quit hogging her, old man."

"Old man, my ass," Greg complains. "I've gotta go. The boss wants to talk to you. Take care of each other, and we'll see you soon."

"Bye," I whisper as the phone is handed off.

"Lara?" Zig's warm voice makes me bite my lip. God, these

guys are killing me. How did I go from having no one to having such a huge family? "Thank you."

I sit up straighter, confused. "What? Why are you thanking me?"

"You kept the kids safe. My boy was a target before he ever left his mother's womb. And you stopped him from becoming one again."

"I don't know if that's true. He might come back and use them to draw me out, or he might just hurt you all to punish me. I feel like I can't do anything right. No matter the decisions I make, someone is bound to get hurt."

"You bought us time, Lara. Time we might not have had before. The kids are prepared and know what to do and where to go if there is an emergency. We have this whole place on lock-down, and Ev is scouring the files on the flash drive for information we can use to bring this to an end once and for all, but there are so many to go through, and we don't have the time."

"What kind of information?"

"Places your father and the other top-ranking men might hide out. If they have a secondary facility. Who their contacts are, and how much firepower they have at their disposal. Even people who you think are loyal to him and whether or not they are gifted—and if so, what those gifts are. There is a lot of info on the flash drive, but half of it is in code that will take time to break."

"I can send you everything I know. I'm not sure how useful it will be. I'm sure he'll have anticipated me spilling my guts."

"I'm not so sure. He strikes me as the kind of man who believes he's untouchable. He'll think you'll keep his secrets because you're his daughter, forgetting that loyalty isn't something you inherit through blood. It's something you earn through kindness. And for an empath, he sure as hell fucked up with you."

I huff out a snort of amusement. "You're not wrong there. I'd better go. I need to talk to the guys about something. Can you say hi to everyone for me? Tell them I'm sorry and that I miss them."

"Will do. Just remember, this isn't forever. You'll be back with us before you know it, only this time you'll do it without having to look over your shoulder."

I nod. "Thanks, Zig. I'll talk to you soon. Stay safe."

"Always. And the same goes double for you."

He hangs up, so I hand the phone back to Crew, and taking a deep breath, I gather up my courage to continue.

"I need to talk to you and Wilder about something."

"Okay. Do you want me to wake Wilder up, or can it wait a while?"

As much as I'd love to put this whole conversation off, I know I'll chicken out if I don't do it soon. "Now would be good, if that's alright."

He stands up. "I'll go get him. I won't be long."

He presses a kiss against my forehead, and I close my eyes, savoring it as I send up a silent prayer that it's not my last one after they find out the truth about what I've been hiding from them.

Chapter Thirty

Wilder

Crew smacks me in the head with a pillow, making me bolt upright and reach for my gun.

"Lara wants to talk to us."

"I could have shot you in the face. I still might," I snap when he yanks the blanket off me.

"Just get your ass out of bed. I don't know what's going on, but she looks pretty fucking freaked."

I look at him for a second and frown before climbing out of bed and heading to the bathroom.

I take care of business and wash up before pulling on a pair of jeans and a faded black t-shirt.

Walking out into the kitchen, I smile at Lara as she walks in from outside and takes the coffee mug Crew offers her.

She takes a sip as she sits at the table. If I wasn't watching her so closely, I would have missed the slight tremble of her hands.

I look at Crew and frown. "What's going on?"

"She spoke to Oz, Zig, and Greg."

"What did they say?" I ask, but he just shrugs.

"Not sure. One minute they were talking, and now she looks like she's about to have a nervous breakdown."

"You know I'm still here, right?" Lara snaps.

"Yeah, we know. So tell us what's wrong."

She clamps her mouth shut and looks down at her mug.

"Talk to us."

She gets to her feet, leaving her cup on the table. She walks to the window and wraps her arms around herself.

"I have two things to tell you. One is my secret. One is someone else's. I'm telling you both because I think you should know. If you hate me afterward, I'll understand. It will hurt like hell, but I'll get it. No matter what, I'd never be able to remember you without remembering how happy you made me, even if it was just for a little while."

"I know you're stalling. We literally buried a body for you. Whatever it is can't be that bad."

She bites her lip, tears in her eyes.

"Lara," Crew soothes, but she shakes her head.

"Nash came to me when we were at the swimming pool."

I stand frozen in shock. "What?"

"Nash is alive. But, and I'm so fucking sorry to be the one to tell you this, Hendrix didn't make it."

"I don't understand. Why hasn't he come to us? He doesn't even know you," Crew questions, his voice sharp.

"He wanted confirmation of something." She runs her fingers through her hair.

"The explosion started as a fire. A fire that burned too hot, too fast. He wanted to know if I knew of anyone with that gift."

"And do you?"

She nods. "When I was a kid, there was a boy who wielded fire. He and his sister were at the Division before they were both moved somewhere else."

"The Division killed Hendrix?" Crew snarls.

"Nash thinks so. The woman they were seeing, we think, was the pyrokinetic's sister. She had the gift of allure."

"Was she sent to target Nash and Hendrix?"

"It seems like it."

"Did you know?" Crew asks, his voice barely above a whisper.

"No, of course not."

"But Nash came to you, not us," he states, anger and hurt in his tone. I almost step in and tell him to cool it, but I'm still in shock.

"I told you. He came to ask me if I knew a firestarter."

"Why didn't you tell us? Why all the secrecy? You knew how worried we were."

She swallows. "He asked me not to. He doesn't understand how he and Hendrix were targeted. Until he can get the answers he's looking for, he doesn't know who he can trust."

"He can trust us. We're his fucking brothers," I snarl.

"Cooper and James betrayed Apex, and now his best friend is dead. He's grieving and not thinking clearly."

I scrub my hand down my face.

"You still should have told us. Hendrix might have been his best friend, but he wasn't just his. Hendrix was ours too, and we deserved to know."

"I know. I'm sorry. I told him I didn't want to keep it from

274

either of you, but he insisted. And when I still said no, he black-mailed me."

"What exactly is he blackmailing you over?" Crew asks as I watch Lara, who is desperately trying to make herself seem smaller.

"He knows about my gift and threatened to tell you about it before I was ready to tell you myself."

"We already know about your telekinesis, so that's bullshit."

"That's my secondary gift. The one I inherited from my mother."

"Wait, you have two gifts?" I ask, thrown for a moment. It's been hard enough to get my head around the possibility of having a single gift, but the thought of people having more than one is more than my brain can handle.

"How many people have dual gifts?"

"Hardly any. It's incredibly rare to inherit both parents' gifts. Usually, a child will get the gift that is the strongest, though not always. I think since the Division's inception, there have been two recorded cases of dual gifts."

"Are you one of them?"

She shakes her head. "No. They're both dead. Avoiding burnout with one gift is hard enough, but trying to handle two..." She shakes her head. "As far as I know, I'm the only one with dual gifts right now, but you won't find me in any database. It stands to reason that there are others out there who hide the fact they are dual-gifted too."

"What's your second gift, Lara? Why hide it?" Crew folds his arm over his chest, but I've already figured it out.

"Gifts are inherited," I say slowly.

She looks at me, fear written in every line of her face, and nods.

"Jesus fuck. You have the same gift as your father." Crew curses.

She nods again, wrapping her arms around herself once more.

"Have you been manipulating us this whole time?" As soon as the words are out, I want to take them back. Her body jerks back like I've hit her, her pain so visceral it hurts to look at her. But I don't apologize because I need to know the truth.

She moves her gaze from mine to stare at Crew, waiting to see what his reaction will be.

"Just answer his question, Lara. We deserve that much."

"The fact that you even have to ask tells me everything I need to know," she whispers and moves to walk away, but I intercept her and grab her arm.

"Let go of me, or so help me God, I'll make you."

I release her and take a step back, not wanting to risk it now that I know what she's capable of.

"Look, let's just calm down a little. Tell us what you did, and we can work through it," Crew tells her softly. Fire flashes in her eyes. That was clearly not the right thing to say.

"What I did was fall in love with two idiots who don't deserve me." When I open my mouth to speak, she holds up her hand to stop me. "Nothing I say now matters. You won't believe what I say, and I don't trust that you'll have my best interests at heart now."

"We are men of our word," I bite out.

"Bullshit. Just leave me alone. I can't be in the same room as either of you right now."

"Fine, run away. It's what you do best, right?" Crew snarls.

She doesn't answer. She doesn't need to. She drops her head

like she's disappointed and heads to the bedroom, closing the door quietly behind her.

As silence blankets the room, I think I would have rather she'd stay. She should have screamed and shouted and slammed the door. How are we ever supposed to sort anything out when her go-to response is to walk away?

"Fucking hell, can you believe this?"

"Honestly, not much surprises me anymore."

Crew throws himself down in one of the armchairs, his elbows on his thighs and his head in his hands.

I walk over to where Lara was just standing and gaze out the window.

"Do you really think she manipulated the way we feel about her?"

I look over at Crew. Instead of answering with a knee-jerk reaction, I think back. "When we first met her, we were drawn to her, but she was standoffish, like she didn't know what to do with us. Then, when we found out who her father was and went off on her, she was pissed. But so were we. She sure as hell didn't use her gift on us then."

"No, it was talking to the guys and seeing her with the kids that made us think differently about her after that. She tried to stay away from us. We're the ones that tried to force a friendship with her, and then she left." Crew groans.

I close my eyes and realize Lara's right. We are idiots.

"After how we reacted to finding out who her father was, I can't say I blame her for not telling us what she can do. When I think back, I can't think of a time she's ever used her gifts—unless it was to calm down one of the children.

"She could have made us forgive her. She probably could have made us all forget that she was related to Penn altogether. She didn't strip our anger from us, even though it hurt her, and she didn't make us develop feelings for her. If anything, she tried to avoid us."

Crew sighs. "We just keep fucking this shit up."

"I think it was hearing about Nash and Hendrix. But still, it's not an excuse." Now it's my turn to sigh. "We're going to need to start coming up with creative ways to say sorry if we keep this up."

Crew nods.

"Let's give her some space. I'm not sure she'll listen to anything we say right now anyway."

"Fine. What about Hendrix and Nash? You think it's true? About Hendrix being dead, I mean?"

"Nash wouldn't leave him behind," I tell Crew softly, even though deep down he already knows this.

"We need to let the others know."

"I know. Maybe Ev can find a way to track him now that we know he's back in the States."

"If what Nash said about them being targeted by the Division is true..."

"Then we'll destroy them," I reply without hesitation. If the Division wants a war, then a war they shall get.

Chapter Thirty-One

Lara

I swipe angrily at my tears. I don't know why I'm crying. I knew they were going to act this way, but I guess a small part of me had hoped they wouldn't.

I look around the room we slept in last night, with me snuggled in the middle of the two men I'm falling hopelessly for. For a moment, I was happy. I knew, given the circumstances, it was weird to feel that way. But I learned early on, in a life filled with storms, to embrace every second of sunshine.

I knew telling them would pull the curtains on all that sunshine, but it was the right thing to do. Even though it hurts that they flung those words at me, I don't regret what I did. Part of me knows they have a right to be pissed. I would be in their place. But just because I understand, it doesn't make it any less painful.

I head into the bathroom and splash my face with cold water before staring at my reflection in the mirror. Is this my life now?

Running, hiding, and hurting people accidentally. How can anyone around me ever truly be safe? Nothing will ever change if I keep doing the same thing over and over again.

Crew's right. I do run when the going gets tough. I still stand by all the reasons I ran, but for once in my life, I want to fight instead of retreat.

I walk back into the bedroom and spot my bag on the far side of the room, next to both of theirs. I rummage through their bags, finding what I might need, including the hunting knife that they swiped from Giles and a small first aid kit, which I shove into my bag.

Blowing out a breath, I try to talk myself out of this crazy idea, knowing it'll probably fail. And yet, I can't keep doing nothing. Acting on instinct alone, I ignore all the voices in my head telling me to calm down and think this through, and gently slide the window up.

When I don't hear footsteps approaching, I drop the bag out the window before climbing out. I pull the bag up my arms and make sure it's secure before I look around, trying to decide the best route. I know I need to avoid the windows at the front of the house, or they'll see me. So I walk around the property, and after telling myself that everything will be fine, I head into the cornfield.

I wait until I am completely invisible to the house before I give a short whistle, knowing Rufio is lying on the porch in the sun. A few minutes later, I hear the jangle of his new collar as he looks for me.

"Come on, boy," I murmur. When he finds me, I drop to my knees and press my face to the top of his head. "Hey there, boy." I stand up and move farther into the field, confident that Rufio will follow.

Once I'm sure I've gone far enough, I slide the bag off and sit down. I dig around inside and pull out the hunting knife and the first aid kit. I open the kit and take out the surgical tape, a bandage, some gauze, and an alcohol wipe. Pushing my sleeve up, I clean the inside of my upper arm with the wipe before I feel for the raised lump under my skin.

Using the hunting knife, I cut into my arm, barely holding back a scream, and search around for the chip. I think I'm going to pass out, but I manage to keep it together. It's a lot harder than I thought it would be—the chip is so small, and my fingers are slick with blood.

In the end, I use my telekinesis to pull it out. Once I find it, I place it on my leg and clean my arm before I place some gauze over it. I wrap the bandage around my arm and hold it in place with some medical tape. I clean the chip using another wipe, then slip the chip behind Rufio's collar and hold it in place using more tape.

Once I'm done, I shove everything back into the bag and keep walking through the field. I don't know how long I've been gone or how far I've gotten, but I sense the change in the air when they realize I'm missing. I sit down and lean my head against Rufio, my breathing ragged as I try to decide what to do.

I've led the division on a wild goose chase so they'd stay far away from Apex. It's the only way to keep them away from the kids. But standing in that empty bedroom, I decided I was done running.

I just want to be me. The only way that will ever happen is if I accept myself first. That means no more hiding from my gift. No more making myself less to make everyone feel more comfortable.

So now I have a new plan, one that will probably piss off

everyone at Apex, and it comes with no guarantees of survival. It's a scary prospect with the probability that I might die when I've only just begun to live. But what kind of life am I going to have if all I can ever do is hide?

I get to my feet once more but stay low as I continue moving. I weave through the cornfield, double back, and start to head the way I came—just a little farther away from the house.

After a while, I hear voices. I pause, holding my breath for a moment, scared to move in case I give myself away.

"She's not here. Fuck, where is she?" I hear Crew's voice. He sounds agitated but mostly worried. I almost stand up and tell him where I am, but then they'd drag me back to the house, and we'd carry on with this stupid game of cat and mouse.

I keep low and quiet, listening to them talk to each other.

"Her bag's missing."

"Fuck!"

"Calm down. Maybe she headed toward that small town we passed on the way here."

"It's five miles from here, Wilder. That's a fuck of a walk."

"She's the most determined woman I've ever met, and we've hurt her. Trust me when I say five miles is nothing."

"I know. But why leave? Yeah, I made that crack about running, but she had to know we were just venting. Yes, we're pissed. We're allowed to be, but that doesn't suddenly change how we feel about her. Why the hell would she put herself in danger like this?"

"Maybe she's leading them away from us again or maybe she just thinks we're so mad that we won't want to be with her anymore. Hell, she might have left so that she doesn't have to stand here while we break her fucking heart. I keep forgetting that she has zero experience with relationships. Especially ones like ours. We're not easy men to love, Crew, but do we really need to make it so damn difficult?"

"It's not like we're doing it on purpose, but I agree that we're the ones with experience. So if we keep fucking up, how the hell can we expect Lara to get it right all the time when she's just figuring shit out?"

"Ugh, I wish I had a manual for this," Wilder complains, making me bite back a grin. Though my emotions feel pretty raw right now, I can tell they're just as confused about us as I am. There's comfort in that. I don't want to be the only person figuring it all out. I'd rather we do it together.

"A manual? Is there a how-to book for loving a woman who has been born and raised in captivity by a megalomaniac father? A woman who also raises kids that she never gave birth to and who loves two assholes like us when she could do better. And let's not forget who's half our age and has not just one, but two gifts," Crew snarks.

There's silence for a moment, and my mouth drops. I can't believe what I just heard. They love me. I don't have time to process the revelation right now, though.

"I'll admit, it seems unlikely that there's a book for that in the library," Wilder drawls, making me cover my mouth so I don't burst out laughing. "Come on, let's head into town. It's not far, and it's not too big that she'll go by unnoticed. If anyone there has seen her, we'll find out. Even better, if they have cameras, we can get Ev to hack them."

I tense at Crew's groan. "That means telling Ev we fucked up. He'll kick our asses."

"I have a feeling he'll have to get in line. I'm going to leave a note in case she comes back. I don't want her to think that we've left her."

"Good idea." I hear Crew say as they move away. "I can't believe she took the dog with her."

I look down at Rufio, who has his head cocked. Thankfully, he remains quiet.

"I'd rather she have him with her than be alone. Rufio might be a big softy, but I have a feeling he'd tear anyone to pieces if they tried to harm Lara."

I don't catch the rest of what they say, but I follow quietly behind them, being careful to keep my distance.

Staying out of sight, I watch as Wilder heads inside, presumably to leave a note before joining Crew, who's in the truck.

I wait for them to leave before I make my way back to the house. I jog up the steps and open the door. I head inside and find the note on the table—the pen he wrote it with right beside the paper.

I lift the note, my hand shaking as I read Wilder's cursive writing.

Lara, we've gone to the last town we went through to look for you. I'm sorry we got mad. Please give us a chance to talk shit out with you. We'll be back soon. Please wait for us.

I close my eyes and feel the dampness gathering behind my eyelids. They have no idea how much they've come to mean to me in such a short amount of time. How much I wish I could stay and let them keep rescuing me, but I can't. Sometimes, you have to rescue yourself.

I let my bag slip to the floor. I only took it so I could shove the knife and first aid kit inside of it. That, and to make them think I took it and ran. I need them away from here for the second part of my plan to work.

Because my father's men are drawing near, and I need to be ready. I don't know how I know that I just do.

I pick up the pen and write a note of my own before rummaging through the bag. I take my cell phone, the one Mallory gave me, which I've kept off all this time, and leave it on the counter before grabbing Crew's phone from where it's charging. A quick look tells me it's at fifty percent battery life, which will have to do.

Looking down at my clothes, I decide to change. I pull on a pair of jeans, a long-sleeved T-shirt, and a hoodie—that should do —then slip on my boots. I loosen the laces so there is some gaping around the ankle of one before shoving Crew's phone inside. I pull the laces tight, then roll my socks over the top of the boot to hide the gap the phone makes. I'm glad the jeans are bootcut, as I push down the legs and make sure they cover everything before standing up and looking around the room.

I can't risk taking a weapon. They'll most likely frisk me, though I can't imagine them being very thorough. To them, I am a weak child who has always done what I've been told. As long as I keep playing Little Miss Meek and Mild, they'll have no reason to suspect I'm there for anything other than being found and brought back. Besides, I am a weapon. A knife isn't going to bring my father down. Only I'm capable of that. I just hope this new-found confidence doesn't go out the window the second the man who donated half my DNA stands in front of me.

Bending down, I stroke Rufio's head and pray it's not the last time I see him or the others. I've done many things I've been ashamed of over the years, things I was scared of or too young to stop from happening. Right now, I plan on making up for all those things.

"Come on, boy." I motion for him to follow me into the bedroom. I snap my fingers for him to jump up on the bed. He does so, circling a few times before he lies down.

I stroke my hand over his head and check to make sure the chip is still attached to his collar.

I bite my lip, questioning if I'm doing the right thing. When I jumped out of the window with my backpack, I'd already decided I was going to let myself be captured. I cut out the chip with every intention of flushing it, but something told me to hang tight, so I stuck it on Rufio's collar for now.

He looks at me with sad eyes, like he knows what I'm about to do, but I don't let it sway me. Squaring my shoulders, I leave the room and close the door behind me. I stand in the hallway wondering if I've finally lost my mind when I realize I can hear a car.

I swallow down the instinct to hide and pray it's not Wilder and Crew. If they've changed their minds and decided to wait me out, I'm fucked. Moving to the window, I see a small cloud of dust as the approaching car kicks up dirt and gravel from the road. I keep watching to see if it's the truck of the men I love that crests the hill or something else when the vehicle finally comes into view.

A black SUV approaches. This is it. Showtime. And what a

show it will be, because if I don't get dramatic now, they might become suspicious.

Taking a deep breath, I open the door and make a run for it. I head toward the cornfield, but I keep my speed relatively slow. I want to get caught, after all.

I hear the SUV come to a stop and the doors open, so I keep running, bracing myself for what's to come. And not a moment too soon. I find myself tackled from behind, a large body knocking me flying and pinning me to the ground. My breath is knocked out of me, and I gasp as I try to suck oxygen into my lungs.

I'm pulled to my feet and spun around to see one of my father's men, Bill, looking at me like a bug he wants to crush.

"Did you really think he'd let a traitorous rat go free?"

"No. I knew he'd come for me, but I had to try."

Bill shakes me before shoving me toward a big guy I don't recognize, but I don't think for a single second I might find any empathy in him.

The guy reaches for me, and when I don't struggle, he moves me in front of him and shoves me lightly, so I start walking.

"If you even think of running, I'll shoot you in the leg and drag you the rest of the way," Bill says from behind me, but I have no intention of running, not yet anyway.

"My father's okay if you shoot me, and you wonder why I ran?" I huff, knowing I've caught everyone's attention. Only a very select few know who my father is, and none of these guys, except Bill, are in the know. My silence was bought through threats, not to me but to the kids coming in and out of my care. Now that they're gone, I just don't give a fuck who knows who my daddy is.

"Father?" the guy walking me asks curiously.

"Yeah, your boss is my daddy."

"Don't listen to this bitch, Phil. She's a lying whore."

"How have I lied? And who the hell to? Up until recently, I'd never left the Division. I was born there, and if my father gets his way, I'll die there. As for being a whore… Tell me exactly how a teenager who is kept away from people becomes a whore."

"Teenager? What the hell is going on?" Phil looks at Bill. Jesus, if the guy driving's name is Will, I'm going to lose my mind.

"I'm seventeen," I lie. "But don't worry. My whoring days don't start until my father has decided who's sperm he's gonna choose for me. He's gotta make sure he doesn't end up with a faulty grandchild too."

I hear the sound of a gun being cocked and shut up. There are many ways to play this, but getting shot won't help one little bit.

"You're weak, Lara. Always have been, always will be. You'd better hope you birth someone stronger than you, or you'll be of no use to us."

I pause, wondering if he knows more than he's letting on. Most of these guys are hired on a need-to-know basis. Bill might know who my father is, but does he know the inner workings of the Division?

"You can call me weak all you like, but honestly, the opinion of someone that has no issue with a child being beaten and raped means nothing to me."

"You won't be a child forever, Lara. Who knows, maybe Daddy will let me shoot my shot with you."

Phil shoves him back. "That's enough. She's supposed to come back alive and unharmed."

I snort at that. "That's sweet, Phil. But Bill knows my father doesn't give a shit. He's worked for him for years. He should also know my father would never let him *shoot his shot*." I glare at Bill. "You're nothing but the hired help. Do you think my father is going to let you fuck his daughter and impregnate her? I thought you were a regular asshole, not a delusional one."

I'm yanked from the side a second before I'm backhanded by Bill. I drop to the ground, my face throbbing. It's still fucking tender from where Giles hit me, dammit.

"You fucked up, Lara. You ran. If you think your father won't punish you, you're the one who's delusional. The kids are gone. He knows he needs a new way to hurt you. That leaves one option." He bends down and cups my face, squeezing hard enough for me to want to scream. "He'll let me have you so you remember your place," he snarls as Phil shoves past him and helps me up.

"He'll kill you for marking her."

"No, he won't," Bill answers confidently.

I glare at him as Phil eases me into the back of the SUV and sits beside me. I send out my gift and center it on Bill. I watch as his eyes dart around warily as I make him feel just enough fear and panic to unsettle him.

He climbs into the passenger seat and turns to look at me. "I'll tell him you fought me and that I tried not to hurt you, but you became hostile. My men will back me up.".

Neither Phil nor the driver dispute his words. I know they'll take Bill's side, even if it's just to avoid getting caught in the crossfire.

"Do what you need to do, Bill. I really don't give a shit. Just know this. The second you try to touch me, I'll kill you." I throw more fear at him and smile when I see him shiver and look away.

I turn and look out the window as the car pulls away from the house. I watch it get smaller and smaller and fight back the tears. I have to stick to the plan. It's the only shot we have. Yet, as the house becomes nothing more than a tiny speck in the distance, I can't help feeling like I've just made the biggest mistake of my life.

Chapter Thirty-Two

Crew

We spend an hour searching around the town for Lara, but nobody has seen her. In the end, we head back. We take the turn toward the house, both of us sitting in silence as we try to figure out where the fuck she would go.

"This isn't like Lara. She knows what's at stake."

"It is exactly like her. You just don't want to see it. You want her to have gotten halfway and turned around because she knew we'd have her back. That's all good except for one thing: we keep fucking letting her down, Crew, and then expect her to trust us. Why should she?"

"Well, there was the whole dead body thing," I mumble as I pull up outside the house.

"We got rid of the body, true. But we didn't save her. She did it herself. And she would have found a way to get rid of him too. Hell, she was the one who suggested the grave."

I jump out and head for the house, slowing when I spot the door open. I take off at a sprint. "Lara!" I yell, looking around the room but not seeing her. I head toward the bedroom, where I can hear Rufio barking.

"Thank fuck," I sigh, knowing she wouldn't go anywhere without him. Only when I open the door, Lara's nowhere to be seen. "Where is she, Rufio? Where's Lara?"

Rufio jumps off the bed and runs toward the front door. I follow him with a frown but stop when I see Wilder at the table with the note in his hand.

"She's gone."

"What?"

Rufio comes running over to me, his head rubbing against my leg as I stare at Wilder, trying to process his words. I reach down to stroke Rufio's head and spot her bag on the floor.

"She's gone back to the Division to deal with her dad. She thinks cutting off the head of the snake will leave them scrambling, at least long enough to have the Division cutting their losses. She knew they'd come. Knew they'd track the chip here and used herself as bait exactly like she wanted to."

"Not exactly like she wanted to because she wanted our help, and we told her no. So instead of having us at her back, she went and did it alone," I snarl.

"She might be alone, but she's not unarmed. And without the kids there for him to use as a bargaining chip, Lara should have the upper hand."

I rub my hand over my face. "How the fuck are we supposed to track her?"

"Same way we always have. Don't start doubting us now. She's relying on us."

"Call Ev. Let everyone at Apex know what's going on and put them on alert. If Penn has Lara, he should be happy, but we're not dealing with a rational man. He might make his move now to take one of the kids to use against Lara. To force her to do whatever the fuck he wants. I'm going to grab our shit and load the truck." I storm back into the bedroom and grab our bags. I gather our things from the bathroom and stuff them into the bags, along with anything I spot lying around the room. I make sure everything is packed before heading out to the main room, grabbing Lara's bag as I pass by it.

I toss them into the back of the truck, muttering under my breath.

"You stupid, stubborn girl," I snap out, hoping she can somehow hear me. I swear to God, when I get my hands on her, she won't be able to sit down for a week.

I stomp back to the house and head to the kitchen for my phone and charger, stopping short when I see it's missing and find a phone I've never seen before.

Blinking, I stare for a minute before whirling around and jogging over to Wilder, who's on his cell phone. "Put it on speaker." He does as I ask. "That you, Ev?"

"Yeah, Wilder was just giving me the rundown. I'm going to pull up all the traffic cams in your area. There's nothing within a four-mile radius of the house, which will make it harder to—"

"She took my phone." I cut him off.

I hear his fingers moving rapidly over the keys of his computer.

"It's not on. But if she took it, then she has to know we can track it. I'll keep trying. As soon as she turns it on, I'll find her."

"It was charging. That's why I didn't take it with me," I tell them, knowing they don't care but needing to say it anyway.

"My guess is she'll keep it off until she gets to wherever they are taking her, knowing it won't be the Division's main headquarters. Then I can track her. You have any idea what we could be walking into?" Ev questions.

"*We?* No, you guys need to stay there. He could be sending men to your location right now. Don't let him gain an advantage over Lara by letting him get his hands on one of you guys or the kids," I bark.

"Fuck you, Crew. Do not ask us to leave you out to dry. We're already missing two brothers. I refuse to lose any more."

There's a pregnant pause as I stare at Wilder, the weight of what we know in our gazes, neither of us relishing having to tell Ev the next part.

"We need to tell you something." I swallow and pull out a chair, sitting down heavily on it. "Nash approached Lara when we weren't around."

Ev sucks in a sharp breath, but I continue before he can ask any of the million questions he probably has.

"There was a fire that led to an explosion, which you already know, but Nash says there was nothing natural about it. He asked Lara if she knew anyone with a gift for fire."

"And does she?"

"Yeah, she remembers a boy from when she was little. She said he wasn't there long. He and his sister were moved. The sister might be Kate, the woman Nash and Hendrix were seeing."

"Where's Nash now? And what about Hendrix?"

I close my eyes and force myself to spit out the words I hoped I'd never have to say. "Hendrix's dead, Ev."

There is nothing but silence on the other end of the line for a minute, except the sound of Ev's harsh breathing.

"Fuck. Fuck!" Ev yells before I hear something smash.

I wait him out, knowing he needs this. When it comes to death, there is no way to soften the blow. The loss of life feels like a sledgehammer smashing into your heart, the echoes of pain destined to be felt for years to come. If someone makes a profound impact on your life, their death is bound to leave a void of equal measure.

"Where's Nash now?" he finally asks, his voice subdued and filled with pain.

"I don't know. I'm not even supposed to know he's alive. He told Lara to keep it quiet."

"He doesn't trust us," Ev states.

"He's been through a lot," I say, defending him.

"He has every right to be cautious. How the fuck did they figure out where Hendrix and Nash were? That wasn't public knowledge, and we moved their base of operations after everything went down with Cooper."

"Originally I was thought James was the most likely reason," Wilder says gently, reminding us of a man we all liked and respected. The Division destroyed him when they planted a chip in his head, stripping the man of who he was and making him a puppet.

"But they met Kate right after Oz and Zig made it out of the jungle. Cooper's cover being blown was likely the reason Kate was tagged in. All she would have had to do is watch and wait. She probably followed them from their base to their knew hideout and simply staged a meet meet-cute from there." He adds.

I rub my hand over my jaw. "Everything has a fucking ripple

effect. Cooper's death put Kate in their path and now we've lost Hendrix, but if Cooper lived, he'd have killed both Oz and Zig. No matter what happened someone was always going to die."

"I fucking hate these guys," Ev snarls.

"I know, we all do. You okay to fill the others in about Hendrix?"

"Yeah, I'll talk to them. You know if Nash holds the Division responsible, he'll track them down and kill them himself."

"And normally, I'd stand back and cheer, but these guys aren't going to be easy to kill, Ev. Their varied gifts make even one of them twice as deadly as Nash is."

"Don't underestimate a man fueled by vengeance."

"I'm not doubting his motivation. But if he's letting his anger rule him, he'll be reckless and make mistakes. Mistakes that will wind up with him dead too."

"There's nothing we can do now but find Lara and hope Nash is already there. At least with Nash there, Lara will have someone at her back." Wilder says, trying to find the bright side.

I want him to be right, but something in me knows this isn't going to play out how we want it to. "I know you want to let the others know, Ev, but we need to figure out which way Lara is heading."

"I'll widen the search radius and run through all the cameras in the area, checking facial recognition. I'll call you back when I have something. Stay safe. I can't keep burying people I care about."

He hangs up before I can reassure him. Just as well, there are no assurances in life, and right now, I can't worry about anything but pulling Lara out.

"Weapons-wise, we have what we brought with us, plus the

cache of weapons we took from Giles. I don't know if it will be enough," I tell Wilder.

"It's going to have to be. We're out of time and options."

"Let's head out. I can't sit here and wait for news."

"We can't. We might head in the wrong direction and then have to backtrack. I don't like this any more than you do, but we can't act without thinking, or we'll only be putting her in more danger."

I walk to the kitchen and pour myself a glass of water. I drink the whole thing, needing a moment to calm down before I punch something. "Alright, fine. Let's talk it out. We're gonna need a plan."

"We have no idea where they're taking her yet or how many people will be there."

"So let's make plans for every possible scenario. It's better than sitting around here doing fuck all."

Seeing the strain on my face, he nods. "Alright. Let's assume that he has a second base of operations in a more secluded area. That main building was about hiding in plain sight. I think they're falling back and assessing the damage before they make their next move."

"Okay, that makes sense and will help us keep innocent casualties to a minimum. We've gotta remember, though, that not everyone at the Division is bad. There will be people there because they have no choice."

"Noted. But our main focus is Lara. If we take out the main people, that will hopefully give the others being forced to stay some options."

I lean against the counter, my eyes falling to Rufio. "Whatever we decide, we'll have to mostly work on the fly. There are too many moving parts."

"We'll need to split up when we find her. One of us will need to get in and get Lara out. The other will have to create a distraction."

We're both quiet for a while, each of us working through all possible outcomes.

"What about Nash?" Wilder asks.

"If we find him, we take him with us. But if Nash doesn't want to be seen, he won't be. His call sign was Shadow for a reason."

Before he can say anything else, Wilder's phone rings. He answers it and puts it on speaker.

"Found her. I'm tracking the car she's in as we speak. It's a little hit-and-miss because, this far away from any major cities, people tend to trust their neighbors instead of putting up cameras to keep an eye on them. I'll text you the coordinates and keep you updated. I'm sending one of the team to meet you."

"Don't. Not until we know what's going on. I'll call for backup if we need it."

He starts to argue, but Wilder cuts him off. "You have the chopper; you can send it if needed, but Crew's right. We have no idea what we are walking into. Right now, anyone else will be a liability."

"Fine." Ev hangs up, clearly pissed.

"I wouldn't be surprised if he sends someone anyway. The man is stubborn as fuck." I curse.

"I don't want to leave Apex vulnerable," Wilder growls.

"We've gotta trust that the guys to know what they're doing. Now let's go get our girl."

He nods as I look around to make sure we have everything and head out to the truck, clicking my tongue so Rufio follows.

I wait for Rufio to jump into the back before closing the door and climbing into the passenger seat. My mind's too scattered to drive. When Wilder climbs into the driver's seat a few minutes later and types the coordinates into the GPS, I feel pressure in the air inside the cab. I don't say anything. Voicing my fears won't make them any less likely to happen. But as Wilder starts the truck and pulls away from the house, I feel the pressure on my chest like an anvil.

I don't need a gift to tell me that we're heading into trouble and there's a good chance that not all of us will make it out alive.

Chapter Thirty-Three

Lara

I pretended to sleep most of the way. Not only did it stop them from talking to me, but it also made them feel comfortable enough to talk among themselves.

They argued quietly, mostly Bill and Phil. Turns out the driver's name is David, not Will, shattering my dreams of a rhyming kidnapping dream team.

David seemed to be the strong, silent type, but Phil and Bill clashed like siblings fighting over who used all the hot water. Bill is still a dick. He's the kind of person that makes you realize why birth control was created. That, and I always had the urge to dip him in hot tar.

Phil, on the other hand, didn't seem so bad, but only in the same way a woman seeing her friend's husband cheat might stay with her own neglectful asshole because he wasn't as bad. I don't usually grade on a curve, but henchmen don't tend to be very nice. Go figure.

They talked about how pissed my father will be, according to Phil, for my rough treatment. Bill argued back that my father was only interested in one thing from me, and that was my ovaries.

I kept my opinion to myself. Nobody in this car knew anything about my father. Nobody but me, that is.

The worst kind of monsters are the ones that know how to humanize themselves. They wear kindness as a second skin, blinding people to the evil beneath it.

When I was seven years old, I failed to stop a moving car with my mind. My father had thrown a ten-year-old boy, who'd been brought in by the Division for just this purpose, in front of the car. The idea was that my fear would kick in and my gift would flare to life, thus saving the boy.

It didn't, of course, and the boy died in front of me before being discarded like trash. He wasn't gifted. He meant nothing to my father or anyone at the Division, but that boy changed my life in the most profound way. He made me realize there was no line my father wouldn't cross, no boundary he wouldn't obliterate to reach his goal, and all the while, I had no clue what the hell that goal was.

Now, after saving Bella from falling off the playset, I wish I'd been smart enough to try to move the boy instead of the car.

When I feel us slowing down, I let the memories of that boy drift away and crack my eyes open.

We seem to be on a large farm of some kind. I can see what appears to be a main house, similar to the one at Apex. Beyond that, there are huge barns and a variety of fields in various stages of growth.

A quick look around shows that there are no other buildings visible in the vicinity. That doesn't necessarily mean there are no neighbors, but I'd put money on there being none within a ten-mile radius.

I see a few people wandering around outside. I don't recognize any of them. When the car stops and Phil pulls me out with his hand wrapped around my bicep, none of them seem surprised. They might not know who I am, but they clearly knew to expect someone.

My boots kick up the dust of the parking area as I'm pulled toward the main house. Nobody says a word. Phil and Bill are as quiet as David, and I don't think it has anything to do with respect and everything to do with fear.

I look around as we walk inside the house, which is dated. But not dated in a way that says it needs renovating, just that it's a family home from a time gone by. I can see a huge pine table and chairs in the kitchen that looks like it would sit twelve. Instantly, I think of the guys back at Apex sitting down and laughing together through meals, the soft giggle of the kids, and the women teasing their men. I wonder if this place holds memories like that—ones filled with love and respect that take the bones of a house and turn them into a home by filling it with life.

A tug snaps me out of my thoughts and leads me away from the kitchen down a long hallway to the back of the house. We stop outside a wooden door. Bill leans over me to knock, his groin brushing against my ass. I lift my foot and stomp down on his foot with my boot, delighting in his bellow of pain.

The door is yanked open just as Bill reaches for a handful of my hair. My father's hand is around his throat an instant before Bill's hand makes contact. A second later, Bill collides with the wall he's thrown against.

I'm not stupid enough to think of it as a father protecting his daughter. He just doesn't like people breaking his toys. He's capable of that all on his own.

"Somebody want to explain what the fuck happened to her face?" my father asks, his voice devoid of all emotion.

"It was Bill. He never was good at keeping his hands to himself," David says, surprising me.

I turn to look up at the man in front of me. He's a handsome guy, but I must take after my mother. Other than our eyes, I see nothing of me in him.

"Hello, Father."

His eyes flash as he addresses the others. "Leave us."

They don't argue. Phil and David simply turn and walk away, leaving me with the person I spent half my life loving and the other half hating. It didn't matter that he never loved me back. As a young girl learning about relationships from movies and stolen books, I tried so hard to be the daughter I thought he wanted. In his own way, he taught me the most valuable lesson of all—that you can love someone. You can love them from the width and breadth of your soul, but you cannot make them love you back. You can keep giving them pieces of you and watch as they get casually discarded like a used tissue, or you can glue your remaining pieces together and reshape what's left into something different.

I'll never be the person I was before. There are too many parts of that girl missing. Parts that got stepped on and lost along the way, but that doesn't mean that I am less now. If anything, I'm more because, even at my weakest, I didn't break. A part of me will always feel the echo of sadness for the girl who just wanted her daddy to love her. But the woman in me is proud that I learned to be strong and to survive when this man buckled and broke.

"Lara." His voice is cold, stern even, but it doesn't make me tremble like it did before.

I stare into his eyes and shut my emotions down tight, letting him gaze into the void of nothing. He wanted a daughter just like him. Well, there is a reason people warn you to be careful what you wish for. I don't speak. I wait for him to step back and let me in so we can get this stupid show started.

He eventually does, moving to sit in a chair next to a large oak desk under a window that has a view of a small yard with flowers. I look around the room and take in the bookcases on one wall and a leather sofa on the other that looks worn but comfortable.

"Take a seat."

I do as he asks and sit on the sofa, glad he opted for the chair. It's hard to be close to someone when you've fantasized about clawing their eyeballs out.

"I'm glad you've returned."

My calm goes out the window. Everything I left behind flashes in my mind. "I didn't exactly have a choice."

"Your place is here beside me."

I roll my eyes. "We both know that's a lie. What do you really want?"

He stands and paces in front of me, his air of calmness disappearing into a cloud of agitation. Interesting.

"You are my daughter. The fact that you just announced that to my men when I've tried to keep your identity a secret is a testament to that. Of course, your place is with me. Much has happened in your absence. Our research and medical files have been largely destroyed. We kept most things in old school files, not wanting to leave a digital footprint."

I laugh to myself—if only he knew—as I think about the flash drive at Apex. He might not have believed in leaving a digital footprint, but thankfully Bella's mom Emma did. She scarified herself to get that information to me for Apex.

"Hmm...such a shame that trying to hide your criminal activities led to you losing everything. I guess you'll have to start from scratch."

"We didn't lose everything. We might have been narrow-minded, but we were not stupid, something you'd do well to remember."

I cross my arms and lean back. When he doesn't get more of a response, he runs his hand through his hair, reminding me of a normal frustrated parent, not the robotic dick he was the last time I saw him. Even more interesting.

"This location is better anyway. More secluded. More space. It will be easier for me to achieve my vision."

I know I should keep my mouth shut, but I'm curious to see if he drank the Kool-Aid he's been selling. "Your vision? The one where you enslave as many gifted people as possible?"

He whirls on me. "I'm not enslaving anyone. I'm freeing them. This place could be a utopia for us. We could all be safe here."

"Too many gifted people in one place would make this whole operation vulnerable. It doesn't matter to me if you believe your delusions or not, but your idea of utopia is another person's version of hell."

"You know nothing."

I jump up, pissed off beyond words. "It's you who knows nothing. You've become everything you hated."

"I'm saving these people."

"These people? We are these people, Dad." He jolts at the moniker I normally never use. "You're not saving us. You're condemning us."

"You're—"

"I was happy," I whisper.

He freezes at my tone.

"For the first time in my life, I had a family. I was loved."

He hisses like I've struck him. "I'm your family," he grits out, but it sounds weak.

"No. You're not. I didn't know what it was like to have a family. I didn't know that love was given freely and without conditions. I learned that there is no such thing as perfection, that people mess up, sometimes big, sometimes small, but families forgive you. They love you through the good times and the bad."

I don't realize I'm crying until I see him stare at my cheeks in confusion.

"You don't understand. I'm doing this for you and your sister. I'm doing it for us, for all of us."

"You take terrorized kids and traumatize them further."

He frowns in confusion. "How? I gave them a mother. I gave them you."

There is something almost childlike in his lack of understanding. In another life, it might have softened me to him, but I've seen too much.

"What about me?" I hit my chest. "Where was my mother?"

He snaps his mouth shut.

"What you're doing here is hunting people and then caging them with threats and coercion. That's not freedom."

"The government would lock us up and make us lab rats. I'm

building an army, so when they come, we'll be ready for them. They won't take another one of my children, not again."

I ignore the tear in my heart his words cause, knowing instinctively it's Salem he's talking about, not me though she was better off without him. He talks about losing her but he made no effort to reconnect until he could use her for his grand plan. He's just another deadbeat father that likes to blame everyone else for his failings.

I laugh instead, the sound mocking and cruel. "You are the government, you fool. You thought you could bring the establishment down from the inside, but instead, you ended up becoming one of them. You're the boogeyman to these kids, not the government."

"That's not true."

"Yeah? So I'm free to go then?"

He moves to the door, blocking it. "You're a child."

"Wrong again. I know it's hard to keep track of your daughter's birthdays, but I'm now a legal adult." I can practically see the wheels in his brain turning.

"There are some people I want you to meet. They understand the vision I have. Then you can see the beauty of it. One of them, Tony, has requested to court you until you are comfortable—"

"No. I know where this is going. I will not let you pimp out my womb so that you can grow your cult of wonder kids."

I move toward him, hoping he'll listen to reason, but any emotion I might have caught on his face was fleeting.

"You'll adjust. You enjoy being a mother. Children love you. We just need to bring the others home. Tell me more about Apex."

"No."

He grabs my arm. His grip is hard and unyielding, and he's

bound to leave bruises. "Where is your loyalty?" he roars in my face.

"Fuck you."

He backhands me, striking me on the same side of the face Bill and Giles did. What the hell is it with men? Do they take a special class in school that teaches them this shit?

I manage to keep my balance, but I feel the skin of my cheekbone split open and my eye throb in time to my heartbeat.

"You will learn your place," he spits, grabbing my arm.

"I already know my place, and it's far from you."

He pulls the door open and drags me down the hallway to another door, this one leading down to the basement. It's dark, but he doesn't turn on a light before he yanks me down the wooden steps.

I somehow manage not to fall. When my eyes adjust to the darkness, and with the sliver of light coming in from the open door, I see a row of large cages. And not all of them are empty.

I don't fight him as he shoves me inside the closest empty one. He pulls a chain from around his neck with a key on it and uses it to lock the padlock on the door.

"Yeah, it's a real Garden of Eden here, Dad," I say sarcastically.

"You just need the children back. Everything will be back to normal then."

"How? Are you going to stick bunk beds in here? Maybe throw in a couple of coloring books for when they get bored?"

He looks at me, but he says nothing as I appeal to him again. I might have my pride, but pride won't save my Lost Ones. "They can play now. They can run and climb and swim and get to do all the things children should get to do."

"They can do all those things here. They'll grow up happy here and have babies of their own. There will be so many gifted people that nobody will ever see us as weak again."

"We were never weak," I say firmly.

He shakes his head and climbs up the basement stairs.

"It's you who's weak," I whisper.

I wait until he closes the door before I move to the padlock. I think of the boy and the car. I'm not strong enough to break the cage, but God help me, I can break the damn lock.

I study it before I bend down and pull the cell phone from my boot. I turn it on. Remembering the feature Salem told me about from when she crash-landed in the jungle, I press the SOS button on the side of the phone. I make sure the sound's off before shoving it back into my boot.

"Umm... Hi. Anyone else awake?"

"You think we'd sleep in a place like this?" a voice replies.

"I'm not sure what to think anymore," I admit before I take hold of the padlock and close my eyes.

I picture what the inside of the padlock looks like. I spent years looking over specs for a million different kinds of locks in preparation for a moment like this. It's not easy. It takes what feels like hours, though it couldn't have been that long.

My head feels like it's been put in a blender, and I can feel blood running from my nose. None of it matters, though, when I hear the click of the lock as it gives way in my hand. I push the door open, cringing when it creaks loudly.

"Hey, what's going on?" another voice calls out.

I don't have enough energy left to open all their locks, but I won't leave them down here. "I'm going to try and get you all out. When I was tossed in here, he used a key to lock my cage. It was around his neck. Is there a master key for all the cages, or are there others?"

"How the fuck would we know?" another voice answers, this one rough sounding.

"I'm just asking, asshole."

"Ignore Jack. He's a dick," a soft voice tells me.

"I get it. I don't want to leave you behind. I'll try and get the key. But if I can't, I'll come back for you. I promise."

"Sure, whatever," the sarcastic voice of who I'm guessing is Jack replies.

I bite my lip to stop myself from cursing him out. I'm pretty sure I'd be a dick too if I was trapped down here.

I creep up the stairs. When I reach the door, I give the knob a gentle twist, hoping it isn't locked. When it opens, I let out a relieved sigh. With the cages padlocked, he obviously felt comfortable not locking this door, too. That also tells me he's not worried about anyone else accidentally stumbling across it. They probably already know what's down there. Resting my head against the wood, I send up a prayer, hoping I get out of this in one piece.

Taking a deep breath, I gently ease the door open, and when I see the coast is clear, I slip out. I go in the opposite direction of my father's office, and instead of heading for the front door like my instincts are telling me to, I sneak upstairs. I check all the rooms, which are mostly empty, and use the windows to get a better view of the property.

It's big, but there doesn't seem to be many people here. I'm not sure what to make of that. I know that most of the medical team was wiped out in the explosion, but that still left plenty of people. Only me and the children lived on-site, with a small staff to see to our needs and act as security.

Maybe this is just the skeleton crew.

I haven't seen any children yet, which is a relief. As much as I think I have the mental capacity to deal with whatever happens today, I know I'm lying to myself. Dragging a kid into it means one more person with a lifetime of nightmares in their head.

I close my eyes, open my senses, and see if I can use my gift to sense how many people are close by. I feel my mouth drop open when the connection hits me bright and clear. I never thought to use it this way, and part of me is pissed at my father all over again. If he had been a good dad, I could have gone to him for advice. We could have worked things out together. But instead, I've come here to kill him in cold blood.

My eyes open on that thought. Seeing him again didn't change how I feel about the man. Instead, it reminded me that, as much as our gifts are alike, we're not the same. Killing him will turn me into someone I'm not and will set me on the same path he's currently walking.

No, I might be able to kill to protect myself, but I don't think I could murder someone. Not if I want to be able to look at myself in the mirror.

An overwhelming sense of desperation washes over me as my options dwindle to nothing. I have to bring the Division down one way or another.

But murder isn't the answer.

Not today, anyway.

Chapter Thirty-Four

Wilder

Lara didn't just turn Crew's phone on. She hit the SOS function that I had no idea she knew about, making it that much easier for Ev to find her. He sent us the coordinates and has been texting us ever since.

I should feel better. I know we could be scrambling right now with no way of finding Lara at all. If it wasn't for her quick thinking, tracking her would have been impossible.

It doesn't change the fact that I'm still pissed off with the woman, though. Why didn't she hide? How could she put herself in danger like this? Did she even once think about how this would make me or Crew feel?

"Why do you look constipated?"

"Fuck you."

Crew studies my profile before speaking again. "You're mad at her."

"Oh, I'm fucking furious. She'll sacrifice everything for the people she loves, but what about her? She just keeps flinging herself into danger. I swear to God, I'm going to handcuff her to the bed when she gets home."

"Well, you'll get no arguments from me."

My cell chimes, so I keep quiet while Crew reads the latest text.

"The Mayfield Farm."

I look over at him briefly, but he's still reading the message.

"That's the name of the place where they took her. Or where my phone is, at least," he mumbles before continuing. "Apparently, it's owned by the Isaacs family and has been for the last five generations."

"More gifted people?"

"Hold on, let me ask." He types the question before sending it and continuing to read the previous message. "There are no cameras on or anywhere near the place that Ev can hack into, so we'll be going in blind. He did say, though, that while he's been researching, he had some of the others in to help. Avery spotted something."

The phone rings before he can continue. He chuckles. "It's Ev." Answering, he puts it on speakerphone.

"Texting is taking too fucking long. Okay, so here is what we have so far. The Isaacs family was approached by land developers four years ago. They were offered a price for the land that was three times over the market valve."

I whistle. "Damn, they really wanted that piece of land. Why there, though?"

"That's what I wondered. I was even more curious to learn

that the family turned the developers down. They wanted the property to stay in the Isaacs family."

"Well, they sold out in the end. Not that I can blame them," Crew states.

"That's just it, they didn't. Only, I can't find a single trace of them. None of the kids are in school, and I can't find anything to suggest homeschooling. The father didn't turn up for work one day, but nobody's been reported missing, and the property is still in their name. The bills are paid on time, but for all intents and purposes, they just up and disappeared one day."

"People don't just disappear. They could still be there. You never said if they were gifted. It would make sense if they were. They could have offered up their home to the Division."

"I didn't find anything to suggest they're gifted, but you know, as well as I do, most people hide their gifts." He sighs.

"Okay, let's forget about the Isaacs for now. Why this property and not somewhere else?"

"Aside from the fact that it's huge and isolated, it's self-contained. There are animals for meat. They grow fruit and vegetables and even medicinal herbs, from what I found on an old website of theirs. The thing that clinched it, though, is something Greg stumbled across in a local newspaper article. The grandfather was interviewed about the area a year before he died. And during it, he mentions that he's a prepper, like his father before him. And that under the house is a bunker."

"A bunker, as in an underground shelter where people can live for years?"

"Yep."

"Yeah, that would definitely make that property very attractive to the Division."

"You said Avery spotted something?" I remind him.

"Right. The Division employs a lot of people. It's impossible to keep track of all of them, but I do have most of their names flagged. Avery recognized a few. All of them are dead, and I've confirmed they weren't onsite at the time of the bombing."

"I don't suppose we're talking about natural deaths, are we?"

"In most cases, they look like accidents or suicide. If it had been only a couple, we probably wouldn't have noticed, but..." His voice trails off as I look at Crew.

"Just how many are dead, Ev?"

"Fifteen that we've found so far. Interestingly, Avery says, to her knowledge, that the few dead she knew were non-gifted."

"They knew about the gifted, though, right?"

"Oh yeah. There's no doubt about that."

"It sounds like a culling," I tell them both quietly.

Crew curses.

"That's what we were thinking too," Ev admits.

"He's getting rid of the non-gifted people who have knowledge of the gifted. Why now, though? Astrid already announced to the world that she's gifted, and others have followed suit. There is no putting the rabbit back in the hat now."

"At first, I thought the bombing had just rattled him. And he'd change locations and pick things up where he left off," Ev says.

"But you're thinking like a rational, sane man, and I'm not sure this guy fits the bill," I admit.

"Lara told us about him and his gift. And after hearing this, I can't help but feel like he's even more dangerous than she realizes." Crew states.

I hesitate for a moment, not wanting to break Lara's trust, but

Ev and the others need to know. If there is any anger, they'll have time to get over it before they see her again.

"Lara's telekinesis is her secondary gift."

Crew whips around to look at me. His jaw ticks as he grinds his teeth, but he doesn't stop me from explaining further.

"Her primary gift is the same as her father's. Only she can turn her gift on and off, unlike Penn. From what she described; it makes me think of it like having dozens of neighbors with their radios on playing constantly in the background. It got to the point where Penn couldn't hear his own radio, so he turned it down low and only listens to theirs. The kicker is he can control what they listen to now that he's not focusing on his own radio."

"I don't even know what to say to that. I don't want to feel sorry for the man, but that's fucked up. Wait, so Lara's an empath too?"

"Yeah, but she can shut out everyone else's radio at will."

"The radio analogy is killing me," Crew complains.

"She's an empath and a telekinetic? Jesus. I knew she was strong, but damn, color me impressed."

I don't say anything, and neither does Crew.

"Ah fuck. What did you guys do?"

"Let's just say we didn't take the news of her gift well," I admit.

"For fuck's sake. Why do none of you assholes ever learn? Let me guess, you accused her of manipulating your feelings for her, even though most of the time she tried to avoid you."

I wince because he's right. Having it said back to us just makes me feel even more stupid.

"We fucked up, we know. But we'll fix it," Crew says solemnly.

"I just hope you get the chance." Ev hangs up, his ominous words floating in the air.

"Tell me she's gonna be okay, Crew. Tell me, we'll get the chance to make this right."

"She's far stronger than we've given her credit for. I'll be damned if we give up on her now."

"You're right. I need to calm the fuck down. I swear I'm going to have a heart attack before the day is over," I grumble.

He doesn't mock me because I'm pretty sure he's feeling the same way. It's hard knowing she's out there facing God knows what without us there.

I think back to the scene at the cemetery and frown. "Did Lara tell you she stabbed that Giles guy?"

"No, I got that from the knife wound in his throat."

"She didn't have enough blood on her," I murmur before smiling. "You know what? I have a feeling our girl's going to be fine."

"Okay, I'm lost. Care to share with the class?"

"I think Lara used her gifts on Giles. I think she either got him to turn the knife on himself, or she used her telekinesis to stab him."

Absolute silence fills the cab before Crew bursts out laughing.

"You're right. We'd be fucking idiots to underestimate her. She's a fighter, and now that she's had a taste of freedom, she'll fight tooth and nail to keep it."

"Good, because once we get her back, we're never letting her out of our sight again."

* * *

We park the truck a mile down the road from the farm and spend the next hour doing recon.

The farm is hidden behind a line of trees, with half a dozen armed guards patrolling the perimeter.

A few other people walk around between the buildings, but otherwise, we haven't seen much. Unfortunately, I haven't seen Lara either.

"We're going to have to go in blind," I say to Crew. We had been hoping Ev would come through and find blueprints and layouts of the buildings, but so far, he's had no luck. It seems that other than the information he found online, there are no records. Even the flash drive had minimal information. The Division has gone to great lengths to keep this place a secret. The question is, why?

"Once we get past the guards, we split up. We don't know if she's in the main house or one of the barns. We're going to have to try and blend in a little, see if we can get a feel for what's going on there. We're trained for this shit, and those people seem like regular Joes."

"Regular Joes that might be able to turn our brains to jelly with a flick of their wrist," Crew reminds me. Though they might not be soldiers, it doesn't mean they don't know how to kill.

"Good point. Alright, we stick together." I look down at my watch. "We have about an hour until it gets dark; we'll wait until then." It's too open to go in now, even with so few people. We don't exactly blend in. Plus, tight-knit crews will all know each other.

"We'll take Rufio with us. He'll scent Lara, no problem."

"Keep him with you. I don't trust those assholes not to shoot him, and Lara would be devastated if he got hurt," I warn him.

318

"Agreed. We go in armed. If we're spotted, we won't get a second chance. Normally, I'd say if they're unarmed, shoot to injure, but everyone here could have a dangerous gift, and we wouldn't know until we're dead." I nod at that. Dead would not be good.

"We don't know how many people are here willingly," he continues. "So try to avoid it if possible. Incapacitating them, though, won't be enough. We'll need to, at the very least, knock them out so they can't use their gifts at all. Our aim is to retrieve Lara. That's it. I know she wants her father's head on a platter, but she's too soft-hearted. I don't think she'll be able to kill him, and that's not because I believe she's weak. It's because she feels remorse. And that's what separates him from her."

I blow out a deep breath. "I'll message Ev, get him to send someone with the chopper now that I know we're not facing an army. Once we have Lara, I want to put as many miles between us and this place as possible."

"Agreed. We can arrange to have the truck picked up later." Crew nods, so that's what we do.

While we wait, we eat the energy bars from our backpacks and drink some water. It's not the most appetizing dinner, but we've had worse. Right now, all I'm concerned about is keeping our energy levels up so we don't make mistakes.

"Did Lara take any weapons with her?" I ask.

"No, but like you said, she doesn't need one. Besides, she might have assumed they'd search her. It's what we'd do if we were grabbing a high-profile target hell-bent on escape."

"We know what we're doing, though, for some reason, this all screams amateur hour."

"Don't be so sure about that. It could all be an act to draw us out. Getting overly cocky will be our downfall."

Once the sun's set and we're dressed in dark clothes that will help us blend into the night, we begin arming ourselves while Rufio watches on from inside the truck.

Crew shoves a gun into the holster at his back before looking at me. "You ready?"

Before I can answer, my phone chimes.

I look down at the message and see that it's from Greg and smirk.

Look behind you.

I spin around and search the darkness just as I see a figure move towards us.

"Thought I better warn you. Getting shot is such a ball ache," he calls, making Crew snort.

"What the fuck are you doing here? You shouldn't be here. You're still healing."

"Fuck you. I'm exactly where I'm supposed to be. That girl is just as much mine as she is yours." I don't say anything to that because he's right. Penn may be Lara's father by blood, but Greg is her dad in every other way.

"Greg, good to see you, man." Crew greets him.

"You too. Now, you find her yet?"

"No, but Ev says the SOS came from inside. If she's there, Rufio will find her."

Greg frowns. "Rufio?"

I let Rufio out of the back of the truck, and he runs over to Greg, who pats him.

"Ah, the dog. Welcome to the team, buddy." And with that, Greg just gained a new friend.

"Right, well, the chopper is a twenty-minute run from here. I couldn't risk putting her down any closer. When we get Lara out, head back to the truck. We don't know what state she'll be in, so it'll be easier to drive over.

I grit my teeth at Greg's words, but I know he's right. We have no clue what those assholes could have done to her.

"Alright, I'm done waiting. Let's go get our girl."

Chapter Thirty-Five

Lara

I used my gift to detect other people and avoid them, somehow turning myself into a human radar. I was tempted to make a beep-beep sound but figured it would defeat the purpose of hiding.

The sun had set, casting the farm in darkness and shadows, the stars just starting to become visible above.

I knew I was running out of time. My father hadn't been to check on me yet, but that wouldn't last. He would want to see if his punishment was working. As soon as he finds my cage empty, he'll have this whole place searched.

In the last ten minutes, I've noticed everyone starting to gather in one of the large barns closest to the house. My naturally paranoid mind was worried at first that we had reached the virgin sacrifice part of the evening before logic set in and suggested it was probably dinner time. Knowing I won't get a better chance than now to look around, I take a deep breath, head downstairs, and slip out of the house.

I keep my head down and walk like I have a purpose and not like someone walking toward their death. Steering clear of the barn where everyone's going, I check the others first. Three of the five have been converted into sleeping quarters; row after row of basic single beds makes me think back to the shelter. These rooms are not designed for families, that much is clear. However, the thought that these rooms could be dormitories designed for children makes my stomach turn.

I hurry outside, needing fresh air more than anything else right now. Bending over, I breathe as deeply as I can before blowing it out, trying to stop the panic attack that's threatening to consume me. Suddenly, the pieces of my father's idea of utopia shift and take on a different picture altogether. The beds, the lack of people here, the almost blasé response to all the medical research being lost.

My father isn't bothered about medical reports because old-fashioned impregnation works just as well. I'm a reminder to him that even pairing the best sperm and egg together can produce a dud, so why waste time and effort?

I stand up straight and try to get my heartbeat under control. I'm guessing the adults here are more persuadable than most, and none of them have aspirations of taking over. The adults, though, are not where his focus lies. It's the children. It always was. They are the future, untainted by the government's greedy hands, and perfect for my father to turn into gifted mini-soldiers who will follow his every command and worship him like a god.

Nausea rushes up my throat, but I swallow it back down and grip the wall to steady myself. When he mentioned me becoming a mother, he wasn't just talking about my offspring but all the children he hopes to have born here. So why the people in the cages? Who are they, and why are they being held like cattle? Unless...

"Holy fuck, he plans to breed them."

I think back to the hostile man and the quiet woman and the dozens of other people who sat silently in their cages, and my legs almost give out.

Was my father going to force the men on the women until they became pregnant? As my mind rebels at the idea, I know deep down it's the truth.

Creeping away from the dormitory barn, I make it maybe four steps before I'm grabbed from behind, and my mouth is covered with a large hand.

My tender cheek protests, the pain making the edges of my vision turn black for a second. I fight it back, not willing to go out like this. I'm about to unleash my gift on the asshole holding me when a familiar voice whispers in my ear.

"We've really got to stop meeting like this."

He releases me, giving me a chance to spin around and stare up at the menace who keeps trying to give me a heart attack.

"Nash."

"What the fuck are you doing here, Lara?"

"It's a long story. Why are you here?"

He glares at me like I'm dumb. "Don't ask questions you already know the answer to."

"You came to kill my father." A statement, not a question. I can see it in his eyes.

"You'll only be putting a bandage on a bullet hole. Eventually, someone will step in to take his place, and everything will come full circle." It wasn't until I realized I didn't have it in me to kill my father in cold blood that I stopped to look at the bigger picture. My father is just one man, and right now, he might be the most powerful, but he's still just a man. When he's gone, there will be others who might not step into his shoes but who will follow in his footsteps.

As long as the government knows of the gifted ones' existence, we'll never truly be free. They will always hunt us, or at least find the opportunities to grab us and use us for the good of our country. My father is just another pawn in a game that's bigger than he is. Maybe he saw it coming all along, and his twisted vision of utopia is the end he sees in sight.

"Maybe. But it will cause enough chaos to keep this generation of gifted safe. When they're old enough, they can work on taking out the newest asshole."

I can't argue with his logic. The truth is often not as comforting as we'd like it to be. Not all stories end with happily ever afters. Sometimes we get a happy-for-now ending, and you can either dwell on the unfairness of it all or play the cards you've been dealt.

I think of my Lost Ones and know that, given time and training, we can make them strong. If they have to face the Division again one day, they'll be ready.

"I understand," I whisper, rubbing my eyes and suddenly wishing I had a pair of ruby slippers that would whisk me back home with the click of my heels.

"I need to get you somewhere safe first."

"No." I hold his wrist, shaking my head. "I need to see this through."

"Lara—"

I cut him off. "He's lost his mind, Nash, and he was never

stable to begin with. He thinks he's building a utopia. This is basically a breeding farm, only the livestock are people. And when he has the children he wants, the adults will become expendable."

"Fuck," he curses, running a hand through his hair. "I can't get them all out. Your father would just use the distraction to escape."

"I know. That's why you'll focus on him, and I'll work on everyone else."

"Lara, you can't. Your father isn't the only zealot here."

"I know, but like you once said, I can be deadly when I need to be."

"You don't have to do this."

"Yes, Nash, I do. For you and Hendrix, for expendable ten-year-old boys, and my Lost Ones waiting for me to come home."

His breathing is harsh as he takes in my determined expression. "Fuck," he curses before yanking me into his arms. He holds me tightly, and I take a second to push some calming energy into him.

"Wilder and Crew are lucky to have you in their lives."

"It's me who's lucky, Nash."

He pulls back, but not before pressing a kiss on my forehead. "That you think that just proves my point. Go before I change my mind. And for fuck's sake, be careful."

He moves to step past me, but I reach out and grab his hand, halting his movement. "I'm glad I met you, Nash. Please be safe. Your brothers love and miss you."

"Lucky," he grumbles, making me laugh as he pulls away and disappears into the shadows.

I take a second to center myself. I feel calmer knowing I'm not alone anymore. Though I barely know Nash, his presence helps me focus. With that in mind, I head back to the main house and keep my senses open to everything around me.

Creeping toward my father's office, I don't sense anyone inside, so I take a deep breath and let myself in. I pause in the doorway, relieved to find it empty but still wary. Knowing my father, he probably has the place booby-trapped.

Braving it anyway, I head straight for his desk and start rummaging around until I find a large, old-fashioned key ring with multiple keys on it.

"Bingo." I close the drawer and head out the open door, only to freeze when I find David standing there watching me.

"David." He doesn't say anything. I'm not sure what to think, but I need to get past him.

"Umm... I never got to thank you for telling my father what happened with Bill. You didn't have to do that. Thank you. I really appreciate it." I give him a small smile.

He smiles back at me, but there's something not quite right about it.

"I knew it," he says quietly.

"Knew what?" I ask cautiously.

"That you feel it too."

"Feel what?"

"The connection between us."

"Say what?" Is this guy for real?

"I felt it the moment we met."

Is it a work requirement for the Division that all employees must be batshit crazy?

"David, I don't—"

David lunges for me, but I don't mess around. I don't let guilt or remorse make me hesitate as I savage his brain.

By the time I'm finished, he's sitting in the corner of my father's office, sobbing as he rocks back and forth, mumbling incoherent words. I don't have time to worry about what I've done. Maybe the guilt will come later, but I like to think I've made peace with this. If I can't accept it's a part of me, then neither will anyone else.

I close the office door and head down the hall to the basement door, easing it open and slipping inside. I slide my fingers along the wall until I find a light switch. I flick it on and bathe the room in an eerie glow. I swallow when I notice there are far more cages than I thought. There has to be at least twenty or thirty people down here.

I race down the steps to the cages.

"You came back," the now familiar female voice states as everyone moves closer to the doors of their cages.

"I said I would."

"You found the keys?" A deeper voice asks.

"Jack the dick, right?" He flushes but nods.

"I'm sorry," he says apologetically.

"Don't worry about it. You're locked in a fucking cage. I figure I can cut you some slack."

He grins, and his gaunt face looks far more youthful than before.

"Okay, I have no idea which key goes to which cage, so bear with me for a little while."

"No worries. We have nowhere else to go," he jokes, making a couple of his fellow captives chuckle.

"Ooh, dark humor. I like it." I take the first key and try it on the first lock. Of course, it was never going to be that easy. I keep going, trying each cage until, ironically, Jack's clicks open.

We both stare at each other in shock before he shoves the gate open, making me stumble back. He grips my arms to stop me from falling and plants a kiss on my lips before lifting me up and spinning me in a circle.

Once I'm back on my feet and the room has stopped moving, I look up at the visibly choked-up man and smile.

"I might have to leave the others locked up if that's the response I'm gonna get each time," I tease, making him chuckle.

I take the next key and start the process over again. This time, the third cage pops open, releasing a woman with pale blonde hair and almost translucent skin, making me wonder how long she's been down here. I assumed this place was being used out of necessity after the explosion. But now, I'm starting to suspect it's been in use for much longer.

"Is this everyone, or are there more captives being held somewhere else?" I ask as Jack helps the woman out.

She tenses and looks at me with tears in her eyes. "The ones who get pregnant end up in the bunker."

I freeze. "What did you just say?"

"The bunker," Jack jumps in, sensing how frail the other woman is. "It's located near the poppy field. I only know that because I wasn't always a prisoner. I believed in the cause once upon a time. But this,"—he nods his head at the cages—"this isn't what I signed up for. He's hurting the people he swore to save." Jack's voice cracks, making the woman beside him wrap her arms around his neck to comfort him.

"Can you two get everyone else out? I have to find the bunker."

"It's guarded," Jack warns as I give him the keys to the cages.

"I'll figure it out. I have to at least try."

He nods before steeling his shoulders. "I'll get everyone here out. Don't worry about us. Thank you…"

"Lara," I tell him with a smile as I jog up the stairs.

"Thank you, Lara. You don't understand what it means to us that you came back."

I pause and turn around, feeling tears spring to my eyes. "Yeah, Jack. Actually, I do."

It took me ten minutes to find the poppy field and another ten to reach it and find the stupid entrance. I had to use my telekinesis to open the hatch, which left me bleeding once more and shaking like a leaf.

As I climb down the steps that descend into darkness, I try to brace myself for what I'm about to find.

What I don't expect is the fist that flies toward my face. Thankfully, I manage to dodge it at the last second, so it just grazes my temple. I kick out, happy when I hear a pained groan before the lights suddenly turn on, temporarily blinding me.

Knowing that it's been done to distract me, I reach out with my mind and make my attacker so tired they can't stand up or keep their eyes open even a second longer. A thud has my eyes opening and dropping to the man on the ground.

Looking up, I glance around the room and spot a man, who I assume is a doctor, in a white lab coat with his hands in the air, watching me warily.

"Who are you, and what do you want?" His voice shakes as I move closer.

My eyes drift to the row of beds. There are five in total, four of them occupied by sleeping women. Heavily pregnant, sleeping women. On the opposite side of the room are five cribs, all of which are thankfully empty, not that it's enough to wipe away the horror of what this room is.

"What's wrong with them?"

"Nothing is wrong with them. They are perfectly healthy specimens," the doctor spits, affronted.

"Then why are they all asleep?"

"They are in medically induced comas, so they don't hurt themselves or their babies."

"Why would they—" I shake my head, remembering that these women are rape victims. I turn my glare on the doctor and allow him to see the fury in my gaze. "You know what happened to them. You know they had their bodies taken by force, and yet you're violating them all over again."

"You don't understand—"

"You're damn right, I don't understand. But then neither do you."

"It's important work," he says, affronted. In these circumstances, a few need to suffer for the greater good of many, then so be it."

I tilt my head and swear that if Wilder were here, he'd tell me I look like some creepy doll from one of those horror movies he likes so much. I snap my gift out and wrap it around his mind, testing his emotions and molding them like clay until the good old doctor feels exactly what these women are feeling, the sense of violation, the lingering pain that echoes through their bodies, and the overwhelming amounts of shame and guilt.

The doctor steps back, the blood draining from his face as he whimpers. "No."

"It's for the greater good that you understand what they went through–what you put them through."

He drops to his knees and cries, but I ignore him. If I focus on him anymore, I'll kill him.

I move over to the women and feel tears run down my cheeks at the injustice of it all. The monitor's beeps beside them; their heart rates strong and steady as mine rages out of control. I know they need more help than I can give them. It's not as easy as me just waking them up. I need a professional to look after them, one who will have their best interests at heart.

I've never needed to speak to Salem, Astrid, and Avery more than I do right now. I bend down to pull the cell phone from my boot and stand just as I'm yanked into someone's arms.

I freeze for a second before his familiar scent envelops me.

"Crew!" I choke out, turning in his arms to look up at him.

"In here," he yells as something soft touches my hand.

I look down and see Rufio sitting beside me, his head bumping my fingers.

I sob and press my head against Crew's chest as I gently pat Rufio.

"Shhh, I've got you," Crew murmurs before kissing me. The taste of my tears on our lips proof of how relieved I am to see him.

A second set of arms wrap around me from behind and I don't need to look to know who it is, but I tip my head back anyway.

Wilder's concerned eyes stare into my watery ones before he leans down and kisses me.

I lose myself in them both for a moment. Just having them here with me makes the rest of the world disappear until a cough snaps me out of it.

I turn my head and gasp when I see Greg.

"Am I getting a hug anytime soon, or do I need to shoot these two assholes?"

I break free from Wilder and Crew and throw myself into Greg's arms.

He grunts, reminding me that he's still healing, but when I go to pull back he holds onto me tighter.

"Alright, old man you can let go now," Wilder complains making me chuckle through my tears.

But Greg doesn't let go.

"Anytime now," Crew snaps.

Greg sighs and loosens his hold so I can look up at him with a watery smile.

"There she is," he whispers before kissing my temple and turning me back into the waiting arms of my men.

My men. I still can't wrap my head around the fact that I get to call them mine.

Though after how I left...

I bite my lip and look up at them.

"Oh no, you don't. That sweet– as–shit expression will not stop me from putting you over my knee and spanking the shit out of you," Wilder warns me.

"Your ass will be so red you won't be able to sit down for a week," Crew adds as Greg walks over to the silently crying doctor.

"My ears need bleaching. Can you guys wait until after Lara tells us what the fuck is going on here?"

"Dr Doom over there has them in a medically induced coma so they don't hurt themselves."

I look over at the doctor who Greg is staring at.

"Why would they hurt themselves?" Wilder asks.

I turn back to see him looking down at the woman beside me.

"I'm not saying they would; those were his words. Something he told me right before he confirmed that none of those babies were conceived with consent."

"Motherfucker," Crew hisses and Greg snarls, fists clenched at his sides.

"There are rows of cages in the basement under the main house filled with people who are forced to...be together, and from what I understand, the women who wind up pregnant end up here."

I wrap my arms around myself, imagining the fear and hopelessness they must have all felt.

"Is he crying like a little bitch because of you?" Greg asks. I look at him and nod slowly, guessing that Wilder and Crew told everyone about my other gift. They must have gotten over it, or they wouldn't have come for me, but that doesn't mean Greg's okay with it.

"I made him feel what they did," I admit quietly.

"Good girl," he praises before punching the doctor in the face and knocking him out.

I stare at him wide-eyed, shocked at both his easy acceptance of my gift and the punch.

"What?" he asks, and I shake my head.

"I need help. We can't leave them here like this and there are other people who need medical attention too. This isn't just about me or Apex anymore."

"I'll make some calls." Greg pulls out his cell as I look up at the guys.

"We need to get you out of here," Crew says softly but I shake my head.

"No. No more running, Crew. This ends tonight, one way or

another."

Before he can argue with me, I reach out and grab his hand.

"I thought I could come here, take out my dad and everything would be okay. It was stupid and reckless, and I was wrong. I knew as soon as I saw him again that I didn't have it in me to kill anyone if it wasn't in self-defense, and I'm okay with that. That doesn't mean I don't want him dead, just that I can't be the one to do it."

"Then let us do it. I have no fucking problem crushing his windpipe," Wilder growls, making me winch.

"As sweet as that offer is, someone's beaten you to it."

He frowns before realization dawns. "Nash."

I nod. "He's hunting down my father right now."

"Fuck. Alright, stay here with Greg and Rufio, and we'll go find him."

"No, I'm coming with you. I shouldn't have let Nash take on my father alone. Unless he takes him by surprise, my father could easily get the upper hand. I'm the only one who can stop him."

"Because you're his daughter? I don't think it means the same thing to him that it does to you," Crew says warily.

I shake my head. "No, because I'm the only one immune to his gift."

Wilder and Crew look at each other and have a whole silent conversation before turning to me.

"Fine, but you don't leave our sides." Wilder folds his arms over his chest waiting for me to argue, but I'm not an idiot.

"Deal. Let's go."

"Greg?" Crew calls.

Greg looks up and waves us off. "I'll stay with them until I can get help."

I offer him a grateful smile before bending down and picking up Crew's cell phone, which I must have dropped, and slip it back into my boot.

Standing, I see Crew staring at me with a bemused look on his face. "What? It's mine now." I shrug. And with that, I turn, and the three of us head upstairs. Wilder opens the hatch, and I crawl through, with him right behind me.

Getting to my feet, I look up and freeze, finding Bill, Phil, and a handful of other armed men in a semi-circle in front of us, all with guns pointing our way.

"Keep moving or I'll blow her fucking head off," Bill tells Wilder. "You too," he calls to Crew, who has his head sticking out of the hatch.

Taking his time, Crew climbs out like he doesn't have a care in the world and isn't staring down the barrel of multiple guns.

"What are you doing, Bill? I thought my father made it clear how he feels about you messing with me."

I hold back on using my gift for a moment. I've never used it on so many people before, and for good reason. The strain would most likely knock me out cold, and there'd be no guarantee it would even work.

"Fuck you. I don't see Daddy around to protect you now." He grins.

"You underestimate me, Bill. I don't need my father's protection," I tell him, and he scoffs. That's when I decide to work on the people on the outside first. I make them think they can't move, and since everyone's focus is on us, nobody notices when they lower their guns.

Nobody but Wilder and Crew, who must figure out what's happening right away.

"This the pencil dick you told us about?" Crew asks. I love that he's playing along and buying me time, even though I've never said a damn word about Bill to him.

Bill's gun points at Crew while I work on the next two people.

"A pencil's probably too long," I quip.

The gun swings back to me as Phil eyes us all warily.

"No wonder you come so hard for Crew and me if this is the best your father has to offer," Wilder teases me, and Bill swings his gun to him, his emotions outweighing any common sense as per usual.

"You really don't know when to be quiet, do you?" Phil sighs. "Look, we don't want to have to hurt anyone, but we really only need you, Lara. Don't make me shoot your boyfriends."

"Oh, really Phil? And you'd just let them walk away I suppose?" The two men on either side of Bill and Phil lower their guns, too, but I have nothing else left for Bill and Phil.

"Wait, their names are Bill and Phil?" Crew snorts as I hear a faint tapping sound coming from behind me.

Tap tap taptaptap

"Now! Wilder roars, and Crew tackles me to the ground.

The sound of gunshots firing has him covering my head.

When the shooting stops, and it's quiet, Crew lifts his head and looks around. Once he decides it's safe, he helps me to my feet.

I look up, and the first thing I see is Greg, his head poking out of the hatch with his gun in his hand. He looks at me and winks.

"Morse code for the win."

"Wait, that's what the tapping was?" I look at Wilder, but he's staring over my shoulder.

I turn and see my father's men all on the ground, blood pooling on the gravel where they lay.

"When Crew tackled you, their compulsions wore off." Wilder explains.

"Thank you for keeping me safe, all of you."

I hear Rufio bark and look at Greg. "Keep him with you. I don't want him rolling around in all this blood."

"You got it." He drops back down out of sight, closing the hatch behind him.

As I move to step closer to the downed men, a commotion to my left has my eyes darting over to see Jack and his band of captives tackling someone to the ground. They might look weak, but rage can give even the most broken of people strength.

Crews pulls his gun and has it pointing at them while Wilder still covers the fallen men.

"It's okay, Crew. These guys are the prisoners. I freed a couple, and they've been freeing the others."

He lowers the gun but remains tense as I step over to the bodies.

Most of them are dead or unconscious and injured—— except for Bill, because, like the cockroach he is, he can apparently survive anything.

I stand over him as he glares up at me, blood trickling from his nose and mouth.

"And now it's you laying on the ground at my feet. My, my, my, how the tables have turned."

I grin as he spits blood at me but misses by a mile.

I pause when I feel the phone in my boot vibrate.

"Where's my father?"

He grins at me, blood coating his teeth.

The phone keeps vibrating, but I ignore it as Bill starts to laugh.

"I don't know what he sees in you, but he wants you home."

I assume he's talking about my father, as he coughs and chokes a little.

"But you already have a home, don't you?" He grins again, my blood turning to ice as Wilder's phone starts ringing.

"Didn't you wonder why it was so quiet? You didn't question where everyone went?"

I look at Wilder, who has his phone to his ear, his face going unnaturally pale.

"Astrid had a vision."

I swallow hard at his words. Astrid isn't a precog like Bella. She's a harbinger.

"What did she see?" Crew asks moving close, wrapping his arm around my shoulders.

"Darkness and death."

The phone at my ankle vibrates again as I whirl back to Bill and press my foot against his chest.

"He's heading to Apex. To get the children?"

"Oh no, it's way past that. He's punishing you. He's gonna take away your home and your reason for living then you'll never feel the need to run again." He laughs again, this time at the horror on my face as the phone continues to vibrate.

"I hope you said your goodbyes."

I yank the phone from my shoe as Crew fires a bullet into Bill's head, making a few in the crowd scream.

"We need to go. We have the chopper; we'll beat him there." Wilder orders as I nod answer the call, holding the phone to my ear.

"Lara?" A familiar voice sobs down the phone, and my heart clenches.

"Delaney?" I reach out blindly and grip Crew's arm, understanding sinking in. She's a sensor. She can tell when people are nearby.

"We're coming. Hold on for me, okay. We have the helicopter; we'll get there first." I reassure her, but when she whispers next, I almost drop the phone so I can scream at the sky.

"They're already here."

Chapter Thirty-Six

Lara

Everything inside me shuts down after that. I'm vaguely aware of people shouting and moving around me. I feel someone shaking me, but I can't find my way out of the paralyzing fear consuming me.

I'm lifted into someone's arms, and I have just enough instincts to hold on to a fistful of t-shirts before I black out.

When I come to, I feel like I've been hit by a truck. I groan and try to move, but realize I'm sitting on someone's lap with their arms wrapped around me.

I look up, my eyes colliding with Crew's relieved ones as everything comes rushing back.

Tears run down my face faster than he can wipe them away.

"She's awake," he says, echoing in my ears, and I realize I'm wearing a headset in a helicopter. I look around and see Wilder at the controls, flying, but I don't see anyone else.

"Thank fuck. You scared the shit out of us, Lara," I hear Wilder say through the headset.

"Apex? The kids?" I choke out.

"The kids are in the panic room. And the guys are holding their own. They've been preparing for this since the day Zig and Oz brought tSalem home. There have been a lot of casualties, but none from our side. Right now, they're at a standoff right now. They can't get in, but Apex can't get out either."

I blow out a shaky breath as Crew leans over and hands me a bottle of Gatorade from the seat next to us.

"Wilder's right, you scared the fuck out of all of us."

"I'm sorry. When Delaney...It was my worst nightmare come true. Everything I gave up. Everything I lost and sacrificed was for nothing, and—"

He cuts me off with a soft kiss before unscrewing the bottle cap and motioning for me to drink. "You have nothing to be sorry for, baby," he murmurs, and I nod.

"Where are the others?" I take a sip from the bottle as he replies, his hand soothingly rubbing my back.

"Greg stayed behind with the prisoners. As much as he wanted to fly back, he knew he couldn't leave those pregnant women vulnerable. He has allies on the way to help; they'll be there soon. And he has Rufio with him, so if anyone tries anything, your dog will eat them."

I nod and frown. "What about Nash?"

Crew shakes his head. "No sign of him, and we couldn't afford to stick around. Greg will keep an eye out for him."

I rub my hand over my face. "If I had killed my father when I had the chance, none of this would have happened."

"No." Crew insists. "He had this planned. Nothing you did was going to change this."

"What do you mean?"

"Your father's men must have already been there waiting for the signal," Wilder says.

I think back to how empty the farm was. It all makes sense now.

"He wanted information from me, but he was attacking with or without my help."

"Yeah. Nobody at Apex has seen him but if he has a chopper or a plane, he'll be there before we will."

"The problem you'll have is getting close to him. The guys can't take him out from inside; he'll be prepared for snipers and things like that. And someone trying to get close to him will be putting themselves in danger."

"The guys are good at what they do," he reminds me.

"I know they are. But my father's a monster. He'll twist someone's mind and send them back in. He won't need to get inside to attack the women and kids if he can turn one of your brothers into a puppet. They'll do it all for him."

Crew grips his hair. "Fuck!"

"Exactly. If any of those guys hurt the kids or—" I blow out a ragged breath. "They'd never forgive themselves."

"You're right. We need a new plan."

"It needs to be me. If I take him out, you can all focus on the rest."

"Lara, please don't ask me to stand by and watch you walk into danger."

"Why? You're expecting me to watch you do it. I don't want to fight with you, but I can handle my dad. I'm stronger than he ever was. You have to trust me."

"He'll be expecting you to turn up."

"Maybe," I smirk. "But he doesn't know I'm an empath and won't see me coming."

"All he has to do is check the chip," he reminds me.

"The chip that I attached to Rufio's collar?" I look at him innocently.

I pull up my sleeve and show him the bandage wrapped around my arm.

"Holy shit. You cut it out?"

"And it's all the way back at the farm," I add with a smile.

He looks at me, shocked, for a moment before his face morphs, and he clenches his jaw.

"Fine, we'll do this your way, but if you get hurt—"

I cover his mouth with mine and pour all my love into it before pulling back.

"I love you."

He presses his forehead against mine.

"I love you too."

"For the record, I hate this fucking idea," Wilder grumbles as we make our way through the dark orchard.

"I know you do. If you have a better idea, I'm all ears."

"Anything is better than this," he snaps.

I grab his arm, making him whirl around.

Crew keeps a look out but hisses for us to hurry the fuck up.

"We don't have time for this, Wilder. I know you want to protect me, but I can do this."

"I can't lose you." He grabs my face.

"I'm not going anywhere, I swear, but this is my fucking home, so you better believe I'll defend it."

He growls and kisses me hard. "I fucking love you."

"I fucking love you, too. Now, let's go save our family."

He takes my hand, and we start moving again. Crew flanks my other side, gun out.

Wilder drops my hand and pulls out his gun too.

We all stop and listen to the sound of gunfire in the distance, little flares of light illuminating the night sky. I swallow, my palms sweaty, and my heart racing, each beat a frantic rat-a-tat-tat. We keep moving, careful to use the trees as cover. When we reach the edge of a clearing, Wilder holds up his hand, signaling for us to stop as he scans the area.

"Okay, go." Wilder orders, gesturing with his hand. Crew and I run as fast as we can as Wilder covers us. And we keep running until, suddenly, Crew stops.

"Here." He drops to his knees and yanks back what looks like grass. But it's actually a piece of fake turf. Underneath it is a metal hatch.

He yanks it up, and when I look inside, I gasp when I see Slade waiting for us.

"It's good to see you, Lara." He holds his arms up to me as Crew lowers me down.

He gives me a quick hug before the sound of a nearby explosion makes me gasp.

"Fuck. They've got eyes everywhere; it's why we haven't used this entrance."

"We'll take care of them." Crew looks around as Wilder steps up next to him.

Slade looks at me. "Can you find your way on your own?" That's when I notice the guns strapped to him.

I nod. "Go, but be careful."

"Tell Astrid—"

I cut him off with a shake of my head. "You can tell her yourself when this is all over."

He smiles and winks at me before holding up his hands and letting Wilder and Crew pull him up.

"Be careful," I call out as they close the hatch.

Taking a deep breath, I turn and start jogging through the man-made tunnel, thankful there don't seem to be any side passages because I'd get lost in a second.

Eventually, I make it to a locked door that looks like it belongs in a bank vault. I pound on it continuously until it swings open. I find myself wrapped up in Zig's arms a moment before I'm pulled away and yanked into Oz's.

"Thank fuck. We've been worried sick."

"I know, I'm sorry."

"You're back now, and that's all that matters."

"Where's Slade?"

I look over at Zig. "He went with Wilder and Crew. They texted you the plan, right?"

He grunts. "Yeah. As much as I fucking hate it, you're right. You're the only one who can take him out. Are you sure you're up for it?"

"To keep you guys and the kids safe? Absolutely."

"Alright, let's go."

Oz walks with me tucked under his arm and leads me into

what looks like a military operations room I've seen in movies. I have to say, I'm impressed. Even with the unlimited funds my father received from the government, he didn't have anything nearly as impressive as this. There are screens everywhere. There's a large table with chairs surrounding it, and that's all I take in before Salem, Astrid, and Avery swarm me.

Another explosion sounds, making us all stop and look up.

"Fucking hell," Salem curses.

"We can rebuild. It's just bricks and mortar," Zig reassures her as she buries her face in his chest.

I look at the screens and see video feeds and images from the cameras Ev must have set up down here and around the property.

Speaking of Ev, I spot him in front of one of the screens and walk over to him.

He looks up as I approach and jumps up from his seat to hug me.

"Aren't you a sight for sore eyes?" He pulls away and sits back down, pointing at the chair beside him as he continues monitoring the screens.

"Can you see where everyone is?"

"It's too dark, but I know where they are. Look, there's Jagger." He points to a shadow peeking out from behind a tree.

"What about Crew, Wilder, and Slade?"

"Slade's out there?" he asks, looking around. I wince as I look back at Astrid, but she gives me a wobbly smile.

"I know what kind of man he is," she says softly.

I nod and turn back to Ev.

"I've got Wilder and Crew—no, wait, that's Slade with him in the left quadrant. Crew is..." He flicks through the screens as the moonlight catches on something. He pauses the screen and laughs. "In the crow's nest."

He zooms in and sure enough, there he is. I shake my head.

"Do you know how many of my father's men are left out there?"

"Not many. Our guys have been taking them out with ease. Unless your father has reinforcements, I'm counting five remaining hostiles. There's still no sign of your dad, though."

"He's here somewhere," I murmur. He has to be.

"Hey, is that—" Oz starts, but Salem finishes.

"Nash." Oh God.

He looks up at the camera near the front door. His whole face is visible, so there is no mistaking who it is.

"Ev, disengage the locks. Oz and I will go grab him and bring him back here," Zig yells as they run through the tunnel toward the main house.

I stay behind with Ev and the rest of the women, my eyes on the camera.

"Why isn't he coming inside?" Astrid asks.

"He might be injured," Ev mutters as he brings up another camera.

"Two SUVs are pulling in," he yells.

"How?" Salem asks, terrified.

"The last round of explosions must have broken through the perimeter defenses," Ev curses, his fingers flying over the keys.

"I'll warn Zig and Oz," Avery yells, running after the guys.

I stare at Nash's face and notice his eyes are unfocused.

The hairs on my arms stand on end.

"Fuck! Your father's on his way up the hill," he tells me, but my eyes are still on Nash.

"No. I think he's already here. Oh God, it's a trap. Warn Crew, Wilder, and the others. My father's in the house."

I run, Salem and Astrid hot on my heels.

I grab Astrid's arm.

"Go to the kids."

She hesitates before changing directions and heading to the panic room. Salem and I continue through the tunnel and upstairs to the main house.

We spill out into the basement.

I hear voices but can't make out what they're saying.

I look at Salem. "I have to go up, but you should stay here."

"My men are up there, Lara. I'm coming."

I grit my teeth, but I don't argue. I'd do the same if the roles were reversed.

We don't bother with stealth. Instead, I run up the stairs with Salem right behind me and fling the door open.

I head right for the front door but change direction when I hear the voices coming from the kitchen.

I freeze, Salem crashing into the back of me and almost knocking me off my feet when I take in the scene.

My father's standing behind Avery, with his hand around her throat and a gun pressed to her head.

"What are you doing here?" He asks me with a frown.

I look at Oz and Zig, who both have their guns pointed at him.

"I live here."

His eyes take me in and then over my shoulder to Salem. His expression softens a fraction before they return to me.

"My girls," he whispers almost reverently.

Salem steps up beside me and takes my hand.

"Get back, Salem," Oz roars at her, but she ignores him.

"Long time no see, Penn. Or should I call you Dad?" She confronts him.

He smiles, and I can't help but feel a little jealous that he's never looked at me that way.

"I couldn't tell you, but I was never far, and you were always in my heart."

I fight the urge to gag.

"Why don't you let Avery go?" she says gently as we both walk slowly toward him.

"She's gifted," he says, like that's the answer to everything.

I stare at Avery's tear-stained face and swallow hard as her hand presses against her stomach. *Against her baby.*

"But she's not yours. I am. Salem is. Let Avery go, and I'll come with you. I won't run, I won't fight, and I'll do everything you ask of me."

He considers my words, his gun rubbing Astrid's temple.

Tears run silently down her face, but she doesn't make a sound.

My fingers twitch with the urge to use my gift on him, but one wrong move, and it's game over for Avery.

We take another step closer.

"I don't believe you."

"You should. There's nothing I won't do to keep my family safe. It's why I ran, to begin with, and it's the reason I'll give myself up."

He thinks it over before he speaks. "I want both of you," he says, waving between me and Salem.

Salem readily agrees as Zig curses.

Gunfire sounds from outside. Shouting and cursing assault my ears, but my father doesn't blink, unconcerned with anyone other than himself.

"We're going to walk out to my car. You'll drive." He points at Salem.

"You'll get in the back with me."

I nod. "Let me swap places with Avery first."

"No. I won't let her go until we reach the car. I don't trust anyone not to shoot you to get to me, but they won't shoot her."

I raise my eyebrows at that, but then he knows nothing about me or the people I love.

"Ev, can you get the guys to stop firing if you can hear me? We're coming out the front door and don't want to be hit by stray bullets." I say loudly, letting him know exactly what route we're taking so he can let the guys outside know.

When the gunfire stops, I know he's told the guys.

"Alright, we can go now. Just be careful, okay? We don't want you to trip."

He walks backward, taking Avery with him.

We all follow. When we reach the door, he orders me to go first.

I squeeze my hands into fists. I shouldn't be surprised by his willingness to risk me rather than himself, but at least this way, Avery is safer.

I walk out and swallow down a cry when I have to step over Nash, lying face down outside the door.

I walk down the steps and wait as he walks out, easing both him and Avery around Nash.

Salem brings up the rear, her eyes red when she takes in Nash.

"Close the door," he orders Salem.

"Lock it."

The keypad beside it activates the locks once Salem types in the code.

She walks down the steps toward me just as my father turns and shoots the keypad.

It makes a high-pitched noise as smoke starts pouring from it.

"That will buy us some time."

"Let Avery go now. You have what you wanted." I tell him.

He looks over his shoulder at me.

"I could let her go. But I'll need a bigger distraction than a locked door. Such a waste."

Before I can absorb his words, he throws Avery, who falls onto the steps with a scream of pain.

Salem runs to her as my father whirls on me, clearly disappointed his favorite daughter just picked her side, and it isn't my father's.

"Sometimes I wish I drowned you at birth."

Once upon a time, those words would have hurt. That was before I found those women being turned into human incubators. Before he hurt Avery.

"Sometimes I wish you had too," I agree.

"Salem was always a stubborn one. But you, you were supposed to be my successor," he spits.

"No. I'm supposed to be your downfall."

His eye twitches and a faint tingle at the back of my head tells me he's trying to use his gift on me. I smirk as a line of blood runs out of his ear.

"Oh, stop. That tickles." I laugh before smashing through his shields with a wave of my power.

"What? How?" He drops to his knees, his expression a mix of shock and awe.

"Surprise."

The sound of a gun firing, followed by screaming, has me looking over to see that Avery's been shot in the chest by one of my father's men, and Salem is pressing her hands over the wound.

I hear a roar of anguish and what sounds like a stampede of people heading our way.

At the sound of a click, I look back at my father to find a gun pointed at my head. I don't have time to feel shocked or disappointed in myself for taking my eyes off him. He gives me a sad smile before he pulls the trigger.

When the impact comes, it's not from a bullet but from a body as Nash tackles me to the ground, knocking all the air out of my lungs.

I sense my father step closer, the gun still in his hand, as he aims and fires two shots. I'm ready this time, though. The bullets stop midair, holding still for what feels like an eternity as my father's expression morphs into one of fear.

"I was never weak," I choke out as I change the trajectory of the bullets and watch as they both hit my father in the center of his forehead.

A wave of sadness crashes over me, but I ignore it as I roll Nash off me and lean over him.

"Nash?" I whisper. He opens his eyes and coughs, blood flicking from his mouth, covering his teeth.

I look down and see a bullet hole in the upper left side of his chest, right where his heart is.

"Nash! Oh God, no, please don't you do this to me."

"It's okay," he whispers with a smile. "I saved the pretty lady."

I sob as I press my hands to his chest to stop the bleeding, but it's pumping out of him too fast.

353

I look up and see Salem doing the same to Avery, but a faint glow around her hands tells me she's healing her or trying to.

Bodies swarm from every direction, blocking my view as some move to help Salem and others come to help me, but I ignore them, looking back down at the man who saved my life.

"Please don't go," I choke out as two bodies drop down next to me.

I sob louder when I realize it's Crew and Wilder, but still, I don't take my eyes or my hands off Nash.

"You guys are lucky," he tells them, his breathing taking on an odd whistling sound.

"I know, Nash. We are so blessed. And because of you, we'll be blessed for many days to come. Thank you," Wilder tells him softly, his own tears running down his face.

Crew bends down and presses his forehead against Nash's. "I've never been so proud to call you my brother. I love you."

"Love you too, weirdo," Nash gasps before his eyes fall on mine one last time. "You didn't think I'd let Hendrix go off without me, did you?"

His smile stays permanently etched onto his face as his eyes glaze over and his chest stops moving.

"No," I whisper.

I look over at Salem, but she's lying unconscious next to Avery.

She can't save him. The thought hits me like a Mac truck.

"No!" I scream, crying harder, my insides feeling raw, my heart breaking into pieces. I find myself wrapped in the arms of the men I love, who do the only thing they can.

They hold me together while I fall apart.

Epilogue

Four months later

Lara

The Issacs family were found buried under the foundation of one of the newer barns. It broke my heart all over again hearing the news. Part of me had hoped that they had found their happy ending far away from that vile place.

Apex had to call in every favor and marker they could think of, from friendly law enforcement officers to private investigators. Even a motorcycle club chipped in to help keep the truth from the media. Never again would we let targets be painted on people's backs just because they had a little extra sparkle in their DNA.

The freed captives and the pregnant women in comas were hidden away until they had a chance to heal and build a better, safer future for themselves. I'd received a letter from Jack, of all people, thanking me again. Not just for saving him, but for restoring his faith in humanity. I didn't know what to say to that, but if it meant he was healing, that was all that mattered.

I'd even managed to return to the shelter, with Crew and Wilder standing dutifully behind me as I hugged a crying Mallory. Their threat about never letting me out of their sight again wasn't so much of a threat as a promise.

The sadness and sense of loss hung in the air for days and weeks—the aftermath of what went down was a difficult truth to accept. Yet, instead of blaming each other and tearing each other down, we all pulled tighter together. I kept my gift locked down, knowing we all needed to grieve in our own ways. And we did so by leaning on each other. We cried on each other's shoulders and eventually, we started the slow process of healing. We said our goodbyes in the orchard when the trees were ripe with fruit and the smell of wildflowers perfumed the air.

Both Avery and the baby were fine thanks to Salem, and though we all felt incredibly blessed that they'd survived, not everyone made it back safe and sound.

Two black slate stones lay in the peaceful silence, the perfect memorial for two fallen soldiers. We had scattered Nash's ashes in the stream that ran across the far edge of the property, setting him free in death the only way we knew how.

There was nothing left of Hendrix to bring home, but Apex didn't need a body to bury or ashes to scatter to remember their love for one of their own.

Goodbyes are always sad, anything with a finality is, but we sat around as a family in that orchard reminiscing, while the children ran around chasing each other. I listened to their stories, saddened that I never got to meet Hendrix, but glad that Nash walked into my life and touched it in such a profound way.

"Woah." Avery grabs my wrist from where she's sitting beside me. Rufio, who is laying across my feet, lifts his head to see what's going on.

"What is it? What's wrong?"

"The baby moved."

"Really? Can I feel?"

"Of course." She yanks me over, making me laugh as I collide with her.

Rufio gets up and walks over to Greg, who is laying on the grass a few feet away with a book in his hand.

Avery places my hand on her bump and lays her hand over mine.

I wait for a minute, but when nothing happens, I start to pull away. That's when I feel it– the tiny fluttering that almost feels like wings against my palm.

"Wow."

"I know, right? Little Bean is a miracle. So why do I feel so damn nervous all the time? I keep waiting for something bad to happen because it always does, and—"

I send a wave of calmness over her, easing her fears and worries.

"God, you're better than Prozac."

"Should I be worried about you two?" Creed asks as he comes to sit on the other side of Avery, kissing her temple.

"Yes, she's the love of my life, and we're planning to elope."

"Like fuck," Crew bellows from somewhere behind.

Creed grins. "Can I watch?"

Crew dives on him.

"Why must you wind him up?" Avery sighs.

"Because it's funny," Creed admits as he ducks a punch.

I get to my feet and break them up by squeezing between them—which I know wasn't the smartest move—and planting a kiss on Crew's lips.

He doesn't waste any time picking me up and tossing me over his shoulder.

I hear cheering and applause as he carries me off to our place, and yes I can say our place now that I've officially moved in with them.

We barely make it through the door before he sets me down and we're stripping each other's clothes off.

As soon as I'm naked, he lifts me up and pins me to the closest wall before gently easing inside me. We both moan.

His hands slide under my ass, he starts fucking me hard and fast.

I dig my nails into his shoulders and hold on for dear life as my teeth find his neck.

I bite down and suck making him shiver and his grip tightens.

"Fuck, you feel so good, like hot silk," he groans before taking my mouth with a scorching kiss.

I let go with abandon, giving myself to this man in every way and with zero regrets.

When he hits a particularly sensitive spot inside me, I come hard, throwing my head back which collides with the wall. I'm so lost in my pleasure that I don't even feel it. And when Crew comes inside me moments later, I know I'd happily wear a few bruises as a badge of honor.

"I love you," I whisper against his lips making him smile.

"I'll never get tired of hearing you say that."

"Good because I'll never get tired of saying it." I pull back and look around. "Where's Wilder? He was supposed to meet us in the orchard."

"Probably still napping. Want to go wake him up?"

I grin. "Time for sexcapades, round two?"

He smiles at me as he lowers me to my feet.

I watch for a second as he pulls the condom off that I never even saw him put on before he slaps my ass making me squeal.

I yank his T-shirt on as I run from him to the bedroom we all share and slip inside.

Spotting Wilder, I smile and climb onto the bed beside him. I trail my lips over his bare shoulder, making him smile.

"What soft lips you have, Crew. New chapstick?" he teases, earning a pillow to the face.

"That will teach you."

"Oh, it's gonna be like that, is it?"

He yanks me down and rolls on top of me before he starts tickling me.

I squeal and laugh, bucking my body, as I try to get myself free. "Oh my God, Wilder, I'm gonna pee. Get off me."

"Not my kink, darling, but I'll try most things once," he jokes.

"Ewww. Crew, save me from this heathen," I yell.

Wilder smirks at me, clearly confident that Crew won't do jack shit until he finds himself being dive-bombed and knocked off the bed. He looks up, dazed, at Crew, and laughs when he sees me climbing onto Crew's back and clinging to him like a koala.

"I see how it is. Just you two wait. I'll get my revenge when you least expect it," Wilder threatens.

"Telling us you'll get your revenge when we least expect it makes us expect it, nut sack," Crew laughs, offering Wilder his hand.

He takes it and lets Crew yank him up. Clearly forgetting he's naked.

"For fuck's sake, dude. Put that thing away before you take someone's eye out," Crew complains.

Wilder looks at him evilly before shaking his ass and doing some hip thrusts. Crew backs up so fast that he almost drops me. I can't stop laughing, so much so, that I've given myself hiccups, making it hard to hold on.

"Permission to abort," Crew yells at me as he reaches the door.

"Permission granted," I yell, but instead of taking me with him he flings me off and tosses me onto the bed.

"Sorry, gorgeous, but it's every man for himself." He blows me a kiss and runs off.

"Dick!" I yell as Wilder jumps on top of me and pins me to the bed.

"Dick you say? Funny you should mention that because I have a dick here with your name on it." He wiggles his eyebrows at me, making me snort, but it quickly turns into a moan when he rubs his cock against my clit.

"Can I take you bare? I want to watch my cum leaking out of you."

I nod rapidly. "I'm on the pill. I want that too," I tell him, my voice hitching with need as he strokes my clit before slipping a thick finger inside me.

"You're all swollen, Lara. Have you and Crew been fucking?"

"He fucked me against the wall. I've never had wall sex before. Ten out of ten. I'll recommend it to all of my friends."

"Ten out of ten huh? Let's see if I can do any better."

He takes his time working me over with his fingers, mouth, and tongue until I'm a writhing mess that's on the verge of sobbing.

By the time he slips inside me, I'm so damn wet I'm soaking us both.

He fucks me with deep, hard strokes, his cock brushing against the tip of my cervix. The tiny bite of pain adds another layer to the pleasure, and my already oversensitive body overloads from the stimulation.

I wrap my legs around him and come with a choked plea as I squeeze him tight and feel him erupt inside me.

Easing out of me, he scoots down the bed and slides his finger inside me, gathering his cum and using it to circle my clit.

"It's too much," I gasp.

"One more, Lara. Give me one more."

"I can't," I cry, gripping the sheets because despite what I said, I can feel another orgasm looming on the horizon.

When he flicks my clit and reaches up to pinch my nipple hard at the same time, I come again, my voice hoarse from screaming.

"That had to be an eleven at least, right?"

I throw a pillow at his head before rolling off the bed and stumbling to the bathroom.

I take a quick shower—so I don't smell like sex— and dry off before walking back into the now empty bedroom to get dressed, slipping on a clean pair of panties, jeans, and a white tank top with a built-in bra.

Once dressed, I leave the bedroom and head toward the kitchen. I hear their voices getting louder as I approach and smile.

"I'm heading back out, you coming with me?" I ask as I slip my sandals on.

They both nod and finish getting dressed before the three of us walk back to the orchard together.

"Clean clothes and shower fresh. What could you possibly have been doing?" Hawk teases as we approach.

Crew tackles him, so I walk around them. Wilder sits beside Greg and Rufio, and absently runs his hand over Rufio's fur as he starts egging them on.

I walk back over to Astrid and Avery, who eye me knowingly.

"Why are the children always so much better behaved than the men?" Salem asks as she walks over to join us, dodging the fighting men.

I hear a tiny war cry and grin. "I think you spoke too soon," I say as Bella and Delaney throw themselves on top of Crew and Hawk, who immediately pretend they've been knocked out.

I look around and see Noah with Oz, who is attempting to get a large kite in the air but the wind doesn't seem to be strong enough. In the end, Oz gives up, picks Noah up, and flies him through the air like an airplane, making Noah giggle. I smile at the sight, my heart warming that Noah is coming out of his shell.

My eyes keep moving until they land on Alfie, who is lying in the grass under a huge oak tree, away from everyone else.

"Be right back."

"Sure thing," Salem replies, taking Aries from Astrid as I walk over to Alfie.

I see he has his headphones on. He's either listening to music or one of his audiobooks, so I don't try to make conversation. I just lie beside him and stare up at the leaves above me.

The last few months have been hard. The sadness at times has been overwhelming but there has also been happiness and love.

One day, this peace will be threatened again. People will come, if not for The Lost Ones, then for their children. The history of what happened before will be lost with the dead, but they'll learn the hard way that we will never back down and we'll never give up.

After a few minutes, I feel Alfie's hand as he wraps his pinkie finger around mine, reminding me that no matter what, we can face anything as long as we do it together.

As a family.

Also by Candice Wright

The Throne of Lies: An Underestimated Novel Book Seven

The Echo of Violence: An Underestimated Novel Book Eight

Ricochet (Underestimated Series Spin-off)

THE COLLATERAL DAMAGE SERIES

Tainted Oaths: A Collateral Damage Novel Book One

Twisted Vows: A Collateral Damage Novel Book Two

Toxic Whispers: A Collateral Damage Novel Book Three

THE PHOENIX PROJECT DUET

From the Ashes: Book one

From the Fire: Book Two

The Phoenix Project Collection

Virtues of Sin: A Phoenix Project Novel

DEATH IN BLOOM SERIES

Coerce

Compel

THE CANDY SHOP SERIES

Dulce

Reese

Lollie

Sugar

SHARED WORLD PROJECTS

Hoax Husband: A Hero Club Novel

STANDALONE

Vices and Vows

Sole Survivor

Acknowledgments

Dez@ Pretty in Ink Creations. – For my awesome cover.

Tanya Oemig – My incredible editor - AKA miracle worker. I'm so grateful to have you on my team. You're amazing and I adore you.

Briann Graziano – Proof reader extraordinaire.

Stacey, Mallory, Marie and Thais – you girls are the bomb diggity.

Julia Murray — my amazing PA, friend and book whore-der

My kids for being epic human beings. Remember I want the fancy kind of retirement home okay?

My OH – For feeding me when I forget and for giving me moral support when I'm running on nothing but caffeine and sarcasm.

My Candi Shoppers– you are the best readers group a girl could have. I love you more than muppet porn.

My readers – You guys are everything to me. I am in awe of the love and support I have received. Thanks for taking a chance on me and on each of the books that I write.

Remember, If you enjoyed it, please leave a review.

About the Author

Candice is a romance writer who lives in the UK with her long-suffering partner and her three slightly unhinged children. As an avid reader herself, you will often find her curled up with a book from one of her favorite authors, drinking her body weight in coffee.

Printed in Great Britain
by Amazon

43347995R00219